# The Tale of the Shadow Dwellers

Carol Johnson

Copyright © 2015 Carol Johnson
All rights reserved.

ISBN: 0996132236
ISBN 13: 9780996132237
Library of Congress Control Number: 2015910539
Carol Johnson, Las Vegas, NV

# 1

## Laura's Gambit

aura held her coat collar close around her face against the cold. She pushed open the elaborate diamond-paned door with her shoulder. The wind followed her in, blowing leaves against her legs and clearing the smoky air in front of the door. She moved aside as two departing patrons pushed past her to exit the theater.

Laura scanned the theater-restaurant-lounge called The Colony, looking for her target. She could sense danger in the gloomy room before she saw the lethal criminal, Eric Mateo, hunched over a back table, engrossed in a meeting with two equally sinister-looking men.

Eric was a big man, dark and menacing. He had a broad forehead and short, military-style haircut. Even at a distance, she could hear his voice, stern and unyielding. He wore black like his bodyguards and business associates. They effortlessly projected the Hollywood image of bad guys. Eric looked up, as if sensing her scrutiny, and turned his ruthless eyes on her.

Laura expected his gaze to pass over her as insignificant, but he continued to stare. Deliberately, she removed the London Fog trench coat, letting it fall away slowly and seductively. She wanted to unveil the white dress underneath in the most tantalizing way she could manage. Finally, she hung the coat on the rack by the door.

Laura had dressed with meticulous care for her visit to this exclusive theater. She would never have approached Eric Mateo in his usual haunts. He seemed to prefer the seedier bars. But this establishment was known for respectability. In fact, it had the remarkable reputation for sophisticated entertainment in a low-rent, industrial section of town. The larger buildings there allowed for the special clientele of The Colony, which attracted the wealthy classes as well as the nefarious underbelly of Rainier.

With a sensuous sway of her hips, Laura walked to a tall, cushioned chair at the bar. The white silk clung to her hips and showed to advantage her long legs. The off-the-shoulder dress drew attention to her gleaming shoulders and long neck. A white silk belt with crystal accents was wrapped around her slim waist, crossing in back and then tying low on her hips. The neckline revealed just enough to stir the imagination. She had taken special care to include a sheer white lace choker held in place by straps tied in a bow at the back of her neck.

Laura settled herself seductively on the chair, crossed her legs, and turned slightly, but invitingly, toward Eric. She had left her hair loose, and it teased at the belt of her dress. She wore little makeup and no jewelry. Tonight she was dressed to catch a big fish. Every detail had to be tailored to attract a rugged, unprincipled mark.

Eric Mateo was a man of lethal secrets, and his specialty was young women. Laura had read the newspaper reports connecting him to illegal gambling and auto chop shops. But these crimes seemed tame in comparison with the evidence her recent investigations had uncovered. Eric Mateo was up to murder—but not the usual kind of murder. The bodies of his recent victims had been pristine, with no apparent cause of death, and they had also been her three best girlfriends.

Laura was an orphan, and those women had brought her into their group like a long-lost sister. She would get justice for her college sisters, even if Eric was too elusive to be brought down by the police.

Eric Mateo was one of a clan of Shadow Dwellers, an immortal who lived off the life force that coursed through humans as an essential part of their blood. It wasn't necessary to kill. In fact, Laura guessed that many Shadow Dwellers lived hidden within law-abiding human society. But some, like Eric, felt superior and entitled. The women he fed on had no real value to him, and so he killed them indiscriminately. When he had stumbled onto her friends' usual Friday night party, he had been insatiable, murdering everyone. That was going to be his fatal mistake.

Laura ordered a cocktail and then retrieved a small jar of amber gel from her purse. It looked like perfume, but it was much deadlier. She loosened the lace choker and smoothed the gel around her neck, applying it with all the sensuality she could contrive. It seemed fitting that Eric should see the means of his downfall—presuming, of course, she was successful before he killed her. Laura had no delusions about this possibility. By coming after Eric, she was tangling with death incarnate. He did not play with his women for long, at least not the young ones.

Laura recrossed her legs and retied the lace choker. She was sipping her drink and smiling absently in Eric's direction, when she felt someone else's attention. She was used to admiring gazes, but this one was much more intrusive than most. Startled, she cast her eyes around the room, looking for the source. At the end of the bar was an intriguing man, staring at her with intense interest.

A shiver ran across her back at his suggestive stare. Laura felt her cheeks warm and her heart race like a foolish ingenue. He was older and more sophisticated than Eric. He wore a tailored, high-fashion Armani suit of soft gray wool and leaned on the bar with a comfortable confidence. He had large, artistic hands with slender fingers. Laura had always noticed hands. She imagined he must be the proprietor, given the deference the bartender seemed to extend to him. He acknowledged her questioning glance with a nod and a friendly smile.

He was beginning to walk toward her, when Eric Mateo stepped between them. Eric completely ignored the other man, and Laura saw the proprietor scowl impatiently behind him. Seeing them together, Laura knew they were both Shadow Dwellers. Their similarities were unmistakable. Unlike her friends, Laura had always been able to sense the preternatural. She hadn't always known what was different, but she always knew something was.

"I'm Eric Mateo. You wanted to meet. Your invitation was clear," he asserted with an arrogance that Laura had seen before. Men of his type, obviously rich and powerful, were always the same. They were so used to the simpering admiration of young, naïve women that they underestimated those who might have ulterior motives. He leaned in close, his sour breath burning her nose.

"I don't know what you mean by invitation. I was admiring your obvious authority, but I never imagined you would come over." Laura lightly stroked his arm and leaned closer so her hair brushed against his cheek. Eric smirked, making the intended assumption. *Really, men are so easy,* Laura thought. Bat an eye, show some leg, and the target was easily acquired.

"I'll buy you a drink. Join me at my table?" Eric gestured, not to his original table, but at a booth, which offered some privacy. Laura saw that his associates had left, and only one bodyguard sat a few stalls away. She couldn't help but be relieved. The fewer the witnesses, the easier her mission.

"I'd love to." Laura giggled and looked down shyly. "I'm Laura."

She rose out of her chair, intentionally brushing against him. Laura knew that the more excited Eric was, the more likely he would give her an opening early on. He was pulling her to the new table when the man in the Armani suit blocked their path. The proprietor smiled, but his eyes held a challenge that couldn't be ignored. Eric gave the stranger a withering sneer.

"Move!" he demanded with clear contempt. The blatant emotion crackling between the two men silenced nearby conversation. "We have nothing to say to each other, Renard. Get out of my way!"

"With pleasure," Stephan retorted. "But I will speak with this woman first." He pulled Laura out from under Eric's arm before the other man could stop him. "We have business."

Instead of confronting Stephan, Eric turned to Laura. "Join me after Stephan is done playing games. We have much to discuss." He smiled then, in a way he must have thought was sexy; to Laura, he just looked more dangerous. His grin was rigid, and his eyes flashed like a hungry predator's.

Laura suppressed the shudder prompted by the memory of finding her friends cold and dead. Stephan led her a short distance away. His warm hand on her bare arm and his velvet voice were distracting.

"You must avoid that man. He's dangerous, even lethal. Your life is at risk," Stephan whispered urgently.

Laura could hardly argue. Eric was obviously not someone a nice girl tangled with. But Laura wasn't a nice girl, and she had to settle with Eric tonight. So she decided to fall back on another ploy: the foolish daredevil. "I like dangerous." She pouted, lowering her eyes and fluttering her eyelashes. "Tame men are boring. Besides, I know Eric's type. They're like wild bears. If you know the rules, then they play nice." Laura tried to avoid looking directly into the man's eyes. She couldn't risk his uncovering her subterfuge.

But Stephan wouldn't be ignored. He leaned forward, putting his face in her line of sight. His need to dissuade her was etched clearly in his features. She jerked away, realizing he was too close to her neck. The gel had to be extremely lethal if it was going to work before Eric could seriously hurt her.

Stephan took hold of her wrist. The warmth of his hand was appealing. She looked up into his face and saw her attraction echoed in his surprised expression. He let go of her abruptly.

Still Stephan persisted. "He's responsible for the disappearance of women more experienced than you. Do you expect me to stand by and let you become his next victim?"

Laura decided to give this man a sliver of truth. "I know how dangerous he is. That's why I'm here."

Laura turned away before Stephan could respond, walked toward Eric with her arms extended, and shrugged. She wouldn't give Stephan any further opportunity to interfere, and she couldn't explain any more without putting her own life in danger.

Eric smiled, supremely satisfied. Laura slid onto the cushioned seat next to the big man. A drink waited for her on the table, and she took a long sip to steady herself. Eric stretched his arm along the back of their seat and pulled her closer.

"Don't remember seeing you 'round. New to the city?" he asked, stroking her arm. With each pass, his nail dug deeper, finally leaving a thin streak of blood. Oddly, Laura felt no pain, only a vague sensation of pleasure. Absently, she watched her blood drip down her arm.

Laura knew that the Shadow Dwellers were usually attractive, but Eric didn't have that strange mythical beauty that automatically lowered natural defenses and suspicions. His appearance was rough and mangy. Still, she felt disoriented. She realized that Eric was exerting some type of influence. She moved away from him and shook her head, trying to dispel her disorientation.

"Do you need another drink?" Stephan asked. He had come up to the table. Ignoring Eric's scowl, he laid his hand on Laura's. Through the fog, she felt the familiar tingle of attraction. She came back to her own senses abruptly.

"Didn't know serving drinks was your job. Or is bothering customers your new policy?" Eric complained.

Laura expected Eric to provoke Stephan into an angry confrontation, but the club owner only smiled, bowed, and moved away.

"Now where were we? Oh yes, you new in town?" Eric repeated, leaning close to her, his eyes only inches away.

Laura thought his eyes seemed too large. But her mind was still clear, and the injury on her arm began to ache. It was becoming urgent for her to get this thing done. She pretended to take a long drink, but let only a few drops of the liquid into her mouth. Then she planted a crooked, boozy smile on her face.

"Yes, I just started with a new airline. I'm here for one night on this trip. You from these parts?" Laura wouldn't reveal anything factual about herself. She didn't want Eric or anyone else to be able to find her later. There could be no chink in her armor.

"I've been around. Me and my boys have made a few profitable deals. Just purchased an old compound on the edge of town. I can show you 'round the city. You won't be disappointed," he promised with a wide, toothy grin. His teeth were unusually white, considering his breath. But Shadow Dwellers always did have immaculate teeth.

Smiling sweetly, Laura played with the straw in her drink. The places Eric knew would count her as a new menu item.

"That'd be super," she purred. She took his hand, turned it over, and stroked his palm. "I can tell your fortune." She followed the lines on his hand lightly with her fingertip. "You have a deep lifeline, which means long life. And here between your thumb and forefinger..." She stretched the skin of his hand. "It's perfectly smooth. Uh-oh! No children."

"Hey, that tickles," he objected. He snatched his hand back and rubbed his palm. "I don't believe that crap. The future, the past, what difference do they make? Right now is what's important."

Eric bent over and boldly ran his tongue down her jaw, like a restless animal marking its prey. He tangled his hand in her hair and pulled her head back, stretching the lace of the choker. With one quick yank he ripped the choker off, exposing her naked throat.

Laura heard a low growl from Stephan, who had returned to the bar. She had to get Eric out of the club before she started a brawl. "Let's blow this place, honey," she cooed. "I work better alone."

Extracting herself from Eric's grip, she stood up. Fortunately, he seemed willing to follow her. He kept staring at her newly exposed cleavage. As a result of his rough treatment, the top of the dress had been torn as well and now hung several inches lower. Eric eagerly propelled Laura to the door. She managed to snatch her coat off the hook before he pushed her outside.

They had walked down two short blocks before she spotted a long, shiny black limousine sticking out of an alley. It was big and bulky, like the man beside her. Despite her dedication to this course of action,

Laura swallowed hard. She had never gone up against a man as powerful and notorious as Eric. She couldn't help wondering if, despite her best efforts, she would become his next victim. She was completely unprepared for his offer.

"Ya know, you're just what the doc ordered. I need a more acceptable rep. You're classy and sexy, and you'd get me points with my business partners. Blow that airline. I'll make it worth your while." He took out a wad of cash.

The fact that it was after midnight and they were in a dark alley went a long way to convincing Laura that this man was real trouble.

"Fifty thousand must be more than you make in a year. All I want is a few months. So, do we deal?"

It surprised Laura that he was asking instead of telling. Then she realized that without her cooperation, he couldn't impress his friends. As she studied his face in the light from the limo's open door, he blushed. Laura almost laughed, but laughter would very likely have ended her mission. The blush was *the tell*. He was serious. He probably thought her class would rub off on him. Maybe he even respected her.

"Sure, baby," she promised, shoving the money deep inside her purse. "I'll be your wingman."

Laura slipped on her coat before climbing into the backseat and then placed her purse on the floor next to the door. She might have embraced the advantages of gaining access to Eric's world and more criminal Shadow Dwellers, except that the phantom cries of her friends were too loud to ignore. They deserved justice in a world that Eric could manipulate too easily.

Eric instructed the driver to head to his new place in the hills and then settled back. They quickly reached the outskirts of the city. Recklessly Laura kissed Eric, rubbing her chest against his arm. He groaned and returned her kiss unwillingly.

Drawing back, he objected, "Hey, babe, let's wait till we get home. We can get to know each other real well."

But Laura couldn't wait. At his house, there would be bodyguards ready to defend their boss. So she pushed her neck against his mouth, her blood beating loudly in her ears.

Fortunately for her, Eric was used to indulging his hungers. Taking his time, he licked the long carotid artery in her throat. Then, he pushed his teeth deep into her neck and started sucking. Laura gritted her teeth against the pain and waited. She found the obvious sexual undertones of his action revolting. Killing this animal was worth every risk and any discomfort.

She began to feel lightheaded. He was feeding too quickly, and despite his intention to keep her alive, she feared he wouldn't stop in time. Not killing took a discipline that pigs like Eric never acquired. Suddenly, his eyes flew open, the whites filling with dark-red fluid. He choked on the blood that gushed from his mouth.

"Pull over now!" Laura shouted at the guard. "Something is wrong with your boss!" She inserted all the terror and panic she could muster into her voice. She had to keep the driver off balance.

With Eric bleeding out of every orifice, Laura calmly pulled a syringe out of her purse. The driver jerked the vehicle onto the shoulder and slammed to a stop. Before he could turn around, Laura leaned across Eric, jammed the needle into the driver's neck, and pushed the plunger down. Eric had taken almost too long to react, and she could only hope the driver would succumb faster. He screamed at the sudden pain and tried to grab the offending syringe. She calmly plucked the needle out from under his searching fingers, capped the point, and concealed it in her coat. She couldn't leave any evidence.

Laura jumped out of the car before the driver could retaliate, but she needn't have worried. The drug was doing its evil work with surprising efficiency. Both men were slumped over in pools of their own blood. Every blood cell had exploded into a thin fluid that flowed easily from their bodies. Like their victims, they had been drained dry.

Laura studied Eric and his driver for any lingering signs of life. They both showed the peculiar translucence that was customary for Shadow Dwellers at death. Gideon Lord's cleanup crew would dispose of all evidence of their murders to avoid triggering any retaliation by Eric's crew.

Laura walked away from the vehicle and removed her blood-spattered coat. Luckily, the dress underneath would pass casual scrutiny.

She scanned the street, searching for Monk's black van. She had spotted the familiar vehicle on the way out of town and was glad for the unexpected backup. She made the signal that all was clear by putting on his silly bright-red cap. He had insisted on this stupid sign, and she kept it well hidden in a secret pocket of her purse. He pulled up a few moments later.

Monk had become Laura's closest confidant after Gideon Lord, now her patron, had found her investigating the deadly world of the Shadow Dwellers alone. Monk was Lord's most trusted soldier, and he relied on him to keep curious bystanders away. So Monk went the extra mile to appear more menacing. It helped that he was already big, bald, and forbidding.

Laura knew that their work made friendships rare. Monk had even driven his family away so they couldn't be used against him. She had taken an instant liking to the big man, seeing his loneliness through his show of intimidation. Laura showered him with the sisterly affection denied them both. In return, Monk watched over her with the loyalty of a bulldog. They had created a resilient friendship in a world of peril.

Monk jumped out and opened the passenger door, leaving the van purring quietly. But Laura ignored the car door and threw herself into his arms. Chuckling softly, Monk lifted her into a great bear hug.

"I feel like I've been soaked in sewage," she said.

"Lord won't be happy about this, Laura," Monk grumbled as he put her down. His eyes twinkled, softening his next words. "Eric is too well connected for his disappearance to be kept a secret for long. You're lucky Eric didn't snap your pretty neck before you got him."

Monk's voice always surprised Laura. It was not what she would have expected from a man who looked like him. He spoke with a deep, melodic English accent that was soothing, and Laura took comfort from his concern, despite the censure.

"Lord is worse than an overprotective father. He'd prefer I do nothing but stay safe and live a quiet life. But, Monk, I still have nightmares about Grace, Ellie, and Pam." She whispered the names, her voice stricken and haunted. "I can imagine what they must have felt in those last moments, when they knew they were going to die." She scowled at the idling limousine. "These creatures can't be allowed to kill without retribution."

"You should give Lord more credit," Monk urged. "If not for him, you'd probably be dead. He's the one who prepared you for the unique dangers of fighting Shadow Dwellers. If you hadn't run headlong into their secret world, exposing yourself as their enemy and making yourself a target, he wouldn't have had to interfere. You should never underestimate your enemies, youngling." He hugged Laura again.

Laura relaxed into his embrace. Truth be told, Eric had come close to draining her before the drug had disabled him. She would have to alert Lord that his concoction was not as effective with master Shadow Dwellers. Master Shadow Dwellers were older, extremely clever, and had the capacity to do great harm. It seemed they also clung to life with great strength as well.

"Now he wants to see you. I think it would be wise to go tonight." Monk stared at her with grim determination.

Laura wouldn't have put it past him to carry her bodily to Gideon Lord. She nodded disagreeably. She couldn't summon even an illusion of affability when she felt Lord's rules tighten around her like invisible shackles.

# 2

## Stephan Renard

Stephan stood next to Jon, his right-hand man, and watched the beautiful young woman and the dangerous crime lord leave his establishment. Since arriving in Stephan's town, Eric had caused so much damn trouble that many longed for his death. He was drawing attention to their loyal group of Shadow Dwellers, and this attention could force them all back into hiding. But more than Eric, Stephan worried about the graceful beauty in the scandalous white gown. To wear such a dress was an invitation for trouble, and trouble in his world could very likely mean death.

Stephan had watched every breathing man in the bar follow her movements as soon as she had discarded her bulky trench coat. Her unique chestnut hair with glowing highlights and her pale green-gold eyes were irresistible. When she had shown an obvious preference for Eric, Stephan had felt a sickening dread. Why were humans so eager to end their fragile lives?

As an immortal, Stephan had lived many lives, and each one had brought him more wisdom. But even as time stretched out before him, he longed for the vivaciousness of the short-lived humans. His human friends had lived each moment with a ferocity that lit Stephan's long, dark life. Eric was stupid to imagine that their kind were superior. But brash Shadow Dwellers were always too self-obsessed to see the truth. Their solution to immortality was to fill their profound emptiness with violence, blood, and sex.

Stephan had long ago found his answers with the humans themselves. What he could do at his leisure, the humans had to fit into a few short years, and so there was an energy that ignited their blood. But more than this, he envied their devotion to each other and their willingness to die for a higher good. Humans laughed and loved, worked and played, in a world where many factors were outside their control and something as simple as a violent storm could end their precious dreams in an instant. It was this ardor that called to him.

His last human loveling had filled his life with humor and the unexpected. He had tried to maintain the usual immortal detachment, but she was just too endearing. When she had died a sudden death, it had broken his heart. He could not bear the thought of a similar fate for this strangely appealing new girl.

"Find out who that woman is! I'll be back as soon as I can," he barked.

"I'm on it!" Jon called to the back of his disappearing boss. Jon had been with Stephan for many years and was completely trustworthy.

Stephan dashed out the entrance and searched the empty street frantically. His small, nondescript car was parked in a special spot in front. He could have purchased a flashy, expensive vehicle, but he shared the habits of all those of his race. He needed to remain invisible. What his people had to do to survive, humans would never permit, and for that reason, they lived in a secret society. So while his car had every high-tech feature known, its appearance was shabby.

Stephan caught sight of Eric and Laura walking into a dark alley and watched as they climbed into a black limousine. Eric didn't hide his love for ostentatious vehicles. Casually, Stephan maneuvered his car into traffic while the other vehicle gained speed two streets away. He knew he could easily keep up with the limo, which had the maneuverability of a Greyhound bus.

The closer the two vehicles got to the forests outside Rainier, the more anxious Stephan became. Suddenly, the limo swerved and the driver pulled off the road onto the shoulder. Even at a distance he could see Laura press something against the driver's neck. Then the girl jumped out of the limo, and the driver slumped forward. There was another slumped figure in the backseat, and Stephan guessed that he must be Eric. He was horrified to see Laura's gray trench coat covered with blood. He expected her to show some sign of injury, but it became obvious that she was unharmed. She stripped off the ruined coat and put on a bright-red Christmas hat.

Stephan turned down a dark side street and out of sight just as a black van parked near the stalled limo. He turned around and pulled forward far enough to see the van and the limo. Stephan watched, fascinated, as Laura flew into the arms of a big, hulking bald man, dressed all in black, who held the passenger-side door open. She embraced the man with all the affection one would bestow on a long-lost brother. The man returned the embrace with obvious affection.

With enhanced senses, Stephan listened to their muted conversation. The stranger, whose name, he learned, was Monk, chided the girl for her recklessness. He took the bloody coat, apparently more worried about smearing blood on her than spreading it to his own clothes. Stephan started nervously when he heard them both mention Gideon Lord.

Lord was well known among the Shadow Dwellers. He was one of the few humans who knew of their existence and still lived. Many young ones had tried to terminate him, only to find their own lives cut short. Lord knew their ways and kept an army well equipped to protect him. Much to the Shadow Dwellers' consternation, he also kept a force of hunters who would step in if they became too bloodthirsty.

In a way, Lord did them a favor. The Shadow Dwellers survived by remaining in the realm of myth. Unfortunately, the new babies tended to be reckless and got into trouble easily. By killing the more vicious ones, Lord's army helped the rest of his people remain fiction rather than fact.

Stephan learned that this woman's name was Laura and her target had been Eric. He could only imagine that Grace, Ellie, and Pam—the women Laura had mentioned and obviously loved—were among his latest victims. He smiled in the dark car, well satisfied. Eric had been a thorn in his side, and he was glad to finally be rid of him. Regrettably, Eric's empire would fall to one of his underlings, and Stephan knew that the new boss might be more violent than Eric had been.

Laura had climbed into the van, and it was casually pulling away, interrupting Stephan's introspection. Hastily, he started his car and surreptitiously followed. After traveling several miles, the van turned into the long private drive of Gideon Lord. Stephan knew better than to follow onto grounds that were crisscrossed with special night-vision surveillance. He cursed softly and pulled behind a stand of trees, several yards south of the gate. He wondered if Laura actually lived here. If she worked for Lord, he would have to dig deeply to find real information about her. She had taken a terrible risk confronting a man as notorious as Eric in public.

For several minutes, Stephan watched the closed gates, feeling defeated. For some insane reason, he had to know who Laura was, but he couldn't wait there indefinitely. There were people watching his activities. He would just have to get someone back there before she left.

Stephan quickly retraced his route, parked back in the spot reserved for his private use, and hurried into the theater.

"Jon, come to the office," Stephan directed.

Jon was behind the bar serving customers. Stephan waved one of the more attractive waitresses over. "Misty, I want you to watch the bar." He didn't explain further. Misty belonged to Nicolette and could be relied on to further only her mistress's agenda.

Stephan opened a door behind the bar, and both men entered his office. He collapsed into a tall black leather chair behind a mahogany desk. Jon remained standing, waiting. Old-world manners required he wait to be addressed by his superior.

"Did you find any information about the girl who left with Eric?" Stephan asked tersely. It still infuriated him that he had to leave that beautiful creature at Lord's.

"She gave us a credit card to run a tab. But the name was bogus. Grace Lambert is dead." Jon's voice cracked with disappointment.

Stephan recognized the name. It made sense that Laura would use aliases when hunting, but two? She had told Eric her name was Laura, while she gave Grace's credit card to Jon. "Grace Lambert is probably the reason Laura left with Eric."

"Laura?" Jon asked.

"Her hulk of a partner picked her up and used her name. The woman referred to a friend named Grace. Did you get a cause of death?"

Jon looked embarrassed. "I—um—just assumed it was a dead end. I'll look into it." He headed for the office door.

"No," Stephan barked. "I don't want to alert Nicolette to my interest. She would read way too much into your activities."

Jon turned back to Stephan with pursed lips and a raised eyebrow. "Way too much? Just why are you interested anyway?"

"I don't know." Stephan confessed with surprising familiarity. He had a special relationship with Jon. While Jon treated him with the respect accorded a person in authority, they both exchanged confidences and advice frequently. Stephan had turned Jon into a Shadow Dweller, and in return, he had earned Stephan's trust and become his right-hand man. Eventually, Jon became the brother that Stephan never had. "I've known many beautiful women, but I've never seen one take on a vicious Master Shadow Dweller."

"You mean Eric?"

Stephan nodded. "She had Eric dancing to her tune in short order. Are we so easy to manipulate?" He shook his head helplessly, recognizing that he, himself, had fallen under her spell. "She works for Gideon Lord. Some big guy, maybe one of his lieutenants, took her to Lord's compound after she killed Eric and his driver."

"She killed Eric?" Jon asked incredulously. "Shouldn't you warn Nicolette? There's certain to be trouble with Eric's empire up for grabs to his goons."

"She would see the girl as a threat and maybe even consider acquiring her." Stephan reasoned with a flash of distaste. Nicolette's girls lived a painful existence. "So we wait to tell her. Look, I'll take over the search for the identity of this new girl, and you go to Lord's estate and follow her when she leaves. I want to know where she lives. Misty will cover for you here. The most important thing to remember is let no one know what you're up to, especially Nicolette. If she asks—which she is certain to do—tell her you're investigating a possible business merger. I'll tell her the truth if I have to."

Misty popped her head into the room. Her face was etched with nervous agitation, and her eyes were filled with a hopelessness that marred her pale beauty. "Nicolette would like to see you out front. She wants Jon to retrieve a bottle of her favorite wine from the cellar," she mumbled before retreating.

"And so the diva commands," Stephan quipped, rising with a tired sigh. "I have a bottle here in my office. I'll handle Nicolette. Go out the back way. It's important that you get there before Laura has gone."

Jon didn't hide his relief at avoiding Nicolette and wasted no time heading for the exit.

As Stephan neared their usual table, Nicolette rose to greet him. Her red hair always fascinated him. It was so lush, containing strands of various shades of luminescent red color, that it immediately drew attention. She was dressed in the most expensive designer clothes and carried herself with a polished sophistication. Nicolette had told him about her life as a courtesan. He knew that between her looks, her voice, and her poise, she could have easily become a world-renowned performer. But she, like Stephan, had to conceal her unique nature. There could be no public image.

Instead, Nicolette had cultivated a careful selection of the most artistic women she could find. She kept human female performers because only they could enter the public world and demand high fees. But the clever ones were changed into Shadow Dwellers and forced to obey through the use of special coercions. Their hunger could bring pain as easily as pleasure.

Nicolette pulled Stephan down next to her on the cushioned couch and brushed her cold lips against his cheek. She snuggled against him, sighing with satisfaction. Stephan knew that Nicolette was totally enthralled with him. Usually he liked her public demonstrations of devotion, but tonight he felt a new discomfort that made him restless and irritable. He forced himself to relax and poured her a tall glass of very expensive Cabernet Sauvignon. Nicolette loved strong red wine.

"Here, I've brought a bottle of your favorite. I recently acquired a special vintage from an accomplished collector of rare wines. I hope you like it." He poured a second glass for himself. His heightened senses allowed for a special appreciation of rare wines. Food, on the other hand, was impossible. Shadow Dwellers couldn't digest food.

"You're always thinking of new ways to please me. I'm fortunate indeed," she cooed, seemingly unaffected by his uneasiness.

Stephan and Nicolette had started a liaison after the car accident that killed Chloe, his last mistress, a human. In fact, if Nicolette hadn't been with him that night, he might have suspected her involvement. If she had killed his Chloe, Stephan would have made certain she paid for that mistake.

Stephan's devotion to Chloe had made him quite a spectacle in his Shadow community. She had filled his life with so much happiness that he hadn't cared what anyone thought. Often, he would return to their shared lodgings to discover that she'd planned some new adventure. From a murder mystery weekend with costumes, to hiring a troupe of actors to enact an ancient Greek play and banquet, to a country party filled with musicians and philosophers, there was always some new entertainment to excite his imagination. It had taken him months to recover from her death, only to find Nicolette eagerly waiting.

Tonight, Nicolette kissed him possessively before raising her glass in a toast. Her eyes were shining with adoration. "To our great love. May it reign supreme, above all other loves."

Stephan remained quiet and took a small sip of his wine. He felt embarrassed by this excessive display of emotion, which overshadowed her sophistication and made her appear foolish.

Nicolette gestured to a stagehand. The lights dimmed, and a wisp of a girl came out onto the platform wearing a thin white shift. The cloth clung to her young curves, bringing her pale face into stark relief. Her hair was long and white and floated in an artificial breeze created offstage. Nicolette had ordered a stage backdrop of dark, looming trees and a misty, silver moonlit lake. Stephan wondered at this strange scene until the girl began to sing. Her voice was like a bird's, trilling in a silent forest. At first, it was light and sweet, and then it became lonely and sad. She held his complete attention as she sang a trio of intensely provocative love songs. When she stopped, the tones of her last song lingered in his mind with an eerie finality.

The Colony was open all night, attracting patrons who conducted their lives in the protective darkness of night. This evening, the audience had stilled during the girl's performance, their idle conversations dying at the first notes. When they rose into a standing ovation, the talented girl fled off the stage. Nicolette nodded at the stagehand. The curtain dropped, marking the end of the performance.

"I was looking for you earlier, Stephan," Nicolette complained prettily, as she stroked his thigh. She never seemed to get enough of touching him. "I saw Eric in the lounge and you at the bar earlier. I know he's a constant irritant to you, so I arranged for Blythe to sing her soothing songs. But you disappeared. Where did you go?" she asked innocently.

Stephan had no intention of telling Nicolette about following Laura. She would never allow his attention to linger unopposed on an attractive woman. He wouldn't only have to keep his activities a secret, but he would also have to make excuses to keep her at arm's length to avoid discovery. He appreciated that this task might prove impossible. Nicolette looked on their liaison with the avarice of a starving octopus. She would not be put off easily. Desperately, he racked his brain, searching for some reasonable explanation for his absence. He decided on a version of the truth.

"I followed Eric. He's become increasingly dangerous, killing more and more often. If he isn't stopped, he'll bring the police down on us all. It's time to take action."

Nicolette's lips thinned with displeasure. "Eric is out of control. There is nothing he won't do to win, no act of savagery he won't try, and he's recruited a very large crew. Don't take him on, Stephan. For now, he's leaving us alone."

Stephan was disappointed at her shortsightedness. One day, Eric would have tried to dominate all the Shadow Dwellers in Rainier. Stephan knew he would have been forced to kill the rapacious reptile sooner rather than later. "For now," was all he said. For now, he wouldn't tell her about Eric's murder.

The front door banged open, loudly heralding the entrance of a dwarf, who strutted over to their table. Stephan rolled his eyes and gritted his teeth. The newcomer was Nicolette's troll. At least that was how Stephan mentally referred to the good-for-nothing snitch. Whenever Nicolette needed a spy, she used Noel. The reference to Christmas was just a cruel joke. Noel couldn't be further from the friendly elf of Christmas lore, except for his fluffy white hair and whiskers. His beady little black eyes missed nothing. He was forever underfoot, nosing in on any activity that might gain him some advantage.

"I have news, Mistress," he chirped proudly. "Your opportunity has come." The little man glared at Stephan and then tugged Nicolette off the couch and up the long aisle. "We need privacy," he insisted.

Nicolette went willingly, steering Noel into Stephan's office. Apprehensively, Stephan watched the door close. He had secrets, and her little spy had an uncanny knack for uncovering secrets. After an eternity, Nicolette appeared and glided slowly toward Stephan, stopping at a spot across the table from him. She was smiling, but it wasn't a happy smile.

"Noel has been following Eric for weeks," she confessed bluntly. "I feared he might be planning an attack. You and I have been accumulating too much wealth, and Eric couldn't help but covet our profits. But Noel has witnessed something very interesting." Nicolette's expression turned malicious. "It would seem that our problem has been handled."

Stephan knew that Noel must have seen him following the limo. His vehicle was very familiar to the troll. Stephan had been too preoccupied with Laura to notice the little worm. He cursed mentally.

"Eric is dead?" he asked, not willing to show his hand yet.

"Don't you know?" she countered. Her eyes held the sure knowledge of his deception.

"I didn't actually look. I just assumed he was," Stephan admitted, dropping all pretenses.

"Well, our problem has been solved by our old watchdog, Gideon Lord. Eric fell neatly into the trap set by his weapon."

Stephan raised his eyebrows at this reference. "Weapon?" he echoed.

"Our little white-gowned seductress, of course. She managed to bring down Eric without firing a single shot. She lured him away from his army of guards and assassinated him on the way to his compound. Noel checked his body before Lord's crew arrived. Now we have a way to stir up enough trouble to deal with Lord for good."

"No!" Stephan hissed in a harsh whisper. The angrier he got, the quieter he became.

Nicolette backed off, looking surprised and then nervous. Stephan commanded greater power, and thus more respect, than most Shadow Dwellers. He was older than even Nicolette, so her caution was natural.

"You know that Eric would have killed us both to gain leadership of the city," Stephan reminded her sharply. "I've already hired extra security. Now he's gone, and we're blameless. His crew can't move against us. Gideon Lord did what we both needed done. If you act against him, you will force my hand," Stephan promised, deliberately leaving the actual threat to her imagination. Still, an icy fear collected in his chest. To bring the Houses of the Shadows against Lord would mean that all of Lord's people would be massacred and Lord would make sure it happened publically. His people would have to leave Rainier. This he would prevent for as long as he could.

"Relax, lover," Nicolette soothed. "I guess we don't need to kill Lord. Time will do that all too soon. One of the Shadow Houses will get tired of his interference. But do we announce Eric's murder?"

"No! The longer it takes for his men to discover the truth, the more time we have to minimize collateral damage." Stephan insisted with little hope. It would be like trying to slow a flash flood. "His reckless Shadow men are so damned destructive. They act like there's no code of secrecy. Soon enough, his potential successors will fight for his territory, and with luck, we'll be able to stop a full-out war. Only a strong leader can temper the battle to come."

Unfortunately, Noel knew the truth, and there were others who would pay as handsomely as Nicolette for his information. If only Stephan could extract that stone in his shoe permanently.

"What of the girl?" Nicolette asked. She eyed Stephan speculatively.

Unfortunately, she knew about his fondness for human girls, and Laura had made an impression. If ever he could have been an actor, now he must prove to be a good one.

"She's Lord's problem. What happens to him happens to her." Stephan tried to appear indifferent. Furtively, he watched Nicolette and saw her shake her head. "What do you want to do?" he asked cautiously.

"She would make an exciting addition to my collection. I might even consider turning the little chit," Nicolette purred, her eyes flashing darkly.

Her answer turned his stomach into a burning pit. Shrewdly, he said nothing. But saying nothing and doing nothing were two entirely different things.

"Come, enough of humans. Let us enjoy the evening." He gestured for her to join him at the table. Nicolette was still standing stiffly.

"Why did you follow her?" she snapped bitterly. "Noel said you made it easy to follow Eric's killer since you trailed her all the way back to Lord's mansion. He had no explanation for your behavior."

"She'd just killed our greatest threat. I wanted to know who she was. Wouldn't you?" Stephan growled low. She was the only one who ever challenged him repeatedly.

"But why follow her in the first place?"

"You are such a suspicious minx," he cajoled, changing tactics. "Look, Nicolette, I followed Eric and his new friend because I was curious. There was no master plan or chicanery. Now, can we please continue with our evening, or do you want to call it off?" It had taken Nicolette many months of concentrated effort to gain entry into his private life and its privileges, so he was sure she wouldn't risk losing it now.

"Of course not! Besides, I have another acquisition you might enjoy." She forced a smile and gestured at the same stage manager; the lights dimmed, and a rainbow spotlight lit a fairyland backdrop on stage. Into this fantastic scene entered a woman of exotic oriental beauty. With her intricate, acrobatic gymnastics, she lured the audience into a world of new and exciting dances. Her flexibility was astonishing, her balance phenomenal, and her grace seductive.

But Stephan was too distracted to notice. He had allowed his mind to wander back to the bewitching Laura. Not only was she strangely appealing, but she was a clever warrior. He remembered her long, flowing hair and her curves exposed by the taunt, brilliant silk. He was quite embarrassed when Nicolette had to repeat her question.

"Do you like her, Stephan? Shall we invite her downstairs?" Nicolette's eyes were dilated in the dim stage lighting. Her expression was wild and hungry.

"Downstairs" was Stephan's private apartment. It suited him to be close to his business. When he needed time to himself, he had his secret workshop far away from prying eyes.

"Not tonight. Let's just keep it simple, shall we?" he pleaded, sounding more regretful than he felt. He was getting tired of her sexual games. He finished the fine wine in one gulp and slid out from behind the table. He gestured to one of his bodyguards to handle the management of The Colony. Jon was still gone. Nicolette followed close behind, bumping into him at the curtained door to his quarters.

Once downstairs, the two Shadow Dwellers fell into each other's arms with practiced ease. Their clothes dropped away effortlessly. Stephan always enjoyed the first moments when his bare skin slid sensually over Nicolette's. They both knew about the special delights of their species, and each had intimate knowledge of the other's unique preferences.

When Shadow Dwellers drank the animated blood of humans, they also drank the memories, intense emotions, and heightened sensations created by erotic experiences. In fact, it was the ability to manipulate these memories that gave the Shadow Dwellers power to influence humans. They could call up intoxicating past events and enthrall their victims into complete amnesia, leaving only an echo of remembered ecstasy.

Now Stephan and Nicolette each called up remembered images that most delighted the other, sharing the blood that carried these memories. He felt Nicolette sink her teeth into his thigh and drink. She filled his mind with the pleasures she had taken from the two new women entertainers, lulling him into a sexual trance. But she was greedy, and he began to experience a growing weakness.

Stephan dragged her roughly off his leg. He bit down hard on her neck, and she moaned with pleasure. He replaced the blood she had taken so recklessly, feeling the powerful thrust of energy that came when the spirit blood flooded into his body. Finally, both were sated and they dropped into the deep sleep of the Shadow Dwellers.

Shadow Dwellers didn't sleep in the same way that humans did. But they did have to regenerate their physical and mental faculties, and these times came on them irresistibly. In fact, it was their death-like sleep that had gone a long way toward creating the myth of the undead.

When Stephan roused the next morning, Nicolette was lying across his body, her arms and legs tangled with his. Remaining motionless, Stephan took in the darkened apartment. He had chosen underground for its absolute security. The only access was the long stairway under the theater and an escape tunnel in case his enemies attacked. He had used tricks of the movie industry to replicate shifting sunlight, breezes, and tinkling water to give his dark world the illusion of being above ground. Thick, plush carpeting covered the floors, making bare feet an adventure in sensual pleasure. Several expensive paintings of international hot spots hung on the walls. Hot-red, burgundy, amber, and white harmonized to bring a vital animation to the space. He felt warmth, even though the rooms were slightly cool.

When Nicolette rolled away restlessly, Stephan slipped off the bed to take a shower. He didn't want to face any more interrogations or recriminations. If she started in on him again, he would have to shut her down more firmly. Maybe she would figure out on her own that her bad attitude was preventing any possibility of a permanent joining, which she was advocating with increasing pressure. When Shadow Dwellers married, it was for a lot longer than a human lifetime. The celebration of this event was so important that it was carried out with a grandeur not soon forgotten. With Nicolette, it would be an unimaginable hardship.

# 3

## Gideon Lord and the Trust

aura faced Gideon Lord, looking very much the disobedient schoolgirl. By some miracle, her white dress was still presentable, although the lace choker had been a lost cause. She shifted uncomfortably, unable to conceal her nervousness.

Lord began pacing, his face tense with frustration. Finally, he stopped and turned to her with clear disapproval.

He was a tall, thin, older man with thick silver hair that was now disheveled, suggesting hours of worry. His voice was gruff, his eyes astute, and his chin determined. He didn't tolerate nonsense. He had a definite European quality that contributed to his air of authority. Despite his look of disappointment, Laura tried to maintain an attitude of righteousness.

"He deserved worse, and you know it," she declared, unnerved by the protracted silence. "While you're planning your next strategic move, victims continue to pile up. If he hadn't taken me in his limo tonight, he would've found someone else to kill." Laura peeked at Lord furtively just in time to see him flinch. Lord had taken the role of her father almost from the moment Monk had brought her in.

"I'm trying to keep you alive, you little miscreant. An endeavor you're making exceedingly difficult. We would've handled Eric, as you well know. You're afraid that I would've chosen another operative to deal with him, and so you acted first. You made yourself an instrument of revenge, which clouded your judgment with emotion. You're lucky you survived."

"With all due respect, sir," Laura protested, "your methods aren't working. At least, not in the long term. If you want to win this conflict, overt armed combat will never work against Shadow Dwellers. They have all the advantages of greater strength and sharper senses. You need to handle them in a way that's designed to use their weaknesses against them.

"They want our blood and all that it contains. So, I lure them in with the promise of our richest, strongest emotions: the fever of passion and the fire of great happiness. When their guard is down, they're vulnerable. They would never consider me—a mere human woman—a threat. I'm too young, too frail. So they lower their defenses, and I take them down. With my blood, sure death comes to those animals." Laura held up the vial of Lord's new blood catalyst chemical. "You know I'm right, or you wouldn't have given me this weapon."

"Yes, you've definitely found a way to get close to criminal Shadow Dwellers, and yes, I did give you the poison gel," Lord agreed. "But Eric was exceptionally dangerous, and you were lucky he didn't kill you first. But more than that, with his death come serious consequences. His men won't let his disappearance go unchallenged. Even if we destroy the body, there will be reprisals. Have you made some plan to protect our agents from the fallout?"

Laura dropped into a chair, for the first time repentant. She had forgotten about Eric's minions. She decided it was time to reveal a plan she'd been molding for weeks. It could have a serious impact on the community of Shadow Dwellers: their food would become their worst nightmare.

"I've recruited a small group of young women who can be trained to bring down criminal Shadow Dwellers. When I organized a concert series last fall, I met three very talented, yet-to-be discovered women. Kate and Tanya are amazing singers who can charm the most recalcitrant criminal. Mina is a musician and an exceptional dancer. She writes good music. All three are willing to help me in my quest to get justice for criminal victims. More important, they're young, and the Shadow Dwellers do like the young ones. These ladies will be underestimated, making them lethal weapons. We'll act as an elite squad operating undercover. All we need is your resources and leadership."

Laura waited for Lord's list of objections. She kept her eyes downcast, afraid he would find her proposal impulsive and foolhardy. She looked up to find him studying her speculatively. Then, to her utter surprise, he agreed.

"I think your idea has potential. For so long, we've used armed soldiers to battle these creatures, only to create a war that never ends. But you might really be on to something. I'll want to vet your candidates, of course." He looked deliberately at Laura, and she nodded. "We can use simulated conflict scenarios to test their skills and ability to improvise. And I've strengthened the gel, so there's less chance of getting killed before it works.

"But I have bad news. My cleanup crew did dispose of Eric's body, but someone was leaving when they arrived. I don't know how soon the murder will be reported to the Shadow community. I can only hope Eric's men will hold off long enough to get your patrol up to speed."

Laura had been fighting against Lord's rules for so long that she was a bit dumbfounded by his sudden surrender on this issue. But rather than examine this precious concession too closely, she pulled out her phone and started making calls. What she hadn't told Lord was that she had already started training her recruits. Also, they needed time to develop unique personae to attract Shadow Dwellers.

Within an hour, the three women were standing in Lord's library ready to enter the echelons of his elite force. Lord explained that they were expected to live at his house during their initial training period and would be paid generously for their service.

Lord studied each woman critically, finally nodding his approval. Laura had deliberately chosen women who would satisfy a wide range of appetites. There was a clever, petite Asian geisha; a tall, regal, blond Viking; and a curvy, flirty, black vixen. Laura would be the mysterious creative siren.

"Each of my operatives has chosen a code name to maintain her anonymity." Laura pointed to each one in turn. "Mina, the geisha, plays a number of musical instruments; Kate, the Viking, has a voice as clear and sweet as a mountain stream; and Tanya, the vixen, is a singer who can stir the audience's emotions." Each girl nodded when her alias was mentioned. "Our team will be called the Trust because we survive only if we can trust each other to stand together, and our safety hinges on keeping our existence secret."

"And you?" Lord asked. "What is your talent?"

Laura blushed uncomfortably. She had always been outspoken regarding the assets of her friends, but when it came to singing her own praises, she was clumsy. "I-I'm another s-s-songwriter and stylist," she mumbled and then forced herself to speak more clearly. "With my experience in photography and theater, I'll help the women with provocative costumes, realistic backdrops, and imaginative songs coordinated to a common theme. It's my responsibility to make sure we're attracting our targets. My code name is Conductor."

Lord nodded and waved Monk closer. "Monk will act as liaison between us. Once you're in the field undercover, he'll provide you with anything you need: money, tech, weapons, anything."

"But they might recognize him as one of your men," Laura objected.

"He's kept a low profile since the current crop of Shadow Dwellers came to Rainier. He's one of my best bodyguards and your loyal friend. I'll not let you start such a dangerous operation without him. He'll keep you alive no matter what it takes. Still, we'll need to consider additional men to guard the other women. Monk can't watch all four of you at once, especially if you split up."

At this, a roar of objection rose from the new recruits. Laura could see that her ladies didn't want male protection. But Lord was resolute.

"Look, I know that you're all impressive," he soothed. "But men will bring unique and valuable skill sets to your team. The more expertise you have available, the better your chances of success."

"Monk has saved my neck numerous times," Laura agreed. "We need backup to handle the unexpected."

Grudgingly, her team accepted this last condition set by Lord. Laura remained behind, while Monk accompanied the new recruits through an intricate inlaid door to a hidden elevator that led to Lord's underground training facility. Laura expected her team to qualify for fieldwork easily. They were already accomplished at basic defense skills. She wouldn't wait for male counterparts. That would be Lord's headache.

Laura glanced at her watch. It was well after 2:00 a.m., and the thrill of the hunt was fading. Ever since preparing to engage Eric, Laura had been pumping pure adrenaline. Her senses had become hypersensitive, her heart had accelerated, and her mind had sharpened as soon as she'd entered The Colony, automatically formulating response strategies against possible exigencies. When Monk insisted she come back to Lord's, fear of his disapproval had maintained her high adrenaline levels. Now that everything was in process, a wave of weariness passed through her. She took a cleansing breath, rubbed her eyes, and rotated her shoulders, trying to ease the new heaviness.

"I'm going," she announced suddenly, turning toward the door.

Monk had returned and was now waiting by the exit. "The women are being processed," he told Lord over Laura's head. "Their first training session will begin tomorrow. May I take you home?" he asked, reaching to take Laura's arm. "I already sent someone to retrieve your car."

Laura sighed with relief and felt some weariness lift. She was glad Monk had taken charge. She let him take her down to Lord's cavernous garage. Monk was a fan of fancy cars. His usual high-tech black van was perfect for subterfuge, but now stealth wasn't needed. Monk stopped in front of a long, red hot rod. Laura eyed the flashy number dubiously.

"You've got to be kidding. Can you even fit in that thing?" She raised her eyebrows askance. Sports cars were notorious for having tight, narrow seats.

"I had it customized," Monk assured her, clearly not offended by her reference to his large size.

Monk's shoulders and chest were so muscled he looked like a football player on steroids. He usually wore a long black coat to hide the true extent of his size and strength. He had taught Laura that being underestimated went a long way to winning a battle, a tactic she was now using with gusto. He held the passenger door open for her, let her slide in, gently closed the door, and then rounded the car to climb into the expanded driver's seat.

Monk drove with single-minded focus. He was never chatty, but when he drove, he spared no attention for anything else. She held on with both hands as they swerved around tight curves and barreled down straightaways, full speed ahead. At any moment, she expected to hear the familiar wail of a pursuing siren.

Finally they turned up her driveway, and Laura felt a flush of happy anticipation. She could see her little cottage peeking out from underneath the familiar crown of trees. This was her secret haven, far from the dangers of hunting Shadow Dwellers. Now that they had safely arrived, she perceived a benefit to Monk's wild driving. No one could have followed their mad dash through the empty streets and narrow roads without alerting Monk.

When she was patrolling the city, Laura usually stayed with Lord. His compound had security measures that she could rely on. But during her downtime, she stayed here, where her heart was. There were three structures, a main cottage and two cabins for staff and friends. The three buildings were surrounded by flourishing gardens.

Laura watched Monk leave before she opened the front door. She moved quickly through the dark house, going directly to her bedroom. She stretched out on the bed, letting the quiet room slow her racing mind, deliberately relaxing her tight, tense muscles. Even though she was tired physically, her brain needed to slow down before she could sleep.

Three names, three silhouettes, three personalities spun in her mind: Eric, Stephan, and Lord. Three powerful, dangerous men tugged at her emotions, demanding attention. For Eric, all she felt was unqualified relief. He was gone, and the ghosts of her friends could finally rest. Since the tragedy that had taken their lives, her dreams had been filled with their pale, lifeless bodies and their cries for justice.

Laura had met Grace, Ellie, and Pam during her enrollment at Rainier University. The three women had traveled together from a small community in Kansas. They'd seen Laura standing alone, waiting to register for classes and had come over to introduce themselves. The four had quickly become close, finally moving into a house together. They shared homework, honors, holidays, and heartbreak—until that unforgettable night a lifetime ago.

In retrospect, Laura recognized that fate had saved her on that terrible night. She should have been there. She would have been there if not for a series of misadventures that had no rhyme or reason. Why had that cat run out in front of her? Why had she decided to stop for gas? Why had that old lady stumbled while she was waiting at a light? It seemed that something, more than the obvious, had been afoot that night. In the end, she had survived, but she had lost her dear roommates.

When Laura had finally arrived for their usual Friday-night party, all those months ago, the house had been dark, and she had seen a black SUV roaring away from the house. A sharp stab of fear had twisted her stomach. She'd automatically memorized the SUV's license plate number and had even managed to catch a glimpse of the driver, an obviously dangerous man.

Warily, Laura had parked her car a few doors down the street and raced to the house. With her heart pounding painfully, she opened the front door, turned on the lights downstairs using the master switch by the door, and rushed to the living room. She hadn't realized she was holding her breath until it exploded in a gasp of shock at the tableau that lay before her.

Laura's last hope, that her fears had been silly superstition, was replaced by a terrible grief. Tears flooded her eyes. Wiping them away impatiently, she knelt beside the figure of her best friend, Ellie. Hesitantly, she stretched her hand toward the girl, stopping short of making physical contact. Her friend's body showed evidence of a brutal murder. Deep gashes covered the bone-white bodies of all her friends. But there was no blood. When this fact fully registered through her shock, Laura scanned the room feverishly. There was no blood anywhere. All her friends were there, in various contorted positions, but there was no blood. She stood up then, recognizing that she was a witness to something outside the ordinary.

Laura saw the phone lying on the floor next to the sideboard. She reached for the receiver intending to call the police and heard the sound of a skidding vehicle pulling up to the house. Apprehensively, she headed toward the back door. When the front knob rattled, she veered into the study, closing the door behind her. She barely made it before she heard the sound of boots stomping into her house. Laura quietly opened the French doors leading to the backyard, squeezed out, and dashed behind the neighbors' hedge. Once she was safely hidden, she tried to see what was going on. But she could only discern human forms moving around inside, violating her home. She needed to get away and decide what to do.

Laura had made her way back to her vehicle in a fog of suffering. Once inside her car, she sank down out of sight. Parking away from her house had been an automatic precaution, almost as if she knew what was going to happen. It was one of those strange coincidences that speckled her life. She dug through her purse for her cell phone and found it buried at the bottom. She called the police, hoping to catch the intruders before they got away. The dispatcher wasted precious moments trying to establish a cause for action until she used one word: *murder.*

Helplessly, Laura watched as each of her friends was carried outside and dumped into the back of a white van. Of course, their bodies were completely concealed in carpets. But Laura knew that inside each roll was one of her roommates. She raged silently at her inability to take any action. But there were just too many men, and she had no weapon. She cursed when they finally drove away. She could just make out a siren in the distance: too little, too late.

Laura made a fateful decision in her car that night. Her friends were going to be avenged. She followed the white van, staying as far back as she dared while still keeping it in sight. At each light, she slowed, fearing they would notice her car. Once, three vehicles pulled in between them, and she lost sight of the van. But it was late and traffic was thinning. Eventually, the cars veered off, and she had an unobstructed view of the van. She followed it to the waterfront, where it entered the fenced parking lot of a warehouse. She drove to a bushy clump of trees that concealed her car and gave her a partial view of the warehouse.

The intruders made no attempt to hide their activities. They unlocked a rolling freight door and in the glaring interior light, hauled the incriminating bodies into the warehouse. Laura watched in horror as her friends' bodies disappeared into a vat of smoking liquid, most likely acid, which would dissolve all evidence of their sinister deaths. Revolted, she slumped down and waited for the men to finish. She would always remember the terrible stink coming from the vat.

Laura was determined to find the man she had seen driving away in the black SUV. He had to be the killer. In the wee hours of the morning, the van finally led her to a luxury tower of condos. Here, she did enter the building but only long enough to see which floor the men stopped on. It was the penthouse, of course. She easily extracted the owner's name from the young desk clerk: Eric Mateo. Then she left. She had enough information to identify the butchers; time was now on her side.

What Laura hadn't known that night was that she wasn't the only one following these men. Monk had been tracking Eric's activities for weeks and had witnessed the murder of her friends. He told her later that when he discovered that she was also following the van, he feared that she didn't know the true nature of these killers. So Monk had kept tabs on her, and the next time she approached the condo tower, he had intercepted her. Without explanation, he forced her to attend her first meeting with Gideon Lord.

Initially, Laura had fought Monk like a wildcat, fearing that she was about to meet the same fate as her lost friends. While trying to avoid serious injury, Monk had assured her that they were both fighting a common enemy. He had driven her to a house that was nothing short of a castle, with turrets, a defensive wall, and even, absurdly, a moat. Gideon Lord did not disappoint either. He stood as a formidable figure in his impressive library, filled with hundreds of old books, in front of a blazing fire. He exuded an aura of nobility that was intimidating.

Then, in no uncertain terms, Lord laid down the law of the Shadow Dwellers. His deep, resonant voice had echoed throughout the room. Laura remembered that night, when she had learned the truth about her friends' killer, as the beginning of a new life.

"The Shadow Dwellers are a secret race of nearly immortal creatures that live off what is hidden in our blood," Lord had told her. "Human blood contains the life force, creative intelligence, stream of consciousness—or any other name you can come up with to describe an energy that can animate matter—and that conveys immortality to the Shadow Dwellers. This power to convert our blood into virtual immortality can be transferred to humans. Unfortunately, if the Shadow Dweller views us as mere food, he or she will kill indiscriminately and often.

"Ironically, the Shadow Dwellers are not as well hidden as they would like to believe. Every so often, someone stumbles across their existence, and a new element of their myth is revealed. If you're determined to avenge your friends, it's time for you learn what is fact and what is fiction.

"They have a long life span, so they learn to be very resourceful. I have seen them die only as a result of extreme violence or innovative science. If they have elders, they remain a closely guarded secret. Once they learn of your awareness and knowledge of them, you will become a target. Always act naïve.

"One fact of the legend is the undeniable fascination Shadow Dwellers have for humans. This is their Achilles' heel. They learn to manipulate the memories buried in our blood, and use them to dominate us. Once they begin to feed, you had better have your means of killing them already activated because you won't be able to slay them afterward. When satiated, they're more powerful and appear more human. They occasionally take human pets when they need a public image, so beware of humans close to them. If you persist in hunting them without the proper training and weapons, you will die."

"Will you teach me?" she challenged him, her chin raised stubbornly. "Make no mistake; I will avenge my friends with or without your help. But I'm willing to learn anything that will help me achieve this goal."

Lord studied Laura's physique with an assessing glance. "Can you work hard? We don't have time for lightweights."

"I'll do whatever is necessary to succeed," she vowed.

"You're a bit flabby. It'll take time just to slim you down before building you up. Do you work out at all?"

"I jog—with my dogs. I love to run." Laura smiled impishly. Whenever she talked about her animals, she felt a rush of happiness.

"That will help. But our workouts will be difficult and require a sustained commitment. Once you start, you must finish," Lord insisted firmly.

Since he'd obviously doubted her proficiency, Laura had wondered why he'd considered training her at all. But she said, "Agreed."

Ultimately, Lord allowed her into his army to keep her alive. He had reminded her of this fact with every difficult maneuver he showed her. He handled her instruction personally, teaching her skills as quickly as she could master them. Laura embraced the physical challenges eagerly. The harder Lord made the lessons, the more determined she was to adapt and excel. But her favorite subject was the stories of the Shadow Dwellers themselves. He made their history sound like some great legend hiding a greater wisdom. In the end, he became more than a mentor. He looked on her success with the kind of pride she would crave from a father, a role that had been painfully vacant.

With memories of her training days lingering in her mind, Laura drifted into a light sleep. A soft smile played across her lips as she remembered again that her friends could rest in peace. Pleasant memories swirled in her fading consciousness. A vision of Stephan with outstretched arms touched her imagination, and she snuggled deeper into her pillows. Later, she was running with him through a dense evergreen forest, jumping effortlessly over rocks, roots, and piles of autumn leaves. The cool air spurred her to a faster pace. Someone was calling to them to slow down, and Laura reduced her speed. In her dream, she looked back over her shoulder, resisting Stephan's attempts to pull her forward faster.

"Wait! Stop! Please!" came the soft call in the recesses of her mind.

"Stephan, please, we must wait," Laura pleaded, as if he were a dear friend rather than a stranger. "There's someone coming."

But Stephan wouldn't slow down. He released his hold on her hand and ran ahead, leaving her behind in the strange forest. Laura moaned aloud before falling into a dark oblivion.

# 4

## The Last Straw

Stephan was impatient for Jon's report. His bartender had called earlier warning Stephan of his imminent return. Jon had been watching Laura for days, staying clear of the theater and Nicolette. Stephan had been unable to shake off her constant surveillance. She had the instincts of a predator, and he was her favorite prey. Using Eric's death as an excuse, she had hired extra bodyguards. Stephan hadn't missed that their vigilance was usually focused on him.

News of Eric's death had spread like wildfire and raised the expected alarms. Everyone was under suspicion. What he found amusing was that no one considered that the girl in the white dress might be a potential suspect. He had to give her credit. She was the perfect adversary, one that hid in plain sight.

Stephan felt relief replace his impatience when Jon entered the club. He had taken extra precautions to keep Nicolette's ubiquitous spies off Jon's trail, specifically Noel. He only hoped he had succeeded.

"Our little minx has been busy." Jon grinned.

Stephan shook his head slightly when he noticed a guard move within earshot.

"Let's go inside. How was your trip?" he asked blandly. Stephan led Jon into his office without waiting for an answer. Once inside, he activated a jamming device. He had added it at the same time that Nicolette had installed her new security. Finally, he nodded for Jon to continue his report.

"I had to be extra careful. She is one jumpy fish. She spends most of her time at Lord's and is definitely one of his soldiers. Any personal details will have to come through the lady herself."

"So what is she working on now?" Stephan prodded, his frustration trampling his customary calm.

"She's coordinating the activities of a group of young women. I think there are three of them, and they are spectacular. Three flowers, each with her own unique beauty."

"I do believe you're smitten, Jon. Surely you aren't planning an encounter." Stephan chuckled mischievously.

Jon's escapades with the fairer sex were epic.

"Don't be foolish. I'd have to meet them first," Jon quipped with a cocked eyebrow and a Cheshire grin. Then his expression sobered. "But they spend most of their time at Lord's. I believe it's some type of elite force. Because Laura has already taken out one target, these girls might be preparing to take out more—"

"Shadow Dwellers," Stephan finished grimly. "So you think they're after us."

"Since the girl is a hunter, it's logical that the others are as well. It would be better if we took them out now, before they come at us full force."

"You want to kill them just in case? We're not murderers." Stephan found the tendency of his kindred to meet each problem with violence a bit unnerving. "Besides, Lord only kills those who go on killing rampages. Is there a rampage on your schedule?"

"I don't think a rampage would be as fun as it used to be. That is, since the villagers got machine guns." Jon hung his head soulfully, blinking eyes that appeared misty. "Oh, what I wouldn't give for a return to the good ole days."

"You mean when frenzied mobs of villagers would come at us with torches and burn everything in sight, including us?" Stephan chuckled, winking conspiratorially.

"So, she lives with Lord?" he asked abruptly. How would he ever get close enough to watch her if she really lived in that fortress?

"Not all the time. She has her own place with its special brand of guards." Jon smiled mysteriously.

"Guards?"

"Dogs, cats, birds, and several other wild species." This time, Jon laughed outright. "She collects animals. I saw a deer leap her fence to nibble her blackberries, and she made no effort to stop its pilfering."

"Wonderful. How am I going to reach her?" Stephan moaned morosely. While he could hold humans in his thrall, animals were beyond his influence. Their fear would definitely be visible.

Stephan's yearning for Laura tasted sweet and dangerous. If anything, his fear of her elite force made his desire sharper and more focused. He leaned closer. "What have Laura's new friends actually done?"

"Initially, nothing. The new women stayed at the complex, and Laura visited during the day. Yesterday they hired a limo and visited lounges where the Shadow Houses like to hunt, but none owned by you or Nicolette. Lord has to be the one providing Laura with the list. Maybe he doesn't want her around you or your paramour."

"Maybe," Stephan conceded. "How long did they stay?"

"Long enough for a meeting. They were dressed in business attire, not like girls dressed for a night on the town. Then Laura took them to a quiet restaurant for a ladies-only powwow."

Stephan nodded. He walked around his desk, opened a locked cabinet, and retrieved a digital camera phone with multiple features. "Take this. I want pictures of each woman for identification. Send them to my personal cell. Try to get close enough to record what they're planning and send that to me also. Maybe sneak into a club while they're inside.

"Nicolette knows about Laura, but fortunately, she's been too preoccupied with me to ask about your activities. I've never been so grateful for her obsession. In any case, be back here tomorrow. We'll make our final plans for a face-to-face with Laura then." Stephan looked nervously at his watch. It was almost time for Nicolette's grand entrance. "Maybe there's still time for you to leave out the front."

Unfortunately, when Jon ducked out the front entrance, Noel scurried for the still swinging door. Swearing, Stephan grabbed the troublemaker by his collar while he was still within reach, lifted him off the floor, and slammed him with a satisfying bang onto the bar.

"Stay!" he barked, very like an owner controlling his disobedient dog. Out of the corner of his eye, he saw another guard dart forward. "You leave and I'll make it my personal mission to see that you regret it," he threatened with enough deadly intonation to stop the man. "You may work for Nicolette, but you operate unmolested at my pleasure. Do you want to give me a reason to send all of you, including Nicolette, away?" He smiled sardonically. "She wouldn't be pleased."

The offender turned pale and shook his head nervously. He returned to the door that led to Stephan's basement apartment, which Nicolette had taken over. She had tried to redecorate in her own flamboyant style. The result was uncomfortable and unsettling, so Stephan had moved to his office, unofficially.

Nicolette could appear at any moment, so he had to act quickly. Stephan glared at Noel. "Where were you going, and what are your orders? Before you try to lie your way out of answering, know this: I'll know whether you're being honest and take the appropriate steps."

Noel shrugged stubbornly and refused to answer. Stephan took a handful of his collar and twisted it until it closed around the little man's windpipe. Even when the gnome's lips turned blue and his eyes bulged dangerously, he didn't struggle. He didn't even try to draw breath. This creature was obviously used to being tormented. Stephan was ready to give up all hope of getting answers, when one of the new guards broke. He didn't have the stomach to watch the little dwarf die.

"She wants us to follow Jon," he blurted nervously.

"Enough!" boomed from the apartment doorway; the door had opened silently. Nicolette stormed into the middle of the drama, her eyes flashing with a fearsome rage.

She gripped Stephan's arm roughly and roared, "Why are you detaining my men? They have their orders, and your interference will cost them." She twisted her hold, trying to pry his hand off Noel's collar. He released the obnoxious dwarf impatiently.

Stephan stepped back, swallowing a suffocating wave of exasperation. He was tired of Nicolette and her constant attempts to keep him in line. He would no longer stand by quietly while her men spied on his operation. If she wouldn't give him some measure of freedom, then he was done.

"This worm was attempting to follow Jon, my most trusted operative. You will not spy on my activities any longer. I'm not your underling, and I won't answer to you. Noel is lucky I didn't just kill him the first time he crossed me. Then I would have prevented his continuing intrusions into my private life. I want that parasite out of my establishments permanently." Stephan had finally captured the dwarf's attention. He pointed at the front entrance.

"But he's my best man, and I need him. Why do you care what he does? Are you doing something wrong?" Nicolette's eyes sparked with jealously. "Why are you so determined to hide your activities?"

Stephan stared at Nicolette in disbelief. He realized that it was too late. "I will no longer tolerate your ridiculous need to dominate me. If you want a pet lover who'll follow your orders and have no life apart from you, then find someone else. You're through ruling this roost. Take your men, your things, and get out!" he thundered. His righteous indignation exploded as the chains that had been strangling him finally fell away.

Nicolette's stricken expression intensified as Stephan's loud accusations drew stares from his customers. He knew she had spent a great deal of time and effort trying to hook him. Early on, when she had been careful and discreet, Stephan had lowered his guard. But as time passed, her obvious need for recognition increased. Instead of setting boundaries, he'd been complacent. She must have grown used to his easy nature and getting her own way. But she'd made the deadly mistake of forgetting that she could go too far and demand too much, and using her men to spy on him had been the final straw. Yet Stephan was honest enough with himself to admit that Laura had a part in his sudden intolerance.

"But, sweetheart," Nicolette pleaded, fear darkening her eyes. She glanced at his office door, obviously wanting privacy. But he shook his head decisively. There would be no more secrets. Everyone would know where they stood. He could see that she was horrified at the possibility of losing him and her position at his theater.

"What are you saying? We've been happy together. I thought we would surely be bonded in the ancient ritual. You can't want to destroy all we have built. Our colony is strong; our businesses flourishing."

Stephan's heart softened at her pleas. She was right. They had built a vibrant empire, including several establishments that catered to their people's special needs. Many wandering groups of Shadow Dwellers had settled around their safe haven. But Nicolette couldn't leave the subject of Jon alone, reminding Stephan of why *they* would never work.

"What could Jon be doing that you would throw away everything we've built? Is it some new woman? Is it that woman who was with Eric?" Nicolette couldn't hide her jealousy or her desperation for long. "I've every right to protect my interests. If you're chasing other women, then I'm entitled to look into your affairs."

"You just can't leave well enough alone, can you?" Stephan snorted bitterly. "I think I've made it clear that your men are not welcome to investigate me, now or ever, and still you act as if this is your right. Well, I have the right to privacy; I have the right to follow my own interests without your interference. When you decided you should control our life together, you ended any hope of a relationship between us. Get out, or I will have you thrown out!" Stephan knew he had to be brutal in a very public way, or she would never leave.

"N-no. My girls are The Colony's only entertainment! I-I have to stay here to manage them," she whined weakly and then with more conviction. "You can't throw me out!"

"Your girls don't work here anymore. Take them with you!"

"But you can't run The Colony without them! Your clients come here to see their special talents."

"They come here to see me. I'll find new entertainment," Stephan promised, unimpressed by her assessment of her own importance. He had survived without her before and would do so again.

"Please, please, Stephan, reconsider. I'm sorry." Tears filled her eyes. She collapsed at his feet and took his hand imploringly. "I'll stop looking into your affairs. I-I helped turn The Colony into a successful theater. Don't send me away. I'll do anything. Pleeease…"

Stephan looked down at Nicolette, but instead of sympathy, he felt a strange emptiness. He knew she would go back to her old ways as sure as a cat would search for a new mouse to terrorize. At the moment, she was afraid and would promise anything. She would just conceal her schemes, at least for a while. He knew he would be free only if he sent her away.

"I'm sorry, Nicolette, but there's no going back. I might have been angry at first, but now I'm just resigned. I don't love you, and I can't live without love. Now go, before you embarrass yourself further." He pushed her toward the apartment entrance.

At last, Nicolette seemed to accept his decision. Her eyes burned with a new madness as she rose to her feet. "You'll come to regret what you've done here today. I'll make you pay even if it takes everything I have!" she shrieked inches from his face. Then she turned and flounced down the stairwell, waving at her people to follow.

Stephan knew he had made a powerful enemy. Nicolette lived in his world, and she knew his vulnerabilities.

"Make sure she doesn't take anything but her own belongings," he ordered the guards who had always been loyal to him. He didn't want to leave her alone in his theater, but he had to depart before his presence incited her to some bad act.

Stephan allowed himself a few moments to bask in a newfound feeling of freedom and lightness. He had been under her thumb for so long he'd become accustomed to the weight. Now he appreciated its absence. Unconsciously, he whistled a tune as he headed for his car. To his dismay, he caught sight of Noel entering the stairwell to his apartment, most likely to report Stephan's small gesture of happiness.

# 5

## A Friendship Is Born

Lord had given Laura a list of lounges that offered two vital features: they had entertainment, and their clientele included Shadow Dwellers. Laura had noticed that Stephan's name wasn't on the list of owners. Since he owned high-class establishments, she had wondered at this omission.

The Trust had started its first round of auditions after only a week of training. The girls quickly showed proficiency in all the skills Lord required. The list of performance halls was his silent signal to begin operations, even though they still hadn't agreed on male bodyguards. Mina, Kate, and Tanya dressed in high fashion and, along with Laura, visited Lord's suggested establishments, looking for bookings.

As a consequence, Laura learned that Nicolette, Stephan's ex, was on a rampage. After the very public disintegration of her partnership with him, she was terrorizing the other theaters, forcing them to use her girls exclusively. This meant that Laura had a very short list of potential employers. Stephan became her best option.

Laura knew that returning to The Colony would be risky. Stephan would, most certainly, recognize her as the one who had left with Eric before his *disappearance*. She would need to have a good explanation. If anyone learned the truth, she might turn from the hunter into the hunted.

Laura decided to scout The Colony alone. If there was trouble, she would be the only one at risk. Obviously, Lord didn't want her back there, so she would have to go without telling him.

Laura nervously pushed through the front doors and walked directly to the bar. She studied the elegant theater more closely now that she wasn't on a mission. It had the European flair preferred by Shadow Dwellers born in those countries. There were lovely beveled-glass windows that complemented the door and highly polished wood paneling. Special booths along the walls were circular, with high backs that created pools of privacy. Everywhere, staff was preparing the theater for that night's customers. She could hear the rustle of activity behind the swinging doors that led to the kitchens.

Laura felt a reprieve when she spied the man behind the bar. It wasn't Stephan. She was still anonymous. He finished a phone conversation before glancing up and smiling a welcome. Laura returned his smile and moved closer.

"Is the manager in?" she asked politely.

"Not at the moment. Maybe I can help. What's your business?" The man moved from behind the bar and waved her over to one of the circular booths. He turned a small vase at the center of the table, increasing the overhead chandelier's illumination.

"How clever," she chirped, nervously trying to find a comfortable position on the cushioned seat.

Ultimately, Laura perched herself on the edge of the seat and laced her fingers to keep them still. She was taken by complete surprise when Stephan himself suddenly appeared and pushed her further into the booth, blocking her exit. His expression was one of innocent curiosity, his manner informal and friendly. But his blocking her in was unsettling.

"How nice of you to visit us again," he said politely.

"Are you the manager?"

"Yes." He nodded at Jon, and his friend returned to the bar. "How may I help you?"

"I represent a group of performers looking for bookings. Your theater has a great reputation. Are you looking for new talent? Is this your only location?"

"I own four theaters, and all offer entertainment." His smile broadened. "You couldn't have come at a better time," he confessed. "I just lost my main provider. How many women do you represent?"

"Three, two singers and a dancer. We compose our own music, have specially tailored costumes, and construct our own props. A major component of our performances is the illusion created on stage. Each performance is designed to tell a story," Laura explained.

"Could your clients come at four to audition? Perhaps we might have a private dinner later?"

Stephan's interest in her was unexpected. Laura swallowed hard, considering the pitfalls of a personal relationship. A romantic liaison was, of course, out of the question. She could never accept a man who was kin to monsters like Eric, and she would never forget how her friends had died. Even a friendship could create problems. He'd be more aware of her activities and whereabouts. Emotions tended to have a life of their own and might easily create confused loyalties.

Besides, she really didn't want to be responsible for putting Nicolette on Lord's most wanted list. Scorned lovers were notorious for irrational decisions that could end in violence for any perceived rival. She would have enough trouble working among Shadow Dwellers. In the end, she made the only decision that made any sense.

Laura shook her head. "I don't think so. My girls' shows are very time-consuming, which doesn't leave time for friendships. If your interest in me has prompted your offer for auditions, then I think I'd better decline." Laura slid around the other side of the table and stood up.

"Wait! I really do need entertainers. Do come at four," he insisted as he came to his feet beside her. "I'm intrigued by your full-service approach. Singers are easy to find, but vision is rare. Your willingness to compose new music for an entire performance is a godsend. I, myself, do all the engineering at The Colony and could use some outside inspiration. Would you like a tour?"

Leaving prudence to the meek, Laura nodded. Seeing behind the curtain of a prosperous theater was a rare treat. Stephan took her into the main auditorium and across an ornate stage into the back hallways. The performance platform and orchestra pit had only a small part to play in the total mechanics that were required to put on a performance. There was a high-tech control room with dimmer racks in the back, several catwalks, a green room, and modern dressing rooms. A large trap room hid Stephan's most impressive innovations. It was under the stage and allowed invisible manipulation of all the backdrops and props. He could raise and lower several different stage sets, including complex water features in many and meticulous, realistic painted backdrops in all. He had also installed special lighting directly into the scenery.

Laura found herself in awe of his mechanical and electrical adaptations. Stephan was not just a businessman and technician. He had the heart of an artist, and The Colony was where he displayed his most intricate work.

"These are my latest designs." Stephan indicated a corner containing three bulky sets. "I'm trying to incorporate high-tech mechanisms into elaborate architecture. I often improvised at my first theater, in France."

Laura suppressed her excitement. "France?" she inquired, trying to sound causal. The histories of Shadow Dwellers were hard to uncover. She couldn't believe he would so casually reveal his past.

"My family had money, and my father was a patron of the arts in France. He invested heavily in a well-respected opera house, and so I grew up learning everything about his work. I discovered I had a natural talent for adding unusual perspectives to familiar operas. Our theater became popular. Famous performers requested auditions, just for a chance to use our unique stage configurations." Stephan had a contemplative look in his eyes that was tinged with sadness. He blinked several times and refocused on Laura's face. "I've tried to recreate my work from that theater and modernize the sets with the latest technology."

"These are amazing. At least what I can see of them." Laura was only able to see parts of the sets' intricate designs. "When I designed new scenarios for our college plays, I was usually limited to modifying props and sewing elaborate costumes."

"With your specialized experience and my expertise in engineering and architecture, perhaps we could collaborate on some of your shows," Stephan offered.

"That would be fantastic," Laura agreed, forgetting her vow to keep a professional distance. "Some of my most successful costumes symbolize water and snow. I have added crystals and colored lighting to dresses of white fur and Mediterranean-blue silk and produced some great effects. I try to create memorable effects."

Stephan eyes mirrored her enthusiasm. "I've tried risky adaptations. I have a waterfall that's almost too big to control. It uses recycled water spray to create ice formations during the performance. There's a camouflaged bird enclosure that gives the illusion of flying birds, and I've even tried an elephant."

"No, not really!" Laura exclaimed incredulously. "An elephant! How could you possibly get one?"

"The local zoo," Stephan confessed, winking conspiratorially. "For the right amount of money, you would be surprised what even a small theater can accomplish."

"Well, I never had a lot of money. But there's one advantage to doing university productions—unlimited talent. We get young minds willing to think up the most outrageous simulations. I used one design for the inside of a spaceship that was so massive we had to build it outside. We tried to simulate a volcano, but it looked too cheesy."

"The secret is to suggest the features of a volcano without actually trying to duplicate one. I have a simulation over there." Stephan pointed to one of the new sets.

"Great! I still have the technical diagrams and music that use that feature, one of my grand opuses. Kate looks great in front of snow and waterfalls. Could we use the icing fountain?"

Now Stephan laughed.

Laura grew hot with embarrassment. "Oops. I guess I've jumped the gun. You haven't even decided to hire my girls, and I'm already using your scenery. I think I understand why your French theater became so popular. What happened to it?"

"As with anything too successful, others tried to gain control of my designs. One powerful prima donna auditioned for a position at my theater at the peak of its preeminence. I might've used her if she'd been reasonable. Unfortunately, she wasn't going to take no for an answer."

Laura studied Stephan closely. She wondered if this mysterious prima donna was the reason he was here. To be forced into the dark life of a Shadow Dweller because of greed would have been intolerable.

"Did she get what she wanted?"

Stephan shook his head, his expression bleak. "It's impossible to force creative talent. Once I was in her power, I had no energy to create anything. She grew tired of me when my sets broke down and the theater lost most of its clientele. I was able to run away. When I did try to establish another theater, I discovered I would never be free of her greed. As soon as I saw her in the audience, I decided to leave Europe forever. I destroyed my work and fled to America. I don't know where she is today, but if I see her again..." Stephan had a searing fire in his eyes.

Laura felt a shiver of fear. It was time to change the subject.

"But you're here now and, from what I can see, quite successful. I would consider myself lucky to work with these sets. I've never had the benefit of collaborating with a professional theater owner."

Laura's Trust was a testament to her first real family: Grace, Pam, and Ellie. She had gathered a team of talented women who would help her prevent similar murders. What she hadn't expected was Stephan and the realization that her journey could take such an astonishing twist. She saw a chance to gain new skills doing the thing she loved best.

Stephan led Laura back to the entrance of The Colony. "Then, I will see you later?" he asked.

"We'll be here," she promised and extended her hand. He shook it firmly, all business.

When Laura arrived back at the theater at four, her girls were in rare form. They were hired on the spot. Laura immediately began coordinating different elements from her prior work for their first Colony appearances. She would highlight each performer's unique qualities.

During her first performance, Kate looked like a Norwegian goddess in the flowing white costume. It was tight and cut to show her long neck and sleek limbs with a black leather belt that emphasized her small waist. A crystal tiara and jeweled veil captured the light and illuminated the singer. Her seductive pose suggested both vulnerability and availability. Kate sang of brave battles and long ocean voyages with precise pitch and clear tones.

Stephan had added a high-volume mist machine and programmed blue, purple, and white spotlights to suggest the early darkness of a winter evening. His mammoth waterfall, framed by realistic rock cliffs, periodically froze water into strange ice formations before melting them away. Kate looked like she was surrounded by a northern land of extremes.

Tanya's black beauty was a whole other matter. Whereas Kate was ethereal, Tanya was earthy. For her, Laura chose lush red and rich gold. Tanya wore two costumes, one on top of the other. The top costume was made of feathers backlit with tiny lights sewn into the fabric. The feathers caressed her face and hands and covered most of her body. She began her performance with a song of a great love sung in husky, seductive tones. Then the costume fell away, exposing her perfect legs and enticing curves in a tight dress painted with tiny phoenixes and reddish-gold flames. Her moist skin glowed, and her lush red lips pouted flirtatiously. Tanya flipped her long hair back and arched her back sensually while she sang of her one true love.

At Laura's urging, Stephan raised his volcano set for Tanya's performance. High on the back wall of the stage were shifting lights, faux sparks, and steaming fog, which effectively suggested rising magma. Dunes of red and pink sand and rivers of bubbling orange and yellow water, on mobile platforms, fronted the volcano, highlighting the vibrant flames of Tanya's costume. The deafening applause was evidence of the Trust's successful launch.

Laura glanced around the theater and saw Kate and Tanya in the center of a crowd of attentive fans. Monk, who was sitting at the bar, was covertly taking pictures of all known Shadow Dwellers. If any became targets, they would use the girl the fan liked best as bait.

Mina hadn't come on the auditions at The Colony. They had decided to keep her undercover. Fortunately, Stephan hadn't asked about her absence.

Laura was worried about Nicolette. Stephan's ex-consort was creating so much havoc in the entertainment community that she feared Nicolette would become their next target. Even though Laura and her girls were on Nicolette's radar, Mina had worked to remain anonymous. She had gone to Siren's Song, Nicolette's signature club, to see what the female Shadow Dweller was up to. Laura felt a twinge of unease. Mina was working alone, which went against Lord's strictest rule.

Needing his comforting presence, Laura crossed to Monk, who was sitting at the bar. Stephan had accepted the brute only when Laura had made his presence a requirement. Stephan might have plenty of guards, but her girls would be protected by people she knew. Luckily, Monk hadn't commented on Mina's absence either.

"Have you recognized anyone yet?" she whispered to him. She glanced around the room, looking for any of the men documented in Lord's special notebook, the one that listed Shadow Dwellers who murdered humans.

"No. Stephan keeps his people well in line. We might have to look at other establishments." He frowned at a patron who was giving Laura an appraising look. The man suddenly veered around the pair and continued down the bar.

Laura chuckled at the passing man's disgusted expression. "You're not helping advance our mission," she teased. "You'll have to let men approach me sometime."

Monk growled low and dangerous. "If they can get past me," he muttered under his breath.

Laura didn't argue. His desire to protect her was valuable in an environment of constant danger.

"We're lucky Stephan keeps a tight ship. He's giving us a safe place to break in our new hunters. Fortunately, the seedier elements do make an appearance. I was lucky Eric came here."

A sudden commotion at the entrance drew her attention. Two muscular young men entered the theater, bringing in an icy chill. Through the open door, she could hear a howling wind that heralded an approaching storm. The idle chatter of several diners stilled. The newcomers crossed directly to Laura, and the tallest one handed her an envelope. Laura noticed the careful way the men scanned the room, assessing every angle of attack. They were dressed in loose-fitting black. She suspected they could never pass through airport security without TSA requiring thorough body searches.

Laura slipped her thumb under the flap, breaking the seal. Inside was a letter in Lord's familiar calligraphy. It always struck Laura that Lord embodied such odd contradictions. He was a warrior who wrote like a high-society woman.

"Dear Laura: Two bodyguard candidates. Good references and relevant experience. Ready to work. Have your back, Lord."

Laura returned the brief message to its envelope. Maybe his penmanship was like a lady's, but the words were totally guy: brief, focused, and impersonal.

Kate and Tanya joined their small group, attracted by the unfamiliar men. They looked expectant, obviously waiting for introductions. Both men were well-built, with chestnut hair and striking gold-green eyes.

"It's a note from Lord. These are our new guards. He's promised that they're suited to our special needs." Laura waved at the strangers.

"I'm Michael. This is Gabriel." The taller newcomer pointed at the man standing beside him. "We've been briefed on your situation. We're here to help."

Gabriel nodded briefly.

Kate and Tanya looked at each other, smiling conspiratorially, warning Laura of trouble to come. Her girls were comfortable with their attractiveness. Few men escaped their charms.

Turning to the grinning girls, she shook her head deliberately. "I want you two on your best behavior. No funny stuff!" she scolded, trying to sound serious. The girls' antics were really quite funny. "We need more security. Monk can't hope to keep all of us safe. I want your promise that you'll let them do their jobs unmolested."

Tanya glanced at the ceiling innocently, but Kate blushed and nodded. Tanya could fool a judge, but Kate wore her feelings on her sleeve.

It was Tanya who finally said sweetly, "OK, Mom, we'll be good. But they sure look delicious." The men shifted uncomfortably. Abruptly, Laura burst out laughing. She wondered who really needed bodyguards, the girls or these new recruits.

"For tonight, go with Tanya and Kate," she told Michael and Gabriel. "Tomorrow morning, report to Lord's underground gym. I'll evaluate your skill levels in coordinated drills with the women. We need you ready to fight closely in the face of any real threat."

Gabriel followed the girls backstage, but Michael waited expectantly. He obviously thought he would be protecting her. But Monk would always be her personal bodyguard.

"All is quiet. The girls have only one set left. Do we stay or go?" Monk asked quietly, ignoring Michael.

Before she could answer, Michael extended his hand for a handshake with Monk. Monk raised his eyebrows, surprised. It took Laura a moment to realize that few people approached Monk directly. None offered to shake hands. He just looked too menacing.

"I'm here for Laura," Michael announced, moving closer to her.

"I already have a bodyguard." Laura pointed at Monk. "And he is the best."

"Those are my orders, and I intend to follow them," Michael persisted.

"Who gave you those orders?" Monk asked suspiciously.

"Who cares? You're my guard, and I'll have no other," Laura snapped.

"Not anymore," Michael announced implacably. He was apparently uninterested in any opinion other than his own.

"Are you for real?" Laura could hardly believe his insolence. "You're here to assist us. You have no authority."

"I'm here to protect you and your girls from all threats. I need complete access to do that successfully. It's illogical to send me here without it."

To Laura's horror, Monk actually chuckled at Michael's obstinacy. The man's unyielding persistence didn't seem to upset him at all.

Laura wasn't so calm. "That's not your call. You're only the new guy. You do what we tell you."

"Gideon Lord said to show initiative in developing security measures that'll be foolproof. I'm using that initiative," Michael argued, obviously blinded by his own self-importance.

"You're being insubordinate!" Laura shouted.

Monk interrupted the pair by taking control of the conversation. "Did Lord tell you what your duties were?" he asked.

"He sent me here," Michael offered vaguely.

"And?" Monk would not be diverted.

Given no other choice, the man finally repeated his exact orders. "I'm to report to you."

Now Monk smiled. "Just as I thought. Look, I was young and ambitious once. But you're walking into a complicated situation. I am and always will be in charge of Laura's protection. But I'll make you my second-in-command, if you promise to stop 'showing initiative.'"

Michael had the grace to look embarrassed. "Of course, sir," he said without any further posturing.

"Now, I want you to patrol the perimeter and start a photo collection of all the customers." Monk handed him the digital camera. "We'll need them for our library of possible hostiles. Stephan will introduce you to his security men. You'll need to know who has authority to be here in an official capacity."

"As you say," Michael said. He approached a group of patrons who were just entering the theater.

"Well, you're a better man than I. I would have tossed that scoundrel out on his ear," Laura grumbled. "He's going to cause trouble. I can feel it."

To her surprise, Michael glanced back at them at that exact moment.

"First of all, you're not a man, or I wouldn't have so much trouble protecting you. Second, he is not a villain for wanting to protect you. Third, young, energetic men usually need a bit of extra attention. I can handle this one."

"You can handle him only if you know what he is up to. You can't follow him around and do your own job too," Laura pointed out.

"Lord sent him, so he must have references," Monk argued reasonably.

"As far as I know, Lord did only an initial application on them. Have you ever seen these guys at the compound?"

"No, but Lord doesn't keep me up-to-date on all his recruits. Come on; show a little trust," he cajoled.

"Maybe," Laura admitted reluctantly. There was something disturbing about the two men. Laura rubbed her eyes wearily. "But I'm going to keep my eyes open," she said at last.

The lights blinked, signaling ten minutes before the final set of performances. Tanya and Kate dashed backstage for a quick costume change.

"Do you think anything will happen tonight?" Laura asked hopefully, feeling useless. Stephan would run the final performance without her.

Monk raised his eyebrows in disbelief. "Are you kidding? I've never had a quieter duty."

Laura gazed around The Colony, reflecting on Monk's observation. Even though she had blamed Stephan's good management, things had been too quiet. With Eric gone, there should have been a current of discord in the air, maybe even casualties. Someone had to be blamed for Eric's murder. Why hadn't she heard from Mina? They desperately needed an update on what was going on outside of Stephan's domain. She would have to contact Mina herself.

Laura watched Michael help a customer take off her coat. The woman was young, beautiful, and very human. Her escort quickly drew her deeper into the establishment. Michael surreptitiously took pictures of both guests before they seated themselves near the back, away from the auditorium.

While he moved among the customers, Michael would occasionally glance at Laura. She saw something in his expression that made her very uncomfortable. He looked—well—possessive. It was so outrageous, she could hardly credit her impression. When he noticed her watching him, he assumed an expression of bland disinterest. Despite Monk's assurances, they were going to have to keep Michael busy, busy, busy.

"I'm going home. I haven't been sleeping well lately," Laura admitted. Her dreams had become more frequent and disruptive. She desperately needed a full night of uninterrupted sleep. Monk headed toward the door.

"You don't need to come," she objected. She wasn't ready for another wild ride with Monk.

"We can't afford to relax our guard now that we've gone public," he pointed out. "You go nowhere alone. I'll follow you to make sure you get home safely, and I'll check your house. It would take relaxing our vigilance for only an instant for something bad to happen."

Monk was right. They needed to stay alert. She retrieved his high-tech SUV—at his mulish insistence that she take it instead of her own—drove to the front of the theater, and waited until he pulled in behind her. Then Laura pulled out into traffic, leading the way. Monk was on his best behavior, driving her car sedately.

They passed two official-looking trucks a half mile from her house. She couldn't make out the worn logo painted on their sides.

As she turned into her driveway, she spotted a large eagle swooping down on a small gray object in the tall grass. She gasped in alarm when she recognized Misty, her Somali kitten. Roman, her black retriever, rushed at the bird, trying to recapture the disappearing kitten. But the bird flew out of reach easily. Even in the darkness, she could see her second cat, Ariel, a self-obsessed Birman, in the same patch of grass. The feline had long white fur, her face and paws painted black. Laura watched anxiously as Sissy, her Australian shepherd, collected Ariel gently in her mouth and tried to carry the struggling cat back up the road. But Ariel was too heavy and managed to wiggle out of Sissy's mouth. The fleeing cat was immediately recaptured by the returning brawny eagle.

"Oh my god!" Laura gasped, suddenly braking. She heard Monk screech to a stop to avoid hitting her. "My pets are loose!" she yelled.

Another of the official-looking trucks was coming up the road from the opposite direction. Laura watched in horror as Sissy dashed into the road, unaware of the approaching danger. Roman ran after her. The truck accelerated, aiming itself right at her dogs. Laura screamed as Sissy disappeared under the axle, and Roman was knocked into the underbrush.

An uncontrollable fury flooded Laura's body, demanding she take action. She gunned the car's engine, skidded into a 180-degree turn around Monk, and sped after the escaping vehicle. Her only thought—the one that had consoled her since her friends' untimely deaths—was revenge. It had returned with a vengeance.

Laura jammed her foot on the accelerator, forcing Monk's modified car to higher speeds. The scenery rushed past in a blur, and wind buffeted the car, blasting her face though the open driver's window. She easily caught up with the larger fleeing vehicle. Without any thought for her own safety, Laura slammed into the back end of the truck, sending it spinning out of control until it smashed headlong into the trunk of an old tree. She drove past the damaged truck, turned around, and rolled slowly past to assess the danger before confronting the driver. The vehicle doors popped opened, and several men spilled out of the truck, grumbling and looking for a fight. There were too many to challenge, so she sped away before they could identify her. It was lucky she wasn't driving her own vehicle. One black SUV with tinted windows was the same as any other. But she was determined to find out who they were.

With some sanity returning, Laura hurried back to Monk and her injured dogs, but they were nowhere in sight. She pulled over onto the shoulder and walked anxiously to the point of impact. There was a blood trail leading to the drainage ditch. Dreading what she would find, she followed the tracks. There, on a bed of grass, lay Sissy and Roman. Monk had tied his handkerchief around one of Sissy's legs and was examining the black retriever. Roman had no obvious injuries, but was lying flat, panting laboriously.

"I called Lord. He knows people who know people. He found a vet who will come tonight. But you'll need to find your cats." Monk looked sympathetic.

Laura couldn't answer through the lump in her throat. Instead, she knelt by the dogs and stroked them gently. She spoke in a soft voice, trying to reassure them that they were safe. She hated feeling powerless. She didn't know how to bandage their injuries or lessen their pain. Frustrated tears streamed down her cheeks, and the dogs whined and tried to crawl closer to console her.

"Go to the house," Monk urged. "They need to remain calm and still."

Laura couldn't argue with his logic. She reluctantly returned to the car and drove up the long drive to her house. At first, she didn't notice anything wrong. Then she saw her home, which should have been dark, blazing with light. She could see figures inside and heard crashing glass. Black sedans were parked in front of the main house. The prowlers were making no attempt to hide their mischief.

Silently, she let her car roll back down the driveway. There were three new vehicles parked on the road, a sedan near her injured pets and two SUVs north of her driveway. Monk ran over to the open driver's window.

"I've been expecting trouble since I spotted a tail, so I called for reinforcements." Monk waved at the SUVS. "From your immediate return, I'm guessing we have unexpected guests?"

Laura nodded. "Several. We need to do something before they destroy my place."

Laura looked over at Sissy and Roman. She was relieved to see a man with medical supplies working on the animals.

Monk smiled reassuringly. "The doc will have to take them in. Roman has internal bleeding, so he'll need surgery. But Sissy has only superficial injuries and a broken leg."

Laura breathed deeply to relieve the tension from her apprehension. At least her dogs would be safe for now.

Monk, Laura, and the newly arrived guards crept up the long drive and circled around to the back. They used the windows to determine what was happening inside. She counted three men: one in the living area, one upstairs, and one in her back office. They appeared to be wrecking her home. Frantic, Laura started toward the house, but Monk held her back.

"Let the men go first. They can distract the intruders and give us a chance to trap them with minimal injuries," he advised.

Laura nodded reluctantly. She needed to act, not watch. Monk whispered instructions to their small security force, and the men loudly crashed into the house. But the prowlers didn't engage their men. Instead, they rushed out the nearest exits. Laura couldn't believe their cowardice. She saw a shadow scrambling across the roof and then heard cracking wood from the location of her hanging trellis. The idiot used it to escape the roof. Then the black sedans roared down the drive as Laura cursed her oversight in not blocking the driveway.

Monk and his men chased the fleeing intruders, running down the drive and jumping into the SUVs. Laura followed more slowly. She found the vet's vehicle gone and with it her injured dogs. Worried about the other pets, she sprinted back up the drive.

Laura hoped Faraday, her pet bald eagle, hadn't accidently dropped her cats. It would take only a moment of inattention to drop a wiggling cat.

She had found the little, flopping eaglet abandoned on a stretch of beach, safe from human hunters on a protected Indian reservation. It had taken a strong stomach and a stronger cage to keep the eaglet contained long enough to heal his various injuries and allow him to grow big enough to survive on his own. Laura could only imagine what had happened to orphan the defenseless bird. There were moments when she doubted if the little fellow would fly again. But little by little, the eaglet gained strength until the morning she found him flapping against the cage roof.

Laura had hesitated to release the bird. She feared he would be unprepared to hunt in the wild. At least she could keep him safe. But in the end, she had to respect his desire for freedom, a privilege she herself valued. The first time she'd opened the door and stepped aside, Faraday had just looked at her with a tilted head and rapidly blinking eyes. Laura nodded silently and moved several feet away from the door. All at once, the eaglet burst out of the cage and sailed up into a bank of puffy cotton-white clouds. In moments, he popped out the far side and flew higher. Laura watched, stranded on the ground, envious of the wondrous exhilaration he must be experiencing flying free.

If only she could fly like Faraday. It would be beyond glorious. She imagined the wind ruffling her hair and the soft folds of her clothes. She would perform aerial hijinks, feeling the rush of acceleration up and the whoosh of falling down, only to soar once more into the cold, clear sky. She would fly far to see the many wonders visible from above, such as the patterns made by cities and farming communities and follow Faraday to lands unreachable any other way. But she could only watch as the beautiful eagle flew away, vanishing into the clouds.

Laura had become resigned to the loss of her unusual pet, when he returned many months later. He was fat, a testimony to his good hunting skills. At first, he just perched on the roof periodically and watched her play with her other pets. Then, one morning, she came out into the yard and stumbled across one of the miracles of life. Predators and prey might play together.

Faraday swooped down, hovered over one of her little kittens, pulled it carefully into a fist of talons, and flew around in low circles. At first, Laura held her breath, fearing that the delicate kitten might get hurt. But then the bald eagle swooped down to release the kitten gently into the tall grass. Laura wondered if the kittens would run away from the foolish bird. But they only clawed the air eagerly, waiting for the next ride. Her silly eagle was only playing. Laura was mesmerized. Even the dogs watched, their heads tilted.

Only when her foster border collie crawled up next to the kittens, looked up into the air expectantly, and lifted one paw did she collapse into laughter. He was, of course, only a puppy at the time, and Faraday might have been able to manage the dog's weight. But Laura couldn't take the chance. She ran forward before Faraday could try and locked the border collie in the house. She continued to watch the kittens until Faraday tired of the play and flew off. It was this strange behavior that Laura had witnessed tonight when Misty and Ariel had allowed Faraday to carry them to safety. Now she would have to wait until the unpredictable bald eagle brought them back.

Laura circled the house, using the light streaming from the windows to search for any trace of her missing animals. Normally Faraday hung out in his old childhood aviary. Since she always left the door open, he could fly in and settle into one of the rock crannies big enough for a full-sized eagle. Using a flashlight she had retrieved from the garden shed, she searched the dark enclosure, but the aviary was empty.

Reluctantly, she returned to the house. Laura opened the front door, holding her breath. She had heard so much crashing and breaking that she could only imagine what terrible destruction had occurred. She walked into the living room and groaned in anguish. Broken glass was strewn everywhere, carefully selected upholstery had been slashed, and treasured furniture was in pieces. She shot an anxious look at the fireplace mantle, looking for the only picture she had of Pam, Grace, and Ellie. She saw the picture frame lying upside down on the floor. Hurrying over, she picked it up. The photograph was gone and the frame horribly gouged. Opposite the mantle was her glass curio cabinet. The cabinet was empty, and a pile of broken pieces held the door open. She anxiously checked the pile for any intact pieces. Several had been smashed into glass dust. Only a twinkling unicorn, a special gift from Monk, was still whole. He had told her that she had the unicorn's gift for lucky outcomes.

Laura stifled a sob and returned to the main staircase. She placed her foot on the bottom step but was unable to move higher. Her most prized possessions were on the second floor. Unexpectedly, she felt Monk's arms close around her. She didn't know when he had come in, but he often appeared when she needed support. For a few moments, she let his warmth soak into her chilled skin. Then she shook free and continued up the stairs. She wouldn't leave without knowing the exact extent of the damage.

On the second floor, she entered the master bedroom and went straight to a large walk-in closet. A thin wail began at the back of her throat, transforming into a soft "Noooooooooooo!"

She sank to her knees, fingering the stained remains of her favorite green evening gown. She had worn it to her college graduation. Under it was the exotic white dress she had selected for the night she had taken out Eric. Someone had given it special attention. It was viciously sliced into thin, jagged strips. Birthday gifts from mentors and photo albums from her childhood had all been ruined. Tears blocked her vision, and a loud roar filled her ears, drowning out Monk's words of comfort. A huge lump in her throat made breathing difficult and speaking impossible.

At the realization that this had been a deliberate, calculated attempt to hurt her, ferocious rage replaced her grief. She shook with a poisonous need for violence.

# 6

## A New Enemy

Laura felt every muscle tighten, ready to do whatever it took to find the person responsible for this outrage, and then she was overcome with another wave of anguish.

"Why, Monk? Why did they have to destroy everything? Who could hate me this much?" Laura cried. Momentarily overwhelmed with hopelessness, she sank back on her heels.

"Are you sure this was deliberate? Maybe it was just the actions of a ruthless bunch of thugs," Monk pleaded. He handed her his handkerchief.

"I'm sure. The clothes were cut with scissors. The mirrors savagely smashed. Bleach splashed on the carpet, the bedding, and the draperies. All my perfume drained. Things have been destroyed that would have no possible value to an outsider. I thank God that my animals weren't killed." Laura looked at Monk with suffocating despair, her fragile faith in people broken.

"My God," she whispered hoarsely. "This was done by a woman. Only a woman would destroy personal items so vindictively."

"A woman?" asked Monk, bewildered. "But why?"

"That's it!" she continued, ignoring Monk. "Those men must have been hired by a woman. I only need to find out who. But to do that, I need to know why."

"Maybe one of your girls has offended someone's girlfriend or wife. They are seriously gorgeous, and several Colony customers have already promised them expensive gifts."

"It couldn't be that. The girls haven't been here since we went public. This attack was directed at me. This is my house, my belongings," Laura reasoned, trying to find sense in the senseless. "I just can't understand who hates me this much. I haven't gotten close enough to anyone for this." Laura waved at the destruction.

"I'd start looking in The Colony," Monk suggested.

"I agree. The Colony is the only thing new enough and dangerous enough to explain this intensity."

Laura started pacing nervously, and in a flash of inspiration, the pieces finally fell into place. "I know who it is," she announced, meeting Monk's eyes. "There is really only one person who is capable of this level of violence, only one woman who is angry enough to do this."

Monk's expression puckered in concentration and then relaxed. "You're right," he agreed. "Only one. Nicolette!"

"Nicolette," Laura echoed softly. "The only reason to target me is Stephan. Do I just have to work for him to trigger this kind of violence?"

"So it appears. There's no one else who even comes close to this level of crazy."

"She's too dangerous to ignore. I guess it's lucky that Mina has already been watching her."

"Mina!" Monk yelped in surprise. "I completely forgot about her. Damn it, Laura! You've been scheming behind my back again, haven't you? I've come to expect your outrageous setups for yourself, but why send one of your new recruits into the eye of the storm alone?" Tones of outrage had replaced Monk's usual calm voice. "She could already be dead!"

"Calm down, Monk. Mina never came to The Colony with the rest of us. Nicolette has no way to connect her to me."

"That doesn't matter. Nicolette has a reputation for brutality and greed. No woman is safe from her manipulations. If she decides she wants Mina for her private collection, then she could have changed her."

"Ch-changed her?" Laura asked, shocked at this possibility. If Mina was hurt, or worse, turned into a Shadow Dweller, then they were all in trouble.

"You read the reports," Monk fumed. "You see what they did to your house! If something has happened—"

"Let's get to the bottom of this now! Give me your phone." Laura held out her hand, and Monk dropped his cell into her palm.

Swiftly, she dialed Mina's number. The phone rang four long, echoing rings before she heard a click and then silence.

"Mina?" Laura called softly. She had no way of knowing if she could speak freely. "Are you there?"

"Laura?" came the whispered reply. "I had to find a safe place to talk. Is something wrong?"

Laura breathed a happy sigh of relief. She had let Monk's dark premonitions inflame her imagination. She had envisioned the various forms of torture that could have been used against Mina, which was unthinkable.

"There've been some unsettling developments," Laura whispered. "We need you back at Lord's. Can you get away?"

"Maybe. I'll try."

"No maybe! It's no longer safe for you. Nicolette is deteriorating. Get away even if you have to blow your cover. Whatever you have learned about Nicolette so far will have to be enough."

"Relax, Laura. I don't know what's wrong, but things are quiet here. I'm sure no one has connected me to you. So there's no reason for me to act hastily."

"Please just come!" Laura pleaded. "When you hear what's happened, you might agree with me."

"OK, OK. But I'll wait until Siren's Song closes. We can meet to-morrow morning," Mina suggested.

"If you must," Laura allowed. "But please make it early. We'll be waiting at our usual place."

"Roger and out." Mina's laugh was audible just before the phone disconnected. That girl sure did share Laura's love of danger. Laura didn't know whether to laugh or cry.

"She'll rendezvous tomorrow. She's been out of touch for a while, so she's bound to have some valuable information. She might be able to get us inside."

"Us?" Monk repeated gruffly, shaking his head. "If you think I'm going to let you anywhere near Siren's Song after this vicious assault, then you're losing your grip on reality."

"If you think you can stop me, then you're the one who's losing his grip," Laura snapped back. "Look! I have no intention of walking in boldly. The Trust specializes in subterfuge and disguises. If we can't find a disguise that will fool Nicolette, then we shouldn't be hunting Shadow Dwellers in the first place. I'm here to do a job, and I won't let you stop me. I thought you knew me."

"That vampiress is one dangerous predator, and she's currently on the warpath. You'd be a fool to take her on now."

"I can't help that. If my instincts are right, she's already preparing to take us down. We both knew, going in, that we'd be facing danger. Don't wimp out on me now."

Monk growled irritably. She knew that he knew he couldn't stop her, and she also knew he wouldn't let her go alone.

Laura turned away from the wreckage of her bedroom and walked downstairs with new purpose. Fortunately, she could use her apartment at Lord's. It would be too painful to try to salvage anything from the heaps of destruction here. Before leaving, Laura called the housekeeping department at Lord's compound. She asked that they send someone to her house to look for her cats and wait, if necessary, for them to reappear. She assumed that Faraday, kitties in tow, would return once things got quiet again.

Then she left her destroyed home with all its lost memories behind. Laura didn't speak until Monk had navigated the vehicle onto the freeway.

"I just can't understand it!" she exclaimed, shattering the silence. "Why did the men run when they heard us?"

"I imagine that Nicolette wants her identity to remain a secret," Monk offered as a possible explanation. "If she harms you publicly, she risks Stephan's retaliation."

"Stephan...I forgot about him. Why, oh why, did Nicolette have to attack so soon? I wasn't ready to tell Stephan about the Trust. I thought he might be sympathetic. He can't want criminal Shadow Dwellers endangering their safety and their secrets. Now, he'll throw us out for sure. He has enough problems without taking on a jealous ex-girlfriend."

"You underestimate him," Monk said. "You can deny the attraction between you two, but it's obvious to everyone else. Nicolette's spies must see it too, which would explain why she attacked you. When you and Stephan produce a show, you're in perfect harmony. The synergy between you two is remarkable."

"So, we work well together. Big whoopee."

"What you do isn't work. You both create something unique that visibly affects the audience. Your shows for the next month are already sold out. I expect you plan to have new shows after that."

"Not anymore. Now I'll have to hunt Nicolette, which will make working at The Colony impossible. I don't expect Stephan will agree to the assassination of his ex-lover."

"I wonder," Monk mused. "Nicolette is becoming too dangerous for everyone, not just you. But we can't learn anything more tonight. We'll just have to wait for Mina's report."

"Waiting—my favorite thing," Laura moaned. "Still, a bath would be heavenly, and Lord does have a remarkable music collection." Laura decided she would find comfort anywhere she could.

"I'll inform Lord of your return and your desire to be left undisturbed," Monk volunteered. He proceeded to use a special communications link, built into his car, to call the estate.

Lord's compound covered twenty acres and offered many amenities. There was a grand main house, and small apartments were scattered throughout beautifully landscaped grounds. A small chapel and yoga-meditation studio stood in a secluded corner. A secure under-ground gym was used to train his security force and Shadow Hunters. For fun, there was an elaborate pool complex, a modern tennis/rac-quetball/basketball court, and a recreational zip-line course also used for aerial maneuvers. Near the main house, Lord stocked a small store with groceries and basic clothing for various activities. Gideon Lord had designed his compound to be a self-contained sanctuary. Because Laura no longer felt safe on the outside, this provision was heaven-sent.

After Monk dropped her off at her private apartment, Laura decid-ed a brief visit to the chapel might settle her turbulent thoughts. Once there, she found the simple building with its beautiful wood moldings and ornate open windows soothing to her chaotic emotions. She settled herself into one of the cushioned pews. They were a far cry from the hard church benches she had endured as a child. Soft music stilled her restless mind, and a light breeze relaxed her tense body. A whiff of in-cense followed her into an uneasy sleep.

Laura felt herself falling, surrounded by warm currents of emotion. She struggled mentally for solid footing before she sank into a restless sleep. When she roused again, she found herself sitting on a log, float-ing down an invisible river. Laura realized she was dreaming. When Stephan appeared on the log beside her, she tried to move away. But he grasped her arm and pulled her closer.

"Why do you keep running away?" he challenged. "We can help each other overcome the trouble to come.

"Help with what?" she asked nervously.

"You must stop running," he insisted. "We're both in danger."

"How?" Laura hoped for some reasonable reply. But he continued to make little sense.

"I've waited so long," he lamented. "Soon it'll be too late. They're almost here."

When Stephan's expression of sorrow intensified, helpless tears ran down her cheeks. She struggled to break this link of shared emotions and tried to pull away. But his grip tightened, preventing her escape.

"What do you want?" she shouted, panic clipping each word. "Why do you hold me here?"

When Stephan tried to speak, his words were lost in a blast of violent wind. Water crashed across the log, drenching Laura. In the next instant, he was gone, and the log was sinking. She slipped into the water, and its black depths stole all sensation.

Laura awoke the next morning stiff and cold. She scrambled into a sitting position, every muscle aching in protest. She tried to smooth her hair and clothes into some semblance of order. Wisps of her dream flitted through her mind, but they slipped away before she could remember details.

Laura made swift progress back to her apartment, and found Misty and Ariel sniffing at a kitchen cabinet door. Fortunately, someone had left a box of dry and cans of wet cat food on the counter. She bent to the task and in short order had a feast ready. Soon both cats were purring contently as they devoured the tasty morsels. There was a note next to the food assuring her that her dogs were in equally good circumstances.

Laura went into the bedroom, pulling irritably at her wrinkled clothing. While a bath would have been lovely, she was eager to see Mina. So she took a quick shower, pulled on a forest-green exercise outfit that flattered her figure, twisted her hair up into a braided topknot, and headed out.

Laura strode toward the main house, mentally preparing a list of questions for Mina. Even with a bright sun, the shadowed areas remained chilly. Impatient, she took shortcuts through the grassy areas. She could hear the rustle of Lord's various employees working to keep his miniature city manicured. As a result, she was unprepared when someone spoke behind her.

"Does Lord approve of you trampling his landscaping?" Michael asked rudely.

Laura jumped but restrained herself from making a hostile retort. Even though his comment invited conflict, she wanted to respect Monk's desire to utilize Michael's skills. When he gave her an appraising glance, she turned away, intent on reaching Lord's main atrium. But Michael grasped her arm, pulling her to face him again.

"I did a computer search on Stephan's paramour," he bragged, puffing his chest like a bantam rooster. "I heard about your little encounter with her men last night." He ignored her persistent attempts to free her arm. "She has two theaters, one owned jointly with Stephan Renard. Her signature theater is Siren's Song, and it's probably our best bet for finding out what she's up to. We should go there at the earliest opportunity."

Laura found his self-congratulatory tone irritating. Finally, he released her.

"I don't think Monk should come with us," he continued. "He's more useful staying with the girls at The Colony and coordinating the rest of the security team. By joining us, he'll leave the others exposed. I thought of going alone, but a disguised couple would be less conspicuous than a single male."

The more Michael talked, the more Laura wanted to strangle him. She backed away, distancing herself from the little pipsqueak.

"We can leave for Siren's Song around nine tonight when Nicolette's business picks up," he went on. "Right now, we should practice synchronized combat training. Gabriel is already practicing with Kate and Tanya." Again, Michael's eyes swept her figure and he smiled.

Laura had two choices. She could tell him to take a flying leap, or she could use a little finesse. She hadn't become a successful operative by letting her emotions lead her actions. Now she just smiled, thinking of all the things she would like to surgically remove. The smile must have looked convincing because Michael offered a tentative grin in response.

"I don't think so," was all she said and strode to the stairway to Lord's office.

Michael darted forward and grabbed her arm again, preventing her from climbing the steps. Laura stared pointedly at his hand. Then she affected an expression of disapproval to make the inappropriateness of his action painfully obvious. Abruptly, he snatched his hand back, blushing a deep red.

"Where are you going?" he demanded, still trying to gain control of the situation.

But Laura wouldn't give him anything to control. Short of his physically restraining her, she wasn't going to respond, even for the sake of good manners, except to walk a bit faster. She hurried up the steps.

Michael followed, fuming. Finally, she stopped at Lord's office door and turned back to face him.

"While I appreciate your industriousness, you're not in charge of this operation, Monk, my girls, or me. We'll let you know what we need from you. Until then, please find another sparring partner." Laura never raised her voice. In fact, she smiled while she spoke.

Then Laura turned back to Lord's office, opened the door, and slowly went inside. She heard Michael slap the wall before stomping back downstairs.

Lord was deeply immersed in an old volume entitled *Religious Practices in the Yucatan*. Laura knew he was an avid linguist, insisting that books written in their original languages held more information. Most relics of the ancient Mayans and Aztecs had been destroyed. But someone with Lord's unlimited resources could find whatever had survived.

Lord looked up at Laura and smiled invitingly, reminding her that he would always be more than just her boss. Like her, Lord had lost his family early in life. He'd been raised by tutors and guardians, resulting in a man with great knowledge but little sense of family. With Laura, he had tried to make up for this loss.

Lord waved one hand at a small nearby table that held tea service with sandwiches and sweet cakes decoratively displayed. Laura was hungry and devoured several miniature sandwiches without speaking. Gratefully, she poured the steaming tea into a cup painted with nautical designs.

"Monk has told me what happened at your house. I've sent my maintenance crew out this morning to clear away the debris and repair any structural damage," Lord said after letting her take a few sips of the restorative liquid. "It'll take time to replace the items that were destroyed, but I will return your home to its former glory."

Laura smiled gratefully. He really was wonderful.

"I hope you'll take this opportunity to let me share some of my latest discoveries and inventions. I miss having someone as curious and creative as you around. While you're staying here, you could update your fighting skills as well. Michael has volunteered to work with you. He seems to have taken a special interest in guarding you." Lord looked at her speculatively over his spectacles.

Laura snorted with disgust. "That guy is on my last nerve. He's been making it his personal mission to take control of the Trust. What's his story anyway? Are you offering charity to bigheads?"

"He definitely has strong opinions," Lord conceded. "We need people who can rescue you from your risky schemes, especially when you get imaginative." Lord stared at Laura reproachfully.

"We don't have to compromise a good team dynamic for initiative. Where did you find those two new guys anyway?"

"They came in together in response to our recruitment inquiries. Their references were impressive, their employers high-profile men." Lord whistled softly. "Heavy hitters."

"You called their references, of course. I mean, you didn't take *their* word for it—right?" Laura asked indelicately.

An expression of long suffering crossed Lord's face. He rolled his eyes. "Yes, we did manage to function without your guidance. Their prior employers gave them high marks."

"And their tactical training?"

"They're the real deal. You should see them in action before you write them off."

"Look, I just find Michael very, very, very annoying. He's an accident waiting to happen," Laura predicted morosely.

"You might look at dealing with difficult people as an opportunity to improve your skills. This is good practice. Find a way to neutralize him while letting him maintain his dignity, and you have my vote for president."

"Great, that would be *one*. Probably not a landslide win." Laura's eyes sparkled. She knew he was right. Finding a way to get Michael in line would put her in a higher class of successful. Maybe Monk could suggest something before she throttled the punk.

Laura glanced at the wall clock. Mina should be waiting at their meeting place by now, and Lord had to be told about Mina's clandestine activities. Monk had made several good points. Lord wouldn't be happy.

"I have news about Nicolette," she began meekly. "Mina didn't come with us to The Colony for our auditions. We agreed that she could learn more at Siren's Song." Laura hesitated, waiting for Lord's explosion of anger, but the silence persisted, so she continued. "Nicolette was creating too much uproar to ignore. Now that she's attacked my house, I think she might be on the verge of a homicidal rage, if she hasn't murdered already. We have to act, so I called Mina back here to give us an update on her surveillance. She should be here by now."

"I'm glad to hear that she's out of danger." Lord spoke quietly, but his disapproval was obvious. "You might be surprised to learn that Monk made sure that you didn't take on Eric alone. He always had your back whether you sensed his presence or not. Now I learn you put one of your girls in harm's way without any backup."

"It was her idea," Laura defended herself stiffly. Her guilt lay heavy in the pit of her stomach. "We all know this job is dangerous. Why are you and Monk so surprised that we jumped at this chance to collect vital intel?"

"Monk and I have tried to instill in you the importance of implementing safety measures. I foolishly thought you had learned this lesson when you accepted the idea of hiring more backup for the Trust. Now I realize that it was just a ploy to get us to relax our oversight."

"Noooo! Nicolette has never been a target in your book of criminal Shadow Dwellers, so we thought Mina would be safe. Are you saying she has killed humans?"

"The situation with a Shadow Dweller is never static. They're predators and as such have strong impulses. As far as I know, Nicolette hasn't killed humans recently. But I would never assume I had her full history. Her age is unknown to us."

"You're right, Gideon." Laura felt heat flush her face as the wisdom of his words humbled her. "I'm sorry. We thought we were being proactive initiating a plan to watch Nicolette on the chance she would create trouble. But I see your point, and I promise you that I'll take better precautions in the future. Will you come with me to meet with Mina?"

Lord nodded. "Of course. I'm as eager as you to find out what Nicolette is planning. Make no mistake—the attack on you will be addressed, and justice will be sought."

"Our prearranged meeting place is the chapel. It's secluded enough to ensure some degree of privacy," Laura explained. "Monk will meet us there."

Lord took the lead as they left the building. When they reached the chapel, they could hear Monk and Mina arguing.

"You were a fool!" Monk snapped, keeping his voice at a low roar. He sounded like a muffled grizzly.

"How dare you speak to me like I'm a child!" Mina hissed. She was trying to keep her voice down as well. "What is your problem?"

"Enough!" Lord snapped from the open door. "We don't have time for recriminations. What's done is done, and frankly, we're lucky to have someone already on the inside. How'd you manage it? Are you performing at Siren's Song?"

"Not on your life!" Mina's small, perfect features twisted into an expression of revulsion. "Her performers are watched constantly, and the human singers look like they've been through hell. Half her girls are obviously Shadow Dwellers, and I couldn't take the chance that Nicolette might decide to condemn me to that fate."

Laura smiled smugly and looked at both Monk and Lord with a lifted eyebrow. "So it seems that Mina has already taken measures to ensure her safety. Maybe you both underestimated her?" she proffered.

"She got lucky," Monk growled. "You wouldn't be so smug if she had gotten hurt."

"What's going on?" Mina asked pointedly. "The tension in here is stifling."

"Lord has decided that you need to have a male guard as backup at all times," Laura explained.

"But that's ridiculous!" Mina exclaimed. "I only got close because I was alone and easy to ignore. A backup guard might have drawn Nicolette's attention."

"Why don't you start from the beginning?" Lord recommended. "The rest of you keep quiet. If you guys keep shouting at each other, we'll never learn anything."

"I decided the best tactic for investigating a controlling woman is to be as invisible as possible." Mina's eyes flashed with excitement. She really was a perfect agent. She had no fear for her own safety, only enthusiasm for the adventure ahead. "I choose baggy clothes, a pair of ugly glasses, and pinned my hair into a tight bun. I wanted to move around her theater without being noticed, so I applied to the cleaning crew. I thought about being a waitress, but Nicolette dresses them up like little dolls, and I couldn't take the risk of being noticed. Fortunately, the disguise was perfect. I wore a horrible blue coverall, and that was all anyone saw. I could even move around the cells where they keep their prisoners. Nicolette is obsessive about cleanliness."

"Oh my god!" Laura rasped. Prisoners of Nicolette!

"Did you get any information on her plans for us?" Lord asked pointedly.

"She must have recruited some of Eric's old posse. They're all over her theater. It was lucky that you guys made sure we could recognize his men. She really has it bad for you, Laura. She can't let go of Stephan. She talks about him incessantly. I wouldn't be surprised to hear that she's planned some fatal accident for you, Kate, and Tanya. The idea that there are any beautiful women around him drives her crazy."

"She has already acted," Laura admitted. "My house is in shambles."

"I'm sorry," Mina said sympathetically. "I wish I could've warned you. But I didn't know. She does seem to know a lot about what Stephan is doing."

"How does she find out?" Monk asked.

"I'm not sure. That dwarf has private meetings with her every night. Maybe he has spies still working at the Colony."

"Is she continuing with Eric's criminal activities? Handling a network of greedy agents might distract her," Laura suggested hopefully.

"Nicolette is preparing something big. She might be planning a takeover. If she can remove Stephan, then all his businesses will fall into her lap. She's already familiar with his suppliers and customers. If she suddenly reappeared, few would question her. She might even keep him alive, just locked away. He would become her perfect, private pet."

"That's impossible. Stephan is too powerful for Nicolette," Laura scoffed. "He has men everywhere."

"Stephan has civilized guards. Nicolette has unscrupulous animals," Lord warned. "Eric's men are the bottom feeders in Shadow Dweller society. They view killing as a useful tool. Would Stephan?" Lord began to pace. "Do you know when she plans to proceed?"

"Not exactly. But I know somebody who might," Mina admitted. "No caged performer, human or female Shadow Dweller, wants to stay with Nicolette. If we can get her girls out, you might create enough chaos to interrupt her plot and these women might be able to tell you the details of her end game. Also, her girls are the way she holds the loyalty of Eric's men. I don't know how she'll control them if she can't even keep her own performers contained."

"How many prisoners are there?" Monk asked, always the strategist.

"It doesn't matter. We rescue as many as we can," Laura interrupted. She looked pointedly at Lord. "Since a direct assault would cause unnecessary casualties, we need to create a big enough diversion to allow a small group to sneak in and bring the prisoners out. I'm betting that the girls themselves are angry enough and strong enough to aid in their escape."

"Not only strong enough, but already praying for rescue," Mina promised. "You couldn't recruit a better force. These girls are just as determined and just as savage as Eric's underlings."

"It could be like having an army of Trust women ready to take out Shadow Dwellers instead of our small group of entertainers," Laura predicted. She could see the possibilities of Mina's clever plan clearly. "Our problem of subduing Eric's army becomes very simple. I don't think they would kill beautiful women as easily as they would kill Lord's soldiers."

Lord was nodding, and even Monk looked hopeful.

"Mina can bring Kate, Monk, and me in as extra cleaning staff. Lord, your guards could start some kind of diversion in front. With everyone outside, we can sneak in and release the trapped women."

"Nicolette has targeted you specifically," Monk reminded her. "You shouldn't go."

"I'm the perfect distraction. If you think I would stand by and do nothing to avenge myself and stop Nicolette from hurting Stephan, then you don't know me at all. Maybe I'll come up with some tactic that will keep innocent people from getting hurt. Can you live with that?" Laura bristled.

"If it means saving your life, then yes, I can live with that," Lord admitted.

"Well, I can't."

"I won't try to stop you, but I insist you take Michael and Gabriel. Nicolette will have to get through both of them before she can reach you." Lord's expression was as serious as she had ever seen it. She realized that this was his line in the sand.

"Agreed. Maybe Nicolette will do me a favor. While she's trying to kill me, she might teach Michael that his skills do have limits. Now, what do you have on her? Michael found some information, but surely your files aren't so sparse. Could I have a peek into the vault?" Laura smiled wickedly, fluttering her eyelashes. She loved performing, even if she didn't appear on stage.

Lord rolled his eyes at her antics. "If you mean my core files, come on. Mina, I don't want you going back to Nicolette's theater until tonight. No one is going to be at risk again without proper safeguards." Mina tried to interrupt, but Lord held up his hand. "Yes, I know a bodyguard won't work. But there are other ways to protect you that will allow you to remain invisible. Monk, why don't you take our little hellion down to the gym? Maybe a workout will muzzle her reckless enthusiasm."

Monk winked conspiratorially. "It worked with Laura. We can only hope."

Monk and Mina headed for the downstairs gym. Laura ran ahead to Lord's office. She was perched on his desk when he entered.

"So where's the loot?" Grinning playfully, Laura sprang off the desk. She was happy that Lord wasn't fighting her about going to Nicolette's. The possibility that Stephan might be Nicolette's next target made the decision nonnegotiable.

Lord went behind his oversized desk and swung a large painting away from the wall. Behind it, locked in a special metal cabinet, were several thick files. Laura often wondered how he collected such detailed information on a race that was dedicated to secrecy.

Lord pulled out a thick manila folder and spilled its contents onto his desk. On top was a birth certificate from France. But it wasn't decades old; it was centuries old. The name on the certificate was Solange Dubois. Laura was stunned at the dates and the tattered condition of many of the official documents. They didn't look like Xeroxed copies.

"Impressive," she whispered, patting his shoulder proudly.

Laura treated Lord with the causal closeness reserved for family. She wondered why he had never married. He was handsome after a fashion, even if he was a bit long in the tooth. His face was a little stern for her taste and his eyes just a fraction too penetrating. But his voice had the magic of fine music, resonating in the lower registers very much like Stephan's. Abruptly, she realized he was watching her, raising a bushy eyebrow over a slow grin. She hadn't realized she'd been staring at him.

Blushing furiously, she looked back down at the scattered documents. The powerful Shadow Dwellers always made sure that everything they did was legal, which meant inventing identities. Lord had copies of Nicolette's business license and her lease on Siren's Song. There was even a copy of the lease for The Colony with both Stephan's and her names clearly visible. Laura uncovered transcripts of interviews with several workmen who had done a rather extensive remodel of Siren's Song. The prison cells on a lower level were clearly diagramed. Her team would have to find their way down three floors into a subbasement. Lord had even managed to put together a partial list of Nicolette's current stable of talented, beautiful women. Laura shuddered at their desperate situation. Whether human or baby Shadow Dweller, freedom was a right of all sentient beings.

Digging deeper, Laura uncovered several candid pictures of Stephan and Nicolette together. In every photo, Nicolette was touching him, often whispering into his ear. Seeing them together, Laura could understand why Nicolette's obsession had turned into such a terrible rage. Laura realized that Lord was right to insist that Michael and Gabriel accompany her to Siren's Song. She decided it was time to assess their skills as security guards.

The gym was rather large, despite being underground. The upper story was filled with cardio machines, while the main floor contained weight machines and free weights. To one side were spacious glass enclosures ideal for team training sessions. Lord made sure his security was current with all the latest in offensive and defensive combat techniques.

In the central training room, Tanya and Kate were doing coordinated drills with Gabriel. Mina, Monk, and Michael were talking in a small group nearby. Michael kept shaking his head, and finally his voice rose loud enough to reach Laura.

"This is nonsense!" he snapped, interrupting Monk's quiet tones. "Bringing a large group will invite exposure. Only Laura and I should go, and if you insist, Gabriel."

Monk answered in a low, calm voice, his words indistinct. She moved closer to hear.

"I'm the one who discovered Nicolette's plan," Mina admonished. "You're a dung beetle if you think I'm going to miss all the fun. Besides, you don't know where the girls are being held."

"That's my point *ex-act-ly*." Michael enunciated each syllable distinctively. "Why would we help Shadow Dwellers? They are the enemy, and now you propose we put Laura in danger for them!"

"Those Shadow Dwellers are women who are being confined and tortured." Mina was shaking with anger. "They need our help, and they will in turn help us."

"What the hell is going on?" Laura demanded, already smoldering.

"That's what I'd like to know!" Michael spun around to face Laura. "I thought we already had a strategy for tonight."

Laura stared at him incredulously. The last time they'd spoken, she'd made it clear that he was out of line. So, how could he think they had reached some agreement? Tanya, Kate, and Gabriel had stopped training and came closer to listen.

"Monk, what's going on?" Laura asked directly. She would never be able to keep quiet long enough to hear a complete explanation from Michael.

"Michael believes that rescuing Nicolette's stable of women is too dangerous because Mina hasn't collected enough information. He wants to go to Nicolette's with you and Gabe to find out exactly what she's planning. He says you approved this plan."

Laura choked on her frustration, coughing to clear her throat. Gabriel instantly rushed to her side. Unlike Michael, Gabriel had a meek, friendly demeanor. His face was open, his manners impeccable. She realized that he had blended in with the others, while Michael had created trouble. "Would you like some water?" Gabriel asked solicitously.

Laura's cheeks burned with embarrassment. She had let her anger get the best of her. "I'm fine. Please don't go to any trouble. But what is wrong with your brother?"

"How did you know?" Gabriel asked, eyebrows raised in surprise.

"How did I know what?" Laura asked, confused.

"That he was my brother?"

Laura studied both men for a few seconds. "You look alike. I guess I must have automatically assumed you were related. But back to my original question, what is wrong with him? Is he simple-minded?"

Michael roared with indignation. "Of course I'm not simple-minded!"

"Then why can't you understand simple declarative sentences? I explained that your plan was unnecessary and that Monk and I would come up with my team's next moves. Yet you persist in acting like I never rejected your plan."

"You had no better scheme, and I've already scouted the establishment. I'm the best one to guide you," Michael asserted impatiently.

"Mina has been undercover for a week. She's better qualified to lead us to the critical areas of the theater, and she has more information on what's happening inside."

"So she says. But what does she really know? She's found women in cells, she's recognized men hanging around, and she's noticed increased activity. I can get to the heart of the matter in a few hours."

"How?" Laura asked despite herself. So far, Michael had just been squawking like a rooster. Now he was claiming to have some superior skill in investigation.

"Guys talk to guys. One of Nicolette's guards will give me all the facts I need, if I get him drunk enough." Michael's lips curled into a mocking smile as if he had made his point and already won her cooperation. He couldn't have been more wrong.

"You're welcome to make whatever inquires you want. If you think you can find out more than we already know, please go ahead." A small smile played across Laura's lips. "But we are going ahead with Mina's plan."

"What plan?" Tanya asked.

"I'm on board," Kate piped in.

"May I still go?" Gabriel asked calmly.

"You can't." Michael grabbed Laura's wrist and pulled her away from the group. "We need to talk about this privately."

Laura yanked her arm free. "I'll do what is necessary to help those trapped women at Siren's Song," she hissed through clenched teeth. "Your cooperation is no longer wanted."

Michael wasn't going to be dismissed so easily. He set his hands firmly on her shoulders, preventing her from moving away. Monk growled a warning and roughly dragged Michael off her.

"What is wrong with you?" he barked, outraged. "You don't manhandle your boss."

"But she's going to get herself killed. Nicolette is bound to have automatic security measures set to execute anyone trying to help those girls escape. Surely we should protect Laura, even if it's from herself?" Michael looked sick with frustration. But he didn't resist Monk.

At that moment, Lord entered the gym. He was followed by four guards. He searched the room and then headed for their group. Laura guessed he must have seen what was occurring on one of his security monitors.

"What's the problem?" he demanded, crossing the room with remarkable speed. Monk instantly released Michael, who stood his ground defiantly. Lord stared at both men, waiting.

"Michael seems to think he should be the one planning our mission into Nicolette's territory," Laura said.

"He's worried about Laura," Monk explained.

"Do you have a problem taking orders from her?" Lord asked Michael directly.

The man shrugged dismissively. "I will not help her get herself killed," he muttered.

Lord gave him a quelling glance. "Then we will no longer need your services. Monk, escort this man to the gate. We'll mail your belongings to the address you gave on your application. You'll not be allowed back in." The four guards moved into offensive positions, making it clear they were ready to escort Michael out. Michael looked at the men nervously.

"What about Gabriel?" he asked. "Will he have to go?"

"As far as I can tell, Gabriel's performance has been exemplary. I've no problem with him."

"Then I'll stay," said Michael. "We work as a team."

Laura watched in stunned disbelief as Lord punched the young man, who slumped to the floor, offering no further objections. Lord had finally settled the matter of Michael.

"It seems our friend understands only one form of communication," Lord explained. "Sometimes actions can do what talking has failed to accomplish."

Monk carried Michael out, while Laura and her team left the gym to strategize somewhere more private.

# 7

## A New Treasure Found

Stephan had continued to get regular reports from Jon while he rid The Colony of all traces of Nicolette and her spies. During their association, Nicolette had filled several crucial management positions with her own people, and those positions were now vacant. Unfortunately, with her continuing sabotage against The Colony, Stephan had been unable to restore the theater's usual high-quality entertainment. Laura's sudden appearance and her offer to provide entertainers had been a stroke of luck. Plus, having her close would make it easier to learn more about the lady in white.

Stephan took a moment to appreciate the large establishment—his theater home. He had come to this country hoping for a fresh start, safely away from his evil maker. But he had missed the courtesies and elegance of his old life, so he had tried to import some of those qualities to Rainier.

As he looked around, he knew he had succeeded in creating an echo of a fine Parisian opera house in this frontier city. It had the same elaborate ornamentation and drafty dimensions of his parents' establishment in Paris. The huge stage and basement vault was unmatched by any local theaters. The fine brocade curtain had been salvaged from his long-dead parents' opera house. The main salon featured ornate blown-glass chandeliers and gold embellished marble statuettes. The walls were covered in deep red velvet that matched the red runners on the stairways. Black and gold iron, molded into fantastical designs, formed the railings. The bar's alcohol inventory had been decanted into beautiful glass bottles with gold labels and stored in tall beveled glass cabinets. He'd insisted on the finest linens and quality tableware, employed clever chefs, and offered the best wines he could find. He could almost imagine himself back home in one of the more sophisticated men's clubs.

With a sense of pride, Stephan watched his staff prepare The Colony for the evening's festivities. The wood bar had been polished to a high sheen. The freshly washed chandeliers sparkled with reflected light.

He was reviewing the night's specials when Laura arrived and led her people through the dining rooms to the auditorium. Tonight, for the evening performances, she had selected a tropical backdrop with real palm trees and bubbling ponds surrounded by large, flat rocks.

Since Laura was the busiest of her group, he was surprised when she reappeared. Watching curiously as she approached his table, he noticed her abnormal appearance. She was dressed in dark slacks and a black turtleneck, an outfit perfect for clandestine activities. Something was afoot. Stephan hoped for a private conversation until he saw two strangers following her. The man was scanning the room nervously, while the woman stayed close to Laura. Laura was definitely up to something.

It was good business to schedule regular employer-employee meetings, and he was glad when Laura had requested this practice herself. Unfortunately, she was usually accompanied by Tanya, Kate, and/or Monk. In fact, she had avoided being alone with him since their first interview. Tonight, however, she sent the man and woman away.

Laura slipped into the seat opposite Stephan and clasped her hands together between them as a sort of barrier. He was distracted by the delicate curve of her wrists. Before he could stop himself, he brushed her fingers softly in an absentminded sort of greeting. He wanted to feel the warm pulse of her skin. For the first time, she didn't jerk away.

Laura had twisted her hair into a thick braid, and long tendrils hung around her face. He brushed one behind her ear. Her hair was like living silk, and its softness tickled his palm. Her scent swam around him, reminding him of lush foliage rich with the aroma of earth. A smile teased his lips.

"Is something the matter?" Laura asked, confusion lighting her eyes.

"You have the most enchanting scent," Stephan admitted vaguely. "Are you wearing perfume?"

Laura blushed. She didn't handle compliments well.

"Ah…no…not tonight. Occasionally, I'll use a light perfume, which can cling to my clothes. That must be what you smell."

"Must be…"Stephan mused.

"I've made all the necessary arrangements for tonight's performances." Laura spoke in businesslike tones. "Tanya will perform 'Lost in Paradise.' It's the story of an unlikely friendship in a big cat sanctuary. We recorded the chorus earlier. Unfortunately, the musical is too short to fill the entire night. Since Kate is taking a much deserved night off, you'll have to use one of your other acts."

Stephan had been planning to spring a surprise on Laura for some time. With her sudden change in routine, he decided to put his plan into action.

"That won't be possible," he lied. "Our usual relief performers are filling in at my other theaters."

"Then we'll just have to repeat last night's performance," she reasoned, an edge of impatience souring her tone.

"That won't work either. We've already broken down the scenery for tonight. I have an important business party coming, so I need a full program. The music helps put my clients in a more receptive mood."

"Then what can we do?" she agonized.

"What about you?" Stephan suggested quietly, his excitement hidden behind a mask built from centuries of subterfuge. He offered no enticements. Instead, he watched the play of emotions on her face. Her first reaction was so obvious, he had to fight not to laugh. She looked utterly disgusted. Then she became quiet, thinking. She was probably searching for some reason to avoid performing. He wondered if she would go so far as to lie.

"I'm not very good. I could never hope to project the vibrancy of Tanya or the sweetness of Kate. You've been spoiled with the best of my girls. Why do you want me?" she fussed. "You would do better to re-schedule the meeting."

Laura looked over at the bar, taking a deep breath. Watching her, Stephan knew that if he insisted, she would force herself to go on stage. In the end, he didn't even have to ask again.

Laura's girls hadn't seemed aware of the heightened senses of the Shadow Dwellers and often spoke candidly without taking extra precautions to protect their privacy. He'd overheard Tanya complaining one night about Laura, who had had professional training but refused to sing. Stephan had wondered at this. If she was even passably good, then why didn't she fight for stage time like most performers? Instead, she seemed content to handle the numerous details required to stage a complicated production. Tonight, he wanted to find out whether she was good or not.

"I have business later," she hedged unhappily. "If you want me do this, then it'll have to be early."

"Done!" he agreed immediately. It would be unwise to give her time to find a loophole.

When she slid nervously to the edge of the seat, he stopped her by placing a hand on her wrist. "Where are you going?" He nodded at the dark clothes. "You're dressed for something serious."

Laura gazed at him speculatively. Then a faint illumination lightened her skin, and her eyes grew darker, disrupting his focus. He shook his head, dismissing his observations as a trick of the light, except the glow got brighter. He felt a sudden strange lassitude and a willingness to let her go without explanation. Stephan was familiar with many of the mysteries of the magical world. His own people were proof of them. But Laura continued to surprise him, even when he was already impressed by her.

"I'm going to Siren's Song," Laura announced, getting up from the table.

Stephan was relieved at her obvious honesty. After Eric and then Nicolette, he needed people he could trust.

"We have friends who work there. I'll bring my own security."

Stephan had instantly disliked and mistrusted Michael. He had seen the young man watching Laura with an expression that could only be called hungry. Michael wanted to possess her.

"Will Michael be part of your security?" he inquired casually.

"No, thank God." Laura frowned. Turning toward the auditorium, she continued, "I'll go and tell Tanya that I'll be performing first. When do you want the *one* performance?" She made it clear that she wouldn't perform a *second* time.

"Nine. But I must warn you, I think Nicolette imagines that you're somehow responsible for my rejection. You'll need your bodyguards on high alert tonight."

"Why would she act against me?" Laura asked, her eyes refocusing on Stephan's face.

Stephan felt disloyal speaking about Nicolette's obsessive devotion. He had never broken the confidentiality earned in his intimate relationships. But Nicolette was a real threat, and Laura needed to be extra vigilant. How his ex-lover could cling to the illusion that she could still control The Colony and him, even from a distance, was a mystery, but cling she did. The reports from his spies made this clear.

"Nicolette doesn't like attractive women around me. It doesn't matter if I'm interested in the woman or not. She and I joined forces after I suffered a tragic personal loss. But I never loved her, and she couldn't forgive me for this ultimate betrayal. So, she suffocated me with her controlling jealously, forcing me to send her away. I hoped distance would give her the chance to find new happiness. What I hadn't anticipated was that she wouldn't let me go.

"Since I'm beyond her retaliation, she might take her feelings of betrayal out on you. If she killed me for no better reason than jealousy, our people would punish her. But you are fair game. Please reconsider going to Siren's Song. It's her most protected lair." Stephan couldn't hide the plea in his voice. He knew that Nicolette was capable of great violence, and she was a mature Shadow Dweller, powerful and cunning.

"I have to go, Stephan, despite the danger." Laura looked sympathetic but stubborn. "If she's my enemy, then I have to try to neutralize the threat. She might try to harm my girls in an attempt to get to me. Does she really believe that you and I are lovers?" she asked bluntly. "I mean, we've only recently become acquainted. How could we possibly be involved?"

"Facts don't matter to a scorned lover," he reminded her. "Nicolette doesn't need the truth to be jealous or lethal. All she knows is the pain of losing the one person she has wanted above all others.

"Besides, she has reason to be suspicious. I do find you compelling. You have a gift for creating musical stories and a fire for finding justice that dispels the darkness of my world. You bring me the triumphs won in a life that was stolen from me." For the first time in a long time, Stephan felt moisture in his eyes. He had thought he had accepted his situation. But Laura was like a beacon back into a world he had only visited so long ago. "The centuries dull the idealism and fascination of youth," he added thoughtfully.

"I'm sorry. But a personal relationship between us would be impossible. I would never give up living openly in human society," she confessed. She looked away for a moment and took a deep breath. "Your people killed my friends," she blurted, her voice constricted. "I know what you are. I'm sorry your people are restricted to coming out only at night and hide in the shadows. But I love the vivid colors of sunlight. I love the laughter of children. I love the challenges in a mortal, human relationship. I love the opportunities available in the world to anyone who dares to take a chance. One day, I'll leave Lord's and pick up the threads of my old life. I'll return to human society, a journey that you could never make."

Stephan should have been discouraged by her logic. It was indisputable. But in his dark world, love was the only thing that gave him hope. Besides, people with seemingly insurmountable differences could find ways to share happiness, and he just had to hope that Laura would one day want to try.

"I can't stop you if you insist on going to Siren's Song," Stephan muttered, scrambling to his feet. "I can only hope that Nicolette will stop short of starting a war because you can bet, if she harms you, there will be one."

"Don't act rashly on my account," Laura begged. "Besides, I think I might be able to outsmart a disturbed, crazy-jealous woman. Now, I have a lot to prepare."

Laura walked toward the auditorium without waiting for his reply. Monk greeted her by the stage door. Stephan was grateful that Monk was her primary protector. His loyalty was indisputable and his strength formidable.

The time before Laura's performance passed with excruciating slowness. Stephan completed his usual duties, distracted and impatient. Twice, he snarled at Jon.

"Are you going to tell me what's bugging you, or are you going to continue to act like a horse's ass?" Jon finally barked, stung by his friend's rudeness.

Stephan hung his head, embarrassed. Jon was, in every important way, the closest thing he had to family. "I'm sorry, old friend. Laura is going into that she-devil Nicolette's lair," he confessed morosely. It was a relief to talk to someone he could trust, someone who already knew all his secrets. "I tried to talk some sense into the little twit, but she has the determination of a stampeding elephant." Then Stephan's face lightened, and he broke into a crooked grin. "She's agreed, Jon. She's going to perform—actually sing on stage."

"You mean Laura, our reticent whiz kid? Now that's an accomplishment. I never imagined you could or would succeed in cracking that particular nut. She avoids the spotlight tenaciously."

"She agreed to fill in once, tonight, and that opens the door. I just wonder how good our secretive songbird really is. Tonight at nine, I want no interruptions. I'll watch from my special perch." Stephan nodded toward the ceiling.

Stephan had built an enclosed box above the bar, giving him an enviable view of the stage. He could watch, completely unseen, above the paying audience. Tonight, he would record Laura's performance just in case it really was the only one. Only Jon knew of this perch. It had been hard to keep its existence from Nicolette, but Stephan had needed some secrets of his own.

Jon glanced at his watch. "I suggest you get moving. It's almost time."

Stephan climbed the concealed stairs—accessible only from his office—to his lookout and dropped into one of the comfortable chairs just in time to see the flashing red light signal a warning before curtain. He set the recording device and waited.

Pale-blue light filled an empty center stage. Mina pranced out wearing a chiffon gown of emerald green and the feather mask of a great mythical bird. She ran with the grace of a rushing river, lifting her arched feet in clean crisp jumps before launching into seemingly impossible somersault combinations. At center stage, she lifted one knee and began twirling a dizzying number of times with her leg in various stages of extension—just off the floor, curved back, curved forward, and then extended straight up—never losing her balance, never missing a beat. Then she back-flipped three times in succession before collapsing into a forward roll that ended with her jumping up into another series of pirouettes. She made each successive combination more difficult. Mina had been trained as a classical ballerina, and she was delightfully light-footed. She flew across the stage in her most strenuous sequences as the music rose in a crescendo and then glided out stage left when the song abruptly stopped.

Several charged moments later, a sweet, lilting voice wafted in from stage right. Laura skipped out on stage in a sapphire costume. Gray and white strips of lace decorated the skirt and rippled like cresting waves. Spotlights flickered across her costume and artificial wind ruffled her skirt, enhancing the illusion of white water. While her costume was stunning, her voice was the true prize. It showed years of disciplined practice. She sang in perfect pitch, projecting clear, light tones that created a sympathetic response in Stephan.

At first, she sang of the terrible storm that had trapped them on the island shown in the stage backdrop. Stephan could hear the character's terrible loneliness. Then she sang of her own true love, a young man of impossible beauty who was forever out of her reach. Her voice echoed in the theater as she ran through a series of intricate, provocative verses.

When Laura's song faded, Mina joined her at center stage. Thunderous applause, so unusual in the middle of a performance, engulfed the two women. Mina held a dance pose like a human statute, and Laura froze, staying in character. When the clapping died down, they continued their performance.

Laura sang about the isolated culture on her tropical island, about a simple people who lived and loved with their innocence intact. The music filled Stephan's heart with an impossible longing for that simple island life, and he felt an ache of loneliness.

Stephan had become so engrossed in Laura's surprising performance that he was startled by a sudden strangled sob of obvious suffering. Alarmed, he scanned the murky darkness below him. He saw a figure sagging against the wall, enveloped in a cloak. Stephan knew the familiar form too well to be fooled by her disguise. It was Nicolette.

All eyes were glued to the stage, and none saw the cowering figure concealed in the shadows beside a window drapery. But Stephan had an unusual vantage, and she was clearly visible. He could even see her glowing eyes. They seemed to consume all that was left of her sanity.

Nicolette looked terrible. Her face was skull-like, her lips thin, her eyes sunken, and her cheekbones jutting. He could hear her ragged breathing broken by an occasional quivering sob. Her arms held her body as if she had no other in the world but herself and Stephan's broken promises. She swayed, and he feared for one terrible moment that she would collapse.

Laura's voice surged through the audience, the notes of her song rippling like skipping stones. Below him, Nicolette gasped in what sounded like physical pain. Fearing the worst, Stephan rushed out of the box and jumped down the stairs to his office. He opened the door just in time to see Nicolette run toward the exit, her teeth bared like a feral animal's, her pupils dilated, her eyes blood red. She sprinted out the front entrance of The Colony, blind to Stephan's presence.

"My God!" Jon whispered from the far end of the bar. They exchanged a look of shock.

Stephan now knew, beyond any doubt, that Nicolette wouldn't rest until she saw him ruined. He couldn't even imagine what she had in mind for Laura. Even if she didn't blame Laura, she would kill her now.

# 8

# Siren's Song

Laura exited The Colony stage stunned, applause still ringing in her ears. She had stopped singing in public when she discovered her greater talent lay with staging performances.

"They liked me! They really liked me!" she told Monk, spinning and grinning.

He smiled in return. "Didn't know you had it in you, did you?" he teased.

"I've always loved singing, but you're right. I didn't think anyone would react like that. You know I still practice," she admitted, embarrassed. "Not because I want to perform. But because it brings me peace."

"You should accept the compliment. You were good, pet." Monk shook Laura playfully.

"Enough," she said, blushing. "We have to get going."

"Always business when you want to avoid compliments," Monk needled in a stage whisper.

Laura steered Monk into the largest dressing room, looking for Mina and Kate. By continuing to perform, Tanya would cover their absence from any Siren spies. Mina and Kate were already waiting to leave.

Laura quickly shucked her costume and redressed in her own dark outfit. Letting Mina perform had been a risk, but who paid attention to janitors? Still Laura hoped listening to Mina hadn't been a fatal mistake.

"I've rented a van so Nicolette won't be able to recognize the vehicle. There aren't any windows, so you can change into your disguises on the way," Monk explained. "Mina has already loaded the specialized gear. She's also drawn a floor plan of all the underground levels at Nicolette's theater."

"Underground floors?" Gabriel asked, watching Mina nervously. "Closed-in underground floors?"

Monk studied the young man. "Are you claustrophobic?"

"No," Gabriel whispered, avoiding eye contact. "I can handle it."

Laura looked to Kate. "Are you OK going underground?" she asked, worried that she might share Gabriel's fear.

"Ready and eager," Kate reassured her. "Finally we get to do something besides hanging around here. I was beginning to wonder if we were ever going to see some action." Kate's Viking ancestors would have been proud.

"I'll give you all a briefing on the way there." Mina glanced toward the rear exit and then looked to Monk for permission to exit.

Monk led the small group out the back to a long black van parked in the very last row. Everyone piled into the vehicle while Monk got into the driver's seat and then roared out of the parking lot. Mina pulled several black satchels into the center aisle and dumped out their contents. She flung maintenance overalls to each person. They fit easily over their dark clothing.

"Wait." Mina interrupted their preparations and pulled out a selection of loose-fitting cocktail outfits. "I want the option to switch into evening clothes, if necessary. It is a nightclub, so we might need to blend into the crowd." She also pulled out high heels for the ladies.

Laura groaned. Men always did luck out in this regard.

"As maintenance workers, you can carry a small backpack," Mina continued. "I think the ladies should bring these items." She shoved a pair of high heels and the cocktail dress she had selected for herself into one of the satchels. Then she laid out touch-up makeup, a lock kit, one gun, two small knives, a flashlight, a miniature gas mask, and one of Lord's atomizers so everyone could see them. "The atomizer will knock-out the prison guards."

Mina handed Gabe a smaller satchel. "The same for you, Gabe, except I think you can skip the dress and heels." She smiled as she held out masculine evening attire.

Laura took one of the dresses, a pair of sandals, and a backpack. She quickly redressed and loaded her pack with the remaining necessary items.

Meanwhile, Mina set up a video player and projected a floor plan of Siren's Song onto the ceiling. The display magnified miniature replicas of various entry/exit points and labeled each room.

There were four levels. On the top floor were the nightclub, dining room, main security office, and stage. The second floor handled all the tasks necessary to produce a floor show, provide gourmet meals, and stock a cosmopolitan bar. Two rooms were secured to monitor the upper floor and store guards' personal items, weapons, and equipment, as well as provide a private break area. The third floor housed Nicolette's apartment and included an expanded office for several personal body-guards. She was definitely obsessed with security. The fourth floor was their destination. It was in essence a dungeon with concrete cells and a guard station.

"The girls are kept here," Mina said, pointing to the fourth-floor plan. "The only time they're let out is to perform. Despite the con-crete walls and locked doors, the cells resemble small apartments. There are well-stocked bedrooms, bathrooms, kitchens, and living rooms. Nicolette needs her performers ready to do their best. Stark cells would only produce pale, lifeless women who would entertain no one. There's a guard station at the only entrance to this floor.

"I've been working on the fourth floor for the last week, cleaning apartments when the girls are performing on stage. I'll need to report to my supervisor to see which cell-apartments are assigned for tonight. I'll get your access badges then."

Mina turned up the magnification on the screen, and several stairways became visible. "We can take this one out." She pointed to a continuous stairway that led up one side of all four floors. "Unfortunately, there's no access going down. The top door only opens out. We'll have to navigate all four floors as maintenance staff to get down to the girls."

"What about security?" Laura asked.

"Lord's diversion at precisely eleven o'clock is intended to distract the monitor guards long enough for us to sneak out," Gabriel explained. "But we won't know if it's working until it's too late."

"The whole plan does hinge on a certain degree of luck," Kate observed, winking. "But Lord is formidable. He'll come through."

Laura looked to Mina for any additional information.

"Getting by the cameras is the real genius of my plan," Mina continued eagerly. "This time of night is when their defenses are at their weakest. Everyone, even the guards, will be distracted by the performers, and there's regular traffic in and out of the dungeon floor. Our disguises should get us by the cameras. Even if there's an occasional glance at the security monitors, we'll be ignored unless we act suspicious. This stairway..." Mina pointed at the one-way ventilation exit. "...has only one camera, and I can tape a thirty-minute rotating video clip over the lens. I've done this before to make sure it worked."

Laura looked thoughtfully at Gabriel. "We'll have to be extra vigilant of both guards and Nicolette's nefarious traps. Mina has gone in as a cleaning woman without problems, so I think the way in will be safe. But the ventilation exit is unknown. Once we release the girls, we'll be more vulnerable."

"Look, ladies and gents," Monk offered from the front, "we're committed, so let's just focus on problems when they happen."

"How close are we?" asked Gabriel.

"Up ahead," whispered Laura. Now that they were close she could almost feel Nicolette's malice. Siren's Song gleamed in the darkness ahead.

Mina came up behind her, and her whisper sent ripples down Laura's spine. "Turn into the street before the theater," she guided Monk. "The employee parking lot is behind the main parking area."

Monk turned left and parked as far from the parking lot lights as he could manage. Luckily, he found a large tree branch whose leaves shrouded the van.

Laura judged each member of the group for readiness. Not only were they all prepared; they were as amped as she was. They moved quietly out the back of the van and walked toward the theater in a stealthy fashion, scanning the area for witnesses.

Mina's exasperated laugh stopped everyone. "You are maids, people, not an invading force. Please try not to look so…organized."

Laura and Monk smiled sheepishly.

When they neared the back door, Mina took the lead. She disappeared inside, closing the door securely behind her. The others waited outside for the all-clear signal.

As usual, Laura found waiting excruciating. She began pacing to relieve her anxiety, and eventually, Kate and Gabriel copied her example and followed behind. The two looked like baby ducklings following their mother goose. When Monk finally burst out laughing, they stopped, looking confused. But Monk refused to explain. Laura prudently stopped pacing, and her second string, Gabriel and Kate, reluctantly followed suit. As minutes began to feel like hours, Mina reappeared.

"It's a go. We're lucky. Nicolette has called up four of her best girls, and they're already performing. I told security that I'd need more help. Unfortunately, the head dog will only authorize two extra maids." Mina looked Monk up and down. "I'm sorry, Monk. You, I can't explain." She gave Laura, Gabriel, and Kate an once-over. "I think I should bring Gabriel. These women have been taught to distrust other women. With a guy, they might be more willing to risk escape."

Mina looked critically at Laura and Kate. She tugged on Laura's cheap wig and shook her head. They hadn't had time to buy quality disguises specifically for this mission. Laura saw the writing on the wall— she was a threat to the safety of her team. If Nicolette came across her, she would most likely see through the wig and glasses.

"I'll stay," she offered in defeat. She really had wanted to face Nicolette head-on.

Then she had an inspiration. "Wait a minute! We can use my notoriety to our advantage. Bringing Nicolette's slaves out of the theater is our greatest challenge. But if I make an appearance, no one'll be thinking about the girls in the dungeons. If anyone can keep Siren's Song in chaos, it'll be Nicolette's nemesis in person: me. I'll wait until just before Lord's men arrive. They will give me my way out!" Laura couldn't help grinning. Finally, she would have the upper hand over the she-devil who had ravaged her home.

"It will definitely keep Nicolette and her security busy," Mina agreed. "We may get out of this unscathed after all."

"Call me when you've released the girls," Laura told her.

Behind her, Monk's low growl warned her that she had one more person to convince.

Stephan knew about Nicolette's deteriorating voice. She still practiced enough to be a presentable singer and used Siren's Song for occasional performances. Tonight, she had heard Laura's singing talent for the first time. He shuddered, recalling the downfall of others who had stirred her jealously. With a jolt of dread, he remembered that Laura was heading for Nicolette's club. Stephan dashed into the auditorium of The Colony, only to find the performers gone and the auditorium roaring with applause.

"This is unbelievable!" He turned a stricken face to Jon, who had followed him. "Laura's planning to go to Siren's Song. We must stop her." He headed for the dressing rooms backstage and found Tanya in the hall.

"Where is she?" he blurted desperately, noticing several partially opened doors. "Where is Laura?"

"They left," she told him. "I've never seen people change clothes so fast."

"Who accompanied her?" Stephan demanded.

"Mina, Kate, Gabriel, and Monk," Tanya answered with equal gruffness.

At least she wouldn't be alone. But human agents were small hope against a raging Nicolette and her Shadow Dweller minions. He returned to the main lobby and dashed out the front entrance, preparing to run all the way to Siren's Song, but Jon caught his arm, steering him toward his car. He struggled against the restraining hand, worry blinding his reason.

"Drive!" was all Jon said.

Desperate to get moving, Stephan dragged Jon toward his car. He would've preferred the release of running, and it would have been faster since he wouldn't be restricted to streets. But he might need to transport Laura and the others.

Without warning, three of Nicolette's guards blocked the path to Stephan's car. Jon growled dangerously when he recognized his old nemesis, Amos. The other two were known for their savagery. Stephan choked on his frustration at this intolerable delay. He had to find some tactic to neutralize these men quickly.

The three intruders fanned out and walked toward the two men. Stephan crouched, readying himself for the battle ahead. A commotion behind him signaled the approach of a large group of partygoers. The tipsy crowd staggered to the curb in front of Stephan's car. Nicolette's guards instantly straightened and tried to look like innocent passersby. Their black leather outfits made this a challenge.

"Jimmy, give me your cell!" a pretty blond pouted. "We have to call a cab. Who knows how long they'll take?"

"Aw, Susie. Let's drive. My car is right over there," a clean-shaven young man protested. He stumbled when he tried to point at a car parked down the street. Stephan could see a very expensive red convertible in the half-light.

"No way!" Susie retorted. "My life is worth more than that hot rod. Give me your cell!" she repeated and grabbed the phone out of his pocket. She turned away to dial.

Stephan was reluctant to alarm these strangers. Cautiously, he tried to push past the three goons to alert his security inside The Colony. But Nicolette's men persisted in blocking them. Twenty painful minutes passed before Susie's cab finally appeared. In the confusion of the cab's arrival, their adversaries finally dropped their guard long enough to allow Stephan to act.

He whispered to Jon, "Get backup! Hurry!"

Jon dashed back into The Colony, barely evading Amos's lurch toward him. Fortunately, the partygoers lingered, arguing over who would pay for the cab. They decided on Jimmy, despite his protests. Then they crammed themselves into the small cab, and it drove away, visibly rocking.

As soon as the cab was out of sight, one of the invaders attacked Stephan. The goon placed an arm around his throat and tightened it while another held him immobile. At the sound of breaking bones, Stephan felt his senses fog and awareness slip away. He was in the thrall of the Shadow Dweller healing process. Usually, he could overcome these affects for a short time. But somehow, this time, he was unsuccessful. When he awoke an unknown time later, he found himself on the sidewalk with Jon watching him.

"It's about time!" Jon fretted. "Our men took Amos and his men downstairs. They won't be causing anyone trouble anytime soon."

Stephan was too agitated for polite conversation. Silently, he ran to his car, jumped into the driver's seat, and gunned the engine. Jon slammed the passenger door shut seconds before the car sped away from the curb.

On that long frantic drive down dark, tree-lined streets, impeded by grassy center boulevards, time felt like sand trickling out of an hourglass, one grain at a time. Stephan tried to calm his mind, but it was impossible. Instead, he stomped on the accelerator, and the car jumped forward in a violent burst of speed. One tire got caught on the boulevard curb, and he lost control, fishtailing wildly. Only his superhuman strength prevented them from slamming into a steel light pole. Jon cursed loudly, and Stephan forced himself to slow down. He could do no good if they never got there. He only hoped that Nicolette hadn't gone directly back to her signature club.

Kate and Gabriel followed Mina back inside, all three carrying backpacks. Laura's enthusiasm faded when she found herself once more waiting outside. After a few minutes, she and Monk decided to go back to the van. Standing at the back door was too conspicuous.

Laura climbed into the back of the van, while Monk sat in the driver's seat, watching the back door. She would use the time to prepare for her climactic meeting with her royal highness, queen of all she surveyed, Nicolette. She decided looking sexy would create the most mayhem and give them the greatest advantage. So she selected a dress that was just a smidgen too small. It was made of red silk with delicate lace at the breast and waist. She released her hair and let it fall down her back. She wondered how Nicolette's male guards would react. Would they be as focused as when they met a male invading force? She did pin her long bangs back so her hair wouldn't interfere with a quick retreat. She needed to be able to run and climb unimpaired. She was thankful that also meant she didn't have to wear the high heels, even though they were the epitome of sexy. Instead, she put on jeweled gold sandals with low heels.

Laura carefully applied seductive black eyeliner, false eyelashes, and bright-red lipstick. She thought of the white lace choker she had worn to unsettle Eric and decided to draw attention to the Shadow Dwellers' one weakness—their hunger. She looked among the discarded dresses and finally found one with pink lace accents. It was a bit too girlie, but it would have to do. She cut off a long piece and tied it around her throat. Then she examined the total effect in a hand mirror.

"Perfect." She winked at her reflection, and her green-gold eyes sparkled back at her, delighted at the confrontation ahead. The gold highlights of her chestnut hair glowed in the dome light.

Monk turned around and looked at her. "Just what do you think you're doing? Nicolette is already prepared to eviscerate you!" he snapped impatiently.

"I'm trying to unsettle her. What better way to get Nicolette's goat than to look sexier than her?"

"You should say: What better way to get yourself butchered? The angrier she is, the more determined she'll be to squash you like an irritating bug."

"We'll have a large enough army of her very motivated victims to bring her down, Monk. But I'll have my revenge first. Don't you remember what she did to my home?"

"I remember," Monk growled, scowling. "This is still a bad idea."

Laura shrugged and turned back to the pile of supplies. She found a cloak and a bag large enough to carry a Taser and pepper spray for closer encounters. Just then, her phone rang.

"We're waiting at the bottom of the stairs," Mina whispered. "We got past the guards, and the girls are eager to escape. Thank God for Lord's halothane atomizers. We filled their station, and the men dropped like flies. Luckily the air-conditioning unit cleared the space before we released the girls. I don't know how much time we have before we are discovered, but I think speed is the best option."

"Get ready. When the witch and her minions are engaged, Monk will text you."

"Roger, roger," Mina whispered nervously. "Hurry."

Laura gathered her nerves and jumped out of the van. Monk followed close behind.

"We stay together?" she asked softly.

"You couldn't drive me away." Monk's expression was grim and hard.

In that moment, Laura fully appreciated how much she depended on him.

She strode purposefully toward Siren's Song. Luckily, the parking lot was clear. Laura and Monk open the back door furtively and walked down a service hall without encountering any resistance. Laura could hear muffled sound ahead. As they left the service areas, she was astonished at the opulent transformation.

Siren's Song was the most overstated nightclub Laura had ever seen. Thick, rich purple brocade covered the walls. Gold thread was woven into scandalous portraits of laughing courtesans entertaining rich clients. Plush gold carpeting effectively absorbed all sound. Heavy purple curtains separated the rooms, and antique candelabra provided the lighting. Several cubbies concealed overstuffed divans covered in gold velvet.

Laura peeked behind curtains until she found the main dining hall. She was relieved to see that the ostentatious decor had been abandoned in this area. The floors were geometric tile mosaics and the table arrangements clean and simple. Food wasn't a major concern to Shadow Dwellers, so Nicolette most likely left this area to someone else. Only a few customers could be seen in corner tables. They were locked in deep conversations with their companions. Laura and Monk crossed the room unnoticed.

Laura could hear singing muffled by heavy draperies at the other end of the hall. She carefully stowed her cloak under the draperies and checked to make certain Monk was close behind. At any moment, she expected to be stopped. But no one seemed to be paying attention to them.

The stage area was a return to Nicolette's unique style, with a shiny gold-striped main stage curtain and seats upholstered in purple brocade. *How could anyone be so devoid of taste?* Laura wondered as they crept down the dark aisle and took two empty seats down a side row.

Laura thought she was prepared for anything until she saw Nicolette on stage. The resemblance to the pictures in Lord's archives was unmistakable. But her face was twisted, and her eyes blazed with madness. When Nicolette opened her mouth to sing again, the tones were like razors ripping out eardrums. She was making no attempt to sing on key. The horrible truth was that she was mangling Laura's song from tonight's performance. Remarkably, the audience remained quiet as she continued to screech her terrible parody.

As Laura stood up, preparing to stop this travesty, she heard a disturbance to her right. She looked over and saw several large, menacing men at the end of the aisle blocking their exit. She turned toward the opposite aisle to find more guards. There would be no escape route. How could they challenge Nicolette if they were already her prisoners? Laura sank back down into her seat, frustrated.

# 9

## The Rescue

Finally, Stephan saw the marquee, "Siren's Song," glowing above the familiar establishment. A streetlight created a circle of light in front of the entrance. His stomach burned when he spotted Nicolette's purple sportster. He pulled in behind her car.

Stephan longed to run boldly into the club. After all, Nicolette had come into his place uninvited. But at this point, stealth was vital. Calmly, he led Jon ahead of the patrons waiting in line. He knew the doorman, but more important, the doorman knew him. The employee let Stephan and Jon in automatically. He obviously hadn't gotten the memo that they were personae non gratae. Maybe Nicolette had deliberately left an opening for the reconciliation that would never come.

Inside, it took him a few moments to get his bearings in the dark. He guided Jon to the main auditorium and, to his amazement, found Nicolette herself on stage. The bulky cloak that had concealed her identity at The Colony lay to one side of the stage, crumpled into a ball. Her burgundy dress blazed in the stage light, and Stephan was reminded of the savage violence of his initiation into the world of the Shadow Dwellers. Nicolette's costume pulsated in the rotating spotlight like the blood that kept his race alive. She was singing Laura's song in a gross parody.

Frantically, he scanned the audience. Irrationally, he hoped that Laura wasn't there. But that hope was futile. Laura and Monk were already trapped by Nicolette's henchmen.

Stephan looked back at Nicolette, who was glaring at Laura. She continued her terrible mockery of Laura's song. Her hate and envy warped the music's sweetness. Even though Nicolette's reputation as a singer was slipping, she still seemed to delight in screeching the lyrics. With each broken note, he noticed Laura wince. Nicolette's calculated cruelty was legendary.

Stephan knew he couldn't rescue Laura against six Shadow Dweller guards. So, he slipped back into the shadows before Nicolette could spot him. Stephan's options were limited. He could call more men, but they might arrive too late; he could challenge Nicolette herself, but killing her in front of humans was too dangerous.

"What now?" Jon whispered behind him.

In answer, a single word rang out, echoing through the auditorium, catching everyone's attention, even silencing Nicolette's macabre performance.

"Fire!"

Stephan smiled. This was just the effective diversion that Monk might try. But his appreciation transformed into alarm when huge flames erupted from under the stage. It wasn't a ruse. The fire quickly engulfed the heavy curtains and wood floor. In mere moments, Nicolette was framed by a burning inferno. She stood frozen until the flames began to scorch her long dress, and then she cried out in agony.

The panicked patrons were running for the door, creating a churning wall of people. Nicolette's men couldn't contain the panicked stampede and were being pushed back against the walls.

Stephan spied Laura and Monk shoving their way toward a side door. He knew the door led to a narrow hall that accessed the parking lot. But it also contained a booby-trapped floor. Nicolette's club had multiple ways to corner the young women chosen for her stable who dared to try to escape.

Stephan couldn't resist a last glance at Nicolette. His ex-lover tore off the burning strips of her dress and leaped off the stage. He saw her scan the fleeing crowd and pause when she spotted Laura. Desperately, Stephan struggled through the charging mob, trying to reach Laura first. But she was too far away.

Then he noticed Monk waving to get his attention. The big man pointed at the side door and raised his open palms questioningly. Monk must have seen Stephan and realized he had the most experience in Siren's Song. Anxiously, using exaggerated movements, Stephan shook his head and tried to mime a trapdoor in the floor. The other man nodded. He shouted to Laura over the din of the crowd and pointed at Stephan. Once he had her attention, Stephan pointed to the front of the club. She shook her head, obviously reluctant to join the mass of humanity frantically struggling to escape. But when she pointed toward the side door, Stephan deliberately shook his head. Impatient to escape, Monk dragged Laura toward the front.

Stephan was relieved when he saw Laura finally join the escaping crowd. The mass of people, including Shadow Dwellers, would be effective witnesses against Nicolette. She couldn't kill with such an audience. In the Shadow Dweller society, there were rules, rituals, and strict requirements for exacting justice. Even Nicolette, mad with rage, might pause before turning her race against her.

Again, Stephan pushed through the crowd. Eventually, he reached Laura and Monk outside. Nicolette was nowhere to be seen. Impulsively, he lifted Laura high in his arms, ignoring the frown and complaints from Monk. He really had expected that Nicolette would succeed in killing her. The vampiress had always prevailed before. He needed to reassure himself that Laura was still alive and breathing.

Still shaking, Laura hugged him. "Thank God! You...saved us," she whispered hoarsely, shock etched across her features. "She was so angry—so powerful. I was afraid...I had finally gone too far."

Against his better judgment, Stephan brushed his lips across hers. Soft tendrils of her hair brushed against his nose, filling his senses with her intoxicating scent. Laura turned her head and nestled her face against his neck. Stephan felt the familiar stirring of longing as he enjoyed her warmth. He closed his eyes and for a few seconds, reveled in this intimacy. Too soon, he felt Monk pull Laura away. He reluctantly refocused on the activity around them.

The parking lot was clearing. Without warning, a large group of young women ran out of a side door, led by Mina and followed by one of Laura's guards. Stephan instantly recognized several of Nicolette's performers. He had never agreed with Nicolette's methods, but she wouldn't listen to any opinion other than her own.

Laura beckoned the milling group, while Jon separated himself from a group of exiting patrons and joined Stephan.

"We have to go before we draw the wrong attention," Jon warned nervously.

"There's no safe place where that she-devil can't find us." A small blond cowering in the middle of the group spoke out, despite her obvious fright. "She has a special force to keep us under lock and key."

"You said you work for Gideon Lord?" A tall, exotic-looking girl at the front of the group asked a small oriental girl, obviously the leader. "He's the only who can keep us safe."

"Nicolette's guard will come for us, soon." An older, willowy woman moved forward and pointed to the stream of people still exiting Siren's Song.

"You take the van, Mina," Laura insisted. "These girls are too visible here. Monk and I will follow with Stephan and Jon. We can delay any pursuit."

"We're all in danger," Laura's guard exclaimed, drawing everyone's attention. Stephan remembered that his name was Gabriel. "We are stronger together."

Laura looked from Gabriel to the group of women. "You can't be serious," she scoffed. "We won't all fit in the van."

"It would be a tight fit," Gabriel admitted stubbornly.

"Don't be silly, Gabe," Mina said impatiently. "We have to go in two groups. Where am I supposed to take them?" she asked Laura. "Will Lord take Nicolette's girls in, or do you have somewhere else?"

Laura studied the women intently. "Are any of you Shadow Dwellers?" she asked worriedly, and four women stepped forward. "I don't know if Lord will let Shadow Dwellers live in his stronghold."

"It doesn't matter," the tall, exotic woman interrupted. She had stepped forward as one of the Shadow Dwellers. "I would rather have Gideon Lord kill me than live another minute under Nicolette's cruelty."

"I'll take the Shadow Dwellers. I should've done so long ago," Stephan offered, a weight lifting off his shoulders.

"Lord will take them," Monk asserted.

"What about his men? They've been trained to hate my kind on sight," Stephan argued. He felt a growing commitment to help these women.

"Nicolette knows all your safe houses," Monk argued.

"Not all of them. I've kept a few secrets."

"We'll go with her," the exotic beauty insisted, pointing at Mina. "She said we can help keep others safe who've been brutalized like us."

"They can stay at my house in the compound," Laura promised. "I'll call Lord myself to confirm. After that, we'll find a place where all future Trust candidates can stay. With or without Lord, all you girls will be safe."

"I can supply the perfect house for your Trust," offered Stephan, letting Laura take the lead.

"Why would you do that?" she asked. "You don't even know what the Trust is."

"You would be surprised what I know," Stephan shot back cryptically.

The four Shadow Dwellers had glided back to the group of human singers, and the women held hands as their rescuers decided their fate. The van pulled up beside Mina, with Kate driving.

"Get in!" Kate invited enthusiastically. "Time's a-wastin'. We have places to go and people to meet."

The girls climbed eagerly into the back along with Mina. Gabriel remained stubbornly at Laura's side.

"You'll take everyone to Lord's. I'll call ahead to clear the way," Laura promised and gestured for the van to depart.

Kate nodded. "That was my plan all along. That old softy won't be able to turn us away." She tapped the horn before driving out of the parking lot.

Stephan watched Laura make her call. How long Lord could let them stay before their presence stirred up trouble was anyone's guess. With a sigh of satisfaction, Laura hung up.

A sudden eruption of fire captured Stephan's attention. The Siren's Song marquee exploded, sending a shower of sparks shooting out into the black, moonless night, and tumbled off the building. Stephan struggled to understand the behavior of this conflagration. Fires were usually slow creatures, easily subdued—not this one. It whipped into higher and hotter flames on a night with absolutely no wind, consuming the club in record time. Finally, he shook his head in frustration at the unnatural fire, beckoned to the others, and ran to his car.

After unlocking the doors with a pocket fob, Stephan tossed his keys to Monk, letting him drive. Monk shoved his greater bulk into the roomier driver's seat while Gabriel and Jon squeezed into the back, leaving no space for anyone else. The vehicle was not ideal for the bulky bodies of the two men, who worked at keeping fit enough to protect others. After crowding into the passenger seat, Stephan made room for Laura in his lap.

Monk shot out of the parking lot like a bullet and roared down the streets as if all the demons of hell were after them. Stephan was forced to hang on as Monk swerved around every turn at top speed. Laura squirmed uncomfortably as she too tried to brace herself.

"Would you please sit still?" Stephan groaned, when she accidently shoved her elbow into his solar plexus.

At Stephan's complaint, Laura tried to avoid moving. Still, she brushed against his face and chest as she too suffered through Monk's notorious driving.

To Stephan's relief, Monk didn't head directly to Lord's. The Colony was closer, and Monk's specialized SUV was still in its parking lot. In record time, Laura's bodyguard pulled up in front of The Colony and slipped smoothly into Stephan's reserved parking spot. Laura sprang out of the car with all the energy of a cat escaping a filled bathtub. Stephan swiftly followed her, eager to stretch his cramped muscles. Jon exited the car more gracefully and headed for the nightclub. Monk headed for the back parking lot.

Stephan's gaze pulled Laura's attention to him, and suddenly, she stilled. The familiar awareness grew. She looked curious and then confused, as if they were speaking some secret language only they could understand. Stephan expected her to run away, as she had so many times before. Instead, she walked over and stopped in front of him.

For a fraction of a second, her expression exposed a familiar loneliness. He had never seen his own suffering so perfectly mirrored by another. She seemed to understand what it was like to live disconnected from the people around him.

Gabriel stepped between them and broke the spell. He glared at Stephan. "Go back to your own world and your own kind, dark one. She belongs to us," he growled, thrusting his face into Stephan's.

"I what? Who are you?" Laura sputtered. She pushed Gabriel back.

So these newcomers knew he was a Shadow Dweller, Stephan realized. They were too observant.

"She belongs where she chooses to go," Stephan reminded Gabriel.

"We're here for her. She'll come with us in the end," Gabriel promised.

"I'm standing right here," Laura reminded the two feuding men. "Stop treating me like a possession, and, Gabriel, don't ever speak for me again. I didn't accept it from Michael, and I certainly won't accept it from you. Go collect Tanya so we can go back to Lord's. I'll speak to Stephan alone," she demanded, making it clear that the discussion was over.

Gabriel remained in mute rebellion. Laura stood her ground with arms crossed, staring stonily at him. Eventually, he broke eye contact and walked into the theater. When they were both gone, Laura turned back to Stephan.

"I want to thank you again for saving us," she said quietly. "Without the fire, we were goners. There were just too many guards, and Nicolette wanted to hurt me with a ferocity that was intimidating."

Stephan was startled to realize that Laura thought he'd created the fire diversion. "I can't create living fire like the one that consumed Siren's Song," he interrupted. "I didn't start it."

"Then who? It was too convenient and too destructive to be an accident." Laura searched his eyes anxiously.

"I don't know. Look, Laura, there's something I need to tell you. I followed you when you left with Eric until you returned to Lord's compound."

Laura's sharp intake of breath was audible. She wrestled with her shaking hands. "Then you saw what happened?"

"I saw you kill Eric and his driver," Stephan stated bluntly.

"But why did you hire my performers then? I'm your enemy," Laura squeaked and then coughed to hide her discomfort.

"You're not my enemy! I'm not a killer like Eric. He's been an embarrassment to my people for a long time. It's unnecessary for Shadow Dwellers to kill humans. We can drink enough while giving a bit of pleasure and still leave the person unharmed. But Eric was an animal. He treated your people like cattle that he killed for pleasure. It was disgusting. He deserved to be put down."

"Is that why you leave Gideon Lord alone? I mean, you all know about him and his mission to keep Dwellers from killing."

"Every society has its embarrassments, members who behave savagely and without conscience. When a psychopath, sociopath, or criminally insane individual is turned, we're left with a violence that can't be contained. Lord has only taken out Shadow Dwellers who would bring our entire society into the public eye."

"And now I'm doing the same thing. Is that why you let me work at The Colony? To take down your criminals?" Laura looked past Stephan.

He saw dark shadows lurking in her eyes.

"I wanted you at The Colony," Stephan stated firmly, "for reasons that must be plainly obvious. Surely you have some idea how I feel about you."

"I never really thought about it," Laura hedged. "I was so relieved that someone in your world was giving us access that I didn't look too closely at the gift horse."

"Well, there are many reasons why I hired you. I admire you. Without using force, you rid my world of a very dangerous, unpredictable thug. You're beautiful. I think that white dress should come with a warning: wear this at the peril of every male within thirty feet. You're talented. I've never met anyone who could understand my designs, let alone suggest improvements. You're loyal. I know Eric murdered your friends. And you're never boring. Just when I think that I finally understand you, you present new complexities. I have few friends that I can trust, and I believe you could be one, if you ever let me get close."

"So you would help me and Lord?" she asked incredulously.

"No! That would be impossible. I'd be labeled a traitor by Shadow Dwellers and subject to termination. Eric's people are already watching you. I wasn't the only one following you that night. Noel, Nicolette's spy, was there too. He told her about Eric's murder. She knows about you. If I gave them a reason to come after me, they would kill us both with one stone."

"Wh-a-at? But why haven't Eric's men come after *me*?" Laura exclaimed, her eyes dark with confusion.

"I don't think they believe Nicolette. Since she left The Colony, her jealousy has become common knowledge. It's too convenient for her to blame you. Besides, many believe you're too young and fragile to be a real threat. They don't understand that your soft words and shy smile are the real weapons against them." Stephan smiled in a self-deprecating manner, embarrassed by his people's foolish bias.

"So, they don't think I'm a serious threat? This is perfect." Laura beamed happily.

"Don't applaud yourself too soon. Eric's men will target you eventually. It helps that you're under my protection. Action against you means action against me, and I'm the strongest predator in this neck of the woods." Stephan scowled darkly. Any threat against Laura, real or imagined, started his blood boiling. But looking at her, his mood shifted again.

"I would ask a favor," Stephan asked softly, deciding that tonight he would try to make a real connection. He held her gaze, trying to read her mood.

"What is it?" she asked warily.

"There's a private place I want to show you. My secret workshop away from The Colony. You see, it's my fault that you're in danger. Nicolette was my problem, and because of me, she's decided that you're her next victim. My workshop can give you shelter when she comes after you again." He didn't bother to deny this eventuality. "It's on the way to Lord's fortress. But you'll have to send your soldiers to Lord's alone."

Stephan watched excitement battle fear in Laura's eyes until curiosity appeared to overcome her reservations. Still, she hesitated, looking at The Colony's front entrance. He worried that she might insist on bringing at least Monk.

"The invitation is for you alone," Stephan insisted. "You will be safe."

Laura nodded, accepting his terms. He ushered her back into his car before the others could return and convince her to stay. It seemed that Nicolette had done in one night what Stephan had failed to achieve since he'd met Laura. She was leaving with him—alone.

# 10

## The Workshop

After several minutes of silence, Stephan found himself struggling to come up with a way to dispel the awkward quiet that filled the car. Laura stared out the window, watching the rows of trees whiz by in an endless procession. The night pressed in on them, making the small car an oasis in the creeping darkness. Shadows rose in their headlights and, as they passed, fell back into a sea of black behind them. Stymied, he broke the stillness with a question.

"Would you like to hear the story of how I became a Shadow Dweller? It might help you understand why we aren't all villains."

"Are you sure?" Laura asked respectfully. "Your kind is so secretive."

"I think I can trust you. You wouldn't use this information against me, would you?" he asked with a teasing smile.

"Of course not! I am interested, if you're certain."

With averted eyes and a self-conscious smile, Stephan began to speak. His quiet voice filled the dark car. "My father came from a wealthy family, but he wasn't satisfied with the life of the idle rich. Fortunately, his parents let him pursue his aspirations, despite the social stigma. He became a musician and met my mother at a royal concert. She, in turn, was a gifted singer and worked in prominent opera houses. They were both talented enough to win a degree of recognition. As a result, I grew up in the playhouses of Europe. My playmates were clowns and magicians. I eventually learned several magic tricks but never showed any talent for music or dance. However, I loved the mathematical symmetry in architecture and the intricate workings of complex devices. Where my parents were famous for their artistic excellence, I brought new skills to the table. I invented contraptions that enabled their performances to capture the attention of the nobility. With our newfound success and Dad's money, my family was able to buy and modify a modest opera house in the South of France. Between my innovations and my parents' reputations, our theater drew a wide range of interested artists and so attracted the beginning of the end for me.

"When a species, like the Shadow Dwellers, lives for a very long time, they must graduate from the common pursuits and appetites of the young and find a source of enduring fascination. Many are drawn into the imaginative world of talented artists: painters, writers, composers, and performers. This creative horizon provides a stream of exciting innovation that brings something vital into the endless night of Shadow Dwellers.

"One day, a notorious Shadow Dweller found her way to our theater. At first, Ariadne stayed in the shadows, observing the happiness and creative play of my family. I didn't see her appetite for our life grow into an obsession until it was too late. She had some talent, after a fashion. It was enough to gain her an interview with my parents. They offered her a position, but she wanted so much more. She insisted on creative discretion and an outrageous share of our profits. Of course, her demands were refused. My parents foolishly believed that they had a choice and this would be the end of it. They were wrong.

"Ariadne assumed that I would help her steal my family's success, and so she invited me to a quiet late-night dinner. I could tell you of the terror of that night, of the way she played with me like a spider plays with a delicious fly. I could tell you that she drank my blood, not bothering to shield me from the agony that produced, until my life hung by a thread, and then forced me to drink her blood to restore myself, so she could repeat this horrific process again. Ultimately, I passed out and woke to find my spirit broken and my body changed forever, denied the position and reputation my achievements would have won me.

"In the end, I had the last laugh. Once changed, I was of course very sick at first. Ariadne tried to seduce me into following her vicious, ruthless ways, but I never lost sight of my fundamental moral compass. Instead, I pretended that my technical skills had been lost, and I never lifted a finger to help her recreate my beloved theater. She punished me at first, but when a person has no hope, pain just becomes a nuisance.

"I ran away over and over again, forcing her to send her thugs to bring me back. I made sure that I never offered her any entertainment. I followed her orders and suffered through her torture with a numb, lackluster passivity. Finally, she grew tired of me, and the next time I ran away, she let me go."

"What happened when you got here?" Laura asked, her eyes lit with fascination. He had captured her imagination.

"I tried to find somewhere I could coexist with humans while resisting the terrible hunger of the Shadow Dwellers. I buried myself in classical literature by becoming a library security guard and tinkered with electronics to maintain some interest in living."

"Tinkered?" she echoed. She laid her hand on his arm sympathetically.

"We're almost here, and you'll see," Stephan stammered, caught off guard by the unfamiliar feeling of vulnerability. It had been a long time since he'd told anyone about Ariadne.

Stephan turned down a long wooded drive. He stopped twice to remove huge trees blocking the road. He had placed them carefully as a deterrent to curious passersby. Finally, they crossed a rustic bridge into the main courtyard of an isolated mountain lodge nestled in a cradle of old-growth forest. The trees created a thick canopy that not even the sun could penetrate. He parked in front of the sprawling house.

Laura climbed slowly from the car, studying the front of the structure. Stephan retrieved a key from under his steering wheel and hurried to the front door. There, he triggered several hidden switches, and blinking lights appeared in the darkness around the house. Next to the porch, he had built a musical water wheel covered in lights. More lights flashed in the stream, where mechanical fish swam back and forth under the bridge. Laura spun to see more of these lighted features. Mechanical creatures covered with lights decorated nearby trees.

Stephan watched her obvious delight for a few moments before he unlocked the front door and leaned in to flip another master switch. The lodge came alive, and Laura walked into a house with the lights blazing and gas fires already warming the rooms. Stephan didn't like living underground, as did so many of his kind. Instead, picture windows gave views of the lush moss-covered forest. The plush carpeting and walls were a luscious cream. To the left of the door, cozy chocolate couches beckoned in a sunken living room.

Stephan loved art, and he surrounded himself with the best. He had collected detailed scenes of European history. Laura walked up to a painting of a small child, touched the clothes fashioned from textured paint mixed with feathers, and sighed. Stephan meant to offer her refreshments, but he didn't want to stifle her obvious curiosity with the usual courtesies. This place was his ultimate test. How she acted when she entered his secret workshop would determine if they had a future or if he should send her back to the world of Lord and his henchmen.

Stephan led Laura down a long hall to the back of the house. They entered a room that ran the entire length of the building with a picture window covering the back wall. Bright overhead lights illuminated every corner of the room. To hide his prized workshop from curious outsiders, the window was made from glass that allowed one to see out only.

In this workshop, he constructed all that he could imagine and design. Down the center of the room stood long tables covered with contraptions, some with wheels and some with levers. Against one wall, corkboards held drawings. Instead of looking confused, Laura examined two of them closely. To his utter astonishment, she seemed to understand the general idea behind the technical diagrams.

"This is supposed to fly!" she exclaimed, pointing at a weather probe with no visible means of locomotion, "and this is sealed to go underwater." Laura looked around the room. "This is beyond anything I could have imagined. It looks like an old Victorian workshop. Steampunk on steroids. I'm honored you'd show it to me."

"I wanted you to see my real studio. It's modeled after my European one: the last place I knew before the change, the last place I was human. I come here when the darkness becomes suffocating. I know I must live secretly and at night, but what I can't understand is: why would anyone want to?" He asked this last question like a lost child.

Laura could understand the terrible loneliness of keeping one's true nature a secret and put her hand on his shoulder sympathetically. "Why did she take you instead of your parents? I know you were the technician, but your parents had the connections."

"She wanted to know my secrets for creating a realistic world on stage. She ordered me to recreate my inventions. But I built bad reproductions that didn't work well. I couldn't let her evil use my ideas to harm others.

"For the most part, Ariadne lives in a dull, flat world that she despises. But she was still capable of one redeeming emotion: curiosity. She was curious about my work. So instead of killing me, she turned me into a Shadow Dweller.

"It was after I had been a Shadow Dweller for some years that I discovered she wanted more than just this." He spread his arms wide to encompass his workshop. "She did want access to my inventions, but what she really needed was my ability to find something fascinating in everything. She required a reason to continue in a life that would stretch over centuries." Stephan grew quiet, remembering his own struggle to find hope.

"I can't imagine how terrible it was for you," Laura sympathized. "You're stronger than I would have been."

"You'd be surprised at what you can survive. I was."

Laura walked over to the large mahogany desk and glanced down idly at several sheets of textured paper scattered across the top. Before he could stop her, she picked one up.

"These are poems!" she exclaimed happily. "I'm thrilled to find new material. I've been scrambling to satisfy the constant demand at

The Colony." She quickly scanned the paper. "This would be perfect for Kate." Laura hummed fragments of a melody, varying the tempo, and then inserted a few lines of the poem.

"Stop!" Stephan shouted, his pain becoming too much to endure.

Stephan had searched for any outlet for his frustration and confusion about Laura, and the poetry had seemed to help. He had never intended that anyone should read it, and he would absolutely never allow his poems on stage. He had listened as Laura's skills with tempo and harmony transformed his simple verses. As she sang, she conveyed the essence of his deep love frustrated by the constraints of society. It was too hard to let her continue.

"What?" Laura halted abruptly, her eyes slowly focusing on him.

"These l-lyrics are n-not available to use in your shows," Stephan stuttered.

"But they're so good, better than many I've seen lately. We must use them. You want to help enhance our performances, right?"

"No!" Stephan snarled, gritting his teeth.

"You don't want to contribute to our performances?" Laura asked, bewildered.

"Can you be that blind?" Stephan threw his arms up and shook his head.

"Blind? About what?"

"Where do you think these poems came from?"

"The verses are so grand. I'm guessing that the words are about your past. Maybe some girl you knew in France?"

"No." He moved slightly behind her as she faced the desk, leaving a safe distance between them. He brushed her hair back lightly. To his relief, she didn't move away.

"You are so beautiful, so talented," he whispered softly.

She shivered, leaning closer as if to hear better. He sensed that she was attracted to him, even though she might worry that he was too dangerous.

Stephan had gone to great lengths to separate himself from the usual lifestyle of Shadow Dwellers. He wore expensive tailored clothing, treated everyone with charm and courtesy, and lived like an eccentric recluse. He kept his needs as a Shadow Dweller far out of sight. Only his lovers had seen him feed. The others who satisfied his appetite were never sure of what had really happened.

Stephan feared that his next move would be rebuffed, but he had already waited too long. He leaned forward, letting his breath warm her neck. Startled, she turned, and he slid his mouth across her jaw and captured her lips in a deep, passionate kiss. He wrapped her in a strong embrace and used the energy from his last feeding to heat her body. She moaned under his kiss.

Rather than pulling away, Laura pressed closer. Tentatively, Stephan extended his Shadow nature to explore the fire of life that billowed around her. It felt like a raging inferno.

Stephan had always respected Laura, even been a bit overwhelmed by her talents. He had never extended his senses to explore her essence, never measured her as a possible source of life. Now he felt scorched by an intensity that was alien to him. Laura was hotter than any other person he had experienced.

Overjoyed, he tightened his embrace and plunged his tongue deeper. Laura responded wildly, matching his passion with hard kisses, and pressed herself against him.

# 11

## Revelations

Then Stephan made a mistake. He tried to connect with Laura's memories. He wanted to know more about her, and so he pushed to taste a recent experience. He saw the usual disorienting shadows typical of the beginning of the Dweller feeding. But something was wrong. Instead of a gentle fall and hazy images that only slowly came into focus—views that could be manipulated by his need—he found himself in a clear and distinct memory from her first days in college.

Stephan tried to slow the action, to give him time to assess the situation, to no avail. He was solidly stuck in this scene, with no power to shift anything.

Laura stood in the entrance to the administration building, watching various lines of young people waiting for their turn in front of desks labeled "Class Schedules," "Financial Aid," "Add or Drop Classes," and "Extracurricular Activities." Since historical events couldn't be altered, he usually just watched. Now, he wanted to move closer to Laura. But he couldn't move. He struggled against an invisible force that was new.

The younger version of Laura turned and looked directly at him. Abruptly, the invisible force holding him slackened, and he knew he could speak. Could she be controlling this force? Before he could ask, a strange young man ran up to Laura, blocking his view.

"Laura, I can't believe I finally found you!" The man was tall and athletic, with expressive, deep-set brown eyes and short blond hair. He reminded Stephan of a marathon athlete.

"Why did you follow me?" she demanded, stamping her foot impatiently. "I thought I made it clear: we're over!"

"We're not over! You didn't let me explain. I never thought you were a coward," he blurted bitterly.

Stephan saw Laura cringe at the insult.

"I didn't want another argument that would only cause more pain. I was already registered here, and you're going to Yale. Long distance doesn't work, and I wanted to make a clean break. This confrontation will change nothing. Just move on!"

"So I have no say?" he shouted.

Laura backed up, her face tight with embarrassment.

Several registrars were watching them now with unmistakable disapproval, while nearby students were undoubtedly eavesdropping. Stephan burned with an unfamiliar jealousy and took an involuntary step closer. Laura caught his aggressive advance and gazed directly at him.

Then, to his utter shock, she called to him, "What are you doing here?"

Her ex-boyfriend turned to Stephan with a hostile, suspicious expression. "Who is he?" he asked Laura.

Stephan shook his head incredulously. What in the hell was happening? Laura hadn't met him at this point in time. They shouldn't be interacting with him, a stranger. He had to get out of this vision before he lost his way back, before he changed time. He had heard of such occurrences: Shadow Dwellers trapped, their bodies frozen.

Stephan tried to shake his way out, like a dog casting off water, only dimly aware of the argument continuing between the young man and Laura. But his muscles were slow to respond. He didn't feel the usual strength or keen senses of Shadow Dwellers. He closed his eyes and formed a clear mental image of his workshop where he was still kissing

Laura, but fog obscured the image, and he howled silently in disappointment. Despite his hammering heart and twisting stomach, Stephan again concentrated on the vision of his workshop. Only this time, he called to Laura for help.

The scene at the college began to ripple, bend, and darken. The voices became indistinct, and he fell into a cold void. When he opened his eyes again, he was in his workshop lying on the floor. Laura was standing over him, her eyes clouded with concern.

Stephan saw tiny blood drops collecting on her neck. He staggered up, panic flooding his mind, mangling his thoughts.

"What happened to you?" Laura demanded, fear tightening her voice. "You just collapsed."

Stephan's sight was hazy, his hearing dull, and his sensations sluggish. He felt a terrible hunger and a growing fear that he hardly recognized. He stumbled into a chair, struggling to find some explanation.

"I could really use a drink," he grumbled absently.

"What?" Laura exclaimed. "You don't drink alcohol."

Stephan tried to understand what she was saying, but a loud roar had filled his ears and his mind spun. His grip on consciousness was slipping, so he covered his face with his hands and forced his mind to still.

Finally, the roaring stopped, and Stephan cautiously lowered his hands. When he looked up at Laura for a second time, he could see the trail of blood on her neck in vivid detail. The wet blood glistened, and a strand of hair caught in the fluid fluttered on an errant breeze. Whatever had been wrong before was over. He felt his usual vitality coursing through his body, and he stretched his limbs, reveling in his restored agility. But his relief was cut short when he caught Laura absently wiping the blood off her neck.

"I'm so sorry. I don't know how I could have hurt you," Stephan pleaded, looking away. He was startled when she laughed.

"You only scratched me, and then you fainted." She giggled, touching her throat. "People are known to get careless in the heat of passion."

"But you looked upset." Stephan was sure about that.

"You had just collapsed," Laura reminded him. "I don't think my kiss could do that."

"You underestimate your charm. It's no wonder I lost my head." Stephan didn't want to alarm Laura, so he teased her instead, trying to avoid the subject.

Laura looked unconvinced, but she returned to the desk and picked up the poems.

"Well, back to the poems. There are several of them. Surely, one of them isn't personal."

"No," Stephan muttered awkwardly. He really wished he could burn the pages. "They're all about you."

"They're about me?" Laura repeated. She shuffled through the pages, arranging them in chronological order. He wished he hadn't dated the damn things. Then she examined each poem slowly.

Stephan longed to snatch the poems out of her hand, but he could only watch as various emotions played across her face. It had been a long time since he'd cared so much about someone's reaction to his work. Ever since Laura had entered his life, many things had changed.

Mostly, she was quiet and thoughtful. But every so often, he would see a slight smile. Finally, she spoke, granting him a temporary reprieve from his acute embarrassment.

"These are really good. The images are so vivid, so beautiful. But you must know that I'm not the person your poems suggest. You credit me with qualities that are impossible. I'm completely flawed."

Stephan smiled sheepishly. "I got a bit carried away. Strong emotions translate into larger-than-life portraits. But the feelings are real. I've come to know you, Laura. I see your character and spirit every day at The Colony.

Suddenly he blurted out, "I love you," and tensed for her rejection. But her silence encouraged him to continue. "I love your goodness, because it brings light to my life. I love your weaknesses because they show your sweetness and humanity. I love your creativity because it makes our productions so vibrant. Even so, I'm not a fool. I know my poems are silly and overblown, which is why no one else will read them."

Laura answered quietly, hesitantly, as if she wasn't sure she should speak at all. Her attempts to find logic in emotion was endearing to him. She was so serious. "I've loved our time together. Our collaborations are beyond anything I could have imagined, anything I could have accomplished alone. I feel a great attraction to you, but I'm not sure it's enough to overcome the roadblocks between us. I hate that your humanity has been stolen from you. I hate that we're fundamentally different. I'm human and live in human society, while you're a Shadow Dweller forced to live a secret life in darkness. Still, there's something so strong—sometimes I feel your feelings intruding on my thoughts without any warning," she confessed. "It's very unsettling."

Laura looked so young, so confused. Stephan felt old, weary, and pummeled by the vagaries of life. He pulled her into his embrace and kissed her tenderly on the temple. She returned his gentle caresses in kind, stroking his hair.

"You're not imagining things," he reassured her. "I've felt a blurring of the boundaries between us. As to whether we can prevail..." Stephan struggled to find some way to overcome their dilemma. He was caught completely off guard when Laura herself decided to share confidences of her own. Maybe his declarations had managed to crack her shell of protection.

"I've always been different, Stephan. There are things I can do, things I thought everyone could do, that keep me isolated. You see, I didn't have parents to explain what was happening. I'm an orphan." Laura looked forlorn for a second and then caught Stephan's gaze hopefully. "Do you understand everything about being a Shadow Dweller? Do others of your kind explain what you can and can't do?"

"It doesn't work that way. In my case, my maker was too evil to reveal the details of what I had become. As to my kindred, it never pays to reveal Shadow Dweller powers to one who might use them against you. I've been forced to create a fierce demeanor to keep myself safe. Truthfully, I have no idea whether I know everything involved in being what I am," Stephan confessed.

Then he refocused on Laura's story. "Do you really have no idea who your parents are?"

"My family told me they adopted me as an infant. No one knows where I was born, who my parents are, or what talents and aptitudes I might have inherited. Sometimes, I remember a warm face and a gentle voice. I just don't know if I'm imagining them. I do hope I'll meet my parents someday.

"In the meantime, I've learned to avoid personal attachments because they never seem to work. I don't want a messy relationship interfering with my newfound success. Why complicate things now?"

"Romance is the source of great music, literature, and art. Love can inspire us to do amazing things. Surely you don't want to be alone?"

"Until I meet that one person perfect for me," Laura whispered wistfully, "yes."

"One of the popular myths of romance is that there is only one person, perfect in every way, who will fill all our needs. But there are always compromises and allowances that have to be made." Stephan felt exasperated. Surely this was obvious.

"I do expect that all couples have challenges, but you and I are a catastrophe waiting to happen. It's not a stretch to conclude that a romance between us would push me away from my human friends and sunlit activities." Laura's eyes were gentle, even kind.

"They say the most beautiful jewels are formed in the hottest, most chaotic volcanic furnaces," Stephan suggested. "Maybe there is a way for us."

Laura just shook her bowed head. Stephan decided that an alliance between them needed time. For him, time was easy. He could afford to be patient. Besides, he suddenly realized that a declaration of love when Nicolette was on a rampage was a bit premature. Surely things would settle down after they had dealt with her. Surely things would get better.

"What is a harbinger?" Laura asked abruptly.

"A harbinger is a messenger who brings news of some important future event. Why?"

"I had this dream. This beautiful woman called me a harbinger for the Shadow Dwellers. Someone important is coming."

Dreams in the Shadow Dweller world were special. Often, they held the truth behind things as yet unseen. Stephan felt an uncomfortable premonition that trouble was coming.

# 12

## Alexis

As if on cue, sudden violent gusts of wind shook the house, suspending conversation between Stephan and Laura. Locked windows rattled furiously and then impossibly flew open, bringing in icy air. Snowy white fog gushed into the room and mushroomed up to form a wavering figure. The fog solidified into the floating figure of a woman. Her hair hung around her body like a gossamer veil, and her expression conveyed a preternatural serenity. Her features were young and elfin, but her eyes held an indefinable depth. Here was a woman who was both old and young.

She glided forward, her hands open in a gesture of friendship. "Please don't be frightened. I am no threat. Do you remember me?" The apparition spoke to Laura with a voice that was light and whispery, akin to the fog she had been only moments earlier.

Speechless, Stephan could only stare in disbelief. He had heard of the Ancients, but he had never imagined that he might meet one. They usually communicated only through dreams, never in person. But this creature appeared to be one.

"You're the woman in my dream," Laura admitted.

"Yes." The small, delicate figure drifted closer, again like fog. "We are, or shall I say, I am one of a group of ancient Shadow Dwellers who protect our people. I'm called Alexis. Periodically, we must choose new members, those who will lead our kind into the future. Since our choices shape our society and directly affect the human world, we must select carefully. It has been a long time since we have found one who is worthy.

"I've come for you, Stephan." Now Alexis drifted closer to the gawking man. "You have been chosen, and we believe you will change the face of our society.

"But first, you must learn the secrets of the Shadow Dwellers. Not all young ones are allowed to know their true nature. Many are created who would harm our society. So, we must wait for the new ones to grow up and gain some measure of maturity and control. Our powers would be too dangerous in children who are motivated merely by unfed appetites and self-centered obsessions. We must be led by those who would guide us toward a reasoned future. You, Stephan, are one of these special Shadow Dwellers. You've demonstrated the gifted insight that we hope for.

"We're sorry that we left you so long alone." The floating figure's eyes clouded with a profound sadness. "We have watched you struggle and have longed to bring you into the fold. But you wouldn't have survived our teachings unless you were anchored in the material world."

"Why come to my dreams and not Stephan's?" Laura interrupted.

"Yes, the dreams." Alexis continued to speak to Stephan. "Now that you've found a true partner, you'll resist transcending into the great beyond. You'll fight to come back here. She'll be your anchor."

"But Laura will die in a few short years," Stephan objected strenuously. He didn't want this ancient Shadow Dweller pulling Laura into his world before she was ready, especially when the figure's motives were unclear. "How can this benefit an immortal race?"

"A few years? You know something I don't?" Laura quipped with youthful arrogance.

Stephan smiled, despite the seriousness of their situation.

"For a Shadow Dweller, a few years can translate into a human lifetime," Alexis explained to Laura. "Both of you are trying to force your relationship into a conventional model that doesn't fit your unique situation. You are both capable of enjoying a unique intimacy. You have only to reach for it." Alexis looked at Stephan, her eyebrow raised and her eyes probing. "You haven't guessed the truth yet? You have touched her?"

Alexis had used a polite term for the initial probe of a feeding Shadow Dweller. Stephan was too embarrassed to admit his weakness. Instead, he responded to her first question and reflected on her second.

"What truth?" he asked and shuddered at how unhuman Laura had tasted.

"It's her difference that makes her special. It's why she is a perfect anchor," Alexis explained.

"What difference?" Laura interrupted, her eyes shifting from Alexis to Stephan and back again.

"You are immune to us," Stephan confessed. "At least I think you are."

"Immune? Impossible! You came to my rescue from Eric at The Colony."

"That was different. I can't...I mean, I might be able to...but somehow you take over," he finished lamely, unable to translate his experience intelligently.

Laura dropped into a chair, looking defeated. "So, I really am different. I really don't belong here."

"Wait!" the Ancient interrupted, her voice urgent. "Please, there is no time for detailed explanations. The point of no return is approaching. We must begin Stephan's training tonight. Laura, will you set aside your feelings and help Stephan for now?"

Laura shifted uncomfortably and then nodded.

Alexis beckoned Stephan and Laura out into the middle of the room. The fog trailing behind her thickened and formed a cocoon around all three of them. Alexis motioned for Laura to stand in front of Stephan. Then she captured Stephan's gaze with steady, glowing eyes.

"Visualize yourself on a metaphorical cliff between the world of the living and the world of the dead, trapped in physical form. Imagine wandering the Earth without your body. Humans must release their bodies to cross beyond the horizon, but Shadow Dwellers can move between the worlds."

Alexis took Stephan's hands and intertwined the fingers with Laura's. "Now imagine yourself floating. Let your mind carry you upward, weightless."

Stephan cautiously followed Alexis's directions as his grip on Laura's hands tightened.

The figure of Alexis began to dissolve, until there was only a cloud of thick white fog. In this form, she rose and flowed out an open window. Stephan, disoriented, felt a tug on his mind. He sensed Alexis calling to him to follow. He shivered violently as he lost physical sensation of his body.

"What's happening? Are you hurt? What do I do?" cried Laura.

Stephan could hear Laura's frantic questions with difficulty. He felt a compelling, tenacious force tugging him upward, and he couldn't resist its pull. What he thought of as his spirit or essence popped free from his body and hovered near the ceiling. Panicked, he fought for control of his drifting consciousness. With a last glimpse at Laura, who was struggling to gently lower his sagging body, he was jerked away through the window, into the night. Once out of the house, Stephan could see the shimmer that was Alexis pulling him upward.

For the few moments that the Ancient allowed him, Stephan appreciated the view of the valley that hid his workshop and the city of Rainier. Then she pulled him faster and faster, until the scenery was flying past in an indecipherable blur. Finally, the terrible dizzying journey came to an end. Alexis halted in front of a large stone structure nestled in a sprawling, bustling, distinctly foreign city.

She propelled him through the front door, down a long hall, and into a circular room. Mosaics composed of colored tiles covered the walls and ceiling. Nine tall antique chairs circled a central dais. In eight of them sat a Shadow Dweller, who manifested the signature beauty and indeterminate age common to their race. Even though Stephan was a specter, the Ancients focused their gaze squarely on him. Alexis moved to the empty chair, resuming the form she had taken in his studio. She was still a specter, like he was.

"You have been selected..." a great voice began.

Stephan couldn't identify the source of the voice. It seemed to come from the surrounding walls in a hollow echo.

Abruptly, a wave of distress overwhelmed Stephan. Something was wrong. He scanned the room, trying to identify the source of his alarm. It wasn't here. It wasn't close. His spirit automatically began to rise, intent on returning to his body, but Alexis held him back.

"You must stay. All is well." But she, too, glanced around the room nervously. A great pressure replaced Alexis's gentle pull, and he was held immobile. Stephan didn't believe Alexis, but the decision to leave had been taken away from him.

"You've been selected," the voice, tinged with impatience, repeated, "to be trained in the enhanced powers of the Shadow Dwellers. We know you feel betrayed by the one who stole your human life and for this reason don't share our lust for blood. You don't kill easily, you don't languish selfishly, and you don't exist to satisfy a never-ending appetite. You have an eagerness for life that will keep you thriving.

"Alexis has argued that you are the one who will save us from extinction. More and more frequently, our young are choosing violence over tempered wisdom, and our old are becoming bored with a life without virtue or vitality. Thus, our small group contains only the few resilient members of our race. It has been centuries since anyone has shown the character necessary to enter our Vault of Secrets.

"But you, Stephan Renard"—now the voice thrummed with hope—"you are different. You have found a way to overcome the terrible monotony of centuries. So you have been selected to enter our Vault of Secrets and to know the truth of Shadow Dwellers.

"We can't change the actions of your maker. But we ask you to share in the responsibility of safeguarding our race's future." The voice became louder. "Our need is great. Will you help us?"

Stephan couldn't abandon his people to this dark future. "I'll help. What do I need to do?"

"First, you take the blood oath. It will ensure that you follow our rules. All Shadow Dwellers know what will happen if they break this oath.

"The two most important rules are these. You must never reveal anything you learn here, and you must take your place on this tribunal when our need requires your presence."

Alexis pointed to a tenth chair leaning against the wall, partially hidden by a tapestry.

"Exactly what would I be called to do?" Stephan asked, despite feeling outclassed by these Ancients. Since the consequences of violating the blood oath were so extreme, he wanted to know what he was getting into first. His nervous voice echoed around the room, momentarily diverting his attention away from the group of Ancients. When he turned back, their figures flickered like flames on a sputtering candle. Like him, they were astral projections.

"This council does what is necessary to protect the longevity of our race," the spokesman explained. "We act to keep our existence at the level of myth and use our extended powers to enforce our laws."

"I would keep no secrets from Laura," Stephan declared suddenly. He hoped this might exclude him from consideration by the council. While he wanted to help, the Ancients' pretty words didn't fool him for one minute. He had heard the rumors. When the Ancients acted, Shadow Dwellers usually disappeared.

"She is an outsider. Only another Shadow Dweller can be bound with the blood oath," the voice replied. "If you change her, you can tell her."

Stephan cringed at the idea of transforming his beloved into a blood drinker. "She will not be turned, but I must be able to tell her some details if she is to be my anchor," he argued, glaring at the Ancients until they nodded agreement. With each nod, his future was decided.

Stephan couldn't turn his back on his own race. He might not like being a Shadow Dweller, but he was one. Despite the dangers and his continuing reservations, he had to follow this path laid before him. His submissive posture indicated his acceptance.

Alexis came forward with another female council member. She reformed a shaft of her fog into a long sword, which could seal the blood oath when there was no tangible body. She ran the blade across Stephan's wrists, and to his surprise, blood beaded along the cuts. His wrists were just shadows, but there was blood all the same. Next, she used the blade to slice her own arm and the arm of the other Ancient. Instead of red blood, shafts of white light shot from their wounds. The two light streams merged and then penetrated Stephan's cuts, thickening his red blood with white light. A suffocating ache filled his body. His astral heart beat with difficulty, and his astral breath strangled in his chest. He struggled to endure the agony of his blood thickening without revealing his torment. When the anguish eased, he realized that Alexis was speaking.

"I know it hurts, but you must repeat the oath now," she whispered urgently. She lowered her voice further until her words were little more than puffs of air. "They act as if this is your choice, Stephan. But it is not. You know of us now. You'll never be allowed to leave without the oath to protect our secrets. This will be over soon."

The great voice repeated the words required to seal the blood oath ritual. "I promise to keep the secrets of this hall and fulfill my responsibilities to my people. I vow to promote the well-being of all Shadow Dwellers as prescribed by the books in the Vault of Secrets."

As Stephan slowly repeated the oath, the pain lessened, and he could breathe a little easier. When the last three words, "Vault of Secrets," echoed through the hall, the other Ancients' astral projections blinked out, leaving only Alexis. "Come when we call," whispered through the room in their wake.

Alexis pointed toward a descending stairway. "This way."

Stephan followed her down the stairs. They didn't walk in the normal sense but floated in the direction she indicated. Alexis stopped at a tall, ornately carved cherry oak door. She took one of Stephan's wrists and pressed his wound against the lock. Tendrils of red and white fog oozed from his wrist into the keyhole. Stephan heard a loud click, and the door swung open. Beyond, he could see a room lined with thousands of books.

She pointed at the jagged red cut on his wrist, which was already coalescing into a thick V-shaped scar. "The scar holds the blood oath and will open any lock in our sanctuary. Everything about our history, culture, biology, and advanced powers is recorded in these books." She gestured toward the many shelves. "If anyone tries to forcibly enter this library, they will be incinerated."

Stephan floated slowly into the room, his mouth frozen into a wide "O." Everywhere they could build a shelf to load with books, they had. He could see rolling bookshelves scattered about. Globes, benches, book stands, and small tables were placed strategically throughout the room. The ceiling was made up of religious paintings on large inlaid panels.

Alexis pointed to a shelf protected by leaded glass doors and a huge red lock. "This is where you will find instructions on how to use our enhanced abilities. I assisted you in disconnecting from your body at the workshop, but you need to learn how to do this for yourself. This is how you will return to this hall when called and to learn more about your powers."

Alexis unlocked the shelf using her own scar and carried a large, very old book across to a mahogany book stand. She opened to the section on astral projection and read the instructions out loud.

"The body must be anchored or the projection will lose its way and be lost forever. Take hold of your greatest possession, that one thing you prize above all others. Ground yourself in this anchor by holding it firmly in both hands. Then open your mind to the vastness and imagine a specific destination far away."

Stephan followed the instructions instinctively as Alexis read them aloud. He pictured holding Laura, building the image in painstaking detail until he could see her perfectly in his mind. Because he was an astronomy buff, he picked the Horsehead Nebula as his first destination. Even as he felt himself surge upward, he saw Alexis lunge for him, grabbing his foot and tugging down hard. Unfortunately, she only managed to get pulled along.

"Younglings," she cursed under her breath.

Stephan laughed in pure exaltation. He was excited at seeing those things up close that for centuries he had just glimpsed. As the Horsehead Nebula was only 1,500 light years away, his own telescope had spotted it on very clear nights. Now, he floated over the swirling cosmic dust, seeing behind it for the first time. To his pleasant surprise, he found a solar system of planets orbiting a yellow star.

Suddenly, Stephan felt something go horribly wrong. As a specter, he had continued to be aware of sensations on earth, like wind, pressure, and temperature. He had expected that in space this would change, and he would have no sensation of atmosphere at all. What happened was far worse. He found himself dissolving into millions of specks of intelligence beginning to drift apart.

Luckily, Alexis had been pulled out into space with him. Somehow she managed to provide the shielding he needed to hold himself together for one last precious second. In that second, he found himself back in the Vault of Secrets.

"I took the risk of a sudden jump for both of us at once because you were dying," Alexis gasped when the world reformed around them. "But we were lucky we made it back whole. It should never be attempted unless death is eminent.

"You'll have plenty of time to explore space and see your astronomical wonders when you have the training to survive," she scolded him. "Now, we must get back to Rainier."

Stephan noticed worry lines wrinkling her ghostly forehead.

Together, they flew away from the Ancients' sanctuary and started the long journey back to Rainier. Stephan breathed a sigh of relief that they were finally returning to his studio. To his consternation, his senses registered greater danger the closer they got. He was relieved when Alexis allowed him to go ahead alone. To him, she had been going unnecessarily slow.

"Visualize your lodge and let go. It's the same process that took you to the space dust. Remember, stick to places on Earth for now." She snorted and then vanished.

# 13

## Nicolette's Revenge

Stephan crumpled to the floor, dragging Laura to her knees, and the lingering mist that was Alexis vanished. Laura pulled free of Stephan and considered her next move.

She gazed around the chamber of curiosities, fascinated by this window into the soul of Stephan Renard. He continued to surprise her. He was not like the other Shadow Dwellers or even like her new friends at Lord's compound. Ultimately, it was his poems that had finally penetrated her barriers. She knew she couldn't let him go, despite all the arguments she had given him. Even in her mind, she was reluctant to admit the truth: she loved Stephan Renard.

Mina was the main songwriter for their shows at The Colony and had composed brilliant lyrics. But Laura knew she wrote about what she hoped for, not what she had actually experienced. So far, Mina seemed untouched by great emotion. She appeared to watch life from the sidelines.

Stephan's words showed a deeper understanding of the whimsy and capriciousness of life. He put his singular concentration and energy into everything he created. Already he had designed several tricky backdrops for Laura's performers. The beautiful, old-world painted scenery, which transported her to a historical paradise, had been commissioned from the best artists available. Stephan didn't limit their artisans to Rainier, either. He had commissioned work from overseas craftsmen as well.

As Laura scrambled to her feet, Stephan automatically pulled his arms and legs into a fetal position. Laura would have left him out in the middle of the floor where she could monitor him, but he looked so exposed and vulnerable. Besides, she didn't want him to wake up and catch her snooping through his studio. So she dragged him into a nearby coat closet, concealed by intricate wall molding. She added a heavy blanket as additional padding in case he thrashed about. Now she would have a few seconds' warning when he returned to his body.

Without any idea of how long she would be left there, Laura decided to explore the workshop thoroughly. She was delighted to be able to snoop without being watched, but she still felt the heat of guilt warm her cheeks.

Stephan had covered one table with miniature models of shows he'd created for her Trust performers. Some she recognized, while others were unfamiliar. They included replicas of a specific performer. Happily, she discovered that the small sets were mechanized. She flipped one of the switches under the table, and a recording of Tanya's deep voice filled the room. Apparently he had taped their performances. Laura examined the dolls closely, confirming their surprising resemblance to her people.

Laura retrieved her phone from her coat, took photos of the new designs, and taped the recorded performances that went with each. Just to be safe, she sent them to her e-mail address. She wanted to show his ideas to her people at their next production meeting. All her shows were collaborative efforts. Even the performers added elements that improved their musicals.

Another table held motorized fish, model airplanes and road vehicles, and other devices, all covered with miniature lights. Each of Stephan's contraptions had some distinctive feature and could perform specialized functions. Water wheels that could generate electricity, flying weather probes, and self-watering planters were on top. Scattered among the gadgets were tools that Laura didn't recognize.

Laura approached a third table, set apart from the others and partially hidden by a tall backboard that reached to the ceiling. She walked around for a better view and gasped. Stephan had created a wall of monitors accessing a wide collection of websites on a variety of topics. Four were set to news stations in New York, London, France, and Hong Kong, while others displayed digital scientific journals opened to recent technical articles. He was monitoring architecture and engineering chat rooms. It seemed he wanted immediate access to the latest scientific innovations. He was connected to museums and libraries around the world. One monitor showed beautiful paintings currently being exhibited at the Louvre. She imagined that this artwork would inspire his own work. It was a Renaissance man's paradise. He had even taken advantage of the Internet's anonymity to engage in a discussion on a philosophy website. She saw replies to comments he had posted earlier. Here, at least, he could enjoy stimulating discourse without fear of discovery.

Satisfied with her exploration, Laura returned to the stack of poems. The language was raw with emotion. She skimmed the lines, blushing at the intimate window into his thoughts. With work, they would make great songs. She tried to commit them to memory, reading each one over and over, mouthing the words. Unfortunately her memory was notoriously unreliable. Finally, she tucked them safely out of sight on the shelf above Stephan's folded body. Maybe she could convince him to let her copy the verses before he destroyed them.

Laura was scanning the smaller tables for unusual inventions when she heard a noise behind her. She assumed Stephan and Alexis had finally returned and turned with a smile already forming on her lips. Nicolette's cold, brittle smile and smoldering red eyes greeted her. She was surrounded by several big men. Laura recognized two of them from her night with Eric. Mina's report had been spot-on.

In the space of one breath, Laura darted across the room and sprang through the window, which was still open from Alexis's visit. She knew she was risking serious injury—the window was fifteen feet up—but

Nicolette's expression promised that staying was not an option. She fell hard into the bushes next to the building. Luckily they were thick and lush. Immediately, Laura threw herself forward into a crouching run. If the group in the shop had been alone, Laura believed she might've escaped. But there were more men in the backyard, and they caught her easily.

From the window, Nicolette leaned out, her lips twisted into a taunting grin, and gestured for the men to bring Laura back. Roughly, they dragged her up the back stairs. Their brutal treatment guaranteed that Laura would have bruises before this night was over. They held her powerless in the doorway of Stephan's workshop.

Laura felt sick as Nicolette began systematically destroying every model, every invention, every poster board, and every computer. Laura now had no doubt that Nicolette was the one who had broken into her home and threatened her pets. Soon piles of broken glass and machinery were all that remained of the wall of monitors. Laura expected that Nicolette would take the time to examine Stephan's private documents, but she couldn't have been more wrong. The vampiress threw all his files and papers directly into the fireplace and set them on fire. During the destruction, Laura realized that Nicolette was doing all the work. The demolition was hers and hers alone. Her men only watched. What Stephan's thwarted lover didn't seem to notice was their growing disdain and impatience.

Breathing heavily and covered in debris, Nicolette finally confronted Laura. Her glare dissected the younger woman, who felt scorched by her loathing.

"I knew if I followed you I would find you two alone together," she mocked, her lips tight, her rigid jaw prominent. Laura had expected shrieking, but she had to strain to hear the bitter words Nicolette spit through clenched teeth. "He plays the noble, but he's really selfish scum. Still, I will have him under my thumb soon." Nicolette laughed in low, strangled coughs, like a rabid coyote.

"What are you saying? You know Stephan better than anyone. Can you truly believe your own delusions?" Laura whispered.

"Do you want to provoke me? My friends would love a little alone time with you."

Laura glanced at the thugs, holding her breath. She forced her expression and posture to stay flat, even self-confident. The trick was to figure out what Nicolette wanted and leverage that to escape before her own fear got the best of her. Laura guessed that if Stephan asked Nicolette back, all their problems would fade away. Her only hope was to convince Nicolette of a lie: that she wasn't competition.

"You might think you have him," Nicolette was saying, "but he won't want you when I'm done."

"I don't want him. I never did."

Nicolette laughed without humor. "He can be very convincing."

"We just work together," Laura insisted.

"But he brought you here. Nobody knew where he assembled his inventions. This workshop's location is his most prized secret. And yet, here you are."

"Again, for work. There are relationships between men and women that aren't about love," Laura persisted stubbornly.

"Not for Stephan. If his partner is female, then he'll eventually want a romantic arrangement."

"Well, business is the only type of relationship I would have with a *Shadow Dweller*," Laura promised. She made the words *Shadow Dweller* drip with disdain.

"Stephan has spent a long time learning the art of seduction. He's had centuries to discover human weaknesses and exploit them. Do you really think you can escape his emotional booby traps?" Nicolette hissed dismissively.

"Stephan will consider my feelings and act accordingly. He doesn't exploit women," Laura objected, throwing her safety out the window, as usual. She knew that arguing with this crazy vampiress was foolhardy, but she couldn't stay quiet in the face of Nicolette's malevolence—not after Stephan had told her about the violence of his own transformation. Nicolette must be capable of the same cruelty and probably had similar converts. "You, on the other hand, ruthlessly force your performers and guards to obey you. I'm sure they'll find the courage to take back their lives, and you'll ultimately lose. Even Eric's men will support you only for as long as you have something they want. They'll never respect you as their leader. To them, you're just a jealous woman."

The men holding Laura growled menacingly at her comments. She felt their fingers tighten painfully. She resisted the urge to fight for her freedom. She wanted them to become careless and overconfident.

Still, she persisted perversely. "Maybe your insane need to control is why you lost Stephan in the first place. It's certainly why we're here now."

Nicolette was watching Laura like a cat watches the squirming mouse it will soon devour. She ignored her verbal jabs. Laura didn't like the smirk that was growing on her face.

"Eric's men are here for *you*. They want revenge for the murder of their leader."

"They believed you?" Laura stated numbly, hope draining away.

"Not at first. A mere woman being powerful enough to take out such a notorious Shadow Dweller as Eric is unprecedented. But Noel convinced them. He's as mean-spirited and self-serving as they are. When I told them I knew where you were, they were only too happy to come along for their pound of flesh."

"The one thing you keep forgetting, Nicolette, is Stephan. He's the most powerful Shadow Dweller in Rainier's Houses of Shadows. Even if he hesitates to take on Eric's house, he will deal with you permanently."

Nicolette growled, her red eyes narrowing malevolently, her mouth twisting into a gash. "It doesn't matter what you or any human thinks. When Stephan and I meet face-to-face, we'll come to terms, or there will be war."

Laura made one last feeble appeal. She would go to her grave fighting to save Stephan's fledgling community. "What can you hope to achieve by pitting Shadow Dwellers against each other? There will be consequences, consequences that would cost you not only Stephan, but your own empire here as well."

Nicolette scowled impatiently. "What do you know, human? You're only a means to an end. I've had enough of this useless conversation. I mean to make Stephan suffer for turning me out, and you are the best way. Then you are theirs." She nodded at the fidgeting men. "Take her to the van."

They dragged Laura from the house. Screaming for help, she struck out and managed to injure two of the men before they could stop her. In the end, they had to tape her hands, feet, and mouth and carry her.

They tossed her into the back of a box van, and one of the men covered her face with a smelly cloth, rendering her unconscious. Only when the rocking of the van threw her against the unyielding metal wheel well did she rouse, crying out. She valiantly tried to stay conscious long enough to figure out where they were taking her. Unfortunately, the van had no windows.

From the lack of city or traffic noise, she guessed that they might be heading into the forested backcountry around the city. The passenger beside the driver fiddled with the radio, but all she heard was static. Finally, he turned it off. If only they had been in a movie, Laura lamented, trying to relax her fear with the absurd, then someone would blurt out their whole plan.

She did manage to determine that all the men were Shadow Dwellers, not just hired muscle. Lord had trained Laura on the identifying characteristics of Shadow Dwellers. Their skin was too smooth, their hair too thick, their features too regular. With a few exceptions, they usually had no blemishes or other flaws that normal humans learn to accept. Laura found the plastic perfection of these men ugly. She liked the warmth and sensitivity of those who had learned to accept their weaknesses and blemishes. Shadow Dwellers rarely showed any sign of emotion. These guys sat in the van still and cold as boulders. Only Stephan seemed to thrive in the changing world of humans. According to him, most Shadow Dwellers shunned change as untrustworthy.

When the van swerved suddenly, Laura slammed against a sharp object. She couldn't control the resulting moan of pain and she couldn't maintain consciousness when she smelled the sweet odor of chloroform.

# 14

## A Woman Scorned

Stephan visualized his beloved workshop easily. Instantly, the space around him blurred as he accelerated, and the landscape was devoured by motion and darkness. With Alexis's warning for patience fresh in his mind, he suffered the long period of disorientation that characterized this form of travel. When he could make sense of his surroundings again, he found himself lying on the floor of a small closet. He happily escaped the cramped room. With anxiety already twisting his thoughts, he scanned his workshop. Laura was gone, and only a terrible ruin remained.

Stephan moaned at the complete annihilation of his beloved sanctuary. He could see the pure hatred of the perpetrator in the degree of violence evidenced. Everything had been pulverized. Stephan rushed to the table that held the models for future performances, hoping for something salvageable. The replicas were in pieces, and the scenery was unrecognizable. He searched for his desk, finding only rubble. This piece of furniture had been with him the longest. Stephan stirred the blackened fireplace, forlornly looking for any scrap of recognizable verse. But there was nothing. His anger at the immeasurable loss here was only equaled by the obvious evil of the jealous vampiress responsible.

There was only one person who could have done this. But how had Nicolette found his workshop? He had gone to great lengths to keep it secret. He could imagine his ex-paramour's eagerness to get revenge against him. This was the result.

Stephan hoped that Laura was still unharmed, because he had no doubt that Nicolette had finally captured her archrival. He racked his brain for how best to find the two women. He wasn't fool enough to imagine Nicolette would return to any known location. His only option was to get his spies out looking for her.

Stephan pulled out his cell phone and called Jon at The Colony. His bartender answered after only one ring. Stephan brought him up-to-date on two pressing facts. First, Nicolette had Laura, and second, she had demolished his workshop.

All at once, loud voices roared in the background, and Gabriel's voice replaced Jon's. "Where the hell are you? What have you done with Laura?" he demanded.

"Don't you guys go home?" Stephan grumbled. "Nicolette has taken her. Now put Jon back on the phone. We have plans to make." He was angry at the man's interference but also ashamed for taking Laura away from their protection. If only he had known Nicolette was so close. The time with Alexis had been too short for any other possibility.

"What plans?" Gabriel growled. "You've lost our girl, and you must help *us* find her."

"I don't know exactly how to find her. Nicolette will have gone underground to hide. She'll set up false trails. Actually, we can cover more ground if we work separately. It'll increase our chances of discovering Laura's location."

"We've rescued several of Nicolette's slaves," Gabriel reminded him. "They might know something important, something we can use."

"You mean those abused women who were kept in cells available to entertain Nicolette's men? The women who couldn't wait to run away from Siren's Song?" Stephan asked skeptically.

"Women can be very resourceful. Celeste was Nicolette's favorite and only recently kept in the dungeons. She couldn't stand by and see her friends tortured and thought she could sway Nicolette. She was wrong. However, before she fell out of favor, she might have learned of a location that Nicolette could take Laura to."

"Where is she?"

"Lord did grant them asylum. And these women are no cowering, wounded waifs. The four Shadow Dwellers are eager for battle. They want to bring their former mistress down. If you want to confront Nicolette in her new hideaway, you would be stacking the cards in your favor by using us as backup."

"You have a point," Stephan agreed. "We can use Celeste and her friends. But if the girls don't already know, they're too recognizable to go looking for her."

"True," Gabriel replied. "So, while you do that, I'm going to question the girls at Lord's for intel."

"Let me join you," Stephan offered, realizing that Gabriel had the best plan. "I trust Jon to coordinate my men at The Colony. Tell Lord that I'll meet you at his compound. We should coordinate all our efforts for the best results."

"Then we work together?" Gabriel's delight was obvious.

"Yes. I think you have a proposal that could get us the answers we need, fast."

Gabriel didn't waste time responding. Stephan heard a loud crash through the receiver and pulled it away from his ear. "We have work to do!" he heard Gabriel shout, and then Jon's composed voice came back on the line.

"They're gone, thank God. Now, what do I do?"

Before Stephan could answer, he noticed a scrap of paper on the window ledge above the phone. "Hold on," he told Jon. As he read the note, he barely recognized the disfigured scrawl as Nicolette's. Her usual careful writing was gone. Nicolette was deteriorating. He had to be ready for anything.

"Come to our place," the note read. "Tell no one. We'll keep her company. Might not like results." The last words were an empty threat. He knew that as far as Nicolette was concerned, Laura was already dead.

Stephan had seen similar tactics used by Shadow Dwellers who foolishly believed they could control everything through threats and violence. Nicolette had tried to use him to fill the void created by her lack of trust, and now she used building a bigger empire with Eric's men. But he knew she was still empty, and feeling betrayed, she couldn't let go of her hatred.

"I'm going to Lord's to recruit those rescued Shadow Dwellers," Stephan explained to Jon. "Nicolette left a note here. She does have Laura and has taken her to an old cabin we bought together, the one near Angeline Falls. Get as many men as you can, while still leaving enough to guard The Colony. I have no way of knowing if our scheming vampiress is up to more than one thing at a time."

"Where do we meet?"

"Snoqualmie Pass on east I-90. There is a truck stop at the Snow Lake exit near the summit. Give me about one hour at Lord's and one hour to get to the truck stop. I think Lord, Monk, and Gabriel will be motivated to act swiftly."

"With Laura's neck on the line, I agree. I'll bring enough supplies for everyone, just in case we find ourselves in the midst of a real war."

"Knowing Nicolette, I think that would be wise."

"Call me if you learn anything?" Jon asked unnecessarily.

"Of course."

Stephan headed for the one place that might have escaped Nicolette's wrath. His Jeep was parked in a garage that wasn't visible from the main house. Its four-wheel drive was perfect for the backcountry. With Laura in her grasp, she might have focused on the house alone. Luck was with him. He found the vehicle unmolested.

Stephan arrived at Lord's well-protected main gate unable to calm his growing nervousness. To his knowledge, no Shadow Dweller had ever entered Lord's fortress before Laura rescued Celeste and the others. He found himself imagining all kinds of dangers inside, from booby traps to hostile men hidden behind every dark tree. To his relief, Lord himself answered when he triggered the intercom at the gate.

"Come in. Come in." Lord's accent automatically put Stephan at ease. It reminded him of a time before he had become a Shadow Dweller. "I look forward to working with you. Gabriel tells me you can see into the minds of your kindred."

"Not exactly," Stephan said evasively. How did this strange Gabriel know so much about him?

"Well, no matter. I'll observe with great interest."

Lord directed Stephan to a masculine library with comfortable furniture and calming green tapestries. Books lined two walls, and a mosaic of photographs covered the third. An artistic array of windows made up the fourth. As they were on the third floor, they had a spectacular view of Lake Washington sparkling in the moonlight.

The four Shadow Dweller women were waiting in the shadows created by a free-standing bookshelf. Stephan knew that this was the way of his kind, hiding in the shadows unseen, and therefore remaining relatively safe. Shadow Dwellers quickly learned that becoming the center of attention brought many problems, including jealousy and wrath. Extreme emotions often led to painful consequences. This and the possible genocide of his people were the reasons for their dedication to secrecy.

One particularly beautiful woman, unknown to Stephan, smiled and approached him. So Nicolette had kept a few secrets of her own, he mused.

"Really, you all are such babies," Celeste scolded, gesturing for the others to join her. "Nicolette was the one who hurt you. Stephan is here to help us."

"We aren't afraid, Celeste," an Asian girl objected. "Caution is always a good beginning position."

"Please, come here," Stephan said gently. "It seems that Nicolette has kidnapped Laura."

Instantly, the group of girls glided forward, alarmed.

"The girl who saved our lives?" Celeste asked impatiently.

Gabriel was right. She was anxious to get her revenge. Stephan saw her rage clearly.

"Nicolette left a note revealing her location and urging me to come quickly," Stephan told them." But her emotional ploy won't work. I'm not rushing there alone and unprepared. Do any of you have any information that might help us take her down?"

"Why wasn't I informed of Renard's arrival?" Gabriel shouted, bursting into the room. He glared at Lord. "This was my idea."

"You're here now," Lord said smoothly. "I arranged for someone to inform you as soon as you were available."

Gabriel exhaled doubtfully and turned to Stephan. "What have you learned?"

"We're just getting to that." Stephan looked at the girls hopefully.

"She has Eric's men," Celeste volunteered. "In fact, she'd been working with Eric for several months before his death. She insisted she was just bringing in extra money, that Siren's Song was draining her resources too quickly. If you want to go up against her, you'll need a powerful team, and I'm perfect to be on that team."

"She's been getting detailed reports about your nightclubs. I don't know her source," the Asian girl offered.

"She thinks you'll get back together," another quiet voice revealed.

"The only way to stop Nicolette is to kill her," Celeste declared soberly. "She'll never leave Laura alone. We should just storm her new hideout and take everyone out." Her eyes flashed with a thirsty gleam.

"I don't think a headlong assault is the best idea," Lord objected.

"I agree," acknowledged Stephan reluctantly. The idea of taking her down in a blaze of glory struck a sympathetic nerve. "But we don't have time for a more subtle approach."

"At least do a two-prong assault," Lord urged. "If you distract her, then another force can come in the back."

"Good idea." Gabriel turned to Stephan. "The girls could get close to Eric's thugs before they put up their guard, leaving you to confront Nicolette."

Celeste and Stephan nodded together.

"I have Jon mobilizing my best men. We'll meet him at the Snow Lake truck stop near Snoqualmie Pass. We can split our forces there."

"I can bring men," Lord offered.

"No!" Stephan smiled to soften his gruffness. "Nicolette is my responsibility, and I don't want the deaths of your men on my conscience. We will use only Shadow Dwellers."

"Laura is a member of my team, and these Shadow Dweller women are under my protection. Do you really think I'll just sit on the sidelines?" Lord clicked his tongue and arched an eyebrow. "Would you?"

Stephan laughed at his own temerity. "You might have a slim point."

The tension in the room relaxed. For the next hour, they finalized communication and timing issues. With Lord acting as technical liaison and his men as decoys, it would be an "easy breezy" success. Or so Stephan hoped. Unfortunately, Nicolette had a bad habit of pulling rabbits out of hats when cornered.

# 15

## Nicolette's Obsession

When Laura awoke the second time, she was on a cold, hard floor. Penetrating drafts seeped in through invisible cracks, and she shivered uncontrollably. She could hear the squeaking and scratching of nearby rodents. She hated sewer scavengers, and rats were at the top of her list of repulsive creatures.

Laura took stock of her physical condition. The ropes were cutting into her wrists and ankles, and they were numb from lack of circulation. She struggled to straighten her position and restore some circulation. Laura ignored the pain until her bonds stretched enough to allow her to sit. She was able to use the coarse rope to rub the tape off her mouth.

Seeing her prison only aggravated her nerves. It was a concrete basement with a stark electric light and shallow pools of water on the floor. A furnace and hot water heater were supported on wood blocks to keep them above any drainage. A long, narrow window was painted black. Laura braced herself against the wall and rotated the ropes on her wrists, trying to loosen them.

Her heart jumped when she heard a key rattle in the lock, and the door opened. A human guard came in carrying a tray of food and water. Why Nicolette bothered was a mystery.

She took a long drink of the water he held up to her lips to relieve a terrible thirst. Without untying her, he gave her a few bites of food. When her vision began to blur, she realized they had drugged her again. She smiled slightly as she slipped into a consuming darkness. She was glad to escape worrying about a situation she could do nothing to change.

When Laura's mind swam to the surface for the third time, she was no longer in the basement. She was tied to a chair in a richly furnished living room. The roaring fire in the fireplace made the room uncomfortably hot. Above the black marble mantle was a remarkable portrait of Nicolette.

In the painting, she was lying on a chaise lounge, her skin rosy and healthy. Her red hair was drawn to emphasize the mixture of warm vibrant shades of red. All the trappings of a woman who used her looks to gain wealth and status surrounded her. The painter had captured her youthful excitement. The young Nicolette gazed expectantly out a nearby window. As Laura studied the painting, she could find none of the characteristics of a Shadow Dweller. She realized it must have been painted when her captor was still human. Laura had forgotten that Nicolette was once as human as she was. Unexpectedly, her heart ached for this girl who would soon lose her humanity and ultimately her sanity. Laura forced herself to turn away. She had to remain hard-hearted toward the woman who was planning to kill her.

This room mirrored the one in the painting. The brocade velvet couches, delicate lace tablecloths, and heavy damask curtains were all identical to those in the portrait. The carpet and tapestries showed a definite Spanish influence. Laura had not expected to see tasteful European elegance.

Suddenly, music blasted from hidden speakers. Nicolette swept into the room, singing the chorus of a popular song and smiling with triumph. She shouted the verses with all the arrogance of a grand operatic singer, ignoring the discordant notes. Obviously, none of Nicolette's sycophants had the courage to tell her that she couldn't sing. Laura was thankful when the woman stopped.

Nicolette reached for Laura's arm and tore off her watch. A small rivulet of blood trickled down the back of her hand.

"Ouch! What the hell?" Laura's eyes watered from the unexpected pain.

Nicolette's smile was self-congratulatory. "I still have allies at The Colony. Planting the bug in your watch was ridiculously easy."

"I won't be caught unawares again," Laura promised, forgetting there wouldn't be a second time.

"We don't need to use bugs on you anymore. You've already revealed more than I could have hoped for."

Laura growled with disgust but didn't speak. She wouldn't give Nicolette the satisfaction.

Nicolette only grinned wider. "Of course, I heard your little chat with Alexis. Every mature Shadow Dweller knows about the Ancients and their hidden powers. Now I'll be able to blackmail Stephan into revealing their secrets."

"Stephan doesn't need those mysterious powers. He already has the strength to stop you," Laura sneered. Of course, this was an empty threat. She didn't know what Stephan could do to neutralize this wart on the butt of God.

"It doesn't matter what he can or can't do. You, my sweet, will make Stephan tell me everything I want to know. With the Ancients' secrets at my fingertips, I'll finally have the means to realize my every desire. Noel's value skyrocketed when he pointed me at you."

The gnarled dwarf, Noel, appeared, puffing out his chest like a bantam rooster. This was the first time Laura had seen Nicolette's notorious spy. The bushy white hair bursting from his head, ears, and chin seemed contrary to what she had heard about him. She looked closer. Long, narrow scars marred his pale, bruised skin. His grin was an ugly sneer revealing missing teeth. This little man had lived a life of terrible violence. But his devotion to Nicolette was plain to see. His eyes had the same terrible red tint. He skipped to her side and clutched a handful of her jacket like some doomed demon child.

"It was Noel who planted the listening devices. It was Noel who found Stephan's workshop. He's been following you since you took out Eric. No one knows your movements better than he does," Nicolette taunted.

Noel leered at Laura, licking his lips.

Nicolette gripped Laura's jaw cruelly, forcing her head back. "What do these idiots see in you?" She tilted Laura's head right and left, examining her from every angle. "You are such a common girl. You're too young to be entertaining or useful. Yet, stupid men keep sniffing around you." Nicolette's grip tightened, and Laura feared that her jaw would break. "What is it?" Nicolette shouted. "Why did Eric let you kill him?"

Laura thought the question was rhetorical until the Shadow Dweller shook her chin again. "Well?" she shouted.

Laura knew that her success was based on reading people well enough to guess at their inner thoughts and desires, but she would never give Nicolette this insight.

"It must be...um...all men find..." Laura stammered, searching for some explanation the vampiress would accept. "All men like to be pampered and flattered. How is different for different men."

"And Stephan? What about Stephan? Do you con him with beguiling lies? By now, he should be tired of you dreary mortals. Why does he still want you?"

Laura knew that she should give up. Nicolette would never be satisfied by her explanations or believe that humans might have some attractive quality. But Eric's men were waiting for her. As long as she kept Nicolette talking, they were shackled.

"Maybe he just wants someone who treats him with respect." How could she put this delicately? "Someone who'll let him follow his own ideas of how to build an empire."

"I do that! I worked hard to help him create the best of everything," Nicolette shrieked defensively.

"But *you* determine what that looks like." Mina had given Laura an earful about the frustration that had led to Stephan and Nicolette's breakup. Very little escaped the staff of a busy theater.

"You should have stayed away from him!" Nicolette snarled.

Laura braced for more violence.

"It took so long," Nicolette cried plaintively, suddenly exposing a surprising vulnerability. "He was so enthralled by his last human playmate. I had to pay dearly to get her out of the way. Stephan was already suspicious of me, but he never recognized the alliance between Eric and me—a hellish alliance I used to get around Stephan's foolish attachments."

"Eric—you used Eric against Stephan's girlfriend?"

"When the little nitwit was gone, Stephan was finally mine. We sang the songs of love unique to our kind. You humans know nothing of true bonding. Shadow Dwellers experience a total union of thoughts, emotions, and memories. How could your stupid marriage ritual possibly compare? But in the end, he found you." Nicolette gagged on the last three words. Her grimace twisted with a fierce rage.

"You're right; I don't know about Shadow Dweller relationships." Laura had to find a way to shake Nicolette's idea of using her to manipulate Stephan. "Take Stephan. I don't want him. He can be so annoying."

Instead of helping, Laura's words sent Nicolette into a frenzy. The only warning Laura had that something violent was about to happen was a blur of movement that exploded into blinding pain when Nicolette slapped her. She moaned and fought the darkness that swamped her. By the time she could see again, everything had changed.

Finally, Stephan had come. He was standing in front of an open window, his posture strong and unyielding, like an avenging angel. He stared at Nicolette contemptuously. She scrutinized him with a mixture of longing and lust. Laura saw only a few of Nicolette's men blocking the exits. She heard sounds of fighting through the window close to her chair. Stephan had not come alone.

Stephan turned away from Nicolette and studied Laura, his allegiance plain to see. She hated to see him expose his weakness for her so openly. It only gave Nicolette confirmation of the success of her plan to trap him.

"Are you all right?" he asked.

"So far. She knows too much, Stephan. She's more dangerous than we thought."

"What does she know?"

"Ask me, Stephan." Nicolette walked over to Laura and tied a scarf around her mouth. "This should take care of any more interruptions," she purred. Stephan's presence seemed to enthrall her as effectively as a snake charmer. "I know the Ancients have chosen you to be their newest member. I know they believe you'll be our best leader. I, too, have seen how quickly weaker Shadow Dwellers break down. You do seem immune to it. Together, we could lead our people into a new future."

"Not we, Nicolette. Laura and I. If you really know everything, you should know that too."

"The Ancients made a mistake. Laura can't be the harbinger. She is a mortal who will die soon enough. I'll be at your side for eternity."

Laura wanted to laugh at Stephan's expression of distaste until she realized Nicolette would probably kill her if she did.

"You're deluding yourself. You keep hoping for something that'll never happen." Stephan looked at her with pity.

"But why, Stephan? Why do you prefer humans to us? Humans are just food. You and I are of the same race."

"Because it's a Shadow Dweller like you, Nicolette, who has condemned me. A self-obsessed vampiress sentenced me to this nightmare of unrelenting hunger and isolation. I'm alone, Nicolette. I don't belong to the human world, and I refuse to live the life of a Shadow Dweller. Do you really think I would ever bond with you? Never!"

"But you're working with the Ancients to help Shadow Dwellers. If you hate us, how can you?" Nicolette whispered, the pain of his rejection stark on her face.

"How can I act for the good of many, when just one has condemned me?" he clarified. "The fact that you ask this question shows that you wouldn't understand the answer. Sometimes principles are beyond a selfish person's understanding."

"You're the blind one." Nicolette's face became as hard as granite and as cold as ice. "This is my lair, and my army is ready for combat. Are you ready to drag the Houses of Shadows into a full-on war? I'll have the secrets of the Ancients before I'm through."

Several of Eric's guards smiled malevolently.

But Stephan had a few tricks up his sleeve. Laura could see the mist that was Alexis outside the open window.

"You've made a serious mistake, Nicolette. Do you think you can control me through Laura? You can't win my cooperation with violence. You'll only guarantee that I'll fight you."

"Don't be stupid, Stephan. We'll be here long after Laura is dust. You'll accept that you belong with our kind after you have worked with the Ancients for a while. With their secrets, there will be none who can stop us." Nicolette reached for Stephan, secure in her mad fantasies, ignoring his outrage.

Laura had been so fixated on the battle between Nicolette and Stephan that she only gradually became aware that Nicolette's smallest soldier, Noel, in a low crouch, was moving. Forgotten, he'd circled around Stephan taking a position behind him.

"I won't let her die," Stephan insisted, moving past Nicolette's outstretched hand, toward Laura. "*She's* the one I've been waiting for. *She's* the one who replaces all others. I hope, someday, *she'll* agree to be my bond-mate."

A terrible cry erupted from Nicolette. "Nooooo! You're mine. She won't spoil our lives any longer!"

With both arms and legs tied, Laura was powerless to protect herself. Nicolette made a dash toward her, while Noel, still behind Stephan, pulled a long knife from under his coat. Stephan leaped on Nicolette, knocking her to the floor.

Meanwhile, the fog that was Alexis released puffs of gray smoke that engulfed the menacing men at the doors. The guards choked and gasped for air, rapidly turning gray and then collapsing.

The main body of the fog surged toward Noel's advancing figure. Instead of taking shape, Alexis began spinning. A hum, like the lonely howl of a great wind, filled the room. Despite the conflict in progress, Stephan, Nicolette, and Noel paused at the inhuman wail. The spinning mass released a wave of searing heat that swept through the room, catching paper and cloth on fire. At the fog's center, a ball of flame grew hotter, eating the cloud until all that was left was a being of fire.

Laura recognized the same unique fire that had ignited Siren's Song. The flame's colors and movements were unmistakable. It appeared that living fire was just another one of those mysterious powers the Ancients kept secret. Alexis must have been backing Stephan up even then.

A blade of fire ignited Noel's clothes and heated the knife, forcing him to drop it. He screamed as the flames enveloped him. Nicolette began to struggle in earnest, not to reach Laura, but to help her suffering dwarf. She kicked ruthlessly at Stephan, striking where he was most vulnerable. Taken by surprise, Stephan released her, which gave Nicolette the opening she needed to jump free.

"Stop!" Nicolette shouted as she dragged the burning dwarf away from the being of flame. "You must stop!"

Laura could hardly believe her eyes when Stephan began to help Nicolette relieve the dwarf's suffering. With the flames smothered, the smoking dwarf huddled on the floor and the fire that was Alexis moved back. Unfortunately, this gave Noel the opportunity to attack. He scrambled for the helpless Laura, completely ignoring his own mortal wounds. He seemed to have no instinct for survival. Why didn't he just run away?

Noel jumped into Laura's lap, and when he opened his mouth wide, she saw the unmistakable mark of a Shadow Dweller. He might be missing some teeth, but the ones he had were all vampire. She would never have suspected that the proud, haughty Nicolette would have given this little worm the holy gift of transmutation. For Shadow Dwellers, changing a human into one of them was the greatest blessing. He leaned over Laura's neck and sank his teeth deep.

"Nooo!" Stephan cried.

With surgical precision, Alexis extended a thin finger of flame that curled itself around Noel's body and burned deep. When the pain forced the dwarf to disengage his teeth, the Ancient pulled him off Laura to a spot in front of Nicolette. It took only a few seconds for the flames to turn the squirming dwarf into a funeral pyre. His mistress tried to extinguish the fire that was killing him, but the flames were too hot, and Nicolette was driven away.

Noel shrieked horribly as his skin darkened and his eyes popped. Since he was an immortal, he did not die easily or quickly. The fire burned away his life extremity by extremity and then organ by organ. It was a blessing when the wailing finally stopped and all they could hear was the crackling of breaking bones. Noel's skull was still discernible, his mouth open in a silent scream, his eye sockets staring sightlessly up at the indifferent heavens.

The sight was too awful to ignore. Laura found herself watching with a sick fascination.

Nicolette's face was a mask of pitiless grief. Leaving a trail of Noel's blood behind, she ran to Laura. "Your interference will end once and for all time," she vowed, her face changing to a scowl of homicidal rage. "I'll enjoy teaching you a few realities about Stephan's kindred!" Then Nicolette sank her teeth into her rival's neck.

Laura felt the teeth sink deep and pain exploded along her neck. Fear and rage blinded her, and her whole body tensed as if with some mighty effort. As Nicolette drank rapaciously, she became lightheaded and felt disconnected from her body. Suddenly, with no sound or explanation, Nicolette stiffened and slumped across her lap.

Stephan had run over when Nicolette attacked and now pulled her unresisting body off Laura. Surprised, he dropped his ex-lover abruptly. Nicolette was frozen into a caricature of death, blood dripping from her mouth.

"What in the world?" he asked, glancing at Laura nervously.

The wide-eyed Laura only shook her head in disbelief. "I don't know."

Alexis nodded grimly. "So the stories are true. We have heard of humans who resist us, who promise death if we attempt to drink. But I have never seen one until now."

"But I have kissed her," Stephan objected, using a polite term for the Shadow Dweller's bite.

"Then she let you, or maybe, more accurately, she didn't activate her defenses. But if you ever try to turn her, it could be bad for all of us."

"That will never happen," Laura promised. "I'll never surrender my humanity."

A loud commotion behind them drew Laura's attention. The remaining guards had run to a beautiful tapestry hanging on a nearby wall. The man in front pulled it back, and they all darted through a specially reinforced spring-loaded metal door, but not before flinging a parting glare at Stephan and Alexis. Apparently, Nicolette had planned for a possible emergency escape, as any smart snake would.

Again, Alexis became a weapon of searing heat focused on the door they couldn't reopen. Laura saw the metal bend and ripple like mercury. Remarkably, it withstood the initial onslaught. Then a red glow at the point of the flames' impact grew to transform the door into liquid. Soon, all that was left was a black hole. Alexis easily floated through the opening to follow the fleeing Shadow Dwellers.


Stephan showed no interest in pursuing Nicolette's guards. With Noel's discarded knife, he sliced through Laura's ropes, pulled off the scarf, and lifted her out of the chair, laughing with relief.

Laura had kept herself tightly in check during Nicolette's assault. But now her defenses fell away like the cut ropes. She stood on tiptoes, pulled Stephan closer, and hugged him tight, experiencing every emotion from shock to fear, grief to relief, and gratitude to curiosity. Tears drenched her face as she released the pent-up emotions of hours. Mentally shaking herself, she stepped back.

"Do you think they'll get away?" Laura asked quietly, staring at the black hole.

"Probably. But they'll be back. You have won the day twice, first with Eric and now Nicolette. They will not be able to let that go," Stephan said, obviously worried. He would never be a decent Shadow Dweller. He couldn't seem to master their deathlike inscrutability. "Are you all right? I knew it was Nicolette who destroyed the workshop. The damage had all the signs of one vindictive bitch. Did she hurt you?"

"Not yet. I think she liked taunting me. She sang first, like she wanted to impress me with her great voice." Laura shuddered. "Then she just questioned me in between threats. She bugged us, Stephan! I don't even know how many."

"Whatever she learned with her bugs doesn't matter. Nicolette never knew the full truth about the Ancients." Stephan raised his wrists and showed her the two jagged scars. "This is the mark of our blood oath, one of the most lethal vows among the Shadow Dwellers. Alexis took me to their hall, and they forced me to take this oath." At his words, the marks swelled and pulsed red-black.

Taking Laura's hands, he stared into her eyes. "If we're going to work together, you need to know truth. Even though Nicolette intended to use you to blackmail me, I could never have told her anything about the Ancients, even to save you. I'm forced to keep their secrets." He bowed his head, looking frustrated.

"You saved me anyway," she reminded him.

"From a danger I caused," he mumbled miserably.

"From a danger Nicolette created. There is too much evil in the world for you to take responsibility for someone else's."

"I don't want to put you in harm's way."

"You don't have the power to stop me from getting into trouble. *I* put myself in harm's way—a character flaw that Monk and Lord take great delight in pointing out at every opportunity. Besides, you forget, the Ancients have already learned that I have a part to play. Harbinger, remember? I don't think you can change my destiny." Laura winked, a small smile curling the corners of her mouth.

He shook his head. "I think the Ancients have overlooked the concept of free will. We do have a choice in what path our life takes."

Laura gestured at the smoking hole that was all that remained of Nicolette's secret door. "Your backup has one powerful punch. I think Eric's men might hesitate before attacking us again."

"There is that." For the first time, Stephan relaxed, and a smile crossed his perfect lips.

Laura's breath caught in her throat. She took a moment to appreciate Stephan's fine looks. He wasn't a Greek god, but he did have the sensitive features of a creative genius. She shivered as she imagined their possible future. Collecting her imagination, she took his arm and headed for the door.

"Let's get out of here," she urged, taking one last look at the portrait above the fireplace. The innocent girl who had been Nicolette was lost forever. "Lord must be worried sick."

"Lord is here with the girls you rescued. They were fighting Nicolette's guards so I could come rescue you."

"But where are they? Shouldn't they be inside by now?"

Stephan frowned and went to the rear window where Laura had first detected the sounds of fighting. She followed close behind, almost tripping on his heels. Gabriel, Celeste, and two female Shadow Dwellers had herded up a group of six men. Lord and Jon were examining two fallen Shadow Dwellers. When the window shutter creaked, they all looked up.

"What happened?" Lord called anxiously. "We saw a terrible fire and would have come if these impediments hadn't been so determined." He kicked the man closest to him.

"The fire is a unique weapon of my new allies," Stephan explained evasively. "Nicolette is dead. They went after her men when they fled through an escape tunnel."

"What allies?" Celeste pressed, obviously confused.

"Celeste, I don't think this is the time for explanations," Stephan admonished, looking at their prisoners. "Do you?"

Celeste blushed at his censure.

"Of course," Lord assured him, ever the mediator. "We need to leave this place. We've no way of knowing when or if Nicolette's minions will come back with reinforcements."

"He's right," Monk agreed. "I'll go with Laura and Stephan."

"Me too!" Gabriel shouted. "The last time I lowered my guard, Stephan dropped Laura into Nicolette's lap."

Stephan snorted but said nothing. The truth was hard to deny.

"I need you to drive Monk's SUV and take care of Nicolette's men," Lord interjected. "I'm confident Monk can keep Laura safe."

Gabriel grumbled disagreeably as he nonetheless led the prisoners away. At Lord's nod, Celeste and her two friends followed Gabriel.

"I'll meet you back at The Colony," Stephan called to Jon. "Will you get our men sweeping the area for strays?"

"Of course. Still, we should be close behind you," Jon promised and motioned several men toward the basement floor.

On the journey back, Laura tried to relax, but it was a useless effort. She was painfully aware of Stephan. His long fingers on the steering wheel and his comforting scent teased her thoughts. Monk shifted restlessly in the back. He had made it clear that he expected Laura to join him in the rear seat. She had silently declined.

Stephan's workshop had not only captivated Laura but changed her mind about him. On every table, she had seen the evidence of a lively mind. Stephan had not left the mortal world behind, despite his altered state. Instead, he had used his long life to sharpen his skills in human professions that interested him.

When Laura had started working at Stephan's theater, he had introduced her to his world of creative innovation. He encouraged her to expand on her designs and used many of them in his own productions. So to pass the time until they reached her beloved Rainier, Laura let her mind rearrange the design elements in Stephan's lost workshop displays.

Rainier was built on four hills surrounded by a number of suburbs. Rows of evergreen trees lined inner-city streets, creating a forest atmosphere even in the center of the city. She appreciated the familiar mosaic of mirrored glass skyscrapers downtown. Each building had its own unique shape and color, adding an artist's touch to an architectural playground. Finally she was close enough to see the bay sparkling in the lights cast by the skyscraper cityscape. The Colony enjoyed an exclusive location right on the water south of downtown. She shivered when the moon was suddenly engulfed by dark clouds.

# 16

## Reflection

When they reached The Colony, Stephan couldn't sway Laura from returning to Lord's compound. He tried to convince her that he was better equipped to protect her, but she wouldn't be persuaded. He did notice that she watched him with a new intensity.

"Stephan, I know you mean well, but Lord has an army at his disposal." Laura placed her hand on his arm reassuringly. "He would want me to come home to tell him what happened."

Stephan covered her hand, enjoying this new familiarity.

"Besides," she reminded him, "the Ancients are chasing our enemies. They would be wise to put as much distance between Rainier and themselves as they can. Do you think they want to fight the Ancients?"

"No one fights the Ancients for long. But Eric's men might know about my knowledge of the Ancients' powers. They would come after us for this secret alone."

"Maybe so," she allowed. "But that doesn't change my decision." Laura climbed out of the car and headed for the back lot with Monk.

Stephan trailed after her. Short of tying her up, he couldn't stop her.

"Laura, everyone's been asking questions," Monk said. "You need to be ready for questions."

"Please, don't repeat my mistake," Stephan implored the big man, "and underestimate our enemy. I don't know what Nicolette told her followers about the Ancients." Stephan felt a twinge of pain squeeze his heart as the blood oath was awakened. Obviously, Monk was not allowed any knowledge about them. He had to wait a few seconds until it subsided. "Be vigilant, and be wary," he warned vaguely and walked back into The Colony.

Jon returned thirty minutes later. Stephan waved him over to one of the more private tables. "I need a new studio with all the amenities. Do you have the phone number for that real estate agent who did such a good job finding the last one?"

"I'll take care of it," Jon promised and glanced out the front windows.

Stephan followed his gaze and saw the light changing as morning drew closer. Reluctantly, he rose from the table and went down the stairs to his apartment. He felt nothing for Nicolette's death as he made preparations for the Shadow Dwellers' inevitable daylight sleep.


Monk insisted on using his armed vehicle to drive Laura to Lord's compound. An employee would follow with her car. As Monk pulled away, she watched the sky lightening; it was almost morning.

Laura knew she would have to prepare for the confrontation ahead. Lord was an adroit interrogator. With each mile, she shuffled through various stories; some were variations of the truth, while others were complete fictions. She had to make the story good, or Lord would see through her explanations. The journey to the compound was over too quickly.

Monk parked in the courtyard, and they walked together to the front vestibule. The house was dark and quiet. Monk had told her that Lord was waiting in his private office.

Laura lagged behind Monk as he led her through several halls to Lord's private rooms. Their employer collected unusual mirrors, and they passed several striking ones. Their footfalls were muffled by the thick carpet, maintaining the characteristic quiet of the house. They entered the open door of his office unnoticed.

Gideon Lord was standing over a magnificent oak desk covered with open manila folders. He was examining several pieces of paper, scanning each one quickly. Her mentor didn't look like his usual unflappable self. Instead, his hair was disheveled, his shirt open, and his sleeves rolled up.

They must have made some discernible noise because Lord lifted his gaze and instantly straightened up. He ran his hands through his hair, forcing the errant strands into some order.

Laura began her report without preamble. "Nicolette was a full-blown homicidal maniac who made one too many mistakes," she asserted brutally.

"She is dead?" Lord asked skeptically.

Laura only nodded.

"It's time for you to tell me how you ended up at her mercy, little lady," Lord required. "I rely on you to keep me informed while you move among the Shadow Dwellers. Despite our safeguards, you keep getting yourself tossed right into the heart of danger. First Eric, then Stephan, and now Nicolette. What is it about you that attracts danger like cats to catnip?"

Laura flushed. His assessment was painfully accurate. She was bringing more trouble to Lord than she was helping him eliminate.

"I didn't want Stephan's attentions. I mean, he's been polite and protective, but I didn't encourage him," she blurted defensively. "Then to have Nicolette kidnap me for some imagined romance. How could I battle her fantasies? It was impossible."

"Maybe you should start at the beginning," Lord suggested. "I know you rescued Celeste and the girls. They have made quite an impression, by the way. I don't think I'll have a problem keeping them at the compound." Lord smiled a secret smile. There was definitely a story there. "Then I helped rescue you from Nicolette's hideout. What happened between?"

"Stephan took me to his private workshop," Laura told him. She had decided she couldn't lie to Lord. She just wouldn't tell him everything.

"Nicolette found me there and took me captive." God, she hoped she could keep their secrets.

"And you think there was no basis for her jealousy?" Lord asked skeptically.

"We work together," Laura protested, looking at the floor. "The workshop was just a visit, not an assignation. Besides, Stephan isn't human. He lives at night and is forever isolated from people. I could never live this kind of life." Given the new seriousness of her attachment to Stephan, Laura knew that Nicolette had every reason to be jealous. But she couldn't confess this to Lord. He could lock her up until she came to her senses—or more specifically, his senses.

"He was human once," Monk objected. "In many respects, he still is. His manners, his empathy, his courtesy, his attitude, and his intentions all respect our society. Why are you being so judgmental?"

"We hunt Shadow Dwellers," Laura reminded him. "What's gotten into you? Did Stephan turn you to the dark side?"

"I have my own mind, infant. Not every Shadow Dweller is my enemy, especially Stephan. He's given us unprecedented access to his people." Monk looked offended at Laura's lack of gratitude.

"You're right, of course," she mumbled, genuinely contrite. "I've tried very hard to keep him at a distance, and still Nicolette came after me."

"His interest in you is obvious," Monk observed bluntly. "That would be enough to ignite her anger."

"He took you to his workshop," Lord added, "an action he probably reserves for his most trusted friends. It's notable that it was at the workshop that Nicolette abducted you. Maybe she especially didn't like you being there. How did she find you?"

"She had me bugged!" Laura spat, disgusted.

"How could she? We check you for bugs regularly," Lord objected.

"She had one of her spies watching The Colony, ready to act when circumstances warranted. He was a mean little dwarf," Laura explained. "They chose a watch I rarely wear here."

"Where was Renard when she broke in?" Lord asked.

"Yeah! He watches you like a hawk," Monk agreed.

"He had stepped out," she admitted, hedging.

"Stepped out?" Lord repeated, his brow furrowed. "He took you to his workshop and then left you there?"

Laura looked at her feet, trying to control any telltale indications of her evasions. "Yeah, he was unexpectedly called away," she muttered. "I enjoy exploring alone. I didn't really mind."

Laura hoped they wouldn't question her further on this point. Under no circumstances would she give the Ancients reason to come after her new family, specifically Lord and Monk.

Lord ran his fingers restlessly through his hair again and gave her a meaningful look. She didn't believe she had fooled him with her vagueness. When he changed the subject, she started to breathe again.

"What happened next?" he asked finally.

Monk snorted in disgust.

"Nicolette and her men ambushed me," Laura complained, feeling a bit foolish. Lord had taught her techniques for setting up early warning alarms, especially when in enemy territory. Once Stephan left, that should have been her first move. "I can't believe I was taken so completely by surprise. Nicolette loves to smash things. When she found the workshop, she completely annihilated it." Laura lowered her voice to a whisper. "Her capacity to destroy is terrible. Gideon...It was just like my house."

"What about her men?" Lord asked, moving from behind his desk.

"Stephan believes they will continue to come for him and me."

"Why?" Lord probed.

"Revenge?"

Monk clenched his fists. "I just hope they try."

"No, you don't," Laura warned. "Shadow Dwellers are formidable foes. Several coming here would only lead to death and destruction."

"Laura's right. Shadow Dwellers would strike a heavy blow," Lord agreed. "But they still haven't conquered us."

Laura sensed a new intensity in Lord's manner.

"Have you ever wondered why they don't win once and for all?" Lord went on. "I think we have some advantage that we're unaware of. Maybe

Laura has the key, or maybe there's still more to learn. Until then, I'll gather the reports from our informants, personally. If Nicolette's men surface in our world, I'll know."

"Let me know if you hear anything, Gideon," Laura pleaded. She was afraid he would keep her in the dark to protect her. "Have you finished wiring my house with surveillance?"

In the past, Laura had insisted on privacy at the cottage where she kept Faraday. Now she wanted foolproof security measures. "I want you to keep an eye on me."

"Yes, my girl, your cozy little house has been wired, and the cameras are sending video to my private security office. You have the option to turn on the audio at the house. We still haven't replaced everything that was destroyed, especially the sentimental items. But it's ready for you to move in."

"Thank you. I really want to go home. I would kill for a hot shower." Laura went to Lord and, ignoring his usual reserve, gave him a hearty hug.

Monk trailed after Laura when she left to retrieve her car. He waited silently, looking at her hopefully. Laura could see concern written all over his face. He must have been crazy with worry while she was missing. To appease his apprehension, she waved at the car.

"Come then," she offered generously and gritted her teeth for the drive ahead. His evasion tactics would cost a pretty penny at any amusement park.

Lord's housekeeper-bodyguard, Franklin, greeted them at the front door of her house. He was a bit of a contradiction, unusually short with bulging muscles. He seemed more suited to bodyguard than housekeeper. But her place was spotless, and mouth-watering aromas filled the alcove. Laura was happy to find Lord's choice of servant impeccable.

While Franklin returned to the kitchen to finish breakfast and Monk went upstairs to check the house for hidden microphones, Laura collapsed into an overstuffed recliner. Alone at last, tears streamed down her cheeks as she contemplated how impossible her chance at happiness had become. She feared the complicated life promised by a besotted

Shadow Dweller and the deadly intention of Nicolette's vengeful minions. She had only wanted justice for the women who had treated her with such kindness and generosity and who had dispelled the terrible loneliness that had engulfed her at Rainier University.

Her gray kitten jumped onto her shoulder, purring loudly, and licked her chin. Her long fur tickled Laura's nose. Sissy and Roman, her recovering dogs, settled at her feet and stared at her with wide eyes overflowing with devotion. Lord must have arranged for Franklin to retrieve her pets and bring them there to welcome her.

A little while later, Laura heard Monk enter the den. His footfalls were unmistakable. She had slipped to the floor with her back against the chair, surrounded by her pets. The dogs were lying against her legs, and both cats were curled up in her lap. Her pet eagle clung to the recliner back, squawking in response to Laura's trilling. Their unwavering affection would go a long way toward healing her mental anxiety. She felt grateful tears replacing the tired ones. Monk remained quiet, guarding her like an eternally patient mountain.

When Monk finally left her to Franklin's care and her animal friends wandered off to places unknown, Laura hauled herself up off the floor. She felt calm but discouraged. She couldn't fight Nicolette's army, and she couldn't understand Stephan's situation. Sleep seemed like a very good idea.

Laura awoke from a dreamless sleep rejuvenated. She pulled on a robe and bounded downstairs, heading for the kitchen. Franklin had left a note with instructions, a dress box with a card showing Lord's name, and a delicious meal of roast beef on homemade bread and fruit salad. After eating, Laura spent the remainder of the day setting up her home. Lord had replaced items but not laid them out. When she absently glanced at the wall clock, she was surprised to discover that it was almost time to return to Stephan's club. She fed her pets dinner before racing upstairs carrying the dress box.

Laura slipped on the high-fashion, dark-red, sequined gown, feeling deliciously sinful. The silk slid over her curves luxuriously. Her gold high heels encouraged a posture that showed her figure to its greatest advantage. She twisted her hair into a intricate chignon, leaving strands hanging around her face. When Laura finally glanced at her reflection, she was pleased with the result. She just had time to load her purse and choose a coat before the doorbell rang. Monk was right on schedule.

On the drive back to The Colony, Monk tossed a new phone into her lap.

"This cell phone can't be bugged or tracked. Lord is switching out all our electronics and installing special antispyware. A nice added feature of this phone is that it'll disrupt any listening device within several feet of it."

"But how so soon?" She'd mentioned Nicolette's bugs to Lord only this morning.

"He's been working on this new technology for a while."

Laura slipped the slender device into a hidden pocket of her gown with a sigh of satisfaction. "I'm going to call it quits early. With any luck, I might enjoy one night of peaceful sleep."

"Sounds like a good idea," Monk agreed. "And I have a few errands to run for Lord. He's decided we should take a few more precautions."

Laura raised an eyebrow, hoping for more details, but Monk had shifted his attention to the high-performance vehicle he was driving. The sports car hummed like a well-oiled musical instrument. He spent the car ride gleefully darting around sharp turns and charging down straightaways. He slid to a stop in front of The Colony and leaned over to open her car door and let her out. She barely had time to thank him before he skidded off at high speed. Chuckling, Laura turned toward The Colony entrance. Monk looked like a cartoon character with his massive bulk perched in the cramped driver's seat of the convertible.

Laura entered the club on light feet. She wanted her presence to go unnoticed for a little while. She walked into the auditorium eager to see what production was planned for this evening. She was delighted to find clever new modifications in process on the stage. The platform had been extended out into the seating area, and the musicians were now seated on both sides. This allowed the performers to walk out into the audience.

New scenic backdrops had been expertly painted. Laura couldn't decide where the three-dimensional aspects gave way to the actual painting. To the left of the stage were bunches of exotic flowers arranged in antique vases and a cage of exotic birds. The addition of live animals always added to the illusion that the audience had been transported away from this crowded theater into another land. She had seen the central spotlights mimic all times of the day, including the vivid colors of a setting sun. She imagined bright-yellow, autumn-orange, fiery-red, and red-violet lighting on the new backdrops and her performers.

Finally ready to talk to her friends, Laura walked to the back dressing rooms, only to discover Michael and two strange men trying to push Kate and Tanya out the back.

# 17

## An Old Foe Returns

The evening after Laura's kidnapping, Stephan left his apartment and eagerly headed upstairs to The Colony's main salon. Already customers were quietly talking at several tables.

Stephan let his body relax against the lushly upholstered bench of his private table. Images of his visit to the Ancient stronghold came easily to his mind. He could hardly credit the powers that Alexis had shown him.

Stephan had always laughed at the myths that circulated about his people. The religious aspects were, of course, silly superstitions. But he now understood the images of bats, wolves, and mist that accompanied the vampire legends. Unlike humans, he wasn't restricted to one physical form. He remembered the fierceness of Alexis's fire and the malleability of her fog. Were these the only forms his people could take, or were there others? He was eager for future lessons.

Stephan shivered at the memory of the beautiful Horsehead Nebula where he had been transformed into millions of specks of confused intelligence. Was this the fate of all Shadow Dwellers? Since they didn't die in the usual way, did they just float apart? Was there really no heaven, no final, peaceful resting place? Had they traded an illusion of immortality for the real thing?

Jon came over carrying a glass of Stephan's favorite wine. "Laura's girls are preparing for tonight's performance. They've asked if you have any last-minute instructions." Jon handed him a worn leather briefcase.

Stephan drew out two sketches and studied them thoughtfully. One was of Roman palaces with groomed gardens and exotic birds, and the other was of mountain glaciers illuminated by rippling night lights. He thought it might be time to test the versatility of their two top performers by switching sets. Tanya would sing to Northern Lights sparkling on snow, while Kate would serenade Mediterranean royalty lounging in opulent surroundings. Performers dressed as servants or as arctic wildlife could appear to increase the drama of the show. He would leave the lyrics and music to Laura.

Stephan couldn't remember when he'd last felt a part of such a diverse and creative team. Shadow Dwellers rarely worked among humans without drawing attention. Lovesick employees were always a challenge. But Laura's girls were unaffected by his appearance. As he remembered the many little moments of camaraderie, he shivered. Shadow Dweller hunters were not advisable companions for a Shadow Dweller.

Finally too restless to sit still, Stephan returned his diagrams to the briefcase and stood up. Soft music was coming from the auditorium. Curious, he followed the bits of melody to discover Tanya and Kate huddled over the stage piano. Tanya was scribbling furiously.

Stephan greeted the two women with a careful smile and cautious hugs. They seemed to take special delight in returning his greeting with effusive compliments, excessive touching, and cheek-kissing.

"Enough, enough!" He laughed, backing away from the affectionate, teasing women. "You two should be required to wear a sign: 'Warning, approach at your own risk.'"

Tanya set her hands on her hips and feigned a hurt expression. "Now, Stephan, we're just trying to be friendly. You act like we're a menace. Have we harmed anyone? No? In fact, you could do more to protect *us.*

Last night, it took forever to wade through the mob of fans. If we're the threat, why do *we* need the guards?"

Stephan chuckled generously. "OK, OK. I'll give you this one. But someday you two will be unmasked. You're not as vulnerable as you pretend."

Tanya blinked innocently. A small smile tickled the corner of her mouth.

"Come on, Tanya," Kate interrupted, pouting. "We have several songs to rehearse before show time."

Stephan looked at the girls hopefully. "I have these set designs already converted to backdrops with corresponding lighting and trapdoor cues. If you can write appropriate music, then we could surprise Laura tonight." He withdrew the poster boards for their examination.

Tanya studied the diagrams, already shuffling through the songs on the piano. "I think I have two songs that will work for the arctic scene," she revealed thoughtfully.

Kate checked out Tanya's first selection and sang the chorus. "We need to adapt the chorus to the backdrops," she suggested. She sat at the piano and played the song, substituting various different verses.

"There is one thing," Stephan blurted uncomfortably when Kate seemed satisfied with the song alterations. He had never tried to direct Laura's team. "I'd like you two to reverse roles and take the other's usual locale. Tanya, you would sing among northern lights, and you, Kate, would perform opposite Mediterranean royalty."

Both women clapped their hands and said together, "Wonderful!"

"A change would make things more interesting. No one wants to be typecast," said Kate.

Tanya nodded vigorously. "But only if I get to wear one of those long Viking gowns. They looked scrumptious. Now, let's play the lyrics of the songs for the other set."

Impatiently, Tanya shoved Kate aside, accidently knocking her off the piano bench onto the floor. With her usual good humor, Kate grinned and jumped up. "You always were pushy," she scolded, feigning a stern expression. "I get to see the songs too."

"Do you have the cue sheet for changes in the lights and set?" Tanya asked suddenly. "We can stage the song to match those changes."

"In my apartment," Stephan replied. "I'll get them."

Stephan looked at the clock behind them and realized he had only a short time before Laura arrived. He was excited to see her reaction to these new shows. Quickly, he headed for his quarters.

Stephan couldn't help smiling as he entered the apartment. When a soft cough issued from the gloom in one corner, he swung around nervously. Scowling, he studied the darkness, realizing that he should have been able to see the intersecting walls. Instead, there was only a curious blackness. He guessed it could only be one person.

"Why the theatrics? A simple hello is the usual convention," Stephan quipped, suppressing his own apprehension. Nicolette had certainly managed to unnerve him.

For the first time, Alexis came forward in her true physical form. No more fog or fire illusions. He had assumed that she must be hiding some disfigurement behind her spectral facade. Becoming a Shadow Dweller didn't always eliminate scars and deformities. The process of changing had a perversity all its own. But Alexis was young and beautiful. In fact, he had never seen a Shadow Dweller so young.

"It took a few days for my attendants to bring my body here. I'm stronger closer to my body, and I need all my strength to corner your ex-paramour's army. I don't normally travel from my home because...well, because of this." Alexis swept a hand down her figure. She was not only young, but slight, in the manner of those born in ancient times.

"But your small stature would lull your adversaries into a false sense of security," Stephan said. "With your enhanced strength and superior cunning, you could easily overpower them."

Alexis looked impatient. "I'm not referring to my size. My deformity is my age. No Shadow Dweller is allowed to transform a minor any longer because of the hell I live every day. I made sure it became one of our laws and is punishable by death for both the master and the new Dweller."

Stephan could see the shadow of terrible sorrow in the Ancient's eyes.

"Buy why kill the child? He or she is innocent."

"Because a child Shadow Dweller faces a life filled with ridicule and abuse. Historically, these children retaliate with extreme violence or commit suicide on their own.

"You see, children have no status in society. They can't own property, conduct business, or contract services. Children aren't respected or taken seriously. They'll not be recognized professionally or allowed to contribute to society. Children have no chance for intimacy that isn't tainted by the accusations of abuse. Even if, by some miracle, I was to find my perfect love, we would have to keep our relationship a closely guarded secret or risk criminal prosecution. I lived this waking death until I was rescued by the Ancients. They took pity on me and adopted me into their inner sanctum. There, they taught me how to craft a body that resembles an adult female and how to fool humans into believing it's real. But it will never compare to the life I would have had if I had been allowed to mature to an adult before I was frozen in time as a Shadow Dweller."

Stephan's sympathetic expression only seemed to anger the child Dweller. Alexis turned away and delivered, in frustrated tones, the news that had brought her to his apartment.

"The Ancients' tribunal unleashed the blood curse, which has incapacitated all those who were joined to Nicolette by blood. Eric's men are the only threat. They won't fight us, but that doesn't protect you. We did learn one piece of useful information."

Alexis pulled a wand-like device out of her oversized bag and then waved it down Stephan's body. Several times, he heard a distinctive bleep, once at his watch, once near his pockets, once at his belt, and once at his shoes.

"That stupid vampiress," he snarled. Nicolette had been a very busy girl. By the time he had returned to The Colony that morning, the rising sun had pushed the knowledge of Nicolette's microphones out of his memory. Now, he would have to scan all his possessions.

"We've found Nicolette's listening devices everywhere," confessed Alexis. "We can't rest until we find everyone who enjoyed her confidences and therefore knowledge about us."

Disgusted, Stephan ripped off his belt and watch. He took off his shoes, flipped them across the room, and dumped his pocket contents onto a nearby coffee table. He carefully recovered all four bugs and added them to the pile of three that Alexis had found in the apartment while she waited for him. Then she smashed all seven into dust, smiling evilly. Having warned Stephan, she left to continue the pursuit of their enemies.

Stephan retrieved his cue sheets and the bug device Alexis had left. He knew Laura's girls would have been too tempting a target to resist bugging. He hurried to the auditorium to check on them, only to find it empty. All that remained were music sheets scattered on the floor where they could easily be damaged. He knew the girls were disorganized but not enough to mishandle the music.

Stephan stood still and extended his senses. He recognized Laura's muffled voice, pitched in anger. "Laura?" He tried to project his voice without shouting. "Is that you?"

In response, all noise ceased. Alarmed, Stephan darted down the aisle, jumped over the steps, and raced up the staircase to the right of the stage. Sounds of scuffling from the back resumed.

"Tanya? Kate? What's happening?" he shouted, anxiety distorting his words.

"Stephan, back here!" Tanya cried.

"You won't get away with this! Have you lost your mind, or are you just an idiot?" Laura was using all the diplomacy of a sledgehammer, which seemed to be her fallback position. Stephan increased his speed and burst in on a chilling altercation.

Tanya and Kate were already dressed for their new performances. They must have decided not to wait for the cue sheets and come back there to change. Laura stood protectively in front of her friends, her legs planted stiffly, her arms akimbo.

She looked like an avenging angel in a dark-red, sequined gown. Even in the dappled light, the sequins flashed at her slightest movement. Her hair was piled high, clammy curls sticking to her face. Michael and two strange men were looming in front of her, slowly forcing the three women back toward the open rear doors.

"Insulting me—probably not your best idea. You *will* be coming with us." Michael reached for Laura, forcing her closer to the rear door. Stephan could see a dark-paneled van whose windows were, ominously, painted black. Its rear doors stood open. "Shall we go? Or do we fight?" Michael smiled, his eyes smoldering.

"You have the upper hand only in your disturbed mind," Laura said. "We're in Stephan's theater, which is filled with his guards." She nodded toward Stephan.

"Long before Stephan could stop us, we would kill one of you three. He is powerless to save all of you." Michael's gaze swept Stephan with obvious contempt. His two accomplices closed in around Tanya and Kate.

"Why?" Laura exclaimed incredulously. "What do you want with us?"

"Not us. *You.* I've been trying to separate you from the herd since I got here." Michael shook his head impatiently.

"Me? What possible value do I have to you?" Laura glared at Michael, her breath coming in quick, angry gasps. "What is your obsession with me?"

"There are so many reasons." He looked her over with gleaming, predatory eyes. "But still so full of yourself."

Without warning, Michael grabbed Laura and twisted her arms behind her back, effectively holding her immobile. She groaned as he pushed her wrists upward.

Stephan gagged down his outrage and ruthlessly held himself back. He needed an opening before he could attack. Fortunately, patience was a lesson learned well when one lived many lifetimes.

"Get away from her, you maggot," Tanya snarled.

"You're never getting out of here with her," Kate promised.

Stephan's augmented sight detected blood oozing from under Michael's grip. Despite his resolve, he took a menacing step forward.

"One step closer and Laura is going to get seriously hurt." Michael hauled her toward the door.

"Just try it, you little worm." Laura kicked his shin, hard.

Michael collapsed onto one knee but didn't release her. He dragged her down to her knees in front of him and thrust his face inches from hers.

"I'll have you one way or another." Michael's eyes softened, and Stephan realized that the stupid fool actually had feelings for Laura, who looked nauseous.

"You're deluded. I'll never *cooperate*." Laura's nose wrinkled with repulsion. Then she spoke softly, forcing Michael to lean closer. "Michael, you are dealing with forces you don't want to anger."

"You mean Shadow Dwellers?" Michael spat dismissively. "I know all about them. Nicolette's spies tried to recruit me during my first night at The Colony. They admitted working for Eric and then Nicolette. As long as they get paid well, they follow orders."

"I wasn't talking about Nicolette's people! There is magic greater than the Shadow Dwellers of Rainier—magic that will smash you like the bug you are."

"I don't have time for your stupid deceptions," Michael hissed. He heaved Laura onto her feet and shoved her out the rear door hard enough to upset her balance. She stumbled and fell to the rocky ground.

Stephan ran forward. Time had run out. Tanya and Kate started struggling against Michael's guards, keeping them occupied for a few precious seconds. Michael threw Laura roughly into the back of the van before Stephan could reach them. His enhanced hearing caught the unmistakable crack of Laura's head hitting metal.

The rage that filled him then went beyond any he could remember. A red haze and a deafening buzz distorted everything. His need to stop Michael consumed his reason and caution.

Stephan raced to the van and slipped his fingers along the under chassis, searching for solid framing. Michael had climbed into the driver's seat, and the engine roared to life. But before he could engage the drive, Stephan tipped the vehicle onto its side, leaving the van's wheels spinning uselessly. He hopped onto the upper side of the van, tore the passenger door off its hinges, and tossed it several feet down the alley. Looming over Michael, he roared with satisfaction.

"I'm so tired of men like you," Stephan snarled. He dragged the wiggling kidnapper out of the vehicle and easily pinned Michael's flailing arms. "You think you have the right to exploit women. You think your sick desires entitle you to do anything." Stephan raised Michael high over his head, ready to snap his spine like a twig on his knee.

"Wait!" Gabriel's voice was unmistakable.

Surprised, Stephan grudgingly lowered Michael. He dropped his prisoner brutally to the paved driveway. Following him off the van, he trapped Michael's wrists in an iron grip.

Gabriel, who had taken command of Michael's men, came forward. "Please, let us take him. He's one of us."

"She's mine!" Michael railed, without any regard for his safety. "She's for me!"

"Shut up!" Gabriel demanded furiously. "Haven't you done enough damage?"

"You have no authority over me, Gabe. She doesn't belong to you."

"Do you really want to risk the wrath of the director?" Gabriel demanded. "You're going back, even if you fight the whole way. He should have left Rainier days ago," Gabriel complained, turning to Stephan. "By staying here, he's sacrificed everything. His men will make sure he gets home this time."

"Why should I release Michael when I can deal with him permanently?" Stephan's rage would not give up its target so easily.

"Because I believe you're an ethical man. Murdering Michael is not justice. Will your conscience accept this? I can promise you won't see him again. Please, let us take him." Gabriel's usually calm features were rigid with anxiety.

Stephan knew he didn't have to cooperate. His superhuman strength made killing as easy as breathing. But he also knew that Gabriel was right. Damn principles anyway.

"Take him then," he blurted, shoving Michael at Gabriel. "But if I see him again, I will finish what I started here."

Gabriel nodded enthusiastically and hauled Michael to his feet. With the help of his men, he propelled Michael to the end of the alley.

Michael argued the whole way. "I won't go back. This is my mission. You can't do this to me. Guys, help me," he pleaded. His struggles and pleas had no visible effect. If his henchmen had ever been loyal, they weren't any longer.

"You cowards!" he shouted. "I'll return, and when I do, your betrayal will be repaid in spades!"

Ignoring his threats, they forced Michael into the back of the car they had arrived in.

"Your time in Rainier is over," Gabriel snapped with uncharacteristic brutality. "Consider yourself lucky we got here before Renard killed you."

One henchman climbed into the driver's seat while the other stayed in back. The wheels of the car screeched as it roared away, and silence returned to the alley. Gabriel had remained beside the tipped van.

Stephan climbed into the van and knelt beside Laura. She was holding her arm protectively against her body. Gently, he eased her guarding hand away and extended the protected arm to examine the extent of her injuries. She winced when he touched her wrist. He used his extraordinary sensitivity to delicately trace the condition of the wrist's bones.

"It's only sprained," he announced, grateful his rampage hadn't aggravated her injury.

With Gabriel following, Stephan guided Laura to the theater's main dressing room. On the way, he paused to release Tanya and Kate, who were pounding on a locked closet door. Stephan could only imagine that Gabriel or one of his men had locked them in to keep them from interfering again. He directed Kate to retrieve a first-aid kit and used the ace bandage to carefully wrap Laura's arm. Impatiently, Laura squirmed under Stephan's ministrations.

"What in the hell was Michael talking about?" she finally retorted, glaring at Gabriel.

"He has become a loose cannon," Gabriel explained grimly. "He meets beautiful women and imagines them to be part of some elaborate fantasy. So far, Michael hasn't broken any laws—at least not to my knowledge. You were lucky we caught up with him. He seemed excessively fixated on you."

Laura's shudder was visible. "He wouldn't have succeeded. I have too many protectors."

"He had infiltrated Lord's sanctuary," Gabriel reminded her.

"You underestimate Lord. In short order, he got rid of that slime bag."

"And Michael is not your only problem." Gabriel looked genuinely concerned. "You can use all the security you can get. I'm here to protect you."

"And what do you get?" Laura asked suspiciously. "This isn't my first rodeo. You come out of nowhere, with Michael as your partner. You have some reason for being here."

"Lord pays well, and we've learned that putting ourselves in interesting places gives us interesting opportunities."

As Stephan expected, Gabriel was a pro at saying nothing.

"What's so interesting about Rainier?" Laura persisted.

Gabriel only smiled and shrugged. "That remains to be seen."

"Who is the director?"

Stephan considered Laura and Gabriel's verbal swordplay silently. Several times, he wanted to take over the questioning but guessed that Gabriel would not be so forthcoming with him.

"He's your boss?" Laura asked, visibly frustrated at Gabriel's nonanswers.

"The director's role in our organization is more complicated. He's not a traditional boss. He assigns missions but leaves the details to us."

"I thought you worked for Lord?"

Gabriel didn't answer immediately. Instead, his expression became thoughtful.

Stephan took this opportunity to try to shake his glib answers. "Where are you from? What is the nature of your organization? What is so interesting about Laura?"

Gabriel shot Stephan a look that would've withered flowers. Stephan blinked, trying to look sincere.

"As I've said, the director is not our boss. He just offers us opportunities. We do work for Lord. There really is no mystery," Gabriel replied, answering Laura and ignoring Stephan.

Stephan had to accept Gabriel's vague explanation. But he would remain vigilant. He watched Laura shake her head with an expression of disgust and turn away. It was clear she had abandoned any further hope for useful information.

"It's getting late," Tanya chirped. "We need to prepare the stage for tonight. The new songs need to be set to the lights and set changes."

"The cue sheets are on the piano along with a bug detector. It seems Nicolette is more resourceful than we thought," Stephan said. "You'll need to check your personal effects."

Kate and Tanya looked at each other nervously.

"Don't worry," Laura assured them. "Lord has already checked your rooms at the compound. You only have to worry about what clothes you brought here."

Both performers shook their heads.

"Now you must tell me what you plan for the new backdrops being set up on stage. They are magnificent!" Laura said.

Laura's ability to go from chaos and conflict to the mundane details of their show was awe-inspiring. Stephan knew he had met his match, if ever there was such a creature. He laughed silently at his own skepticism.

# 18

## Connections Discovered

Laura hated being powerless to discover Gabriel's true motives. All she could do was wait until some event brought down his house of secret cards. Until then, she would enjoy her favorite thing, the unveiling of a new performance.

Stephan left to coordinate the technical elements, and the girls hurried to finish their own preparations for that night's show. Laura sat quietly in the auditorium while the stagehands finished setting up the stage and the customers filled the theater. Only one hour later, the lights lowered and the performances began.

Kate's excitement at being on such a lavish stage decorated to resemble a great European opera house was clear to Laura. She posed on the new extended platform dressed in an expertly tailored crimson-and-white silk dress. Her hair was braided into an elaborate chignon sprinkled with rubies. Skillfully, she infused her voice with an energy and pure tone that enhanced the song. The chorus celebrated honor and valor, while the verses teased the audience with promises of intrigues yet to come. Laura was struck by the range of emotions expressed in the poetic phrases. She was lucky she had found such a gifted talent still undiscovered.

When the last notes of Kate's song died away and the curtain slowly lowered behind her, the audience rose in unison, clapping furiously. Kate bowed gracefully, their thunderous applause booming around her. Then she retrieved the enormous collection of flowers thrown onto the stage and glided off.

After a brief intermission, the curtain opened once more to reveal Tanya at center stage. Laura had expected scenery in Tanya's signature style. Instead, the singer was standing on the prow of a Viking sailboat, dwarfed by the looming shadow of an immense glacier. She was dressed in a gown accented with gold threads woven into a Scandinavian design. Spotlights created the rippling green and white wave patterns of the aurora borealis.

Tanya sang a song of heroic forces fighting an epic battle, baring a stark emotional intensity that was magnificent. She leaned toward the audience, daring them to live a life of legend and courage. When she finished singing, the applause was deafening and Laura joined in excitedly. Stephan had been right to switch settings, and his sets and technical trickery were impressive. The new shows were refreshing and riveting.

Laura headed for the dressing rooms, eager to share her excitement at Tanya and Kate's success. She took the shortcut that ran under the stage to the rooms behind.

Both Tanya and Kate were considered headliners, which granted them the privilege of private dressing rooms, but they chose to share so they could exchange confidences. There was also the matter of ardent fans. Tanya had admitted that pushy fans were put off when another performer used the same space.

Laura found them laughing at the energetic adulation they had just received. While the girls changed behind elaborate screens, Laura looked for a place to sit. Everywhere were piles of underwear, wigs, and other personal items. She wondered how they found the essentials fast enough to appear on stage during set changes so beautifully adorned.

Finally surrendering to the futility of her search, she dumped the debris off a chair and sat.

Tanya and Kate might be messy, but they were also engaging and good-natured. They made friends as easily as Laura found trouble. They swept her up in an affectionate group hug as soon as they had thrown on enough clothes to be decent. Laura laughingly pushed Kate's hair out of her mouth and nudged Tanya's elbow out of her side.

Mina, Celeste, and Monk came bursting into the room. Monk tried to hold the women back by blocking the doorway, but they only pushed past him. He could have prevented them from entering, but he wasn't heavy-handed with girls. They took full advantage of this strict code of conduct.

"How are things for you at Lord's?" Laura asked Celeste. There had never been an opportunity for a conversation, since Laura had quickly replaced Celeste as Nicolette's prisoner.

"Perfect," Celeste confessed. "Freedom has a remarkable healing effect, and Lord's men are happy to help. But enough about our accommodations. When can we start working for you? Animals like Nicolette must be stopped, and your organization is the ideal way to exploit our special talents.

"Mystique, Haven, and I can give you insights into our world. For example, the Shadow Dweller transformation refines more than just our physical appearance; it also amplifies whatever special talents each person already possesses."

"But how can you work against your own people?" Laura asked, perplexed.

"Extreme cruelty is a powerful motivator. Besides, you're just neutralizing Shadow Dweller evil. In my mind, we'd be a special kind of police. Laura, our savagery runs deep." Celeste took Laura's arm anxiously. "There are terrible acts of violence kept secret from humans. We must stop them." She had an intensity that might already be obsession.

"Of course you're welcome to help us." Laura had hardly dared to hope that she would gain such obvious loyalty. "We're getting the details worked out. You'll begin work soon."

An intercom system, wired into each dressing room, suddenly delivered the warning bell for the next performance. Tanya and Kate hurried behind their dressing screens, and Celeste pulled Monk out of the room. Mina followed the Shadow Dweller.

Kate came out wearing a surprisingly modest white dress. Her hair was braided around an elaborate crystal tiara. Usually performers wore wigs to provide fullness, but Kate's hair didn't need one. However, she was a bit too thin, so her costumes were designed to compensate. A little support here and a lot of padding there and every eye in the house would be glued to her.

Tanya emerged from her corner in a brilliant yellow gown. Unlike Kate, Tanya needed padding like a Caribbean beach needed sand. However, she was on the short side, and so wore high heels to appear taller. She too had jewels sparkling in her hair. They both looked like exotic royalty. Stephan had an amazing collection of costumes and jewelry.

As if on cue, Stephan came into the room. "You guys are going to miss your cue if you don't hustle and you're going on together. We need to keep surprising your fans."

Laura followed Stephan to the control room, which was elevated to allow a better view of the stage. She loved watching the workings of the technical side of a theater this sophisticated. The Colony was a good training ground.

Stephan always handled the controls for a first performance. After an hour of observation, Laura couldn't help being impressed. His timing was flawless. Each transition in sound, lighting, and prop changes went seamlessly.

Laura switched her attention to The Colony owner himself. Even in the half-light, his chocolate eyes glinted playfully. His enjoyment in this aspect of musical productions was obvious.

Stephan was wearing a white shirt open at the neck. Its brightness contrasted dramatically with his dark skin. His complexion was an intriguing peculiarity. Shadow Dwellers were usually pale and cold. But Stephan carried the genes of his Mediterranean background, and the transformation to a Dweller hadn't altered them. His dark coloring suggested a world of wealth, prestige, and power.

"Laura?" Stephan repeated, snapping her out of her reverie.

"I'm sorry." She smiled sheepishly, trying to recall his half-heard words. His European accent was musical, and his mouth caught her gaze. She glanced down self-consciously, licked her lips, and brushed a lock of hair behind her ear. "I liked all the performances tonight," she offered, hoping he'd been talking about the show.

Laura found her fascination embarrassing. Stephan was, of course, extraordinarily good-looking. Most Shadow Dwellers were. They used their physical beauty to draw prey and enthrall protectors, like chameleons use their changeable skin to hide in plain sight.

"Thanks for earlier," Laura blurted, finding a safe diversion.

"What?" Stephan asked, puzzled.

"When you stopped Michael from taking me," Laura explained. "I never trusted him. He was too arrogant, too willing to push others around. I barely knew him, and he tried to take over. Who does that?"

"Young, naïve men," Stephan suggested. "They can overstep themselves under the false belief that confidence equals success."

"That's what Monk said. But Gabriel said Michael might have hurt me—permanently." Laura couldn't suppress a shiver.

"He would have failed," Stephan stated emphatically.

He wrapped his arm consolingly around her shoulders and gave her a reassuring squeeze. Then he gently stroked her hair, and Laura relaxed under his soothing ministrations.

Troubled by questions that had clouded her mind since childhood, Laura wondered if Stephan might have some insight. "I feel like an outcast all the time. I never fit in with my adoptive family. Now these strangers act like they know me."

"I, too, have been an outcast," Stephan confessed. "My parents are long dead. But yearning for a family can cripple your judgment and cloud your ability to see the truth. Case in point: Nicolette. Even if these men know something about you, they have their own agenda. You must be careful."

"OK, so I proceed cautiously. But that doesn't change the facts. They might know something about me. They could explain why the Ancients think I'm a harbinger and other things."

Laura took a deep breath to collect her thoughts before continuing, but Stephan interrupted her. "We shouldn't talk about the Ancients here. They guard their privacy fanatically, and I don't want the blood oath getting nervous." He extended his wrists. The white marks were stark in the half light. The veins were extended and red.

"Where?" she asked.

"I have rooms downstairs," Stephan admitted.

"OK," Laura agreed without hesitation. What the hell? Trouble was her middle name.

Stephan led her out of the control room and down a circular staircase. He nodded at Jon as they passed through the bar to a doorway blocked by heavy curtains. Jon slipped past them to take Stephan's place in the control room. Laura followed Stephan down the stairwell behind the curtains to an alcove in front of a suite of rooms.

Stephan flipped on the overhead light, revealing beveled-glass French doors. Smiling, he opened the doors with a flourish. Tentatively, Laura entered the stylish quarters. The apartment was surprisingly cozy, despite its location. It had an open floor plan that revealed all the rooms, including the bedroom and bathroom, in a single glance. She turned to Stephan with a furrowed brow.

"Why did you include a kitchen and a bedroom?" she asked innocently.

A dark look crossed Stephan's face, and he snorted impatiently. "You believe the stupid rumors."

"But of course you're different," she reasoned bluntly. "I know you were human once, but that ended long ago. Why do you need a kitchen when you don't eat? Why do you need a bedroom when you don't sleep? In fact, why do you need any of the trappings of a human apartment?"

Laura was surprised by the disappointment that crossed Stephan's face. She had put her foot in it again.

"You're wrong. We have the requirements of a physical body, so we do sleep," he retorted. "Even if we don't need to eat food, we can enjoy the sensations of taste. In fact, all our senses are amplified. Thus, all pleasures are heightened."

"I didn't mean to offend you. I do have more to learn about your people." With this reassurance, Stephan visibly relaxed. "May I look around?" she asked tentatively.

"Of course." He waved a hand of invitation.

Laura's first impression revealed an understated, comfortable living space, a far cry from Nicolette's Siren's Song. She wondered how they could have reconciled such a huge difference in style. The kitchen had the latest in dining technology but was shiny and unused, discrediting Stephan's protestations. The living room decor was elegant, expensive, and very masculine. The floor plan gave the impression of open spaces. All in all, the apartment looked very efficient.

Laura jumped nervously when a long-haired gold cat leaped onto the kitchen counter. Its soft ears perked up at her presence, and its tail whipped impatiently in the manner of a pampered pet.

Laura watched the cat warily. She'd been scratched before. But this one only purred loudly and padded down the counter to leap onto the back of a nearby chair. Lightly, it jumped into the seat and settled into a purring mass.

"A gift from Alexis. She said I needed more intimacy in my life."

"Really," observed Laura. "How is that working out?"

"I'm not sure. So far, we've agreed to respect each other's space. She seems satisfied with getting fed frequently and having easy access to the outside."

Stephan absently rubbed the scars on his wrist. "I need to warn you, the Ancients expect you to practice the same level of secrecy as my blood oath requires of me. I try not to mention them at all. All Shadow Dwellers know of their existence, but details are vague and unreliable. Since Nicolette's men might have gained information from her listening devices, they've sent out their Centurions to silence them."

"Centurions?" Laura repeated. "You mean Roman soldiers?"

"That's what Shadow Dwellers call those who've been tasked with enforcing our laws. They've pledged to serve the Ancients' tribunal and in return are given special concessions."

"Laws?" Laura spat in a most unladylike fashion. She shook her head in disgust. The memory of losing her friends flared as painfully as when she'd found their bodies. "Where were your laws when innocent girls got killed? Where were your laws when your kindred vampires took over criminal enterprises and murdered at will? Vampires seem incapable of living under the rules of civilized people." Laura used the derogatory synonym for Shadow Dwellers, *vampires*, with great relish.

Stephan flinched as if she had struck him.

"Easy, Laura. I'm sorry Eric murdered your friends. But you're being unfair to the rest of us. We have criminals just like you do. Since our populations are small, we must choose our battles.

"Laws are necessary, especially in a secret community like mine. New Shadow Dwellers are more violent, so the Ancients try to restrain them by making it illegal to teach young ones any of our more advanced abilities. Also, any attempt to expose our society publically is a grave crime, and children are not permitted to become Shadow Dwellers because they don't have the same freedoms and protections as adults. These are but a few of our laws…But we came here for you," Stephan reminded her. "What 'other things' were you referring to upstairs?"

"You knew that Eric was a killer but did nothing to stop him." Laura wouldn't be diverted so easily. She wouldn't accept his lofty ideals when they didn't translate into action. "Where were your *laws* when he was killing my friends?"

"It's not that simple. If I had acted against him, his men would have retaliated and many of the people under my protection would have died."

"So you let him continue to kill humans because you didn't want more vampires killed? What kind of sense is that? Eric was a real criminal, and yet you and your precious Ancients did nothing. Your justifications fly in the face of the truth."

"I know it must seem that way to you. But Eric wasn't the worst Shadow Dweller around."

"Tell that to Pam's, Ellie's, and Grace's families."

"We have laws, Laura. They just don't work all the time. Do human laws always stop your criminals?"

"Maybe not. But it seems that killing is an occupational hazard of your kind."

"Loss is never easy. I would bring back your friends, if I could."

At his words, Laura felt a suffocating wave of grief engulf her. Tears streamed down her cheeks, and she found it difficult to breathe. Embarrassed, she turned away. Stephan was not a murderer, no matter how many of his kin were. She had to watch her quick anger and sharp tongue.

Stephan tried again to turn the conversation to safer topics. "So, what can Michael and his kin explain to you?"

This time, Laura embraced his desire to move on. "It's this." She raised her arm. The glow in her skin was slight but perceptible. The apartment's artificial light made the pink shimmer even more preternatural. Laura had hoped that she'd imagined the illumination. But it was there for all to see. "I first noticed it on Gabriel. I'd concluded that it was just a trick of the light until I saw it again, on me. This has never happened before."

Stephan touched her arm. "Interesting."

"Have you seen this before? Could it be some form of magic?"

Before Stephan could answer, Laura's phone issued a jarring ring. It was the protected phone Monk had given her.

An instinctive apprehension touched Laura. Too many unexpected adversaries had threatened her team. She was as jumpy as bare feet on snow. She jerked her phone out of her dress and accidently dumped her purse's contents onto the kitchen counter. Coins and cosmetics rolled across the polished surface and dropped onto the floor. The sound of breaking glass was audible. The scent of her perfume wafted up from the floor.

Anxiously, Laura scanned the display screen.

"Who is it?" Stephan asked.

"Lord," she replied, suddenly reluctant to connect the call.

Stephan took the phone out of her shaking hands. He flipped it open, set the receiver on speaker, and laid it on the counter.

"This is Lord." The voice was strained and barely recognizable. They could hear commotion in the background. "They're here," he managed before the line went dead.

Laura picked up the phone, hitting the redial button repeatedly. Stephan snatched it from her before she managed to break it.

"You have to give it time to make the call," he scolded and hit the appropriate button.

After the redial function had the opportunity to dial the full number, he held the phone out to her. She heard clicking as the phone attempted a connection. But when it should have started ringing, there was only a dull pop and then silence. Not even a dial tone.

"Oh...my...God!" Laura moaned.

She swept her belongings back into her purse and knelt down to retrieve the fallen items. She used a tissue to scoop up the broken articles and dumped them into the trash. Satisfied that she had collected her scattered possessions, she straightened, snatched the phone out of Stephan's hand, and jammed it back into her purse. In her fevered haste, she lost her grip on the purse, and it fell, dumping everything again. She wept in frustration, fearing that each new delay would result in more harm coming to her work family.

"If only we had some idea what was happening. If only he'd told us who was there. How could anyone get past all his security measures?"

"Let me get this," he volunteered, gathering all the fallen items at blinding speed. Accelerated abilities did have their uses.

"You're going to help us?" she asked bleakly.

"Of course. Lord isn't my enemy," Stephan reminded her. "He provided sanctuary to Nicolette's slaves and gave me men to rescue you. Lord is the only human who is helping my people remain hidden. Between our psychotic criminals and the popularity of the vampire myth, we're barely staying under the radar. Whatever has happened to Lord must be linked to both our troubles. You and I are in this up to our necks."

Stephan handed her the purse, and they both ran out of the apartment and up the stairs. Laura headed across the lobby for the front door. Fortunately, there was a performance in progress, and the entryway was vacant.

Monk was standing outside, as imposing as a massive rock. His expression could only be described as murderous. "You disappear with Stephan again, and I'll bury you in a root cellar. I tried to be patient when you left with him the first time." His voice shook as he struggled to maintain control of his temper. "I have no time for any more reckless behavior."

Monk was unconsciously flexing his fists. His bloodshot eyes darted from Laura to Stephan and back again. Laura worried that he might act impulsively. She knew he could no more harm her, his protégée, than he could levitate. That left Stephan as the only release for his frustration.

"There's trouble," Stephan informed the big man. "Lord called Laura; his transmission was cut off before he could tell us what was wrong."

"What?" Monk blinked, and his hands relaxed. "When?" He put his huge paw across Laura's shoulders protectively.

"Just now. We're headed there."

"Then what're we waiting for? But we take Crusher. I figured this SUV would be better protection after I dropped off Laura."

Crusher was Monk's latest project. He had few interests but one serious passion. He was totally consumed with modifying cars. He equipped them with every bell and whistle available that was useful to his security work. Crusher was the latest in a long line of very unusual vehicles. It was rumored that he'd installed some serious arsenal and shielding. Given the circumstances, Laura was grateful Crusher was on hand. They would need options if a full-fledged battle was in progress. That night, Laura wanted to be ready for anything.

Monk led them around to the back of The Colony where he'd parked his current "militarized" vehicle. There, several tall male Shadow Dwellers approached Stephan and requested a private conversation. They were dressed in dark clothing and walked with a silent fluidity that made them natural spies. After a brief whispered exchange, Stephan returned frowning.

"Nothing," he hissed. "They're my best trackers, and still, they found nothing. Let's get going."

The Crusher was an ML350 Mercedes SUV. Monk had a special attachment to German cars. He had replaced the front bucket seats with a long bench. It allowed three people to sit up front. A sensible modification if loading soldiers was a priority.

The reinforced automobile gleamed with enough polish to sparkle, even in the muted light, which wasn't the best presentation for a stealth vehicle. Laura coughed to swallow her laughter when she caught sight of the name of the car painted in yellow letters on its roof. Stephan raised an eyebrow until she pointed at them. Then he too smiled. Monk noticed Laura's gesture and had the grace to blush. But instead of defending himself, he just opened the passenger door for Laura and then circled to the driver's side.

Crusher's engine purred to life so quietly Laura wasn't sure it was actually on. Then Monk switched on a series of electronic screens. The dashboard was so filled with LCD displays that Laura could imagine them in a commercial airline cockpit.

"How long will it take?" she asked nervously.

"We need to avoid police and speed limits," Stephan insisted.

"You both need to take a breath," Monk admonished. "We're going into an unknown battle against an unknown foe. You should learn Crusher's special features in case you have to use her as a weapon. I know you're anxious. But outside of any personal weapons..." He looked expectantly at the two. Both shook their heads. "This car is your only mechanical defense. Don't you think you should know something about it?"

"Maybe," Laura admitted sheepishly. They really did need weapons of some kind.

Laura didn't miss Stephan's sudden keen interest in the car. To him, it would be a mechanical mystery, an area right up his alley.

"What does this do?" she asked, reaching forward to pull a blue knob above her knees.

"Don't touch that!" Monk yelped in alarm. "It releases oil from the back. Let me show you how to operate this baby without ejecting all its artillery."

Monk adjusted several knobs under the largest screen. Immediately gradients of color tinged its view of the parking lot. "This is an infrared sensor scanner. It shows the heat signature of unseen adversaries. This radio can monitor local law enforcement." Monk turned on a shortwave radio and tuned across several channels. They could hear the chatter of various police stations. There was no mention of trouble at Lord's compound. "If necessary, you can call for reinforcements.

"This control might prove useful if we're targeted by heavy gun-fire," Monk explained. He flipped several white levers, triggering panels that banged into place, covering the car with an effective shield but, remarkably, allowing an unobstructed view of the outside. "Hardest transparent material Lord could find. I don't think it's even on the market." He switched the levers back, and the panels retracted. "The rest of the controls release specialized weapons." Pointing to a different button for each weapon, he listed several. "This red one releases water and an electrical charge. The green lever controls a concealed gun on the roof. The yellow button sends out a spray of razor-sharp throwing stars, and the orange one sends out an EMP pulse to knock out electronic devices."

"With that arsenal, we don't need personal weapons," Stephan observed and chuckled.

Laura wasn't surprised. Monk's resourcefulness was legendary. Crusher was good news for their small rescue squad.

Monk pressed a small gray button next to the gear shift.

Laura stirred uncomfortably in the car. "What in the world?" she asked, pressing her hand against the seat. "Is this seat heating up?"

"That's a noncombat feature," he explained, grinning mischievous-ly. "But it's great for a Sunday drive in icy weather."

Laura had seen Monk joke with his troops prior to going into battle. As a result, his fatalities were the lowest in Lord's force. The greater the bond within a group, the better they fought as a focused unit.

"You just want to show off, you big mutt," Laura teased, enjoying the moment of levity.

"Maybe," he replied, feigning innocence. "But I did want to show you everything. Who knows when some auxiliary feature might come in handy to distract the enemy?"

Monk engaged the purring engine and glided out of the parking lot. If ever Laura had imagined a car could move gracefully, then Crusher did. Since Lord's compound was outside the city, Monk took the next freeway on-ramp, and they were soon speeding down Interstate 5. Fortunately, traffic was light. Laura idly glanced at the speedometer, and her eyes widened in shock. She decided it would be better if she didn't look at the speedometer again and instead prayed they would arrive at their destination alive. Like Monk, she just wanted to get there. It was his problem if they encountered cops looking for speeders.

Every minute stretched into an eternity as Laura fought to sit quietly between Monk and Stephan. During Monk's explanations of Crusher's features she had been distracted, but now all she could think was, *Go! Go! Go!* Despite Monk's warning to leave the controls alone, she began fiddling with the police scanner. Monk eyed her sternly but allowed this one nervous activity. While his attention was distracted by several hot rods honking behind them, she twisted the color saturation on the infrared monitor from deep red to emerald green. Monk growled a warning at her. But she could not sit still.

Laura pressed an innocuous-looking white button hidden under the dash, which she suspected might be a radio tuned to real stations. Music soothed the savage beast, and her beast was running amok. Loud metal creaks signaled the start of the shield panel extension. Vainly, she pushed the white button again, hoping to stop the process. It didn't work.

The moving panels blocked the front windshield and threw the car into a wide spin. Instantly, Monk swung the steering wheel into the spin in an attempt to straighten the vehicle. Instead, the car fishtailed onto the gravel shoulder and began to slide wildly. With visibly gritted teeth, Monk held the steering wheel in a white-knuckle grip, struggling to get

Crusher under control. He pumped the brakes, gradually slowing their careening speed. Fortunately, Monk had stayed on the left shoulder, out of traffic. Once his speed was manageable, he brought the car to a complete stop. Laura was clinging precariously to the seat, while Stephan hung on to a strategically placed handle. Monk jumped from the car, panting like an enraged dog.

"Of all the stupid, reckless, dangerous stunts! What have you done with the good mind your creator gave you?" he roared.

With each colorful expletive, Laura winced. She made no attempt to defend herself, which was the perfect reaction to dampen Monk's outrage. After one more carelessly aimed insult, he finally saw Laura's tortured expression.

"Ah, well, yes," he stammered, suddenly looking acutely guilty at his brutal words. "Probably just a lapse in good judgment. I should've warned you about that second shield control. Only had it installed in case the upper levers broke off."

Laura was happy when the panels finally retracted back into the vehicle, hiding her transgression. It seemed that once they had extended completely, the white button did retract them. The car stood idling innocently. She still glared at the vehicle.

"Lord's time is running out," Stephan warned, looking remarkably composed for having survived a near-fatal car accident. Laura was grateful that he didn't comment on her blunder. "Do you think you can continue?" he asked Monk.

"Of course I can continue," Monk snapped hotly. "I'm not some namby-pamby baby. I've faced adversaries that would make your blood run cold."

Stephan smiled and turned away.

Laura was grateful when they were on the road again, speeding toward Lord's.

"Here." Monk handed a handheld receiver to Stephan. "This is set to his private frequency. The signal is scrambled and can't be blocked. If he's near a phone, he'll answer."

Stephan tried connecting several times, but there was only static.

"He must have his receiver off," Monk decided. "Otherwise you would hear background sounds."

"Something is not green in the Emerald City," Laura muttered nervously.

She fell into a brooding silence. By some miracle, they encountered no police as Monk tore up speed records getting out of town. Finally, they were pulling up to the gate of Lord's compound. Monk punched in the code, and the gate swung open automatically. They drove to the main buildings, Laura scrutinizing every shadowy movement. Monk's infrared monitor displayed several human-shaped hot spots. The problem was she couldn't tell if they were friend or foe. When Gabriel and Michael appeared dragging an unconscious Lord to the main house, Laura realized they had arrived too late.

# 19

## Traitors among Us

Stephan struggled weakly against Gabriel's two henchmen as they hauled him to the detention cells. He should have been able to escape. He was a Shadow Dweller. He could bend light poles. He could throw old-growth trees across rivers. He could outrun a truck. But they'd dosed him with some kind of sickly-sweet spray when Laura, Monk, and he had charged into Lord's home. He had instantly collapsed. Whenever he showed anything like his normal strength, their strange skin illumination flared, breaking his concentration long enough for a repeat dose of the disabling spray. Laura was right; the illumination was some type of magic, and magic was a serious weapon.

Michael and Gabriel had taken Laura away to a different area, and Stephan was consumed with worry.

"Where's Laura? Why are you here? We will stop you!" Stephan raged almost incoherently at the silent guards who watched him.

Silently, the men injected him with enough tranquilizer to bring down an elephant, threw him into a cell, and slammed the reinforced metal door. Stephan heard the deadly finality of heavy steel bars sliding into place. It was obvious that Lord's cells had been designed with

Shadow Dwellers in mind. Now, he was well and truly powerless. Still, he was conscious, so there was hope.

Stephan heard Monk's familiar roar coming from a nearby cell. He didn't bother to yell coherent threats; instead, he just howled savagely and banged the door in protest. Stephan let Laura's loyal protector work out his frustration without interruption.

Despite Monk's uproar, Stephan heard others moving in the cells around him. He wondered how many men had been caught unawares at the Lord compound and brought here. He peered out the small window embedded in the steel door. He could see several similar doors and the stairway that led up. They had taken him to a basement detention area.

A commotion began at the top of the stairs. Stephan felt sick when he saw Lord tumbling down the steps to thud heavily onto the cement floor. There was blood everywhere. His beating had been brutal. Two strange men hauled him back onto his feet and shoved him into the cell opposite Stephan's.

When the men were gone, Stephan realized that Monk had gone quiet. He could see the beady eyes of Laura's favorite bodyguard peering out the window toward Lord's cell. In fact, each window in each door showed a pair of disembodied eyes—every door except Lord's.

"Gideon?" Monk cried. "Are you hurt? They captured Laura. We've got to escape!"

Nothing happened. Lord didn't appear at his window or answer Monk's appeal. As the silence continued, Stephan turned away from his own window. Bitterly, he kicked his chair into splinters. He hoped he wouldn't be there long enough to want to use that sad substitute for sitting furniture. The drugs might block his powers, but his mind was still restless.

Monk was surprisingly patient with his employer and let several more minutes pass in silence. Stephan was ready to call out himself, when Lord spoke at last.

"Who's here?" he asked.

Stephan could see his bloody fingers hanging on to the window's grill, gripping hard enough to turn white. A paroxysm of coughing erupted from the cell. Lord's fingers vanished, but bloody prints remained.

"Gideon? Are you all right?" Monk barked.

"Just...a...minute," Lord gasped. His words were punctuated with more coughing. Finally, Stephan saw Lord's fingers on the window grill again. He repeated his question. "Who's here?"

"I am," Monk said.

"I am," repeated several male voices. After each admission, the voice supplied a name. It was a lengthy list.

"I am," Stephan chimed in reluctantly when the room went silent.

Lord spoke again before Stephan had to identify himself. "Yes, I saw them bring you and Monk in," he confirmed gruffly.

"What's happened?" Stephan called. "I thought Michael was forced to return to their home base. How were they able to take so many of you hostage?"

Unexpectedly, Lord swore. The long list of expletives that issued from the educated man was impressive and the images evoked explicit. "Those scoundrels used pretense to gain access," Lord admitted miserably. "Gabriel used my fear for Laura's safety to get me to lower my guard. They brought a small army, and we were taken completely by surprise. If I had managed to reach my control room, they would be the ones in these cells."

Stephan heard long, shuddering breaths emanate from Lord's cell. He imagined that Lord blamed himself for allowing the capture of his fortress.

"What do they want from Laura?" Stephan asked, voicing the fear that tortured his soul.

Laura seemed to be at the center of this whole thing. He bet they did know something about her past. It was the only explanation for their maniacal interest. Who brought an army to kidnap one girl? Stephan realized he had played right into their hands by releasing Michael instead of killing him.

Fortunately, Lord had managed to obtain some insight into the invaders' motives. "Michael talks about Laura like she's the Holy Grail. He seems to think he can use her to gain some elevated position at the *Institute*, whatever that is. Since she is trained as a hunter, his plan to subdue her is a fool's paradise.

"As far as Gabriel goes, it's anyone's guess. He seems extremely interested in my fortress. He used some very persuasive techniques to learn the passwords to computer files and the location of key cards. Fortunately, I had all the sensitive information deleted a week ago. Michael, whom I kicked out for manhandling Laura, had been too interested in my secret files, information that was too critical to leave vulnerable.

"There is definitely some connection between these men and Laura," he went on. "I might believe they were related except for the way Michael looks at her. I can only hope that Gabriel will protect her, but I don't know who has ultimate authority. Why in God's name did you bring her here? You delivered her right into their hands."

"She got a call from you on that phone you gave her," Stephan explained defensively. "We couldn't have stopped her."

"I made no such call," Lord muttered regretfully. "It must have been Michael. He listed mimicry in his résumé, and I gave Gabriel a similar phone a few days ago."

"How many of them are there?" Monk snarled, pounding the door. "And how many of us are there? I counted ten in these cells."

"I can't be sure," Lord offered. "I was taken out early on. But some of their soldiers are different. They must be magical." Breathing heavily, Lord withdrew from view. The chair in his room creaked.

Shaking his head, Stephan sat down on the floor with his back against the wall. He was studying the cell for possible weaknesses when white smoke began to ooze under the door and then spun in a soft whirr, like a ghostly child's top. He could smell the familiar clover scent of his favorite Ancient, Alexis. Eagerly, he jumped up.

"What's that?" Monk demanded suspiciously.

The smoke grew denser, shifting into the vague shapes of familiar objects, like puffy, white clouds. Then, instead of taking a human shape, it changed hue from white to inky black. He was growing impatient with Alexis's antics until words formed in the air.

"Spy listening" was the first drifting message. "Don't talk," she warned unnecessarily. "Get you out." The mist turned from black to transparent, taking on the shifting textures and colors of the cell. Then she flowed back out under the door.

Stephan heard the faint click of his cell's dead bolt withdrawing back into the wall. He opened the door quietly, trying to shake off the effects of the strange drug, and looked for any immediate threat. The corridor between the rows of cells was empty, and the eyes at the other doors were gone. He walked silently to Lord's cell, deciding to release him first. But when he looked through the small window, the cell was empty. Confused, he turned away from the door. The familiar mist hovered in front of Monk's door, before the big man quietly exited.

Monk opened his mouth, but Stephan silenced him with a finger to his lips and a violent shake of his head. Monk's eyes opened wider, but he obeyed. Stephan pointed at the stairs. With raised eyebrows, Monk pointed at Lord's cell. Stephan shook his head and shrugged his shoulders. Monk took a few precious moments to check the empty cell for himself before he followed Stephan. Both men raced up the stairs as silently as possible. But someone must have seen them because they heard a shout from behind. Speeding up, they flung themselves through the upper door, and Monk took the lead. He guided Stephan to a side door that opened into a small study. Cursing as he tripped over a partially concealed chair, Monk snapped on several lights.

"There's a spy in one of the cells. I didn't want to alert him to our escape," Stephan explained in a normal voice. He hoped they were hidden, at least for the moment.

Monk grabbed Stephan by the collar. "Where is Lord?" he snapped.

"I don't know. I found the cell empty." Stephan laid a calming hand on the man's shoulder. "I would have released him, if he'd still been there. He's our best chance of success since he knows the secrets of this place. We must find Laura."

"And be captured again? We're outnumbered. We need a plan first."

"Can we stay here? Isn't there some kind of central surveillance?"

"Yes, there is," Michael mocked from the doorway.

He strode in with his usual arrogant confidence. Two guards followed, blocking the only exit. Stephan felt his stomach twist and burn at the ease with which he'd been played for a fool. He longed to suffocate the miscreant.

"You conniving, lying snake. Is your dog-and-pony show usually so effective?" Stephan snapped recklessly.

Michael smirked. "It did work rather well."

"So what the hell do you want? Rainier has nothing worth your attention." Stephan hoped Michael was conceited enough to flap his jaw indiscreetly.

"Rainier doesn't and you certainly don't," Michael agreed contemptuously. "Even Lord is merely an obstacle. I don't know why Gabriel bothers searching his computers. But Laura is a pearl of great value, only she doesn't know it yet. I'll enjoy explaining."

At the mention of Laura, tempers exploded. Stephan heard a strangled cry, and the huge charging figure of an enraged Monk knocked him aside.

Monk tackled Michael, slamming him to the floor. The two guards circled the wrestling men, looking for some way to neutralize Laura's bodyguard. They began viciously kicking and slugging him. Stubbornly, Monk refused to release Michael, despite the savage injuries that started to bleed. Stephan dived into the fray, knocking the guards off Monk. Stephan easily snatched the handcuffs hanging from their belts and locked them together using the heavy desk leg as an anchor. It was good to have his old strength back. His Shadow Dweller nature had finally neutralized the drug.

But before Stephan could incapacitate Michael, he heard a chilling, ominous sound. A deep, hollow roar, like the echo in a bottomless cavern, vibrated through him. Stephan turned slowly, reluctant to discover the source of this unearthly sound.

# 20

## A New Kind of Warrior

Two towering manlike creatures came shuffling through the door. Seeing the strange brutes in person, Stephan knew why Lord's voice had sounded so bleak. They were much taller than ordinary men and much bigger. They had vacant, vacillating eyes and gray, spiky hair. Even without touching them, Stephan could see that they didn't have the pliant skin of Shadow Dwellers or humans. They were made from something more concrete, more unforgiving, that left a trail of crumbling chunks across the floor. The creatures walked stiffly and mechanically, as if controlled by something other than their own free will. Stephan thought they might be animated stone. But how did one animate stone?

One creature stomped over to the three men, reached down, and lifted Stephan into an unyielding grip. Despite his every effort, Stephan couldn't dislodge the tightening fists. He felt the pressure build into a pulverizing agony. He couldn't expand his chest to breathe, and his heart strained to beat. Stephan continued to punch at the creature's arms, hoping for a miracle. To his amazement, he managed to knock large chunks of the limbs loose. The pressure eased slightly, and Stephan felt a surge of hope.

But then, a strange dark energy radiated through the creature and new gray stone grew over the wounds, making the appendages even more massive. The pressure increased with renewed vigor.

Through his quickly darkening vision, Stephan could see Michael's men resume their vicious assault on Monk. They must have retrieved a hidden key to their handcuffs. Monk, covered in blood, his battle growl growing weaker, continued to fight. Without hope, Stephan prayed for a miracle, realizing he couldn't escape from this foe.

Remarkably, one showed up. A bright-orange beam blazed across his line of sight, hitting the creature square in the chest and blasting free clumps of stone and gravel that showered over Stephan. An expanding, bubbling disturbance erupted under the stone creature's hide, diverting its attention away from him. The creature gazed at its chest in apparent confusion and then anxiety, as if sensing that something was terribly wrong. An ember of red grew under the continuous impact of the beam, finally taking the shape of an enlarged human heart. The organ swelled until, with a horrible soft plop, the entire creature exploded into millions of flying chunks of rock. Any resemblance to a living form was gone.

Stephan lay on the floor, covered in bits of the creature. He could feel a thick, sticky puddle of goo underneath him. Quickly, he scrambled to his feet, trying to assess the situation. The second creature was advancing on him. Its immense foot knocked him off balance, carried him up into the air, and then tossed him across the room. Stephan crashed into a glass coffee table, which shattered into jagged pieces. If he had been human, he would have died instantly. The glass would've shredded him alive. The creature emitted a spine-chilling howl when it saw Stephan rising to his feet. On stiff legs, it pursued him with renewed purpose.

Stephan watched as another orange energy beam hit the second creature. The same curious transformation began and then culminated in the now familiar soft plop that signaled the brute's explosive demise.

This time, Stephan scrambled behind the couch to avoid being hit by flying debris. Fortunately, his injuries from the first explosion were already healing. As soon as the debris settled, Stephan tackled the two human guards brutalizing Monk. He viciously smashed their heads together, rendering them unconscious this time. Then he knelt over the still bodies of Monk and Michael. Their fight was over.

Laura's dearest bodyguard lay in a pool of musky blood. Filled with dread, Stephan forced Monk's rigid fingers to release Michael's neck and heaved his ally over onto his back. Monk's skin was gray, and his eyes were black. He looked dead. But Stephan could still hear the faint beat of life. Michael, on the other hand, was gone. The man's death stare was reflected in his still-open eyes. Death was part of the cycle of life, and Stephan was immensely glad that Michael had finally come full circle.

"Is he dead?" Lord asked quietly.

Stephan jerked around in surprise. Since he wasn't sure to whom Lord was referring, he answered both questions. "Yes and no. Michael is gone, but Monk is hanging on, by a stubborn thread."

Stephan focused on Monk's injuries, shaking his head when Lord offered to help. To slow his bleeding, he propped up Monk's shoulders with pillows to raise his head above his heart. He ripped a loveseat throw into strips and folded them into compresses, tying one to Monk's head injury and stuffing the others under his clothes over the larger wounds. Monk's breathing became stronger, and Stephan was reassured.

Rising from Monk, Stephan studied Lord for the first time. "What the hell is that?" he asked, pointing at the strange weapon Lord was using as a cane. Lord's grip on the weapon was shaking. Stephan came forward and took the gun before it slipped to the floor.

"Oops," Lord apologized, straightening with obvious difficulty. "The gun was developed by my research department. I thought it might work against Michael's strange creatures."

Stephan lifted the firearm to examine it more closely. The central, super-sized barrel was a combination of four different guns. The smallest barrel was the source of the orange laser blast. Lord described the other three barrels as a rapid-fire machine gun, a Taser without wires, and a magnetic pulse gun that could burn out all electronics in a local-ized area.

"Not the most practical design," Stephan observed critically. It was bulky and thus hard to aim at small objects and moving targets.

"That's a drawback." Lord pointed at the remains of the inhuman intruders. "But as you saw, it was surprisingly effective against Gabriel's curious allies."

"I don't think they had a choice."

Gideon Lord stumbled then, and beads of sweat glistened on his forehead. He struggled to remain standing for several seconds before slumping to the floor. His moan transformed into an explosion of wet coughs, and his face turned ashen.

Alarmed, Stephan knelt beside Lord and loosened his collar. "Is there pain?"

In answer, Lord coughed and fought for air, managing only short, shallow breaths. Deliberately, Stephan patted Lord's back, trying to shift any fluid that might be restricting his lungs. He persisted until Lord stopped struggling to breathe. Then he searched for any sign of bleeding or other injury, concentrating on the vital organs.

Stephan knew he had stumbled on the probable cause when Lord winced painfully at pressure on his right side. He found a suspicious red stain under the man's jacket. He pulled open Lord's shirt, despite his obvious discomfort, to reveal a long gray stone embedded between Lord's ribs. Stephan hadn't been the only one cut when the stone war-riors had exploded. Even disembodied, the offending stone shone with the creature's fading animation.

Stephan pulled the stone free, and bloody fluid gushed out from the wound. Lord moaned and then collapsed against him. Stephan lifted him gently onto a nearby recliner.

"Do you have a first-aid kit?"

Lord pointed weakly at a white cabinet.

Stephan retrieved the kit and found a surprising collection of so-phisticated medical supplies. He felt a wave of relief as he extracted a special wound adhesive for lung injuries, disinfectant wipes, a syringe, antibiotics, and pain medicine. He wiped the injury thoroughly and sealed the edges with the surgical glue. Then he inserted a syringe between the second and third ribs. He was able to extract more of the murky fluid, which Lord protested rudely. He then gave a detailed description of how he planned to take revenge on Gabriel. At least the man was showing signs of returning vigor. Gently, Stephan pulled the needle free, allowing more fluid to drain out. Lord's color improved, and he breathed more easily. He even managed to croak a faint "Thank you." Fortunately, the draining fluid thinned and then stopped on its own.

Stephan covered the gash with an antiseptic bandage and gave Lord an injection of pain medication. Lord continued to mumble curses about his own stupidity in allowing himself to be injured. Stephan decided the best medicine was to get his mind back on the business at hand.

"Do you know where they're keeping Laura?"

"No. They kept us separate," Lord snarled. "This whole thing has something to do with Laura, as I said before. I didn't see it at first, but she knew something was wrong from the first moment she laid eyes on Michael. They came for Laura, and now they have her."

Stephan slumped down on the floor beside Lord. "And now they have her," he repeated.

Monk began thrashing, fighting to sit up. He had obviously regained consciousness. Monk had been so quiet that Stephan had momentarily forgotten about him. He was mortified by his own inattentiveness.

"Shadow Dweller, you got any tricks in that box for me?" Monk rumbled, pointing to the open first-aid kit, which was surrounded by discarded packaging.

"You stupid gorilla," Stephan growled, trying to hide his shame and relief. "Doesn't anything slow you down? In case you hadn't noticed, you have a serious head injury. You're supposed to be unconscious."

"And let you two drop the ball worrying about me? Not on your life." Monk leaned forward, shifted his weight onto his hands, and slid his hips back until he was sitting upright.

"Hold on, Lieutenant. We can't have you bleeding all over everything," Lord objected.

Monk's head bandage was soaked with blood.

"It not only makes a terrible mess, but it also leaves a trail of blood that anyone can follow," Stephan agreed. He hoped Monk would respond to military considerations.

"OK, OK. Doc, get your hide over here and do your thing. We have people to find and things to do."

"Wait a minute. Let me finish with Lord." Stephan quickly examined Lord's extremities for additional injuries. He couldn't risk either man collapsing from trauma he missed.

"That old coot," Monk scoffed. "Nothing keeps him down for long. How do you think he got so old?"

Lord chuckled from the couch. "It's usually a good thing to have fans, except when they include a gorilla. You just wait your turn, you malcontent. Without me, you'd still be living in a tent flexing for food."

"Not flexing, boxing," Monk corrected. "And I was winning when you recruited me. I might've been a world-class fighter."

"Ha! You never had the heart to be a coldblooded combatant," Lord maintained. "As soon as Laura came on board, you adopted her like a lost kitten. If any of your opponents or their promoters had learned of your soft heart and appealed to your good nature, you would never have won another match. They would've kept tricking you into letting the other guy win. You're a good fighter, but you need something to fight for. Laura gave you a purpose that had more meaning than mine."

Monk glanced away and muttered inaudibly.

"You've done all you can for me, Stephan. Slap a bandage on Monk, and let's get out of here."

Stephan carried the first-aid kit over to Monk and pushed him back against the pillows. He removed the clumsy bandage from around his head and cleansed the area with antiseptic. Monk snatched some spare wipes and cleaned his hands, neck, and face vigorously. He watched closely as Stephan pulled out the tube of surgical glue.

"This is wound sealer. I've never used it before today, but its efficiency in first-aid applications is undeniable."

"That's right, Doc," Lord confirmed, using the same moniker as Monk. "It's versatile, waterproof wound cement. You completely cover the wound to prevent infection. The healing process itself eventually pushes the glue aside and replaces it with skin. Of course, some use a bandage for appearances." He patted his side.

Stephan squeezed a long bead of the goo along the deep gash in Monk's scalp. He spread it thickly and then waited a few minutes for it to bond. They needed to keep the wound from bleeding. Despite a rebellious Monk, Stephan applied a few stitches to hold the edges and surgical glue to various gashes in different places on his body. Monk passed on any pain medication. Stephan had to admit a growing admiration for the stamina of Laura's champion.

Monk struggled to his feet when Stephan finally moved away. "Can you travel yet, old man?" Monk demanded, frowning at Lord. "Or should we leave you here to recuperate?"

"Not a chance," Lord protested. "Besides, I'm the only one who can show you how to find Laura." Lord got to his feet too quickly and swayed precariously. "Just a bit dizzy. Give me a moment."

After shaking himself like a dog casting off water, he walked across the room. He reached up to a top shelf for a black statuette of Alexander the Great and twisted it toward the back. With a click, a disguised door in the wall popped open.

"You've got to be kidding!" Stephan laughed. "I didn't realize we were in a gothic novel."

"Gabriel gave me the home court advantage." Lord shrugged, obviously pleased. "This house has many built-in secrets. C'mon."

The three men clamored through the door and into a narrow hall. Lord took the lead to guide the others. They climbed up four steep flights in total darkness.

"Gabriel has made a serious mistake coming here," Lord attested. "I've spent years modifying this house. If I'm free to move about, no outside force can prevail for long."

He opened a door at the top of the stairs to reveal a room filled with surveillance monitors and other high-tech equipment. Lord entered the room with undisguised glee. His injuries didn't seem to be slowing him down now. Stephan could tell that he thrived on new technologies. They were probably one of the central reasons for his continued success. The two of them shared this predilection. Stephan's gadgets ran The Colony.

On the monitors, Stephan could see multiple views of Lord's compound. He studied them intently, looking for Laura, Gabriel, or one of Gabriel's goons. Lord adjusted various controls, and soon all the computers were active. The monitors began flashing through several pre-programmed sequences.

"Here's the main control room. Gabriel was directing everything from there. I was trying to override his commands when I caught sight of you and Monk battling Michael."

Stephan looked at the video of the main control room. It was empty. "Well, Gabe's gone now," he noted with disappointment.

"What about Laura?" Monk asked impatiently. "Can your surveillance find her?"

"The last time I saw her, she was with Gabriel. As far as I could tell, he was keeping her close." Lord adjusted a large knob, and the scenes changed more quickly. Every corner of the compound was revealed. Stephan could see his own impatience etched in Lord's and Monk's tense faces.

"Stop!" Stephan barked suddenly. "Go back." The fast flow of images reversed and halted at his urging. One monitor showed a group of outsiders heading for a curious vehicle. The dark truck had no passenger windows and oversized wheels. The windshield and rear window, necessary for driving, were so heavily tinted it was impossible to see in. A long ramp extended from the open rear gate. A rainbow of flickering lights and vapor issued out the rear door, partially obscuring the ramp.

A tall man, obviously in charge, was leading a group of strange individuals into the back of the truck. The group walked slowly, in a stiff, lurching fashion—very much like the animated rock creatures—up the ramp. When they had all disappeared into the truck, the tall man pushed the ramp back into its slot and closed the rear doors. Then, he climbed into the front seat with two other men and drove the vehicle out of the courtyard. Stephan had scanned each individual who entered the truck. None were Laura.

"Why are they leaving?" Monk asked.

"Maybe they got what they came for," Lord speculated, his brow furrowed with worry. He waved at the surveillance room. "They can't find us. These rooms are shielded from their cameras. But I think we were just minor obstacles in their way. When Michael and his stone monstrosities were killed, maybe they weren't ready to accept those casualties. Maybe they have to report back—"

"Wait!" Stephan interrupted. He'd continued to watch all the monitors while listening to Lord. "Turn your cameras back to the room where Michael was killed."

Lord typed in a few instructions, and the den reappeared on the main monitor. The room was empty, except for three pools of blood.

"Damn!" Stephan slammed his fist on the table, creating serious cracks. "They're gone!" Someone had carried away the two unconscious men, and even Michael's dead body.

"Now we've got them where we want them," Monk mocked sarcastically. "Gone! Roaches always do find the smallest cracks to crawl out through."

"I could have extracted information from the guards," Stephan lamented.

"I don't think you're cute enough to charm them into revealing their hideaway." Monk's wisecrack eased the pain of Stephan's failure to act while they still could.

Nevertheless, tension lingered in the room. Losing Michael's men meant they had no immediate way to find Laura.

Stephan smiled painfully. He did enjoy the warm camaraderie of Monk and Lord. "I've turned more heads than your grizzly mug. You'd be surprised what I can uncover with surgical questioning."

"Maybe," Monk conceded amiably.

"There's a way to see if Gabriel and Laura are still here," Lord interrupted, excited.

He started to fuss with his keyboard, typing rapidly. An image of Laura appeared in front of a black grid. Her face and form were outlined in white. The image melted into the grid behind it, and the screen went dark. For several moments, nothing happened. Then different views of Lord's luxurious compound rotated past. The last image was again the picture of Laura. Two words appeared beneath it: "NOT FOUND." He repeated the same process with a picture of Gabriel. The result was the same: a final image of Gabriel with the words "NOT FOUND."

Stephan swore softly.

"They can't be gone!" Monk thundered. Stephan watched incredulously as he smashed a mouse into pieces and knocked several keys out of an ergonomic keyboard.

"Stop!" Lord bellowed, interrupting his rampage. "Get control of yourself! You know Laura needs reason, not emotion. Would you put her at more risk to indulge your anger?"

"It's not like that," Monk mumbled, flushing a deep red.

Stephan appreciated Lord's tactics for getting Monk to calm down. The man was definitely quieter. Then he had an inspiration. "Do you record your surveillance?"

"Yes," Lord answered absently, still studying the screens.

"Can you find the last images of Laura in the complex?"

"Of course!" Lord's eyes lit up, and he bent over the keyboard eagerly.

The center monitor flickered until a view of the main control room reappeared. The scene started scrolling backward in time until the counter read one hour earlier. Frozen on the monitor were Gabriel and Laura surrounded by several men. The scene resumed going forward at a normal rate. Behind him, Stephan sensed Monk's impatience.

He watched the image of Gabriel studying his own surveillance monitor intently. In the background, Laura was struggling against the bonds that bound her to a chair. Gabriel suddenly growled his disgust. Stephan turned his attention to the miniature monitor. Gabriel was watching the battle between Michael and Monk. Again, he heard the soft plop of the exploding rock creatures. Gabriel kicked a chair viciously, sending it skittering across the floor.

"We go now!" he bellowed. Two muscular men looked at each other nervously, and then untied Laura and hauled her to her feet. They lifted her out of view, hardly allowing her feet to touch the ground. Gabriel shoved several folders stamped "Confidential" into a briefcase and followed the guards.

Monk looked sick.

"I wonder what that viper found to steal," Lord hissed. Abruptly, he jumped up and moved to another desk that held a larger computer attached to several peripheral devices.

He typed furiously until paper began pouring out of the printer. Stephan picked up a few sheets and saw plane, train, and boat schedules. Beneath these top sheets were passenger manifests.

"Gabriel and that strange truck must be headed to the same destination," Lord concluded grimly. "They both have unusually large complements. With any luck, they're heading back to their headquarters, and the organization that created those stone creatures has to be remote enough to keep away from curious regulatory agencies. If I can find a combination of men and a woman going to the same obscure location, I might locate our culprits.

"You boys go find us some wheels while I collect and analyze transportation data. Their base might be closer than I think. If not, we have an airplane that can carry our own land transportation. It'll be nice to have the advantages of a high-tech armed vehicle on the ground. Monk should be able to find something that will meet our requirements. He cares for my cars almost as fervently as he fusses over his own. Besides, I can't risk Monk smashing up any more equipment."

"We drove his latest marvel here. A fortified vehicle called Crusher II. So let me in on the secret. How can a shiny black-and-yellow SUV be an effective stealth weapon?" Stephan grinned like a prisoner who had finally served his sentence. Humor was a missed commodity in his dark life.

"Hey," Monk objected with a red face, "that's one of my best efforts."

"We need stealth only if they don't know we're coming. Most Shadow Dwellers know we're coming," Lord admitted. "Besides, he puts a lot of work into his creations. Why not a few embellishments as well?"

"OK, OK. All in good fun, as they say," Stephan conceded, giving in easily. "So, Monk, let's go find another masterpiece."

Monk growled, acting offended, until one corner of his mouth twitched up into a half grin. "Follow me, Dweller."

Monk charged through the house with the speed of someone on home turf. Stephan, on the other hand, was slowed by unexpected turns, stairs, and narrow doorways. Finally, Monk stopped in front of an interior garage-sized door surrounded by decorative black molding. Even if this door only opened into a garage of cars, Lord had instilled in it a definite aura of elegance—another predilection he shared with Lord. With a comical "ta-da," Monk flipped a switch, and the door rose into the ceiling.

Inside, Stephan gazed upon a car owner's paradise. The garage contained an assortment of world-class vehicles. The spacious black-tiled display floor had enough room for ten classic cars. The collection featured a polished black diamond Shelby Mustang GT500; a celestial-white Corvette in mint condition, glowing like snow in the half light; an Italian racing-red Jaguar Supersport reported to purr into life and jump to high speed in record time; a misty silver Rolls Royce Phantom ready to impress a gorgeous woman with high standards; a viridian-green Aston Martin One-77, lean and mean; and a Champagne MG RV8 that rivaled the brilliance of the crown jewels.

Stephan now understood why Lord indulged Monk's passion for cars. All the vehicles were in pristine condition. The four English cars, the Rolls Royce, the Aston Martin, the Jaguar, and the MG RV8, were very expensive. Stephan theorized that Lord must have spent some time in England to be willing to shell out the pretty coin for these models. The Shelby Mustang and the Corvette were American, which might have been acquired as a result of Lord's move to Rainier. None of these first six cars had the military applications of Monk's Crusher. Stephan turned his attention to the last two vehicles, which were isolated from the rest. These two cars were kin to the Crusher, which Monk had parked between them.

Monk almost skipped as he tugged Stephan closer to the collection, smiling like a Cheshire cat. His eyes glowed with fatherly pride. When Monk spoke again, it was with a distinctive British twang. The loyal bodyguard still had a few secrets hidden away.

He waved at the silent cars. "These are my beauties." He stroked the hood of the silver Rolls Royce. "This is Jules. He's the snootiest, most high-maintenance British car I've ever cared for. He demands the most expensive engine fluids and gasoline, or he refuses to work. But when he decides to run, his engine hums like a classic instrument. His interior is sinfully luxurious and the perfect foil for a lady in a shimmering evening gown and glittering jewels…I call that one Blaze." He pointed at the Jaguar. "He's as fast as a raging fire and makes an impression on anyone who sees him at top speed. The red definitely fits his character. He's our fastest model. But like the Rolls, he's not good on long-distance journeys.

With a definite swagger, Monk strolled over to the Aston Martin. Instead of looking like an old English car, this one resembled a vehicle in a futuristic movie.

"This car is our most expensive lady. She comes in at a cool 1.85 million and has an imposing selection of features. Everything is voice activated, keyed only to a recognized voice. But she does have manual controls."

Monk retrieved a small control pad, the same viridian green as the car, from its glove box. He pressed a series of buttons, and an array of automated functions was triggered one after the other. All the windows darkened first, hiding the interior from view. Then the car started without a key or a driver. A camera mounted on the roof took a series of flash photos while turning slowly. Stephan whistled when the car suddenly changed to a cold, cobalt blue. He jumped back in alarm when it unexpectedly rolled forward.

"If that car starts talking, I'm leaving!" Stephan exclaimed, stifling an embarrassed burst of laughter.

"Can they do that?" Monk asked wistfully.

"As far as I know, only in the movies. But I think it's only a matter of time."

"Well, the dealer assured me that I had all the available features. We call her Contessa because we consider her a member of automotive royalty. Still, she's the only purchase I find too outrageous. No car except one made of gold should cost almost two million dollars. But Lord insisted."

Stephan had to agree that the price seemed over the top. But then, he had his expensive hobbies as well.

"Now this car is the beauty of the collection." Monk turned to the last classic car, the champagne MG RV8, which glowed like liquid mercury. "I call her Princess, because I can't help polishing her luminescent paint job. Lord takes her out when he's feeling melancholy. I think maybe this car reminds him of someone."

Finally, Monk moved past the classic cars to the last four stalls. The slot next to the wall held a steel elevator that allowed Monk to store the vehicles in an underground facility. In the next three slots were the three vehicles that Stephan guessed belonged to Monk, the original Crusher and the two other utility vehicles. They were black and low to the ground. Stephan could only imagine what features they must have.

"These are Bruiser and Baron," Monk explained, pointing at the vehicles on either side of Crusher. "They're older siblings of Crusher, but all have the same basic armament. I've just customize each one with a few unique assets. Bruiser has a high-power engine and is therefore the fastest of the three. Baron is the lightest and best for distance travel. If we have to fly, Baron will be the easiest to load on a plane.

"I've decided to leave the choice to you," Monk offered graciously.

Stephan smiled wickedly. "The choice is easy. Crusher II it is. Really, the yellow letters sold me."

# 21

## Glacier People

Laura found herself in a dream that was half fantasy and half memory. She was dancing in Stephan's workshop. She smiled at the polished grand piano and the tables of complex tools. She looked up at the skylight filled with bands of dense stars visible only when one was far from the bright lights of city life. The large moon kept drawing her attention. She had seen colored moons before, but this blood-red moon was different. She could sense the promise of approaching danger that threatened all she cherished.

Laura stirred restlessly, fighting to regain consciousness. She was alarmed to find that she couldn't open her eyes or move her limbs. Mentally, she thrashed in growing terror. Almost immediately, she felt pain in one arm, and darkness swallowed her screaming mind. Like Nicolette, these captors didn't give her a chance to escape.

In a place with no time or space, Laura saw Stephan lying next to her. His calm expression soothed her anxiety, temporarily. But then his image wavered and shimmered, finally dissolving into millions of specks that blew away in a sudden gust of wind. She drew on all her willpower to fight off the effects of whatever drug they were giving her and forced her mind into a higher level of lucidity.

Laura sensed velocity and knew she was in a vehicle of some kind. Her arms and legs were tied so tight they ached from lack of circulation. She was wearing scratchy, unwieldy clothing. The air was bitter cold and hurt her lungs, forcing her to take shallow breaths. A chill blowing up through the floor was as brutal as blades of ice. She had to force herself to maintain the facade of sleep and strangled a gasp when she heard Gabriel's voice.

"She won't stay under much longer. It's taking larger and larger doses to keep her quiet. How soon until we arrive at the entrance?" Gabriel's voice cracked with annoyance. "Pull over. I want to drive," he demanded suddenly.

Laura felt the car slow, lightly fishtailing as it pulled off the road. The brakes were engaged, but the car continued to skid for a few seconds before stopping. She guessed that they must be on ice.

When Gabriel opened the rear door, a blast of frigid air brushed against her exposed skin, causing stabs of piercing pain. She bit her lip to stifle an automatic trembling reaction to the icy slivers of cold. Laura wanted to learn as much as she could about her companions and the location of their base, but if they sedated her again, she would be unable to judge the feasibility of escape.

Gabriel's buddies were not so restrained or respectful. "Shut the damn door, fool!" a deep voice complained. "It's mean cold this time of year. I'll never understand why the big guy doesn't move south. It'd be so much easier."

"You know, Raphe, that people are more inquisitive down below," Gabriel muttered irritably. "They wouldn't let our organization function without questions and documentation. Up here, people don't ask questions, if they even notice our suspicious activities."

Laura heard Gabriel change places with the driver, who climbed into the back a few moments later.

"The Institute is just a few miles ahead," Raphe disclosed, answering Gabriel's earlier question. "Thank God she stayed quiet. I would've hated trying to explain a struggling young woman to inquisitive strangers."

Gabriel gunned the engine recklessly. The sudden burst of speed caused the van to skid across the road for several feet before finding a straighter trajectory.

"What are you trying to do?" Raphe roared. "There are crevasses everywhere!"

"Stop complaining!" Laura heard Gabriel slap his hand against the steering wheel. "We wouldn't even be here if my quick thinking hadn't rescued Michael and lured Laura to Lord's."

"If this girl doesn't cooperate, your heroic efforts won't matter," Raphe snapped sarcastically. "If only we could have reached her before the Shadow Dweller got his hooks into her. Now she'll fight us tooth and nail."

"Their attraction was so obvious," Gabriel complained.

"What if she's ignorant of her abilities?" a new voice interrupted. "And if she is, then what good is she?"

So, Laura had been right. The strange glowing skin did translate into some sort of talent. She was torn between curiosity and the fear of being forced to fight "tooth and nail."

"We show her, you idiot," Raphe said.

Laura needed to see where she was, even if it meant revealing that she was awake. Playing unconscious had been profitable, but they must be close to their destination.

Feigning sleep, she rolled away from the men, who were still arguing. She silently prayed that the van had a low rear window. What she saw, however, extinguished all hope.

They were traveling on a highway covered with treacherous sheets of ice. Far off, she could make out desolate mountain ridges covered in unassailable layers of snow. A thick, gray cloud cover was so dense it hid any landmarks she might have recognized and navigated. The only sign of life was a group of buildings in the distance dwarfed by an immense glacier. She was utterly and hopelessly trapped.

To her horror, Laura felt tears blurring her vision and falling unchecked down her cheeks. She tried valiantly to regain some composure, but she could find nothing to encourage any further subterfuge.

Defeated and depressed, she closed her eyes, unaware that the men had stopped speaking. As the tears dried on her face, the quiet in the vehicle took on a life of its own. Only the roar of the engine reminded Laura that she was not alone.

"She's awake," Raphe observed dispassionately. He made no move to touch her.

"We're here," Gabriel said. The car turned onto a gravel road and slowed to a stop. "We need her awake anyway. She can't cause trouble here." He was dismissing her as easily as an irrelevant flea.

Laura abandoned all pretense and managed to squirm into a sitting position. She needed to reduce the effects of the numbing cold floor. They were parked at the bottom of a sheer granite cliff below a glacier terminus. The area was bleak and barren. There was nothing to distinguish this cliff from any other in the vicinity. She looked for the structures she had seen earlier, but they were now shrouded in gray clouds. Nothing living could survive long outside in this desolation.

Gabriel climbed out of the van and approached the sheer cliff. He touched the granite in several places, opening a panel totally indistinguishable from the rest of the rock. Then he keyed in a code. Laura was able to see the four-digit pass code quite easily. He didn't seem to care if she knew how to get out. Like kidnappers who didn't wear masks, this did not bode well for her future, and she shivered.

A low rumbling began, which increased in volume until the entire car shook. She braced herself against the backseat to maintain her position.

Raphe leaned toward her and lifted her hair away from her face with a long silver knife. "So nice of you to join us. I told Gabriel we didn't need to drug you," Raphe whispered as if sharing some great confidence. Laura wanted to squirm away.

With efficient use of his blade, he cut off the plastic restraints that held her hands and feet. Then he licked her cheek in the manner of some primitive animal marking its property. It was disgusting, and Laura seethed with a fury more intense than any she had ever experienced. She growled low in her throat like a beast of legend, the sound echoing eerily in the van, a sound so threatening that even Raphe looked unsettled. Then, despite the cost, she spit in his face. Raphe raised his fist to strike her, but one of the men grabbed his arm and jerked him away from her.

In a deep, strangled voice that she didn't even recognize as her own, she finally spoke. "Where am I? What do you want?"

"You are home," Gabriel replied enigmatically through the now-open side door. "It's time for you to meet your family."

Instead of joy at this news, Laura knew a fear that shook her soul. She wondered if meeting her family was worth the price that was sure to follow.

Gabriel nodded at Raphe, and the henchman pulled her roughly from the vehicle and deposited her beside the van. Laura could see that a huge door had receded back into the cliff, leaving an opening big enough to swallow a semi. Gabriel took Laura's arm, while Raphe took his place in the driver's seat.

Slowly, the car edged through the opening and up a small rocky incline. A curious green light passed over the van as it crossed the threshold. Laura could see Raphe holding himself visibly rigid. When the light touched him, he emitted a low squeak. He relaxed only when the light had completed one pass.

Gabriel attempted to push Laura after Raphe through the entrance. But instead of a depressed, sedate woman, he found himself holding an exploding ball of fury.

Laura had been trained to fight. She knew weak spots, from the groin to the eyes to vulnerable nerves that could handicap a foe. She might die trying, but she would die knowing that she had done all she could to gain her freedom. Of course, if she did manage to get away, she would be faced with a wasteland. But she would cross that bridge if she came to it.

Using the point of her foot, Laura kicked Gabriel in the groin. Moaning, he dropped to one knee and released his hold on her. She hesitated before taking the action she knew was necessary. Taking out his eye was the only way she could effectively disable him, or he would recapture her easily.

Laura thrust her fingers straight into his face and expected to feel the goo of a damaged eye. Instead, she felt his iron grip catch her hand in midair. She pulled back, trying to free her hand, but the effort was useless. Changing tactics, she kicked out, targeting Gabriel's knee. He staggered, but his grip on her only tightened. Laura was attempting to strike again with greater force when she felt a prick on her neck. She jerked around, too late to stop Raphe from pushing down the syringe's plunger.

Laura cursed silently, frustrated and helpless. Whatever chemical was in the needle was all they needed to ensure she would remain compliant. To her surprise, she didn't lose consciousness. Instead, her body stiffened into total paralysis, and she fell onto the rocky ground. She could still move her eyes and see what was happening, but she couldn't offer any resistance.

"This is ridiculous," Gabriel snarled. "She's a weaponless woman. We should be able to control her without drugs. How're we going to explain this to Bishop?"

"But not defenseless," Raphe observed. "She was almost free."

"Come on, Raphael. They're waiting," Gabriel barked brusquely, taking a position behind Laura's head.

He slipped his arms under her armpits and lifted her torso, while Raphe supported her legs. They carried her through the strange doorway, and the same green light scanned them all. It paused for several painful seconds, focusing a brighter flash of light on Laura before continuing on. It made her feel intensely nauseated. Laura feared she might throw up, risking worse humiliation. Unexpectedly, Gabriel gestured for Raphe to release her ankles, and he raised her into a standing position. Then he leaned her over, and her head fell forward. She felt her stomach start to relax.

"I remember my first time through security. It wasn't pleasant," Gabriel confessed, patting Laura's back.

She was grateful for his consideration.

The rock entrance banged closed behind the small group, activating several banks of fluorescent lights. Gabriel carried Laura back into the van, her feet dragging on the rocky incline that disappeared into the darkness ahead of them. With surprising gentleness, he strapped her into a backseat. Then he climbed into the front, and the vehicle roared to life.

The engine gears grated as the van rocked and rattled up the steep slope. After several sharp turns over rough terrain, they finally drove onto a relatively flat, straight thoroughfare. Laura wondered if they kept this access road arduous on purpose, to deter intruders. A driveway should have been worn down from repeated use. She had given up all hope of getting somewhere soon, when the van came to a stop.

Laura could feel the rock walls and subterranean ceiling weigh down on her. The stuffy air smelled as if it was being recycled. Laura waited to be carried out of the car, resigning herself to whatever fate they had planned for her. Gabriel came into her line of sight.

"We're going to take you to our superiors," he explained. "Please try to act civilized. If you keep fighting us, you'll be locked in a subterranean cell where you'll remain indefinitely. If you want answers, Laura, behave. Our directors aren't patient or understanding. They don't have time for defiant antics."

Laura yearned to show Gabriel just how defiant she could be. But she had waited a long time to find out why they wanted her.

"I'll behave." Laura was relieved to find she could speak. "But would you neutralize the paralytic? Lying here appears to be the extent of my free will." Laura wanted to sound sarcastic. Instead, her voice was only a hoarse whisper.

Gabriel nodded at Raphe, who drew a syringe out of a medical kit stowed under a seat and handed it to him. Deftly, he inserted the needle into her arm and injected the clear fluid. Laura didn't feel anything for several moments, but at last, an itchy tingling awakened her legs and arms. When her muscles began cramping, she groaned.

"What's going on?" she protested, rubbing her calves and shaking her legs to relax the contracting muscles.

"A side effect of the drug," Gabriel apologized. "Our discoveries frequently have some disagreeable side effect."

Laura tried to stand. A lingering weakness compromised her balance, and she shook slightly. Gabriel helped her out of the car, initially supporting most of her weight. As soon as she possibly could, Laura pulled away from him. She studied her surroundings hopefully. It was a waste of time. They were in a parking garage consisting of nothing but unrelenting gray concrete.

Once Raphe and the two other men had joined them, the small party headed for a vestibule accessing the elevators. The area was dingy, with stained walls and broken floor tiles. The extreme temperatures of this land would only accelerate this deterioration. The vestibule was painted army green, leaving Laura to wonder at the limited imagination of her group of captors.

Once she'd entered the surprisingly large elevator, however, all her concerns about the credentials of these people were swept away. The light, sweet fragrance of scented air and the plush, elegant condition of the spacious elevator impressed her. The moving room was an artistic combination of snow and glass. The walls held faceted mirrors painted with tiny winter scenes full of snow sculptures, snow-laden trees, and towns buried in snowdrifts. The white landscapes contrasted starkly against smoky gray skies. Laura was fascinated with the cozy cabins and regal castles until she noticed that all the scenes were devoid of life. She shivered again.

The elevator moved up several flights before stopping. The men took positions around her, assuming a military stance. Gabriel and Raphe were at her sides, and the unnamed guards stood behind her.

Laura had no idea what was coming, but the elevator's elegance had definitely shaped her expectations. The elevator doors slid back slowly, and the men ushered her forward. She had a clear view of an elegant hallway. Unconsciously, Laura patted her hair and smoothed down the thick wool coat buttoned to her chin. She shook her head at the unattractive garment and began unbuttoning the coat. Unfortunately, her clothes underneath were a wrinkled mess.

Gathering her remaining dignity, Laura stiffened her back and walked down the hall into an atrium, only to stop, awestruck. It was so beautiful, she took a long breath. She could identify grand leafy plants, glass ceilings, and enormous mirrors on silver walls. This world was an aggrandized version of the elevator. Everything sparkled with reflected light, distorting her perception.

Laura struggled to make sense of what was real and what was reflection. She decided to start with what she could easily isolate and looked up. The peaked glass ceiling revealed a panoramic view of a snow-covered mountain range. The snow looked so dark and old that it must have survived from ancient times.

Laura's eye followed the transparent roof joists to determine the dimensions of the atrium. It was long and rectangular. She focused her attention on the furthest wall, saw another room, and detected movement within. Before she could lose her sense of direction and nerve, she walked into this adjacent room, unhindered by Gabriel and his men. Falling further back, they followed her silently.

It turned out to be a beautifully furnished conference room. A large oval table of white marble framed in silver dominated the room, its long side facing the door. Tall, white leather chairs, guaranteeing an aristocrat's comfort, lined the far side. Five robed figures sat quietly in the center chairs, their features hidden in the great folds of their white cloaks. Laura guessed she should probably remain still and respectful, facing the figures. But her curiosity won out, and instead she turned slowly, absorbing every detail of this strange place.

The room was the same shape as the table—oval—with recessed, white marble pedestals lining the walls. The pedestals supported meticulously carved statues of fictional creatures. Secreted flickering lights created an illusion of life. Behind the pedestals were painted landscapes similar to those in the elevator. Laura began to approach one of these displays, lost in its intense beauty, when a cough from the table stopped her.

A voice, deep and relaxed, invited her closer. It came from the man seated in the largest chair. He had let his hood drop back, as had all the others, and his silver hair and brilliant gold eyes held her attention. She made no apology for staring. This man looked like a king, and his indulgent eyes silently beckoned her. Laura never knew how she came to stand across the table from him. She just stood there, waiting, as his masterful voice mesmerized her.

"I am the Grand Creator," he announced, his voice vibrating with a strange vitality, "and these are my archangels." He waved his hand, and Laura turned automatically to the door.

Gabriel, Raphe, and the two unnamed guards came forward at the man's pronouncement. One other man entered the room through a side door. All five positioned themselves on one of the six points of the star pattern on the floor. One position was conspicuously empty.

Gabriel left the group to stand beside Laura, and he took her arm possessively. The "Grand Creator" frowned. Laura sensed that Gabriel was creating an unwelcome disturbance.

"Where is Michael?" the Grand Creator demanded.

"Laura's protectors killed him," Gabriel explained. "They were resourceful opponents."

"There will be an accounting," promised the leader. He rose and came around the conference table to confront Gabriel directly. He stared at the young man with a hard scowl, until Gabriel released Laura. At his superior's gesture, he returned to his place on the floor design.

Laura followed the Grand Creator's next movements with only her eyes. The man studied her closely, circling her frozen form without touching her. She seemed to genuinely intrigue and puzzle him, which served only to confound her further.

# 22

## The Institute

Laura had no illusions about her value. She was just an orphan left to her own resources to carve out a life. But now she was in this incredible room, surrounded by mythic sculptures and being scrutinized by the "Grand Creator."

Laura wanted to snort at this bloated title. Really, one would think that someone who was head of an organization that could build a base into the side of a mountain would have a more realistic concept of himself. The vast universe should have suggested to any reasonable man that he could hardly call himself a Grand Creator. And if Michael and his men were archangels, then she was the Easter bunny and Stephan was Santa Claus. Laura was not the least bit fooled by this man's grand speech. If anything, it had made her lose some of her awe of him.

The four people who'd remained seated at the oval table had removed their cloaks. They were older men and women, with white hair and a worldly bearing. They appeared to be in no hurry to question Laura or to interfere with the man who acted as their leader. Still, their piercing eyes followed the chairman's every move.

One of the women seemed vaguely familiar, and Laura worked hard to remember where she had seen her before. It was absurd, of course. She knew she had never been in this cold wasteland, and from the woman's clothes, Laura doubted she had left this place in some years. Then Raphe crossed her line of sight, allowing her to see the two together. The resemblance was slight but there.

Seeking to distract the leader from his intrusive examination of her, Laura asked the questions that no one seemed willing to answer. "Who are you really?" she demanded, using bravado to mask her trepidation. "What could you possibly want from me?"

"I'm Adam Bishop, the director of the Institute." He waved his hand to encompass the entire complex around them.

"Not the Grand Creator?" Laura snipped. She tried to back away, only to find herself immobilized again. "Would you mind letting me go? Am I really such a dangerous threat?"

Instead of responding to her insolence, Bishop turned to Gabriel. "Are you holding her captive in the security force fields?" he demanded, sounding annoyed.

"If you knew how difficult it's been to get her here, you would have engaged all our security measures."

Laura smiled sweetly as Gabriel described her antics over the past weeks, including the journey here. She was surprised at the coordinated effort used to take her into custody. They really had bungled things. Bishop's benign expression revealed a tinge of irritation.

"I think you should stop trying to defend your actions," the leader suggested, his eyes twinkling at Laura. He obviously saw some humor in Gabriel's many efforts to contain her. "It makes us look incompetent. Just release her. If she can escape out of here, then we couldn't hold her for long anyway. Besides, you know we need her cooperation."

"Just where is 'here' anyway?" Laura asked hopefully.

"First, we should get you released. Gabe, will you handle this?" Even though Bishop phrased the last as a question, it was obviously an order. Gabriel exited the room, muttering under his breath.

As soon as Gabriel was gone, Raphe took his place beside Laura, wrapped an arm around her waist, and pulled her hard against him. She looked at him with such an expression of disgust that he released her abruptly. Unfortunately, he didn't take her rejection well.

Recklessly, Raphe knocked her away so hard that, with the simultaneous termination of the force field, it threw her against the table. She slumped to the floor, dazed. Laura had met self-destructive Shadow Dwellers since coming to Rainier, but Raphe and Michael had far exceeded the worst of them. What about her was making these men insane?

Adam Bishop seemed to have grown several inches. He grabbed Raphe by the front of his shirt and twisted it under his chin. Then he lifted the struggling man, leaving his feet writhing in space. Raphe's eyes bulged as he fought for air. He took hold of Bishop's wrists and pulled down desperately. But he might as well have been trying to stop a tree from growing. Bishop didn't even seem to realize that Raphe was fighting back. Laura feared that she was watching his execution. Then she heard a heartfelt cry.

The woman she had recognized earlier jumped up and raced to Raphe's rescue. Wildly, she kicked Bishop in the shin. Still, the director didn't react. Raphe was turning a distinctive shade of blue. His feet hung limp, and his bulging eyes glazed over. Bravely, the woman hoisted one of the smaller stone statues and brought it down hard on the director's arms. Now, he dropped Raphe, and the disgraced henchman collapsed into a motionless bundle. Frantically, the woman dragged him away from Bishop, who himself had staggered backward. Gabriel reentered the conference room at that moment and helped drag Raphe to a chair.

"If you'd succeeded in killing Raphe, I would've made it my purpose to bring you down," the woman snarled. "In fact, you'd better be careful with all the children or face the consequences."

Bishop shot a frown at Gabriel and then stared at Laura incredulously. Suddenly he burst out laughing. "By God, Gabe, you're right. Our little miss does seem to be a lightning rod for trouble. No wonder you had so many problems."

"I do have to give some of the credit to Michael," Gabriel complained. "When you told us that one of us would get her, he took it upon himself to make sure he was first in line. Now that he's gone, I can only imagine what my brothers will do. Their courting skills resemble the mating habits of a hormonal grizzly. Speaking of our little troublemaker…"

Gabriel realized that Laura was still lying on the floor, obviously hurt. He knelt beside her and moved his palm slowly above her body. She could feel warmth follow his hand.

"What happened?" he asked anxiously.

"Your brother's tender attentions," she replied dully. "They're as effective as your force fields."

"Not for long," Bishop promised.

A guard came in carrying a strange device, a long rod attached to a square box with knobs and levers. A glowing screen was affixed to the top of the box. Bishop moved the rod along Laura's limbs, just above her skin. Twice, he snorted, and Laura guessed he had found some injury. Then Bishop twisted a knob, and the rod began to glow. He placed it on her skin at the two places he had indicated, her left wrist and right shoulder. The action was not without discomfort, and Laura couldn't suppress inhalations of pain.

"This knits the bone," Gabriel explained. "But you must move carefully for a little while."

"But I thought you would…?" Laura began, eyeing Gabriel. She had felt the warmth generated by his hand and sensed its healing properties.

Gabriel jerked his head slightly, and Laura instantly cut off her question. Unaware of the exchange, Bishop carried the device back to a guard, who took it out of the room. Laura tried to stand and found that her pain had almost completely subsided. She was relieved. Being helpless in this fortress was her worst fear. Her second worst fear happened next.

Gabriel took her arm in the same manner as before. "I'm ready to proceed," he said cryptically.

Laura was done playing nice. She threw off Gabriel's arm.

"I'm not!" she cried. "What the hell is going on?" Laura stared pointedly at Bishop. "Now really, you must know I'm not going to mate with whomever you happen to choose. I suppose you could rape me. But you mentioned *wanting* my cooperation?"

"Gabriel, you're wrong about our intentions concerning Laura," Bishop explained vehemently. "We're not a breeding farm looking for new stock. Really, between you, Raphe, and Michael, I can only imagine what Laura must think of us. Now bring her over here to the full-length mirror. It's time to enlighten our guest."

Bishop stood behind the two young people reflected perfectly side by side in the mirror. Their kinship was stark and unmistakable. The both had the same green-gold eyes, the same high cheekbones, and the same defined chins. Even their builds were similar. Laura had been trying for so long to distance herself from these dangerous strangers that she had missed what now seemed painfully obvious. Then Bishop released his bombshell.

"You're an archangel, Laura. You belong with us. You're home at last," Bishop proclaimed. "A female archangel is new to us. That's why these men chase you relentlessly. To be able to bond with one of their own kind was, before now, impossible."

"No!" she exclaimed, stepping back. Laura felt the blood drain from her face. Her eyes darted to the young men still standing in the star formation. They looked as happy as children on Christmas morning. She shook her head numbly. "I don't belong here."

But even as Laura tried to reject Bishop's revelations, she saw her familiar features echoed in Gabriel and the other men. They could be her brothers. Laura's mind raced for some alternative explanation. She had wanted so much to embrace the benefits of family, but these people had treated her so badly that now she couldn't stomach the obvious.

"You use words that mean nothing to me. What are archangels? What is a grand creator? What is this place? Whether I'm one of your kind or not, I have no intention of becoming trapped here."

"Calm yourself," Bishop urged. "Damn! I should've retrieved you myself. Gabe is usually so convincing that I thought he would easily persuade you to come here. I should've guessed that you might be immune to his special charms. I promise you'll get a full explanation. But first, a guided tour?"

Without waiting for her agreement, Bishop steered Laura back to the brilliant atrium, ignoring the small troop of directors and archangels who followed behind. Laura felt unaccountably happy when Raphe's female protector joined the group. Bishop walked through a doorway blocked with small mirrors hung on cord. Laura wondered at this strange entry hanging repeated so frequently. It seemed to confuse more than add artistic beauty.

There was a distinct change in the style of the rooms beyond the disorienting mirrors. The otherworldly fairytale aura vanished, and here were ordinary counters and desks. For the moment, the area was unoccupied, but it was obvious that there were tasks waiting to be completed. She could see a letter in process on a computer. A cup of coffee still steamed on a nearby desk, and the lights on the phone system flashed impatiently. However, there were also touches of a grand elegance and affluence. Laura spied sumptuous tapestries and riveting masterpieces on the walls. The floor had an Escher-style geometric pattern of black-and-white tiles that mesmerized as well as amused. She couldn't help but wonder, *Where are all the people?*

Bishop led her quickly through the offices. Even so, Laura came to three conclusions from her brief glimpses of the Institute so far. First, this organization was multinational; there were European, Asian, and American decorations and furniture. Second, great attention was paid to the arts. In fact, some of the talent displayed so casually should have been hanging in the world's great museums. Third, this institute must be old. Whatever had carved out this mountain had done so in the past, using forgotten technology. A large and time-consuming excavation, even in this remote place, would attract someone's attention today, in a world of easily obtained and accessed information. There was also something a bit dated about the costumes the Grand Creator and the other elders were wearing, which suggested they belonged to a time gone by. Bishop looked like an old English lord, and his companions could have easily blended into a French court. By necessity, the archangels didn't share in this dated wardrobe. They wore current clothes that would allow them to blend in to today's society unnoticed.

Bishop finally stopped at the top of a magnificent marble staircase, which rivaled those that graced the great houses of Europe. Down each side, polished Doric columns framed elaborate doorways. Each oversized door featured imposing marble moldings and wrought-gold handles in the shape of lion's heads. Laura wondered what secrets might lie behind each door.

A weak yellow light that didn't originate from any visible source illuminated the staircase. Still believing they must be inside a mountain, Laura tried to identify walls. Much to her dismay, she could not. A thick fog obscured everything beyond an area around the marble stairs. Vague worms of light flashed and wiggled in the shrouded distance. Occasionally, she could smell sulfur concentrated in pungent gusts. Laura felt a chill run down her back. What was this place?

"This is the heart of the Institute. Behind each door is a branch of our organization. Pick one," Bishop offered generously.

Laura pointed to the closest door on the left, and Bishop gestured for her to proceed. Once they stepped onto the top stair, it began to descend like an escalator. They both hopped off at the appropriate moment and walked to the designated door. At Bishop's encouragement, Laura extended a tentative hand to grasp the handle, swallowing heavily. She could feel her heart beating fast. Laura pushed hard against the door, expecting to have to exert excessive force. Instead, the massive slab swung open easily.

"A special mechanism," Bishop explained. "These doors open at the slightest touch. At least they're supposed to, but not all cooperate," he added, winking in an exaggerated fashion.

Through the doorway, Laura saw a radiating light and smelled the sweet scent of flowers. Eagerly, she walked into a delightful terraced garden. The roof was open, exposing the greenery to the chilly, bright sun. She could see a recessed transparent ceiling panel that could be extended when the weather turned bad.

Laura followed the dirt path to a decorative maze of white pebbles at the center of the terraces. She paused for a second to study the maze and realized how each turn in her life had ultimately led her here, to this astonishing place. The garden stretched around her, massive and magnificent, and an invigorating breeze cooled her hot face. She could see beds of large flowers interspersed among other vegetation. Supersized fruits and vegetables were everywhere, and old-growth cedars bordered the garden.

Here at last, Laura saw other people. Several women were collecting the riper produce in large wicker baskets. Laura longed to ask them questions, as she was still suspicious of Bishop. But they didn't acknowledge her presence and soon carried the overflowing containers away.

It was in this garden that the atmosphere of formality constraining the group of trailing elders finally faded. They were smiling, and their chatter cheered Laura. A painfully thin woman with frizzy gray hair and gnarled features appeared on their path and greeted the director effusively. Seeing Laura, she took the role of teacher, one she obviously enjoyed.

"I am Rachel, greenskeeper of the arboretum. Welcome." The woman waved at the many terraces. "This garden is one of our most prized achievements. I didn't know one could grow such oversized produce in these adverse conditions. The food from these terraces allows us to remain predominately self-sufficient, and the concentrated oxygen produced in scattered domed gardens can be used to clean the air in the lower levels."

The agile old woman pulled Laura to one of the terraces and scooped out a handful of thick, dark soil. "This, along with the midnight light and cosmic radiance, allows accelerated growth and produces those." She pointed at a basket of strawberries the size of oranges that lay unattended at the end of the row. "The flowers are my addition, even if they have no utility beyond their sweet fragrance and lovely blossoms."

At this, Laura sniffed the air, appreciating the multitude of scents. Rachel waved at one of the female harvesters, beckoning her over. The woman approached and at Rachel's direction brought the basket of strawberries along. The greenskeeper handed one to Laura, her eyes silently urging her to taste it. Laura took a small piece into her mouth. At the first bite, her mouth was flooded with a sweet juice. She continued chewing with relish.

While she ate the delicious strawberry, Rachel guided her through several terraces, stopping every few minutes to identify specific plants. Periodically, sprinklers watered the vegetation, creating puddles in the rich soil. Finally, they stood before a plant as large as a primordial tree, with corrugated white leaves and copious blossoms. Rachel picked one of the vibrant flowers and handed it to Laura as a final gesture of friendship. Laura threaded it into the top buttonhole of her coarse coat, adding a touch of beauty to the ugly garment.

Rachel led her back to the maze where Bishop was waiting. He escorted her back by way of a narrow dirt path, through a side door hidden behind a cluster of evergreen bushes, and into a new section of the Institute.

Laura grinned happily when she saw the endless rows of books. Every wall was covered with shelves, and beside the bookcases were ladders, small tables, and groups of chairs. Most of the books looked like serious texts, but there were sections containing children's books, picture books, and novels identified by their bright, busy covers.

It was here, in this library, that Laura made another startling discovery. She could hardly credit that children would live in this remote compound, but there were small groups of kids everywhere. One class was obviously completing schoolwork, while another group of younger children sat in a section full of colorful furniture and children's toys. The teacher left this group under the watchful eye of an older child and approached Bishop. She pulled him to one side, leaving Laura to explore a tall bookshelf.

Somehow, the presence of children relaxed Laura's guard. Carelessly, she reached up to take a book that looked interesting, and the entire shelf dropped so she could retrieve it easily. She jumped back, giggling at her startled reaction, and was soon testing this feature with enthusiastic gusto. When she held her hand close to the bookcase, the shelves slowly rotated. She waited, motionless, until the entire contents of that wall of books had slid by.

Laura was distracted from her experiment when the whispered conversation between Bishop and the young teacher became loud and angry. A second woman, with steel-gray hair, hustled over to Bishop and shushed the two quarreling people.

"Really, Emma, we have a guest," she scolded in a loud whisper. "You must exercise some self-control. What I have to endure! Do children ever grow up?" she lamented, in a voice loud enough for all to hear.

Bishop smiled indulgently. He was obviously fond of the older woman.

"But, Gwen, the children! Why does he bring a stranger among the children?" Emma challenged.

"Yes, yes, yes," Gwen agreed soothingly. "But she is only one woman. You can't really consider her a threat?"

"I suppose one person is permissible," the young woman admitted reluctantly. "But the others will have to leave. I'll not spoil what little time the students have here. You know how important library time is and how rare."

Laura had been so absorbed, she had forgotten about the small troop of silent followers.

Emma stared pointedly at the group of elders with one hand on her hip, creating a formidable barrier with her round frame and stern expression. She wore a ruffled smock covered in swimming turtles and playing bunnies. It was hard to imagine a more perfect outfit for children. Laura smiled, in spite of her precarious position.

Gwen turned a questioning look toward Bishop, and he waved the rest of the group back through the door. Soon, only Bishop and Laura remained. Emma nodded, satisfied. She took Laura's hand and pulled her deeper into the library.

In the central lobby, an administrative counter offered stacks of library maps, and several computer directories beeped invitingly. Painted on the floor were footsteps in various colors. On a hanging bulletin board behind the counter was a color-coded legend. Yellow stood for philosophy and mathematics, green for biology and botany, blue for climate and astronomy, purple for fiction, and so on. The colored footprints fanned out from the center counter like spikes on a bicycle wheel. They led through arched entryways, painted the same color as their footsteps, to hallways of books. While the instructions seemed designed for children, the stacks of books would rival a university's in terms of quantity and diversity.

Abruptly, a younger child left her group and approached Laura. Her eyes were large and luminous, filled with an unrestrained curiosity. She tugged on Laura's clothes earnestly.

"Ariel, please, you must wait to be introduced to guests," Emma gently admonished the small girl.

But Laura was so charmed by the courageous child that she offered her Rachel's flower before she could run off. Ariel's face glowed with delight, and her mouth opened into a wide O. She reached out tentatively for the fragrant, oversized bloom.

"Is this for me?" she asked, her eyes shining with incredulity.

"It matches your lovely eyes," Laura praised. Delicate accents on each petal mirrored the violet of the girl's eyes. "It really is perfect for you. Please take it."

Little Ariel needed no further encouragement. She plucked the flower out of Laura's hand and skipped away, her blond curls bouncing gaily down her back. The child wasn't giving the other adults any chance to return her treasure. Laura chuckled at the child's pleasure at something so simple.

Bishop guided her away from the now staring children, with their inquisitive saucer eyes, into a separate section of the library. It was filled with stacks of binders. She could make out several titles, including "Stem Cell Replication," "Recovery of Extinct Species," "Internet Creation and Applications," "Artificial Intelligence," "Cloning Organs," "Modifying Genetic Markers," and "RNA Vaccines." Each stack was at least twenty binders high. Laura marveled at the number of projects.

Bishop stopped beside a table set with tea and finger foods. Laura had no idea how long it had been since her last real meal. Gabriel had kept her drugged during the entire trip there. Her stomach growled at the sight of the food. With a nod, Bishop invited her to eat. Laura reached for the teapot and poured the amber fluid into two gracefully shaped cups. She filled a matching saucer with appetizing treats before settling into one of the cushioned caster chairs. Emma and Gwen waited quietly until Bishop nodded, and then they left.

"Now, it's time to tell you about our institute, and why you were brought here so unceremoniously," Bishop began as he sat down in one of the chairs, took the other cup of tea, and leaned back. "This library contains not only an impressive selection of books from the world's great libraries, but also summaries of all our studies and inventions and documentation of new scientific principles. You see, Laura, the Institute is dedicated to researching science's outer limits. What the outside world might call magic. There are no preconceptions or superstitions here. We answer to no government, so we are not limited by politics or religion.

"When an outside scientist gets close to one of our discoveries, Gabriel and the others bring them enough additional information to make the breakthrough. The insights we share might be seen as divinely inspired. We have been responsible for some of the technological breakthroughs of recent decades. Nanotechnology and advancements in global networking are but a few.

"I know my speech, when we first met, was a bit melodramatic. But in all particulars, it is essentially true. Archangels are messengers of praiseworthy intelligence, and Gabriel and his brothers carry pivotal information to the outside world. While I'm not the only scientist working here, I'm what you might call a Grand Creator ranter than the Grand Creator. Sometimes the myth is enough to impress and convince our new recruits. You, unfortunately, are not the usual recruit.

"We enter the public arena and offer our inventions personally, only when we need additional funding from sympathetic private foundations and/or hope to lure some talented scientist to join our organization. It is hard to refuse an institution that offers superior technical instrumentation and texts containing unprecedented scientific breakthroughs. Once we've opened the door on what we are hiding here, no scientist has yet refused our generous offer. So our advancements have proceeded unhindered. But there is more than science here. Come."

Without waiting for Laura to finish her tea, Bishop ushered her through another side door hidden behind an elaborate tapestry. The door opened onto a stairway hewed out of solid rock. After turning on a dim system of lights, Bishop darted down the irregular steps, forcing Laura to use all her agility to navigate the steep, murky descent. Sharp rocks protruding from the crudely carved walls scratched her exposed skin, and now, she recognized at least one value to her thick, ugly clothes.

Shortly, Bishop exited through an identical side door, and Laura found herself in a brightly lit room. She hesitated, letting her vision adjust to the change in illumination. After several seconds, she was able to take in the unexpected scene. There were several glass windows, but they didn't give views to the outside world. Instead, they allowed a flood of light to illuminate a series of rooms.

In the room where they stood, Laura saw easels holding partially finished pictures. The styles were too varied to belong to a single artist. Through the door on her left, she could see a grand piano and bass cello surrounded by an array of miscellaneous instruments. To her right, through another doorway, were pillars of unformed clay six feet tall.

Laura nodded silently. It made sense that artistic tendencies in all the residents would be encouraged. Creative talent honed in art classes might translate into inspired suggestions for new scientific principles and applications. The only remaining avenue to progress would be a church. Faith, or the belief in things unseen, could assist in making leaps of logic into unproven arenas. But no, Laura suspected that Bishop frowned on organized religion. A lack of faith could explain why the Shadow Dwellers had continued to surprise Gabriel. He didn't believe in the unproven.

Bishop gave Laura a little time to admire the uncompleted artwork before ushering her through the elaborate door that accessed the main marble staircase. The view of the grand staircase, the preternatural fog, and the glowing worms reminded Laura of how little she still understood about the Institute. Bishop led her directly across the large marble steps to another door that accessed a sophisticated laboratory complex. There were steel counters, rows of shelving, computers, imposing scanning equipment, and complex instruments everywhere. Huge, hanging computer screens displayed enlarged graphs and tables of test results so that even the smallest deviations could be noticed. Several white-coated technicians were working at computer terminals.

Adam Bishop had his own agenda, and he gave her only enough time in each department to awaken her interest. Then he returned to the central staircase. They were three floors down from the arboretum. He waved at the continuing pattern of doorways below them. He had shown her the arboretum on the top floor, the library on the first floor, the studios on the second, and the laboratories on the third floor down, and still there were many more doors. Each one held a secret purpose.

"Below us on the fourth floor is a computer complex that would make a hacker drool," Bishop boasted. "There are family quarters on the fifth and sixth floors. Our genetic experiments have produced highly intelligent children, and our scientific recruitment has provided superior genetic material."

Despite Bishop's grandiose tour, Laura listened to him warily. Playing with genetic experimentation, which easily produced ideas of racial superiority, always led to trouble. A dark storm was brewing.

# 23

## The Truth about Laura

"But you must be wondering why we want you specifically," Bishop speculated. "The Institute has assigned its best scientists to exploring human genetic mutation. We've tried to stimulate human evolution by, specifically, accelerating the development of the brain. The brain is the one organ that gives us our unique status in Earth's hierarchy. Gabriel and his brothers are one result.

"Gabriel has unique talents to which you have demonstrated a frustrating immunity. He can influence a person's priorities and steer their actions while appearing unconcerned. He just plants ideas, and people mistakenly accept these new ideas as their own. One telltale sign of his unique mutation is the outward appearance he shares with his brothers. As we have told you, you have the same mutation. Gabriel spotted you quite by accident during one of your college musical productions. The light streaks in your hair, the gold specks in your eyes, and the lightness that can appear in your skin are quite distinctive. Gabriel is the result of generations of experimentation, which we believed were not available naturally. Yet here you are and a female besides. We knew you belonged here, in our special school, under our guiding hand."

"I'm not a scientist," Laura protested. "I have no use for your high-tech academy." She knew it was hogwash to imagine that she might contribute anything to this oppressive, albeit high-minded, institution.

"You are not the *tester*," Bishop clarified, smiling darkly. "You are the *testee*."

"When hell freezes over," Laura shot back valiantly. The storm had arrived, and she was its number-one casualty. "I have no intention of becoming one of your experiments. You can't honestly believe I would give up my life to live in isolation here?" Laura felt her stomach twist with growing panic. It occurred to her that Bishop didn't much care about what she wanted or hoped to accomplish.

Before Bishop could confirm or disprove her estimation of his character, they heard a commotion from the top of the staircase. Laura looked up to find Gabriel and his four brothers taking offensive positions. Eagerly, Raphe jumped down three flights to a position close to her. Gabriel caught Raphe's expression and automatically came directly to Laura's side.

A new voice boomed out. "I don't think they require your cooperation. Once you were brought here, you were never going to be allowed to leave."

Laura recognized that voice. By some impossible miracle, Stephan had found her there, in that frozen wasteland at the end of the world.

Bishop, Gabriel, and the other men spun, looking for the man behind the voice. But there was no one to fight. The voice came out of nowhere.

"The problem with your plan," the floating voice snarled, "is that no matter how many secrets you unravel with your science, there will always be new ones to thwart you. The Shadow Dwellers are one puzzle that you haven't solved, and our hidden powers will be the way we ultimately defeat you. Today, I have come to claim the woman who has earned my protection."

A dense silver vapor billowed with a deliberateness that was unmistakable. It hovered over Bishop and then his men before moving to a clear space, separating into six clouds, and coalescing into human figures.

Stephan and Alexis materialized, along with four big men dressed in mail armor on the art studio second floor.

"You've come! But how did you find me?" Laura gasped.

She felt a wave of hope and laughed despite Bishop's and Gabriel's close proximity. Bishop couldn't hope to win against Shadow Dwellers, could he?

"I think it was a mixture of ingenuity and a lot of help from your friends." Stephan gazed at Laura with obvious relief. "Lord has the nose of a bloodhound and a computer system to rival a small government. He found the travel manifests for Gabriel and his noticeable force's return here."

"Lord is here?" Laura asked happily, clapping her hands. Abruptly, she covered her mouth to stifle her glee, afraid it might incite Bishop or Gabriel. "Then Monk must be here too," she blurted irrepressibly.

"I couldn't have stopped that charging bull."

"But how did you discover this stronghold? It's completely camouflaged."

"As soon as we got close, my new powers kicked in and led me here. It seems that since you are my anchor, I have a sense of where you are when you are in the vicinity. We left a big hole in the outside cliff though, and the others are still storming the citadel."

"Citadel?" Laura repeated, raising an eyebrow.

"Well, in a manner of speaking. His guards are not going quietly." Stephan looked directly at Bishop, smiling smugly. "But I trust that Monk and the others will prevail. They gave us an opening so we could come find you."

Laura tried to rush to Stephan but felt the restraining arm of Gabriel. Unfortunately, she had distracted her rescue team long enough for Bishop to take action. He had darted down one floor and was examining one of the columns on that level. He opened a panel and twisted two dials.

The eerie light in the staircase began to change. Before it had been diffuse and yellow, with electrical flashes and chemical odors. Now the air thickened, and the wiggling lights became brighter and more energetic.

"Shadow Dwellers are not a secret to us." Bishop smirked as he scanned Stephan's group derisively. "Nor is your kind beyond our understanding. This is a perfect opportunity to investigate what your limits truly are. Shall we begin?"

"Stephan! Alexis!" Laura shrieked, fearing the enormity of what her friends might be facing. "Get out! You don't know what these people are capable of!" But they only looked confused.

Desperately, Laura yanked free of Gabriel and ran up one floor to Stephan. But it was already too late. The air around the stairway had grown so thick that she could barely breathe, and she started coughing uncontrollably. Bishop retrieved a mask and rod from the hidden compartment. He pulled on the mask and then lifted the rod into the air. The end of it discharged a flash of electricity that drew the wiggling sparks closer. Then he pointed it at the four Shadow Dweller guards. The lengths of wiggling energy moved with clear purpose. Laura watched as the mythical Ancients, probably the Centurions Stephan had mentioned earlier, struggled against a force that held them powerless. Bishop discharged the rod again, attracting two more cords of electricity, and captured Alexis and Stephan with equal ease.

Abruptly, Alexis returned to her vaporous state. But her actions caused the wiggling energy to transform into crackling sparks that electrified and twisted her mist form. She cried out in pain and transformed back into a solid state. At her cry, the Centurions renewed their efforts to escape with greater urgency.

"What is happening?" Alexis moaned in the soft, vulnerable voice of a child. "Stephan, what is this weapon?"

"It's an electrical field created and controlled by us," Raphe sneered. "If you don't struggle, you might survive." For several minutes, Bishop and Raphe smiled at her friends' futile attempts to escape.

To Laura's chagrin, they didn't use their abnormal weapon on her. Instead, Gabriel pulled her away from Stephan and bound her wrists in an ordinary plastic restraint.

Two elder scientists came out of the laboratory and climbed up to Stephan and Alexis. With a disturbing lack of empathy, they didn't hesitate to poke and prod him. One of the younger lab techs brought a tray of unfamiliar devices and met Bishop beside Alexis. The Grand Creator retrieved two steel shackles, which he snapped around Alexis's neck and waist. Laura could only guess that they were some type of monitoring device. Her rescue party was up to their necks in trouble.

"Take her to lab room 4," Bishop instructed malevolently.

Two brawny technicians carried the child vampire down to the massive door that led into the lab complex. To her credit, Alexis continued to struggle, ignoring the electrical sparks coming from the shackles. Laura guessed that the voltage must be intensifying when Alexis paused, breathing heavily for several seconds, before renewing her resistance. Distraught, she watched the beautiful young woman who had visited her in her dreams disappear.

"Do you really think we didn't know about your pathetic species?" Bishop resumed his taunting jabs. "The only ones who think you're still a secret race are you. We'd hoped to acquire a specimen for study, and you bring several right to our doorstep. I have several pet theories about child vampires. But capturing one had never seemed possible."

"Do you think we'd ever let your filthy race keep our precious Laura?" Raphe snarled hotly. "She's of our blood. You only pollute your victims with your disease, and she's too pure to be contaminated, as you well know."

"You don't know what you're talking about," Stephan snarled. "I'd never try to convert Laura against her will." Even chained and defenseless, he proclaimed his principles proudly.

"I'll take great pleasure in disposing of you when Bishop is finished," Raphe promised. Judging from his smile, it wouldn't be pleasant.

"And guarantee Laura's contempt for all of you." Stephan shot a triumphant glance at Raphe, Gabriel, and Bishop, even as he continued to struggle against his restraints. Laura couldn't decide if he was being brave or suicidal.

"Sooner or later, you'll make a mistake. Sooner or later, Monk and Celeste will come for us. You're just too stupid to realize you've already lost." Stephan's face froze into the death stare that the Shadow Dwellers had crafted into an art form.

Gabriel rocked uneasily.

Bishop took a solid steel baton from the young technician's tray and swung it against Stephan's mouth. The sound of breaking teeth was chilling. Stephan grinned broadly, letting blood overflow his mouth and drip from his chin. He made the perfect vampire poster boy.

Gabriel dragged the protesting Laura away from this grim tableau, down three floors to one of the elaborate doors. She struggled obstinately. Since her hands were bound, she butted his face with her forehead, ignoring the pain. The thought of leaving Stephan to Bishop's mercy without any witnesses was unbearable. But Gabriel only grunted at her efforts, demonstrating the same stoic character as Monk. Laura heard disturbing sounds coming from Stephan, as Gabriel hoisted her over his shoulder and walked through the door. She groaned in defeat when it clicked shut behind them.

Gabriel carried her down a long, dark corridor and through another door, where he dumped her unceremoniously onto a conveniently placed wooden bench. He inhaled slowly and scanned the landscape.

Laura sprang up into a sitting position, looking for some way to escape. They were in a completely artificial environment. The Institute had replicated a huge meadow, with a waterfall, a river, and a lake. There were cement walkways and beautiful landscaped gardens, obviously maintained from plants in the arboretum. The waterfall roared in the distance, and wind gusted from the displaced air. Even the sun, on a much smaller scale, had been simulated, creating minimal warmth.

Gabriel looked back at the closed door nervously, abruptly plucked her off the bench, and loped toward a group of low buildings. He chose a small utility room in the second large building for concealment, shoved her inside, and locked the door behind them. Laura could hear her heart hammering and Gabriel's ragged breathing as he pushed her to her knees in the dark room. Then holding her still, he set his ear against the crack of the door. Exhaling in exasperation, he unlocked the door and peeked out the crack. Immediately, he jerked it closed again.

"Where are you, Brother?" Raphe's voice echoed in a manner that could only be produced by some type of bullhorn. "You can't possibly think I'll let you keep my prize. I won't finish second. Come out, come out, wherever you are. My spies will find you soon enough, you thief."

Laura shuddered at the thought of Gabriel turning her over to his slimy brother. She could still feel Raphe's cold hands and see his cruel eyes. She would do whatever was necessary to get away from Raphe, even if it meant making an uneasy alliance with Gabriel.

She tugged on Gabriel's shirt and nodded at a flight of stairs just visible through a small window. The window was large enough for her to escape, but it would be a miracle if Gabriel could fit through.

"Look, I want to escape Raphe as bad as you want to keep me away from him. Let's make a truce, at least until we're out of here. OK?" Laura held out her hand in the familiar gesture of a handshake. She knew they needed to work together if they hoped to avoid an organized search.

"Seems like the best plan," Gabriel admitted grudgingly. "He has a small army looking through the nearby buildings. It would help if we could put some distance between us and them."

He took a few precious moments to cut off her wrist restraints. Then he silently opened the window. Laura squirmed awkwardly through the hole and fell to the ground in a clumsy pile of arms and legs. Gabriel, on the other hand, used a deliberate order of contortions to wiggle through the small opening with room to spare. He began hopping up the stairs, two at a time, forcing Laura to run after him. They used the buildings as cover, slipping through several without any outcry. She was running out of breath, choking on the disturbed dust of the rarely used passageways. But Laura was too afraid to complain.

When at last Gabriel had to slow and catch his own breath, she immediately slumped down on the ground. They had run through all the connected apartment houses and were standing in a small park next to the thundering waterfall. The roar made Laura feel exposed to pursuers she couldn't hear.

She pantomimed one question: "Where now?"

Gabriel propelled her down a hill, using a branch to restore the disturbed grass behind them and wiping away all traces of their footsteps. Then he guided her through a high thicket of dense, thorny bushes. Raphe would have a real chore finding them here. For a brief moment, Gabriel disappeared into the bushes ahead, giving Laura a unique opportunity to escape. But the possibility of running back into the arms of Bishop and Raphe stopped her short.

Quickly, Laura followed Gabriel, squeezing behind the bushes and hugging a rock cliff. They emerged onto an alpine meadow. Here the Institute's iron fist had relaxed, and a natural starkness overcame the arboretum's lush influence. The trees and bushes on this alpine hillside were stunted, and sturdy yellow grass covered the meadow. Warm summers were in short supply here. The greater cold penetrated her clothing, chilling her hands and face.

A short distance away, thin trees framed a small log cabin. Gabriel escorted her into this small building. "We'll be safe here. There's a warning system if anyone approaches." Gabriel pointed to the one bit of technology in the rustic cabin, a red light above the entrance. "Since the Institute is always on the lookout for curious intruders, we've installed a system of sensors that cover this retreat and the surrounding area. It'll blink if anyone approaches."

The stark cabin was pristine, with only minimal amenities. Laura could see a makeshift kitchen area with a narrow window, a framed sink (thank God for plumbing), and handmade shelves. A small table and matchstick chairs completed the eating area. She was comforted by the wood stove and a large stone fireplace with a cast-iron hook. Through an open door, she could see an old iron bed and faded comforter.

A canvas curtain covered the second larger window in the cabin. Under it sat a secondhand couch and a coffee table buried under old newspapers. Gabriel indicated that she might sit on the couch.

The newspapers were from Thule, Greenland, confirming Laura's worst fears. They had trapped her in a place so remote she had no chance of getting home on her own. Feeling miserable, she slumped back against the couch.

Gabriel bent over the fireplace, and she heard the squeak of a flue being opened. He retrieved four heavy logs from the wood hopper built into the left side of the black rock hearth. Next to the hopper was a box containing kindling and paper. He laid several thin pieces of wood over the newspaper in a layered pattern that would allow air circulation, and lit the crumpled paper in several places. When the kindling was crackling, he piled on the four large pieces of wood. Then he rose, went to the kitchen area, and filled a black kettle with water. He laid out two jumbo cups and put a tea bag and a spoonful of sugar in each.

Laura watched Gabriel with growing agitation. It looked like he was planning to stay for a while. "Aren't you afraid the smoke will reveal our presence?" she blurted nervously.

"Good point." Gabriel returned to the fire and turned several knobs. "This will take care of that," he promised. A fan began to blow softly. "The smoke is being diverted through a water filter. There will be no trace of it above ground."

"We have to go back," she pleaded. Visions of Bishop hurting Stephan in terrible ways crowded into her mind. Imagination could be a terrible thing.

Gabriel placed the kettle of water on the fireplace hook. The fire was crackling energetically, warming the chilly room.

"Of course," he agreed, obviously trying to placate her. "First, let's have some tea. It'll help calm you."

Laura shook her foot nervously, biding her time. What could she do, really? Unless she was prepared to attack him and run into the arms of Raphe, she would have to wait for an opportunity to help her friends.

When the water over the fire was bubbling, Gabriel poured the hot liquid into the two cups and set one in front of her on the coffee table. He seated himself beside her on the couch and stirred his tea. She took

several sips under his expectant gaze. The peppermint tea was refreshing, and it did soothe her frantic thoughts.

"The only way you can help your friends is to gain the support of
some of the other directors," Gabriel explained. "Bishop may seem like
the unchallenged leader, but there are many who would relish unseat-
ing him. He doesn't play well with others." Gabriel leaned forward and
gently swept Laura's hair out of her face. She didn't like his familiarity.

"Why are you willing to help me and my friends escape?" Laura exclaimed. "Since you dragged me here, you've been trying to stake a claim
on me."

"You're right on only one point. I do want you here. In Rainier, your
attention was glued to your Shadow Dweller lover."

"He's not my lover!" she cried.

"We are a special breed, you and I," he continued as if she hadn't
spoken. "I had to get you here with your own kind. But I don't agree with
Bishop." Gabriel's face twisted with disgust. "His methods are barbaric.
He has no right to experiment on people, and I'm not the only one who
thinks this. There is a small group of us who want to get out of here. So,
I put on a show for him until I could get you here."

Laura rose nervously from the couch to sit on a rickety rocking
chair. "What is the Institute really?" she asked. She went on to briefly
summarize Bishop's grandiose description.

"What Bishop told you is fundamentally correct," Gabriel conceded.
He leaned back on the couch, crossed his legs, and sipped deeply from
the cup.

Laura squirmed with barely contained impatience. She forced herself to stop rocking compulsively and took another gulp of tea.

"The Institute is a place to research scientific marvels outside of po-
litical and religious restrictions. I'm one of its greatest achievements,"
he proclaimed, his voice hard and resentful. "As a child, I was studied
relentlessly. My only freedom was to go to school. You see, they wanted
to know the full extent of my genetic oddities. I was never allowed a
childhood or family or friends."

At Gabriel's description of the life that Bishop planned for her, Laura's rocking resumed. "What about your mother?" she asked.

"At the Institute, children belong to the community, not to their parents, and I was their great success. My mother was forced to give me to Bishop early on." Gabriel's eyes stirred with a brutal anger. Abruptly, he slammed his empty cup on the coffee table and sprang up. His easygoing facade was gone.

"They managed to mutate my DNA enough to produce interesting changes. I have a fifth lobe in my brain, which they're still studying. It grants me the ability to convince people to go along with my suggestions. My blood has a higher-than-average concentration of oxygen, so I'm a natural athlete and quick scholar. But the tests are endless. You were right to refuse Bishop. Without fighting him, you would never again be allowed to make decisions about your life."

"But he has you and the others," Laura insisted.

"Yes, and he's experimented on us all. But you're a wild card, too interesting to ignore." Then Gabriel laughed. "It's funny, really. He thinks you're a natural mutation, but he's wrong. You come from here. Your mother faked your death, but many remember that she left shortly after that."

"Did she come back?" Laura asked. When he didn't answer, she looked up and saw the red light over the door flashing urgently.

# 24

## Megatron Scanner

Despite the danger, Stephan was glad they were carrying him to the door where Alexis had disappeared. Bishop's keen interest in Alexis alarmed him. He feared what the madman might do to a child Shadow Dweller. What could he hope to learn that was unique to Alexis?

He groaned when the two guards juggled his weight for a better grip. The strange trance of deep healing was just beginning to cloud his mind. Before disappearing, Bishop had deliberately inflicted savage injuries on Stephan just to test the prowess of his people's legendary healing. But the brutish leader had only scowled at the results.

With Bishop gone, only two guards and Alexis's Centurions remained. If only Stephan could find a way to deactivate the restraints, he could easily escape. But they wouldn't budge.

The guards carried him into a high-tech laboratory. Alexis was already there, strapped down on a table. His mind was beginning to clear, which meant that his injuries must be healed. With the callousness he had come to expect, they flung him onto the nearest table and strapped him down, even though the circular shackles kept him immobile.

Stephan cursed silently at his foolishness in coming there with all the strategic planning of a charging bull. If only he had taken more precautions and brought more soldiers. The tremendous energy harnessed by the Centurions and his anxiety for Laura had blinded him.

"What are the results of the blood scan?" came Bishop's cold, calculating bark. The devil had returned. "We must identify any unique blood factors."

"We've been unable to isolate unfamiliar particles," a timid voice answered after an uncomfortable silence. Stephan heard a heavy thud before Bishop spoke again.

"Out of my way! It's so simple! Just centrifuge the blood, and the parts separate easily."

Bishop's mocking contempt was becoming louder. Stephan heard several slams before the sound of a spinning device dominated the room. He could smell panic from the sweating lab techs. A few excruciating minutes passed with no one speaking. Then the spinning stopped, and finally, frustrated curses broke the silence.

"What the hell! Where are they?" Bishop had dropped his benevolent role as easily as a spider kills its mate.

"S-sir, this is what keeps h-happening. We've run the tests r-repeatedly, but the b-blood shows no abnormalities," the timid voice stammered.

Alexis let out a pitiful moan, and Stephan thrashed vigorously. He could hardly stomach the terrifying reality that they were now experiments of the Institute.

"Take more blood. Maybe this older one has more of the Shadow Dweller factors. Use the megatron scanner," Bishop ordered.

Several of the technicians gasped audibly.

"That probe is unstable! None of the subjects survived," whined the diffident spokesman.

"Since these two vermin have a special capacity to heal, they'll survive its side effects," Bishop asserted. "Try it on the older one first. His results will determine whether you can use it on the younger." Bishop's tone was final. "Now, I'm going to find our newest acquisition. She's the one I've been waiting to study."

Stephan had never heard of a megatron scanner, and he was sure he didn't want to find out what it was. Luckily, the technicians seemed in no hurry to carry out their leader's orders. Only one walked slowly toward a door in a far corner labeled "Hazardous Equipment: Auxiliary effects are severe."

Stephan forced his racing heart and spiraling thoughts to slow. He had to escape before they were hurt beyond repair. Shadow Dweller healing had its limits. He took long, measured breaths, fighting his own panic, but the rattle of a rolling utility cart getting closer derailed his efforts. Instead of fighting his growing terror, Stephan shifted his attention to his last memories of Laura on the marble staircase. Deliberately, he searched for the elusive connection to her that had brought him to this amazing facility. He could almost see her inquisitive eyes as she rocked in an austere room near a loud waterfall.

Then searing pain ripped through every nerve in his body. He couldn't prevent the scream that exploded from his mouth or the cries of revulsion coming from Alexis, as a beam of red light cut into his body.

# 25

## Families

Laura heard Stephan's scream and Alexis's cry as an echo in the dim recesses of her mind. She visualized a strange, bulky machine and a sickly red light and saw the words *Megatron Scanner* for the barest fraction of an instant. She shook her head, trying to solidify the dreamlike quality of the image. But the vision was gone.

Laura ruthlessly directed her attention back to the current danger. The red light was flashing rapidly, almost to the point of solidity.

"I'll go investigate," Gabriel decided. "Maybe I can divert Raphe and Bishop. It's you they want. Hide in the bedroom. If they try to get in, you can always escape out its window." Slowly, Gabriel crept out the back door.

Laura went into the meager bedroom, crouched near the door, and racked her brain for a way to rescue Stephan. She exhaled in surprise when she heard laughter. Through the door, she saw a group of mostly strangers enter the cabin. She recognized Gwen, Emma, and the strange woman who had helped Raphe. There were also several elderly people and even a few young men in lab coats.

"Why did you have to kidnap her?" the strange woman demanded quietly.

"She was in danger from Bishop and Raphe. Bishop was going to start his experiments. It was only a matter of time before he turned his attention on Laura. I had to do something," Gabriel defended himself.

Laura guessed that these two were well acquainted. They were arguing but from positions of mutual respect. Laura studied this stately older woman with green-gold eyes and chestnut hair.

As if sensing her examination, the woman turned to face Laura. Gulping, Laura saw herself, only much older. She sensed both curiosity and a hint of grief in the elder's face. The woman walked over to Laura. Holding her breath, Laura exited the bedroom and faced the women.

"My name is Mary. I'm your mother," the woman whispered abruptly. She laid a hand on Laura's shoulder, her expression wary.

Without hesitation or caution, Laura threw herself into her mother's arms, overwhelmed with a feeling of profound happiness. Her mother returned the embrace with equal enthusiasm. Laura had many questions, but some instinct warned her to let Mary tell her story in her own way. She stepped away to give her mother the opportunity to speak. Mary seemed happy to explain.

"I have cursed my youthful naïveté a thousand times since I was forced to give you up," she began. "I was so wrapped up in the science that I forgot we were creating children, human children. The first babies were boys. It seemed natural that Bishop's tests and trials for Gabriel and Raphe would shape them into strong, resilient protectors. They have learned to endure hardship and overcome adversity, which is proper for a growing man.

"But when you were born, the lie of Bishop's methods became obvious. I could never let him treat you as an experiment and crush all that would make you uniquely feminine. As Gabriel's nature made him strong and protective, your nature, Laura, would likely be to nurture and empathize. I guessed that your genetic mutation might help you telepathically read the thoughts and feelings of others. But Bishop would crush all your gentler tendencies, and you might have become hard and unfeeling. I couldn't risk Bishop destroying your goodness with his stupid tests. So I took you away from this horrible prison and gave you a chance in the outside world."

Laura nodded, her eyes filling with tears. "But why didn't you stay with me?" she asked in a small, vulnerable voice.

"I had to make sure that Bishop never learned the truth. If I disappeared, he might have come looking for me. I don't expect you to forgive me. You've had to find your own way without the support of parents or family. I've missed you so terribly." Mary hugged Laura again, and Laura could feel the tears on her mother's cheeks.

Suddenly, images of Stephan and Alexis's desperate situation blurred Laura's vision, and terrible pain flooded her mind. She pulled away from Mary and staggered.

"What is a megatron scanner?" Laura asked, desperately scanning the newcomers' faces. Tears streamed down her cheeks again, and through a watery veil, she considered the woman who ultimately answered.

"It's a horrible device. I thought it had been destroyed," the woman said, clearly distressed and fighting for control of herself. Her thin white hands wrestled with each other. "Its creation has been kept secret because of its grisly side effects. How do you know of it?"

"Because they're using it on Stephan!" Laura roared. "He's in terrible agony." Her stomach twisted and burned, making her hug her torso in empathy. "Please," she begged. "They'll kill my friends for nothing more important than scientific curiosity. Surely this institution stands for more than that?"

"How do you know what's happening to your friend?" a stout, awkward man pressed. He separated himself from the rest of the group and came forward, his kind eyes sick with dread. His sympathy was reassuring.

"Stephan and I share a special link familiar to Shadow Dwellers. I can sense what Bishop is doing to him. Your grand creator has lost sight of even basic decency. He's become a murderer with no fuss or muss," Laura hissed with pure hatred.

The new man listened quietly, obviously humiliated, and made the decision that would determine all their fates.

"The only way to stop Bishop is to turn off the power that fuels his defenses. This mountain is home to a gigantic lake of magma. It burns an unusual combination of elements that create the living, wiggling energy that feeds the restraints that hold your friends. We can turn it off. But only with the support of your Shadow Dwellers can we hope to subdue Bishop's army of guards long enough to escape this prison. But I fear that if they're using the megatron, then your friends may already be dead."

Laura felt a suffocating anguish at his prediction. But she could not—would not—give up. "We must try," she begged.

"Come then. We have no time to lose."

Laura hurried out of the small cabin and ran back the way Gabriel had brought her. She didn't care who followed her. She didn't care if they met Raphe. She didn't care if they met Bishop. Her distress spurred her into a faster sprint. She had to reach the grand staircase and stop the megatron scanner.

Laura felt a spark of hope when she spied the apartments ahead. She had expected to find Raphe with an army of soldiers searching the area. But everywhere it was oddly quiet. Something must have diverted their pursuers.

Even though Laura was young and fit, the older scientists kept up with her easily. She darted straight for the massive door that led to the grand staircase, expecting at any moment to be stopped.

"Where is everyone?" she asked, glancing around nervously as she turned the doorknob and pushed forward onto one great marble step.

"Your guess is as good as mine," Gabriel admitted from close behind her. "But Bishop is intent on studying you. He will be making an appearance."

Laura shook her head miserably. Then she spotted her nemesis, Raphe, at the top of the staircase next to the arboretum. He was herding the Centurions down the three levels to the laboratory entrance. He hadn't caught sight of her yet.

Laura glanced at Gabriel anxiously and then nodded up at Raphe. Her meaning was clear. "What do we do now?"

Before Gabriel could act, the stout young man rushed across the staircase to the same control panel that Bishop had accessed earlier. Laura had been too far away before to see Bishop activate his strange weapon. Now, however, she followed close behind the young man.

There were three black dials. Beside each dial was a lever inserted into a slot with the numbers zero to ten on both sides. Currently, all the levers were set to ten. Underneath these controls were four buttons: green, yellow, and orange ones and a large red one. The young man pressed the red button and lowered all levers to zero. Then he closed the panel and reset the password. No one would be able to undo his last command without this new password.

In less than a minute, a loud boom filled the huge conical structure. The ceiling exploded outward with a terrible force, exposing the room to the glacier nearby. The temperature dropped drastically, and Laura's breath steamed in the cold air. She recoiled when a loud, desperate howl burst from above.

"Nooooooooooooo! You've killed us all!" Raphe shouted, abandoning the Centurions. He leaped down the stairs to confront the young man. His face was locked in an expression of deadly, purposeful rage.

Without hesitation, Gabriel jumped to intercept his brother. He only had time to tackle Raphe to the ground before events swept everyone into chaos.

The strange illumination in the grand staircase, which had so perplexed Laura, suddenly, horribly, changed. The odd wiggling lights, dimly seen in the mist, popped and cracked louder and louder, until they exploded into blinding flashes of lightning. When she could see again, the disturbing illumination and the shadowy mist were gone.

Impatient to rescue Stephan, Laura scanned the upper level, looking for the Centurions. They stood in close ranks at the entrance to the laboratory with their arms extended. Their alien restraints were popping and crackling like the wiggling lights. Suddenly, they too exploded. Once free, the Centurions easily overpowered Raphe's remaining guards, knocking them unconscious. Gabriel followed their example and rendered Raphe as helpless as his comrades.

Finally, Laura could rescue Stephan and Alexis. But the massive, unshackled forces churning beneath the mountain were not finished. It became painfully obvious that turning off the power that controlled the volcano had produced cataclysmic side effects.

Laura was enveloped in the stench of yellow sulfur gas, and cracking noises came from deep underground. She barely retained her footing as the ground began to roll under her feet. Despite the bedlam, she could hear shouts and protests from the Centurions. She was still four levels down.

Laura squinted, trying to see past the suffocating sulfur smoke. A strong hand caught her arm and pushed her upward. Abruptly, the wind cleared the clouds of smoke, and she could see what all the confusing sounds were conveying. The lovely stairway was crumbling into a central sea of searing, burning magma. Small cracks quickly became terrible gashes.

While the stairway was holding together, Laura leaped up its remaining support structure, with Gabriel following behind. At one point, he managed to pull her aside before she tripped into an expanding fissure.

Recklessly, Laura paused to look back into the red maw of the growing central crater. Her cheeks burned as if exposed to a terrible sun. Despite the danger, she leaned forward to peer down into the bottomless pit. The red glow extended endlessly, as if to hell itself.

Gabriel snorted and forcefully hauled her away, carrying her bodily up to the waiting Centurions. "Get them moving!" he shouted. "We still have to get out of this mountain before it collapses."

The Centurions immediately acknowledged Laura's authority by assembling in a loose military formation and nodding in expectation of her orders.

"They're ready," she observed. "Where to?"

Gabriel led Laura through the door to the labs and down a long corridor. Evidently, she didn't need to issue commands after all. She heard the reassuring stomping boots of the Centurions following behind. When she recognized the large lab ahead of them from her visions, she dashed past him.

"Is this the place? Is he here?" she asked anxiously.

"I think so." Gabriel studied the door. "This is the last place I saw the scanner that Bishop has foolishly chosen to use again. No one will support him now," he said with both contempt and satisfaction.

Laura charged into the lab with the delicacy of a raging elephant. The scanner, with its peculiar whine, held center stage. The terrible red light of the devil machine was peeling away Stephan's skin like melting ice. A golden mass was working furiously to knit new layers of skin, but the rescue party had arrived too late to stop his murder. As Laura watched, the strange golden particles winked out, leaving Stephan to the weak abilities of his lost human soul.

When the alien restraints on Stephan and Alexis exploded into bursts of light, Alexis jumped off the table and barreled into the technician, who was operating the megatron scanner. She threw the poor man across the room, and Laura heard the distinctive crack of breaking bones. Laura's eyes followed the scanner's power cord to the plug in the wall, and she yanked it out. The whine of the device slowly faded.

Stephan was too damaged to move after his restraints fell away. He was breathing laboriously; a long pause of deathly stillness followed each exhalation. Blood was draining into a dangerously large puddle beneath the table. Laura could see his exposed organs and a spreading blackness on his skin that heralded death.

What happened next would remain indelibly imprinted in Laura's memories, a sight never to be forgotten. Alexis laid her body next to the injured Shadow Dweller even as his strangled breathing stopped altogether. Stephan's suffering and personal struggles were finally over. Out of Alexis's mouth, ears, and nose came streams of the alien gold particles. Since Stephan's supply was gone, she gave hers. Laura found the sharing of the healing powers of the Shadow Dweller a miracle in a race that seemed committed to isolation and selfish endeavors.

She watched with growing awe as a golden haze completely engulfed Alexis and Stephan. A strange musical hum grew as the activity increased. When patches of the gold fog thinned enough to allow her a glimpse of Stephan, she saw that his skin had been replaced without scabs or scars.

Laura laughed in pure delight and rushed to Stephan's medical table. She helped Alexis off the table and hugged her fiercely.

"I will never be able to repay you for this," Laura whispered. Her heart swelled with gratitude.

Alexis smiled weakly and offered one cryptic explanation. "If the prophecy is true, Stephan will change the course of my people's history. My life would have been a small price to pay."

Gabriel had remained by the door and looked relieved when Stephan showed signs of rising. "The only escape is back through the mountain!" he exclaimed over the fading music of the healing particles. "There's only one main road to the nearest airport, and this is storm season. The temperatures drop significantly at night. We need to move."

"Are you sure you want to leave?" Laura asked. "Bishop is finished, and this is your home. Maybe some of the Institute can be salvaged."

"This is not my home," Gabriel retorted. "It's merely my cage. I've longed for the opportunity you've brought. Your Shadow Dwellers didn't save only you; they came to our rescue as well." Gabriel's expression turned hopeful. "You will take us? Many have been here so long they have no connections on the outside. For those who were born here, we have no way to support ourselves on the outside. We have no base to begin a new life."

"Us?" How many was he really talking about?

"We've longed for our freedom," Gabriel continued, his eyes focused on some distant memory. "Bishop decided it was too dangerous to let anyone leave once they had learned our location and research. He held at least one of my brothers as a hostage and threatened him whenever he had a mission for us on the outside. In this way, we were forced to return."

"Of course!" she exclaimed, her voice laced with sympathy. "We will sponsor any who want to leave."

Gabriel smiled gratefully and began making a series of phone calls on a handheld satellite phone. From his side of the conversation, Laura knew he was arranging for several groups to meet outside the mountain, including, to her dismay, the children. She had forgotten about the children.

"Will we be able to save all the children?" she asked, worried.

"There was already a plan in place. Families are even now exiting the mountain."

"May I use your phone?" Alexis asked.

Gabriel dropped the phone into her outstretched hand. "Monk and the others will never leave unless we tell them we've escaped," she explained hurriedly.

After several tense moments, she started speaking into the phone in a low and urgent voice and then, abruptly, hung up. "They will meet us at the plane."

"Let's go!" Gabriel chirped.

Another major tremor reinforced the urgency of leaving immediately.

Laura and her Shadow Dweller rescuers followed behind as Gabriel quickly led them out of the lab and through a dark warren of underground passageways. The initial violence of the disturbed magna chamber had subsided, but the underground cracking sounds continued.

One Centurion carried Stephan for a short distance, until Stephan lost patience with this arrangement. When he demanded his release, the Shadow Dweller complied immediately. Straightening his clothes, Stephan joined Laura at the front of the group. He looked as if he had never been injured.

Gabriel, Laura, Stephan, Alexis, and the Centurions traveled through dirty, dimly lit passages that looked like maintenance routes. This stone-hewn track was harder to navigate, but it seemed more direct. Laura rounded a dark, steep turn to discover a second tunnel going back the way they had come. To her horror, Bishop, surrounded by armed guards, came running out of this passageway. He greeted her group with a surprised smile.

"Perfect," he purred. "Now I get to kill you both myself and escape what must be your handiwork." As if on cue, the volcano rumbled louder. "You many have ended my time here, but you'll not get away unscathed."

Laura tried to pull Stephan out of Bishop's line of fire, but his shirt had become painfully hot. "What in God's name?" she yelped. Instinctively, she moved away from him.

"Guards!" Bishop thundered with a distinct edge of panic. He had also sensed the rising temperature around Stephan. He withdrew, letting his guards form a wall in front of him.

Laura continued to retreat as she watched the strange transformation of Stephan Renard. His face was locked into an expression of intense rage that slowly melted into a roaring fire that was igniting anything that was flammable. Even the rock around him began to glow. Alexis and her Centurions had immediately formed a barrier around Stephan when his transformation became obvious. They shielded Laura from the worst of the heat.

"You must stop!" Alexis ordered. "You will kill us all! The Shadow Dweller fire is too powerful for a novice in these close quarters."

Laura heard the growing panic that strained the Ancient's words. The heat in the narrow pathway was becoming unbearable, and finally, Bishop and his men broke ranks and ran back down the corridor.

"I don't think so," Stephan roared. His voice came from pure red flames that burned even higher. He became a blade of red flame that streaked after the escaping Bishop.

Laura forced her way through the Centurion blockage in time to catch a glimpse of the fire that was Stephan engulf Bishop. The man turned toward her, an unholy terror lighting his eyes. Bishop never spoke any intelligible words, he just screamed as he melted into dust.

Laura had to turn away from the sight of Bishop dying. Then the hallway filled with the dying shrieks of Bishop's entire force. Even though her enemy and his men were too dangerous to be left alive, she knew that fire was the worst kind death. When Stephan finally walked out of the corridor, he was his Shadow Dweller self again. But his face was not smug with victory; it was stricken with a profound regret. Obviously, he couldn't kill without conscience.

"We need to go," Gabriel reminded them. "He deserved his fate. Laura, you never knew the extent of what he did to us."

Laura nodded slowly and touched Stephan's hand. He put his arm around her shoulders and inhaled heavily.

"I may not like to kill, but I know when it's necessary," he muttered. "Now let's get out of this hellish place."

Within fifteen minutes, Laura found herself standing outside the cliff entrance. Six heavy-duty vans were standing ready, their humming engines already warming the chilly interiors. Two were overflowing with children. Monk and Celeste were also there, in an SUV that could only be an invention of Monk's.

Laura smiled at all the expectant, optimistic faces. She was grateful to be able to offer Bishop's people a new start. But there was one person she had to check on personally.

As she approached Monk's vehicle, he rolled down the driver's window.

"Thank God you guys are safe," she breathed. "I didn't know how far into the Institute you had gone."

"Nothing will keep me down for long," Monk bragged confidently. "I'll always have your back, little one. It would have been me instead of Stephan, if he didn't have a special means of transport. Turning into mist is mighty handy."

"What happened to you?" Laura asked.

"After Stephan and his team got through, the fighting grew more ferocious, but I was determined to finished this battle and join him."

"Monk took far too many stupid risks to win the day," Celeste retorted impatiently. But Laura could see a sparkle of admiration in her eyes. "Fortunately, Alexis left a squad of Centurions. Also, I had the distinct impression that the opposition didn't have the same commitment to winning as Monk did. Eventually, we subdued the guards who were foolish enough to stay and fight."

"Then we charged into the heart of the compound and found that strange staircase," Monk continued. "On a lower landing, two men were arguing about the best way to find you. One was called Raphe and the other Bishop. They were too preoccupied to see us before they left through one of those huge doors and we followed."

"They led us to an artificial environment," Celeste explained, obviously impressed. "There were apartments, waterfalls, meadows, and s-s-sunlight. It was the first time I had seen the sun in so long." Tears trailed down her cheeks.

"Gabriel took me there for my protection," Laura explained. "But we came out the way you must have come in. Why didn't we see you?"

"Because Bishop must have seen us," Monk replied grimly. "His team darted down a side passageway as a distraction. At the time, we thought you must be ahead of them, so we followed." Monk drew out a small tablet. "I called Lord, and he transferred all the surveillance data he was recording from his plane. He stayed out of the direct conflict so he could feed us intel as we needed it." Monk entered a series of commands on the tablet, and a shadowy image of the Institute appeared. "Lord was using thermal imaging to follow the progress of our infiltration," he said. "Here, I have set it to replay what happened."

Monk handed Laura the tablet and pointed to his team's location behind Bishop's force. She saw two groups of red dots running down a series of hallways next to the row of connecting apartments.

"Unfortunately, their evasion turned out to be an ambush," Celeste confirmed. "They led us down a final narrow corridor and then turned on us."

Monk touched a button, and the tablet fast-forwarded to the ambush. Laura saw one group of dots run down a winding tunnel while the other group followed. Unexpectedly, the dots in the front turned on the dots at the back.

"Then things got a bit dicey," Monk admitted.

A menacing red shadow appeared on the edge of the screen and quickly closed the distance to the first group of dots, the trailing group turned back the way they had come, and the leading group ran down a side corridor out of the screen's range.

"I've only felt that caliber of heat once, and the injuries were terrible," Monk said. "I warned the team that we had to escape or risk death. Thankfully, no one argued."

Laura watched as the red shadow became a solid wave of molten rock and filled both the main corridor and the side passageway used by Bishop. It came dangerously close to Monk's group before the red dots burst out into an open area and ran out of range of the surging mass. Laura used the pretense of handing the tablet back to Monk to study him and Celeste for any obvious injuries. Monk had a large coat across his lap.

"OK, give." Laura insisted and tossed the concealing coat aside. Monk's right pant leg had been cut off, and the limb was wrapped in a thick, white bandage.

"Someone had to be the last to leave, and I wasn't giving that position to anyone else," Monk admitted gruffly. "It's only a flesh wound."

Laura looked at Celeste for confirmation, and she shrugged non-committally. "He's a bulldog who thinks he's indestructible. There was no arguing with him."

"You'll go to the hospital when we get home, or there will be hell to pay, my friend," Laura insisted. A disturbing odor was coming from the leg that suggested infection might have begun.

"Don't worry, imp," Monk reassured her. "I'm as strong as an ox and stubborn as a mule. This little burn might prove nasty, but it won't be fatal. My only regret is I never got to see that son of a bitch Bishop die. Now shall we get going? The hospital is a journey away."

"We found Bishop," Laura interrupted him. "He didn't get away."

"How?" Monk pressed.

"Stephan has a few more secrets besides transforming into mist. I'll never know how we ever thought we could win a war against the Shadow Dwellers. It was a fool's dream." Laura sighed and turned back toward the other trucks.

"Maybe not," Monk insisted to her retreating back.

Alexis and Stephan had commandeered one of the smaller SUVs, and Alexis's Centurions were already in the back. Laura could see Gabriel in the driver's seat of another SUV with a group of his people. As she headed for Stephan's vehicle, Gabriel caught her attention and waved her over.

"I would ask a favor," he said hesitantly. "Would you come with us to help our people navigate your travel arrangements? Some of us have never left this place, and I think your presence might offer a calming influence, especially if you are truly one of us with special abilities."

The implication was obvious. He believed Laura shared his gift to calm others. She hoped he was right. "Of course," she reassured him.

Laura ran over to Stephan's car to explain her new travel plans. When she returned to Gabriel's SUV, her new family cheered from all the vehicles. Then the caravan began the long journey to their new home.

# Epilogue

Laura was surprised at how quickly the Institute refugees made themselves comfortable at Lord's compound. Most had no interest in establishing a presence in outside society. Gabriel had already begun construction on separate living quarters and entertainment facilities. In exchange, all the newcomers had begun training in Lord's underground gym. Laura was amazed by what the newcomers didn't know compared to the number of technical gadgets they had brought, gadgets they had begun to share with Lord and Stephan.

Laura discovered that all of Nicolette's girls had moved to The Colony, among their own people, awaiting word about a new Trust facility. Celeste had taken a shine to Stephan's theater and followed him everywhere. She had quickly mastered the technical manipulations necessary to launch musicals, and except for Laura's artistic collaborations with Stephan, he had left more and more duties in Celeste's hands. Monk had begun hanging out more and more at The Colony. He was often seen in the company of the beautiful Celeste. Laura hoped that her loyal friend would finally end his self-imposed isolation.

With many of Stephan's responsibilities delegated to the girls, he had made his pursuit of Laura his primary priority. He really did know how to dazzle a mere mortal girl. Gabriel was definitely disgruntled, but she was delighted by his inspired entertainments.

Much to Laura's embarrassment, Stephan's disgust, and Monk's absence, Gabriel had taken up the position as her personal guard. He quickly learned her habits and anticipated her needs. At first, she had tried to avoid him but then just surrendered to the benefits of having someone look after her so single-mindedly. Fortunately, he never tried to be anything but a close friend. She had even agreed to accompany Gabriel and a select group back to the old Institute at some future date. Many people, including Mary, talked about returning to Greenland to reclaim beloved possessions, if such had survived.

Laura enjoyed getting to know her biological family, and soon, Mary transformed her life. The older woman had jumped at the opportunity to take on the role of confidante and mentor. Laura soaked up the attention like a desert sponge dropped in water for the first time, and Laura, in turn, helped Mary navigate the wide variety of luxuries and attendant challenges available in the outside world. Laura treasured the quiet words of wisdom and the gentle prodding of her new, much-loved mother. She was thankful she was not directly related to Gabriel and the other enhanced men. Bishop had made sure each archangel was a new genetic line. But they were her family just the same.

Maybe it was time to arrange a return to the Institute. Celeste was really getting on her nerves.

# About the Author

Carol Johnson is a CPA, avid adventurer, and amateur comedian who brings life to her written work with a number of personal and professional experiences. A graduate of the University of Washington, she has also studied science, philosophy, astronomy, and ancient history.

Johnson's forays into the Alaskan wilderness, the temples of Athens, the pyramids of Cairo, cruises to the Caribbean, and many other real-life adventures have served as inspirations for her work and provided the landscapes for her first novel, *The Search for Tomorrow's Treasures*. Two years working at the Bathhouse Theater, twelve years assisting a Foundation that published scientific research, and many years exploring the vastness of space and the human spirit helped shape her second novel, *The Tale of the Shadow Dwellers*.

www.ingramcontent.com/pod-product-compliance
Lightning Source LLC
Chambersburg PA
CBHW071557030726

47593CB00001BA/211